THE ATTACK OF THE ICE REICH
THE RECORD OF THE FIVE RINGS

iUniverse books may be ordered through booksellers or by contacting:

iUniverse
1663 Liberty Drive
Bloomington, IN 47403
www.iuniverse.com
844-349-9409

ISBN: 978-1-6632-3415-5 (sc)
ISBN: 978-1-6632-3414-8 (e)

Library of Congress Control Number: 2021925737

Print information available on the last page.

iUniverse rev. date: 08/23/2022

THE ATTACK OF THE ICE REICH

THE RECORD OF THE FIVE RINGS

PAUL SCHEELER

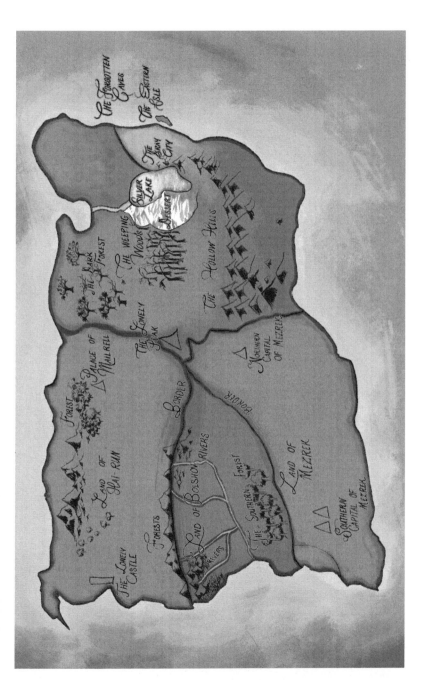

ACKNOWLEDGMENTS

To my sister, Bernadette, and my mother, Ellen, for being the firsts to read.

Thank you to my Dad for pushing me to publish.

To Kat Mason for her thorough editing and insightful feedback. The storyline improved a lot because of her.

To Rachel Croyle, Mae Hickey, and Brandon Woodrum for their support and early comments.

And to Gomdan for everything else.

CHAPTER 1

My Last Moments

Have you ever noticed that when you're about to die, time seems to slow down?

It would be really cool if it weren't also really terrifying.

Right now, as I say these words, I am about to die. And the way I'm going to die is completely unbelievable.

The hopeful half of me thinks that maybe my best friend put a little something extra in the drink he gave me, and I'm not dying but experiencing the world's worst trip.

What am I experiencing exactly?

Well, I just fell from a floating castle made of rock, where I learned I could manipulate matter. I landed in freezing water about six inches from a chunk of ice that would have skewered me like one of my mom's homemade shish kebabs. Now I am floating on said chunk of ice, wondering what will kill me first: the freezing wind blowing across my soaked T-shirt and jeans or the ice monster barreling down at me from about two hundred yards away.

Yes, an ice monster. I don't know what else I can call a humanoid creature whose skin looks as if it's made from flexible ice cubes and who is at least four times as big as I am. Maybe you'd call it a Jotun if you're into Norse mythology. But whatever you call it, I'm pretty sure it wants to kill me.

Suddenly, I remember what I learned a few moments earlier: I can manipulate matter. I'm not nearly as calm as I was when I was in a warm stone room, and my thighs feel a little warmer—and a little wetter—than they should. My heart is beating like a souped-up jackhammer, and my hands shake wildly as I try to do the movements I did above in the floating rock castle, weaving my hands about the way the ring on my finger wants me to move them.

Nothing happens.

Meanwhile, the ice giant is bearing down on me like a quarterback going for the home run. Or is it a slam dunk? I don't really know—I'm awful at sports. In fact, the only thing I'm really good at is playing video games, and they're not coming in terribly handy right now. *Mom, I take everything back about how video games prepare you for life. It's not true. They prepare you to get skewered by ice giants from Jotunheim or from your friend's spiked drink or wherever this monster came from.*

I try again with movement; my fingers are stiff from the cold, and my arms are seizing with fear. The giant can't be more than ten yards away. It's bounding across the open water as if on land.

I struggle again, reaching for the power, pleading for it to respond the way it did only minutes before, but still, nothing happens. Then the ice giant is upon me, drawing itself up to its full height and gazing down on me.

In a moment of terror, my power finally responds, and a few pebbles and chunks of dirt spit from the rock into the ice monster's face. Rather belatedly, it occurs to me I might have power not over matter but only over earth. A cold, rumbling sound escapes the monster's lips, and I wonder if the sound is its version of a laugh. I suppose the situation would be kind of funny from the monster's perspective, looking down on a wimpy kid whose grand defense is to throw a bit of dirt in its face. So much for the stupid ring. I try to pull it off, but it won't budge, so guess I'll die wearing the thing that brought me to this world and ended up killing me.

My eyes move up the monster's long legs of bluish ice to its thick chest and hoary beard of frost. I last find its face, and I stare up into the inhuman, icy eyes of this giant four times my size. I know I'm about to die, because there is no kindness in those cold orbs, only white rage—as white as hot flames and frozen snow. I wonder how I've managed to get myself into this mess. How did it all begin?

It began, I think, with a high school crush, a field trip gone wrong, and a ring I never, ever should have put on.

I don't know if anyone will ever know these last thoughts, but I figure I ought to tell my story before it's all over. This is the story of me, Peter Smythe, and how, at age eighteen, I will die before I'm able to ask out to prom the girl I've had a crush on since seventh grade, before I have my first kiss, before I say goodbye to my mom and dad and the best high school teacher ever, and, most tragically of all, before I get revenge on FireStarter520 for keeping me from Elite Class in *Ghost Army*.

CHAPTER 2

THINGS WERE MOSTLY BETTER LAST WEEK

Things were mostly better last week, though things were never great. That's largely because I have always been kind of a loser, but let's not get ahead of ourselves.

It was a Friday morning, and it began much like every Friday in the Smythe household: with my dad waking me up at five thirty, even though the bus comes at seven thirty. He always wakes me up early so we can eat breakfast together as a family—and I guess because he used to be a marine, and old habits die hard. My mom cooked. We were eating *pizzelle*, which are basically Italian waffles. I'd say they were to die for, but that's too much foreshadowing.

My dad and I sat together at the kitchen table, and I double-fisted Monster energy drinks, trying to keep myself awake, while Mom worked on the pizzelle in the kitchen. The fresh smells wafted through the air, almost making me not miserable. My dad and mom have a routine: she cooks the early breakfast on

Fridays, and he cooks the one meal he knows how on Saturday evenings: pork chops.

Personally, I don't think it's a fair trade—not just because I don't know how my mom is able to function well enough at five thirty to make a small Italian feast but also because my dad's cooking is not nearly on par with my mom's.

You see, my mom is Italian. And Jewish. And also Christian. She's a lot of things, but the main point is that she's a chef, and her Italian cooking is really good. I mean out-of-this-world fantastic. She owns a pastry shop on Smith Street, and her delicacies are so good that her customers have joked about renaming the street Smythe Street, which has yet to happen, sadly.

I finished the first Monster as Mom brought the still-steaming food to the table. I felt my mouth begin to water, and I resisted the urge to reach across the table and grab one of the pizzelle. I waited patiently with my leg bobbing up and down like a jackrabbit's from all the caffeine.

As my mother set a pizzelle on my plate, her brow wrinkled with concern. "You know you shouldn't drink those garbage things. They're bad for your heart."

She still has a little bit of an accent. She came to the United States when she was in her twenties, and she learned English pretty well, but she never managed to get it *perfetto*—I think partly because she's a very stubborn woman unwilling to give up her heritage, even if she left her country. It's probably also why she only spoke Italian to me when I was a baby and still mostly speaks Italian to me.

Then again, she might have spoken Italian to me because my dad had a harebrained scheme to make me into a multilingual prodigy child, so he never spoke English to me when I was a baby either. What languages did he speak with me, you ask?

Homer's Greek and Cicero's Latin.

Yes, no joke. So I was a confused baby, and I think my struggles with the English language all go back to that—Daddy issues, I guess you could say, though not of the usual variety.

I remained mostly silent at the breakfast table, letting my mom and dad do the talking. It was late March of my senior year of high school, and my parents were hearing about all the schools their friends' children had been accepted to. So far, I hadn't received any letters back—except from Harvard, and they'd turned me down, which was not a big surprise. I had applied only because my guidance counselor had forced me to, a decision I understand about as well as multivariable calculus.

I was concerned if I added anything to the conversation, my parents might be reminded of the fact the colleges had forgotten about me and then force me to have a difficult conversation, saying, "What are you going to do with your life? We are concerned about you," and all that.

I didn't want to have to think about what I was going to do with my life if I turned out to be too dumb to make it into college. I guess I could try working in my mom's pastry shop, though I'm not much good at cooking and don't really enjoy it either. I like eating food, not making it.

The two hours until the bus's arrival passed quickly. Looking back, I wish I hadn't been so ungrateful, because that was my last Friday to have Mom's pizzelle and listen to my mom and dad discuss Dante at an ungodly hour.

I stepped out into the fresh morning air, feeling the sting against my neck and cheeks. I cut through the neighbors' backyard with my shoes slushing on the dewy grass and my eyes wandering in a tired gaze across the rows of nearly identical redbrick houses with white panels and gray roofs.

I gathered alongside the other pimpled zombies with their earphones in and smartphone screens glowing brightly, and I didn't look any different. I opened up YouTube and scrolled through my favorites till I found the recording someone had made of *The Odyssey* in Ancient Greek. I let the rhythm of the words wash over me, and I did my best to hide the tears that formed in my eyes, because—this is going to make me sound weird—I'd never heard anything so beautiful.

It's the story of a king lost at sea. With the help of the goddess Athena, he finally makes it back to his home, to the place he belongs. It's a story of longing for home, of growing up, of love and betrayal, of courage, and of all the things that really matter most.

But it's not just the story that affects me; it's the words. I can't really explain it. If you're like me, you'll understand what I mean when I say that words can make you laugh or cry. If you're not like me in that way, well, there's no point in saying anything.

The familiar rumble of the school bus engine sounded from around the corner, and the smell of diesel exhaust filled my nose, waking me from the half-dream state I was in, as I listened to the adventures of Odysseus. I thought of how ordinary my life was and how boring it would probably be until I kicked the bucket somewhere around the age of seventy-nine.

How wrong I was.

CHAPTER 3

How to Make Friends and Enemies

My house is on a hill. To get to school, the bus has to climb the steep hill, round a narrow corner, and then descend into the valley to get to our humble little school, Mormont High. I like to sit near the front of the bus, so I can see the Smoky Mountains in the distance. In late spring, they glow with the sunrise.

A lot of the other kids don't like to sit up front, not just because it isn't cool but also because you get a good sight of Blackstone High, our school's great rival in everything from football to chess. I don't know if it's fair to call us rivals, since there's not really much competition. We always lose. That's mostly because the kids at Blackstone High live in a richer neighborhood, so the school has more money, better facilities, and so on. But I'm not complaining or anything.

Everyone says the Blackstone kids are all stuck up because they have lawyers for parents (that's why their school is called Blackstone, apparently: Blackstone as in Lord Blackstone, which you have to admit is kind of pretentious). But until later that evening, I had never met any Blackstone kids, so I couldn't say for myself whether they were stuck up or just better than we were.

The bus wound its way down Main Street and turned past my mother's bakery before turning into Mormont High. Our school is a miserably square building with drab, dirty walls. It looks a lot more like a prison built sometime in the 1950s than a high school.

The brakes hissed, the doors squealed open, and soon I was pressed body to backpack as I waded through the crowd of students, who all had one goal: to get to their lockers before the bell sounded, signaling the start of homeroom. Well, I guess most of us had the same goal. There were a few kids whose goal seemed to be to make out in plain view as grotesquely as possible, but I tried not to pay too much attention.

Eventually, I made it through the body jam and PDA fests. I slid into my homeroom seat just as the bell sounded. My teacher, Mr. Vex—or Mr. V, as everyone calls him—gave me a disapproving glance as he marked my name down on his attendance sheet. He adjusted his bow tie and suspenders, which he wore over his periodic-table-themed collared shirt, and began to write chemical equations down on the board.

"Barely on time, as usual," whispered a voice from beside me.

I turned to see my friend Resol McGooblias. The few people who notice his existence mostly call him Goober, despite his attempts to get them to call him Sol. He was wearing his usual black hoodie and thin glasses, which covered his dimpled face. In his right hand, he clutched his water bottle, though the people who knew him knew it was actually 120-proof vodka.

I had learned that the hard way when Brutus Borgia, the biggest bully in school, didn't follow the steps in his experiment, and the experiment burst into flames. Instead of following protocol, I grabbed what I thought was the nearest water bottle, and Goober's cries—"No, Pete, not that one!"—reached me too late. I splattered the stuff all over the flames, causing a small explosion, which singed off half of Brutus's eyebrow hairs, something he's never forgiven me for.

"You're dead meat," Brutus had said, jabbing a finger at me.

Goober, like his usual half-inebriated self, had replied, "At least we're not roasted meat," and then proceeded to laugh hysterically at his own joke, which at least explained where I had gotten the alcohol.

It all had been funny until Ms. Schaden, the buxom vice principal, who perpetually wore a disapproving frown on her withered face, appeared, grabbed us by the ears, and dragged us to her office.

Goober and I both had gotten an hour-long dressing down, followed by detention, which was almost a relief after listening to Ms. Schaden for so long. Afterward, we'd gotten an extracurricular punishment from Brutus and his cronies, which left bruises I'm pretty sure still haven't gone away. Goober had made the beating worse by making jokes about Brutus's eyebrows. He had been so drunk that the more Brutus hit him, the more he laughed. I, however, had not been, and as Brutus and company had wailed on us, I'd pleaded with Goober for a solid three hours to stop making things worse. At least that's how I remember it.

I was pretty angry with him for about a week after that, but I can never hold grudges for long, so we were soon back to being best friends.

After class, Goober and I walked to our lockers before going to history.

"So how was chem? You took a lot of notes," he said in his usual flat voice.

"Yeah. I took two pages of notes, which I don't understand and won't remember."

Goober shook his head and put a hand on my shoulder, and I knew he was about to share one of his "life lessons" he considered to be profoundly good advice.

"You just gotta learn not to try, Pete," he said, waving his water bottle through the air as if gesturing to the horizon. "Look at me. I didn't understand anything in class either, and I definitely won't remember the stuff, but I also didn't waste any time writing notes."

I nodded skeptically, wondering what my dad would have done if he'd heard his speech. There was something to what Goober said, I guessed, but I had to try, because my parents wanted me to go to college, and if I didn't go, I had no idea what I was going to do with my life.

"So," said Goober, "are you coming to the game tonight?"

For reasons I don't quite understand, Mormont and some of the surrounding schools play football even in the spring. So in March and April, there are in fact football games.

"I don't know," I said, thinking about the homework I had to get done, as I slid into my desk.

"Come on," said Goober. "*She* will be there."

My cheeks reddened, and just then, *she* walked into the room.

11

CHAPTER 4

EMILY AND THE BLACK DOG

For a moment, my muscles felt weak, and my heart began to race, as it always did whenever I thought about her: Emily Wong, the cutest girl in school, who was hopelessly unattainable. I watched her push back her jet-black hair as she set down her books. Her friend came up to her, and she smiled, with her dimples like craters. Her brown eyes were so beautiful I felt I was going to implode.

"You're drooling," said Goober disinterestedly.

I shook my head and felt my mouth. "No, I'm not," I said, looking over at him.

Goober shrugged. "I was speaking metaphorically." He took another sip from his supposed water bottle. "You gonna ask her?"

I risked another glance at Emily, this time making sure to keep my mouth shut. I was pretty sure she had not noticed my existence any more than a person notices an ant crawling along the cracks in a sidewalk. I was even surer I didn't want her first impression of me to be as some pervert drooling at her.

I watched as she laughed at something her friend said. Her brown eyes sparkled, and her face seemed to go through a million little expressions, each of them stabbing a dagger into my heart.

"She'll say no if I ask," I replied, looking down, feeling aware of how inadequate I was: a C student with no special talents and a social circle about as wide as my ring finger. It was basically just Goober and a few friends we played games with online but had never met. Emily, on the other hand, was in at least half a dozen clubs, the National Honor Society, and marching band. She also somehow found time to read, because she was always carrying a new book with her every time I saw her.

"How do you know?" said Goober.

All the painful thoughts that had just run through my mind played themselves back again. "I'm a loser, Goober, and Emily is *Emily*."

"You think you're a loser? My name is Resol. That's literally *loser* spelled backward. I'm pretty sure my mom was high when she was giving birth to me, and I know for sure my parents were drunk when they named me."

I glanced over at Goober, and for just a moment, I caught a look of pain in his sea-green eyes. But then the moment was over, and his eyes quickly went back to a stone-cold "You can't make me care" look. I thought about saying, "I'm sorry," or something like that, but I knew he would take it the wrong way. Goober and I have a few unspoken rules, and rule *numero uno* is that we don't talk about emotions.

My thoughts drifted back to Emily, to her ridiculous laughter and the fresh floral smell of the perfume she wore, which I could almost taste. I sighed and let my head rest on my fist.

"You've got to lower your standards, Pete," said Goober softly, still nursing his drink. "It's the key to happiness—or at least fighting off the black dog."

"The black dog?"

"It was Winston Churchill's pet name for his depression."

I cast him a sideways glance. That's the thing about Goober: he seems like he's totally checked out and has nothing going on upstairs, but every once in a while, he says something that makes it sound as if he does more than play video games and watch old westerns in his free time. I wanted to ask him more, but before I had a chance, the bell sounded once again, and class began.

Goober spent the class sipping quietly from his bottle and drawing pictures in his notepad. I only caught a glance or two, because he is weirdly private about his drawings, shutting the book whenever he thinks anyone might be peeking, but his drawings are pretty good. I think he might make a good artist or maybe graphic designer one day. He at least has something he's good at.

I put my pencil to the page, scribbling notes about the Peace of Westphalia and all the details, which I could not keep track of. Meanwhile, I tried to keep my mind from wandering back to the world of Homer, in which Odysseus battled against seas, men, and monsters to make it home to the place where he belonged.

As class progressed, a new thought entered my mind. I managed to fend it off at first, but slowly, it grew stickier and more powerful. My brain decided I needed to go up to Emily after class to ask her what I've been wanting to ask her since eighth grade: "Will you go out with me?" Or in the case of this year, "Will you go to prom with me?"

I spent the second half of class imagining the scene over and over in my mind, envisioning all the ways it could go, from a sappy ending in which Emily said, "Oh, Peter, I've been waiting for you to ask me all these years. I was just afraid to make the first move," which was definitely not going to happen, to a horrific ending in which she transformed into a siren, reached a clawed hand into my chest, and ripped out my heart.

At the end of class, I got up from my table and moved toward her. There was a golden moment when she was sitting alone at the desk, packing up her things. Her friend was already gone. I opened my mouth, about to ask her the question I'd been wanting to ask for so long, and—I hesitated. All the possible bad endings rushed before my mind's eye at once.

I stood there stupidly as students brushed past me, and by the time I managed to gain ahold of myself, she was walking out the doorway and on to her next class.

Goober came up beside me and shook his head sadly. "Expectations," he said softly.

In that moment, I wanted to slam my fist into his face for telling me what 99 percent of me already knew was true: a girl like Emily would never go for me. But the anger was quickly gone. I couldn't hate Goober. He was my only friend, and he was, in his weird way, trying to help me—and probably was helping me, since I was never going to get with her.

It was a crushing thought. I understood why Churchill called that numbing sensation the black dog.

CHAPTER 5

THE GODDESS OF WISDOM

The last class of the day happened to be with the one teacher who doesn't either hate my guts or ignore me completely: Dr. Marie Elsavier, my literature teacher. Everyone calls her Elsa, like Elsa from *Frozen*, and they all think they're clever for coming up with the nickname, even though they're just leaving off the last two syllables of her name. I also don't think it's a great nickname, because if we're talking Disney princesses, she's more of a Rapunzel in terms of personality. She's about twenty-seven, with curly dirty-blonde hair, which, unlike Rapunzel's, goes only to her shoulders; big black-rimmed glasses that look more like magnifying glasses, truth be told; and the bubbliest personality I've ever come across. In fact, she kind of seems like she should be a ditz—she talks in a strange mix of brimming enthusiasm and a fey "I'm not totally there" manner—but I'm pretty sure she's actually the smartest person in the school or maybe even in a hundred-mile radius. She definitely could give those lawyers up in Blackstone a run for their shiny pennies.

What makes Dr. Elsavier special is that she knows something about me I would die if anyone else in the school knew. She knows I speak Latin and Greek. I'm not sure how she figured it out, but then again, she is a lot smarter than I am. One day she had me stay after class. After all the kids had left, she leaned forward, adjusting her glasses as if examining a specimen, and said to me, "I know you speak Ancient Greek." Before I could stop myself, I denied it in the same language in which she'd made the statement: Ancient Greek.

I blushed, grew flustered, and tried to deny it, fearing I was about to become a teacher's pet and ergo the subject of even more bullying. I mean, a kid who speaks Ancient Greek is just asking for it. But she clapped her hands, leaned forward, and whispered conspiratorially, "Don't worry. I won't spoil our secret."

We spent the next hour and a half talking Homer and Hesiod. At some point, I think I might have cried as she recited a piece from *The Odyssey*. She said the words as if she had seen the events herself, and her Greek was musical. I could almost taste the salty sea breeze of the Aegean Sea and see Odysseus's ship upon the waves as she spoke. But more than that, she had a strange look in her eyes, one I had never seen before: understanding. She got me—she knew exactly what it was about the words that could make someone cry. Her eyes were a little moist too.

Ever since then, we've had a sort of special relationship. She's somewhere between a second mother and a cool older sister, the sibling I never had. She always seems to know what I am feeling and to understand it better than I understand it myself. I guess I need that, however much I hate my feelings and wish I could be like Goober: placid and uncaring.

We spent most of class that day discussing Ajax, one of Ancient Greece's greatest warriors, who was driven mad by the goddess Athena. After bringing shame on himself in his madness, he stabbed himself in the chest with his sword. An uplifting story. One to match my mood.

Normally, during class, I would participate, answering questions here and there, though not often enough to draw undue attention to myself, because Brutus Borgia was in the class too. But that Friday, I spent most of the time staring at a piece of eraser someone had left on the desk. It didn't take a genius to figure out I wasn't having a good time, even though Dr. Elsavier probably is a genius.

The bell sounded, and Dr. Elsavier had to shout above the mad rush of zipping backpacks as students clambered to leave. "Remember, there is no class Monday, but on Tuesday, you're taking a field trip with your second-bell class."

My second-bell class was history, which meant Emily would be on the trip. Not that it mattered. I felt as if my blood had been replaced with molasses, and I was the last one to pack up my things.

Dr. Elsavier came up as I was slumping my way toward the exit, and she stopped me.

Her brilliant blue eyes searched mine for a moment before I looked down, avoiding her gaze. She drifted back to her desk, still fixing me with the *Elsavier look*: sweet, warm, and clever.

"You want a cookie, Peter?" she asked, opening a drawer in her desk and producing a Tupperware container.

I could tell as soon as she opened it that they were her homemade chocolate chip cookies, because nothing else smells as good, not even Mom's lasagna, which has been known to turn me into Garfield the cat. (If your taste in cartoons isn't as good as mine, Garfield is a cat who really likes lasagna.) The smell of the cookies made my mouth water.

She waved a cookie in front of me, and slowly, I walked over and sat down beside her desk in the chair she had pulled up. I took the cookie from her and bit down mournfully. An explosion of taste overwhelmed my mouth, and I couldn't help but smile a little bit. She gave a knowing look and handed me another cookie, then another, and then the box. The happiness that came from cookies, though, was short-lived, and the grimace soon found its way back to my face.

She looked at me with her dirty-blonde eyebrows arched and her chin resting on her fist in the kind, contemplative look that often comes over her when she is thinking deeply about something.

"What's up, Peter?" she said softly with none of the exuberance that usually fills her voice. "You look a little down today."

I set the cookies back on the table and slumped back into my chair, trying to collect my thoughts. Everything was swirling around. "Thanks for the cookies," I said.

"You're very welcome." Her voice had just enough pep to make me feel a little better despite myself.

I fiddled with my fingers for a few seconds, trying to think of what I was going to say. Could I tell her there was a girl I really liked who was pretty, smart, and funny and whom I didn't have the guts to ask to prom, because I was afraid she'd reject me?

I looked around to see if anyone else was still in the room and then turned to face her. I spoke in Ancient Greek because somehow, I felt a little more comfortable in doing that. Maybe it was because the only people who ever have spoken to me in that

PAUL SCHEELER

language are people who love and care about me: Dad and Dr. Elsavier. Or maybe it was because no one else could have any idea what we were talking about if I spoke in Ancient Greek.

I took a deep breath. "There's a girl I really like," I blurted out. "I want to ask her out to prom, but I don't know how, and I'm afraid she'll say no."

Dr. Elsavier nodded sympathetically. "What's her name?"

"Emily," I said. "Emily Wong."

"It sounds like you really like the Wong girl," said Dr. Elsavier.

I nodded vigorously, ignoring the fact that *Wong* sounded like *wrong*, which my heart whispered to me was significant, perhaps Dr. Elsavier's way of telling me I was barking up the *Wong* tree.

"Really."

"Well," she said, folding her arms, "what do you think a young Odysseus would have done? What if Emily were his Penelope?"

I thought of all the hardships Odysseus had endured to make it home to his wife, Penelope, and all the sacrifice, courage, and endurance. It sounded a little ridiculous to compare my high school crush to the wife of an ancient Greek hero, but in that moment, it felt more inspiring than ridiculous.

Yet I couldn't shake the thought that I was no Odysseus. He had been clever and strong and had help from the goddess Athena, and I was just a dumb kid who probably wasn't even going to make it into college. I told Dr. Elsavier as much. Actually, I said, "I'm not Odysseus; I'm just a loser," in a horribly self-pitying voice.

She shook her head, and her eyes sparkled with wisdom. "No, no, Peter. When I think of you, I'm reminded of Alcibiades's description of Socrates. Maybe you're a little rough on the outside, but on the inside"—she reached forward and tapped my chest, right above my heart—"you have the figurines of beautiful gods."

"That sounds painful." My mind filled with images of figurines sticking out of my chest at odd angles and of blood seeping through the holes they made.

"Not literal figurines, Peter! I mean you have a divine spark in you, something more than meets the eye. You're an Odysseus, Peter. Believe me. I know one when I see one."

Her words stirred something deep inside me, even though the cynic in me was determined to ridicule the buoyant feeling of hope blossoming in my heart.

"Okay," I said. "I think I understand." I would find a way, just as Odysseus had, because it was worth doing. I looked up at Dr. Elsavier warmly and then cracked a smile. "If I'm Odysseus in this scenario and you're my helper, does that make you Athena?"

Dr. Elsavier laughed a clear, golden laugh and tossed back her hair. "Why, you flatter me, Peter! Though I've always thought I had a lot in common with the goddess of wisdom."

Her laugh was infectious, and I managed a chuckle too. The warmth from the laughter spread through my body until I felt much better. I even felt courageous enough to ask out Emily later tonight at the game. Dr. Elsavier and I chatted awhile longer, and I finished a few more cookies.

When our talk was over, she gave me a hug. I know it sounds weird, but you have to understand that Dr. Elsavier is not a normal teacher. She is more like a counselor, older sister, goddess, and surrogate mother wrapped into one kind, bubbly, smart, amazing person.

"Go on, Peter," she said, pushing back her hair and giving me her dimpled smile, which seems to combine both age and youth in one. "Go get 'em."

I left feeling as if I might stand some sort of chance. I headed home to struggle through some homework before going to the football game, where I planned to meet up with Goober. And then, I'd find Emily and would ask her out. My heart was pounding and my palms were sweating when I left the school.

CHAPTER 6

DISASTER AT THE FOOTBALL GAME

Goober and I met outside the ticket box, and after buying hot dogs and overpriced popcorn, we found a seat in the stands right by where the marching band was setting up.

I spotted Emily almost immediately. She was setting up her tuba and chatting merrily with her friends. I considered going down and asking her right away, but she looked kind of busy, I didn't know any of the other band kids, and how awkward would it have been for me to ask her out in front of them? So I managed to convince myself to ask her after the game.

The game went badly, with Blackstone obliterating us, as usual, though I didn't pay attention to the game. I was focused on how cute Emily looked marching with a tuba wrapped around her, with her cheeks reddened from the evening chill. The instrument looked way too big on her, which only made her look cuter.

By the time the game ended, it was dark, and the metal stands had gotten cold enough to make me shiver, even though I was wearing a coat. The elevation of my town is high enough to give spring a later start. Goober, on the other hand, was now wearing his black hoodie around his waist and had nothing on but a T-shirt. He seemed not to notice the cold, staring off into the distance in his usual way. That's the power of alcohol. Or maybe it's just Goober.

Goober and I made our way down the stands toward where the marching band packed up their stuff after the game.

"You're thinking about asking her, aren't you?" Goober said, shaking his head.

"Yeah," I said with a lump forming in my throat as I tried to work myself up to it. She was only a dozen feet away. I could be there in a few seconds if I just put one foot in front of the other. I closed my eyes, rehearsing, and was about stride forward, when Goober grabbed my shirt.

"Looks like you're too late," he said.

"What?" My already throbbing heart jacked into overdrive, and my stomach did a backflip.

Then I saw it. One of the football players was chatting with her—a big guy with a strong jaw and a smile I could never hope to match. She was giving him a look I wished she'd give me.

I stood there gaping like a fool for a few seconds and then turned and stormed away, feeling somehow betrayed, even though I knew I had no right to feel that way. It wasn't as if we were dating. We weren't even friends. She didn't even know I existed! But I didn't feel she had betrayed me; I felt I had betrayed myself with my dawdling. Odysseus hadn't dawdled. *I should have listened to Dr. Elsavier's advice and just gone for it. Why did I have to wait?*

I stormed behind the bleachers, past the hills of dirt from construction that was going on, with my thoughts swirling furiously.

"Hey, Pete, wait up."

It was Goober, and he sounded almost as if he cared; his voice made a rare deviation from his usual monotone drone.

"Pete!"

Goober came up beside me, huffing from exertion, as if catching up with my glorified speed-walking had been a difficult task. Maybe it was for Goober. He wasn't exactly the athletic type: scrawny and all jagged edges, with a diet consisting mostly of Mountain Dew, potato chips, and 120-proof vodka.

"Pete, don't you remember what this place is? We need to go."

I turned to him with my head feeling about as muddled and full of gunk as a two-week-old bowl of Lucky Charms. "What?"

Suddenly, an explosion of light half blinded me as two sets of brights came on. I felt a hand on my shoulder and simultaneously felt ice travel down my spine.

Even before I heard his voice, I knew exactly who it was.

CHAPTER 7

THE FATE OF MCBOOBLIAS AND CHEEKS

Stupid, stupid, stupid. I cursed to myself. *I should not have come back here. I should not have led Goober back here.*

"Well, hey there, Cheeks."

So here's a fun story: I used to pee with my pants down even when standing up, because I thought it was more comfortable. The idea sounded better in my own head, believe me. Unfortunately, my deviant bathroom practices were seen by the last people in Mormont High I would have wanted to see them: Brutus Borgia and his pals. Ever since that fateful hour, I've been known as Cheeks by Brutus and his gang of rats.

I slowly turned to face him. Brutus has a good four inches on me, and his arms have far too much muscle for a kid who's only in high school. Goober and I have long speculated—when Brutus isn't around, of course—how many years Brutus must have been held back, because it doesn't make sense that someone as muscled and intimidating as he is should still be in high school. His jaw is too chiseled, and there is not a hint of baby fat anywhere on his body.

"So, Peter," Brutus said slowly, as if enjoying every word he said, "you like older girls, do you?"

I stared at him with an expression of fear mixed with confusion on my face. "What?"

"Listen here, Cheeks," Brutus growled. "Don't play cute with me."

For a few more seconds, I still didn't get it, and then it hit me like a bag of potatoes—an experience I wouldn't recommend. He was talking about my afternoon talks with Dr. Elsavier.

I reddened because it was crazy what he was suggesting, but reddening was definitely the wrong move.

"Oh ho ho," said Brutus. "Blood flow doesn't lie." He slapped me on my back, massaging my shoulders in a way that somehow felt threatening. "Hey, there's nothing to be ashamed of. I'm actually impressed with you, Peter, for getting such a mature woman to go for you. The only thing I want to know is"—Brutus turned to his companions and did a little eyebrow dance before turning back to me with a crooked grin—"does Elsa know you piss with your pants down?"

Brutus erupted with laughter, and his buddies joined in, slapping their knees and acting as if Brutus had actually told a legitimate joke. As it happened, Brutus's barb was just a warm-up act, because a dozen more jokes soon followed, each filthier and less funny than the one before, until I was blushing half from the nastiness of their words and half from anger.

I could understand why they'd bully me: I was a total loser. But how could they talk about Dr. Elsavier like that? She was kind, and honest, and true.

27

Suddenly, a voice broke through the laughter.

"Don't t-talk to my friend l-like that."

Oh, Goober, I thought. *Just be quiet and let them beat us up. They'll leave us alone eventually.*

Brutus turned to him, still laughing. "Wh-what d-did you s-say?" he said, imitating Goober's high-pitched voice. "S-since wh-when did you become a s-stutterer, McBooblias?"

Goober reddened. "I just don't want you to talk to Pete like that."

Brutus's smile faded, and a dangerous gleam came into his eyes. "What did you say to me, Goo?"

Goober stood up to his full height. He straightened his shoulders, which he always keeps slouched, and then he spoke with deadly seriousness: "I said I don't want you to talk to Pete like that."

"Oh, Cheeks, you're a real player, aren't you? You got a mature woman as a girlfriend, and you've also managed to get yourself a boyfriend." He turned back to Goober. "Is he your boyfriend, McBooblias?"

Goober, who had imbibed goodness knows how much alcohol by that point, scowled. "No, he's my friend who happens to be a boy."

He sucked down the rest of his 120-proof vodka and smashed the tip of his bottle against the ground, forming a jagged knife but cutting himself in the process. He licked away the blood like a madman and pointed his makeshift knife at Brutus and his gang, as if daring them to step closer. Meanwhile, I silently pounded my head with my fist, thinking, *No, no, no, Goober, what are you doing? What are you doing? This isn't a forties western bar-fight scene. We're really going to get our butts handed to us now.*

But Goober, inspired no doubt by his alcohol, seemed intent on making things worse. "Whatcha gonna do, brute face? You gonna try to hit me? You gonna bully us?" He waved his glass dagger around. "La la la. My name is Brutus, and I once got in a competition with a potted plant for the lowest IQ in biology class, and I lost worse than Herbert Hoover in 1932!"

For the next few seconds, Goober continued on like that, spouting the dumbest things I'd ever heard in my life, until one of Brutus's fists landed smack between his eyes, sending him reeling backward. The makeshift knife flew from his hand. One of the bullies kicked it aside before running up to poor Goober and pulling him up by his hair. Goober, however, was not vanquished yet and began to bite and claw at the boy.

"Fly, Peter!" he called out between chomps and scratches. "I'll catch up with you later."

Once more, when the moment of action arrived, I stood there stupidly, trying to figure out why Goober thought I could fly, as I didn't have wings. Just as I realized he meant *fly* as in Gandalf's "Fly, you fools!" one of the boys body-tackled him, sending him crashing to the ground, and this time, three bullies had him: one for each arm and another to keep his head fixed in place so he couldn't bite.

Brutus turned to me and gave a malicious smile. "I wouldn't run if I were you, Cheeks. Not if you want your boyfriend here to avoid getting hospitalized."

My eyes darted around frantically, and I considered shouting for help, but the music from the pickup trucks was blaring, and we were too far from anyone who would care. My shoulders slumped, and I resigned myself to my fate, slowly walking back to where Brutus and the others stood.

He put one hand on my shoulder and then balled the other into a fist, setting it gingerly against my gut the way golfers line up their club with the ball before going in for the drive. He pulled back and drove the fist into my gut. I exhaled sharply as familiar pain exploded through my abdomen. I let out a muted cry.

Brutus shook his fist in the air. "Oh, that felt good!" He held me again and was about to hit when a female voice broke through the air.

"Don't touch him again."

CHAPTER 8

THE GIRL

My eyes flashed to my right, where the voice was coming from. A girl who looked like she was probably a year younger than I was stepped out of the shadows. She had dark hair, olive skin, and soft hazel eyes. She was wearing a flower-print dress that came to just below her knees, and her hair hung loosely. Her eyebrows, however, were drawn in a fierce expression. She looked ready to take on everyone standing there, even though she couldn't have been more than ninety pounds. Brutus could have sent her flying with a flick of his pinkie finger.

I shook my head at her, pleading with my eyes for her to go. Brutus was no gentleman, and I guessed he'd have no problems hitting girls.

He licked his lips and pointed a meaty finger at her. "You stay out of this, or you'll end up like him."

He turned to me with a wicked grin, pulled his fist back, and—

Suddenly, the girl was beside us, and her fist landed on his arm. A massive *crack* sounded in the air, and Brutus went flying backward.

He landed on his butt about ten feet away. With a pained expression, he slowly pushed himself up as his cheeks reddened. There was a dangerous look in his eyes.

He jabbed an accusing finger at the girl. "Get her," he snarled. His cronies surged forward.

I was about to scream, "Run!" but something kept me silent. I was madly curious what this strange girl would do next.

The boys fell on her, and one by one, she sent them hurling backward, each time with the same cracking sound. There was something funny about the sound. It couldn't have been bone breaking or her fist contacting flesh. It sounded more like a balloon popping.

A vague recollection came to me from my freshman science teacher, who'd explained why balloons made a popping sound when they burst—something about pressure waves. But how could that have had anything to do with what this girl was doing? Did she have a high-tech air gun up her sleeve?

That couldn't have been right. And even if it was, how could it explain how a girl who barely weighed ninety pounds could send a two-hundred-and-fifty-pound male flying ten feet through the air? I never had been good at physics, but I was pretty sure momentum was not being conserved. Even if she had that strength in her muscles somehow, she should have gone flying backward too. There just wasn't enough friction on the muddy ground.

I looked up again and saw Brutus Borgia and his forces scrambling. They climbed into their trucks and pulled away while still somehow managing to have enough dignity to make threats at me. Seven boys had just gotten their butts whooped by a girl who probably weighed as much as their little toes, and they still had the nerve to threaten us. Well, as Goober joked, Brutus probably would have lost an IQ competition to a potted plant.

The girl turned around and looked at me with her curious hazel eyes. We just stood there staring at each other. She raised an eyebrow as if she expected me to say something, but my tongue felt as if a sumo champion had decided to use it for a chair. It wasn't going anywhere.

"Ami!" called out a voice.

The magic of the moment broke, and both our necks swiveled to find the source of the noise. It seemed to belong to a boy leaning by the stands. It looked like he was holding a lighter in his hand, because a little flame was dancing in the night.

"Ami! If we're a minute later than we already are, your mother will kill me."

The girl looked between the boy with the lighter and me. "Will you be okay?"

I nodded, holding my stomach. "I've had worse."

She nodded reluctantly and turned with a little kick of her foot and ran off to find the boy, whose lighter still flickered in the night, despite the wind. I could have sworn that as she turned, a little gust of wind lifted her whole body off the ground. But it had to have been my imagination because wind doesn't work like that. My brain was probably not working right after Brutus's fist.

After she wandered off with the boy, I slapped myself. I hadn't even said thank you or asked her name. What was wrong with me? *Whenever a pretty girl looks at you, do you just forget how to speak, Peter? Is that it?*

33

Pretty girl. No, no, no. I pushed away the thought. I was interested in Emily.

Yet there was something about the girl—Ami. Yes, her name was Ami—why did I think I'd needed to ask her name? I'd heard the boy call her Ami. What was wrong with me?

I'm so confused. I held my head, feeling strangely light and warm and dizzy. An ache deepened in my chest. I wished I'd had a chance to talk to Ami longer.

I found Goober and hauled him up, and together we stumbled back home. The whole way, I couldn't get the girl with the flower dress out of my mind. How had she managed to defeat Brutus?

We walked home together, and it was just our luck that a massive storm broke out overhead, with lightning splitting the sky and even striking the earth. We were thoroughly soaked by the time we made it back.

That night, I had strange dreams. In one of them, I walked with the girl called Ami to meet the boy, and it turned out there was no lighter. The flame was dancing on his pointer finger, with no fuel or matches in sight. I turned, astounded, to Ami and found she was floating above the ground, holding out a hand to me as if offering to take me for a flight.

CHAPTER 9

DISAPPEARING DREAMS AND VANISHING TEENS

The long weekend was pretty uneventful right up until Monday night. I spent most of it doing nothing except playing *Ghost Army* with Goober and four other friends we'd met online but had never met in person. Our game play had been described by some as *cancerous* and *broken*, and we were proud of that achievement. It meant we were winning, and there was nothing the other team could do about it.

The one exception to that was whenever we fought against FireStarter520 and his team, who were probably more cancerous than we were, which was really saying something. There had been a few times in the past when I'd thrown my remote against the wall in frustration. But for some reason, he wasn't on that weekend, so the monopoly on cancerous game play that Goober and I had going was once more restored, and no one was going to stop us.

That was, until Monday, when my mom and dad finally came around to the topic I'd been desperately avoiding: the "unfortunate college situation," as my mom gently put it.

It was basically an ambush. I was called to the table for dinner, but instead of finding food on the table, I saw a handful of college rejection letters splayed out. My dad had his reading glasses on, which were perched on the tip of his nose, and had a bourbon in his left hand. My mom had her hands folded. *Oh jolly*, I thought. *I'm really in for it now.*

"Your mother and I have been thinking," my dad said, his voice gruffer from the bourbon he'd been drinking. "We, um— honey, would you?"

My mom put a hand on my father's, and she turned to me with her eyebrows drawn together. "Peter, what if college is not for you?"

A stab of pain blossomed somewhere just below my heart. Even though I knew my mother didn't mean to call me stupid, that was what it felt like. I couldn't even test into college.

I tried to remember Dr. Elsavier's encouragement that I was somehow like Socrates and that even though I might not have looked promising on the outside, I somehow had something special inside, waiting to emerge. But in that moment, I couldn't bring myself to believe it. I let my shoulders slump, and I slipped deeper into my chair.

"Oh, bambino, it is not a bad thing," she said, taking my hands in hers. They were warm, soft, and familiar. "There are other paths in life. I also did not go to university."

I could hear the ice in my father's bourbon glass clinking as he swirled it in his hand, and I knew he didn't feel the same. He was a college professor, and he had raised his son to speak Ancient

Greek and Latin. He hadn't done all that to see me work at Home Depot. I also knew he wouldn't accept my mom's reasoning. It was true she hadn't gone to college, but she was really smart and basically had the equivalent of a college degree from all the books she'd read. I wondered, not for the first time, how parents as smart as mine had managed to produce such a dud for a son.

"Look, Peter, not every college rejected you," my dad said, seeming to find his tongue again. "You do have an acceptance letter from Blackstone Community College. If you put your back into it, you can get good grades there and then transfer to one of the schools you got rejected from."

The way he said *if* made it sound an awful lot like he didn't think I was up to the task. If I had done so poorly in high school, how could I hope to do better in college—even at a community college?

"You do not have to decide now, bambino," my mom said. "But you need to do some research. Find out whether you like Blackstone Community College or whether you should go to— how are they called?—a technical school."

My father nodded. "You have to think about your future, Son. You can't just play video games your whole life."

"It's true," said my mother. "They don't prepare you for life."

I nodded glumly and promised I'd look into it. But when I walked into my room, I saw all the posters of my favorite games staring back at me. I glanced between my computer, where my mom and dad wanted me to do research, and my game console, where Goober was waiting. The decision was clear.

I might not have been able to play video games my whole life, but I could that night. I called Goober, and we got the gang together for a night of games, which lasted till about eleven o'clock, when I heard my mom's voice break through the sounds of gunfire and explosions.

"Peter!"

Her voice was urgent and concerned. I told Goober and the others good night and rushed out to see what was wrong. I'd only heard my mother sound that way once before: when I was about to walk right into an oncoming truck.

I found my mom and dad together on the couch in the living room, staring at the glowing TV screen.

"Did you know them?" my mom asked with her eyes fixed straight ahead.

I turned and saw a local news anchor talking. His expression was grave and concerned. "If you have any information, please direct it to …"

The words faded into noise as my eyes caught sight of the pictures. One was of an Indian boy with a crooked smile and eyes that reminded me of the genius scientists I'd seen in old photographs. Scary smart. The other was of a girl with olive skin, dark hair, and soft hazel eyes.

"Ami," I breathed.

Ami, the girl who had saved Goober's and my butts, had gone missing. I had a strange feeling the Indian boy was the boy with the lighter who had called to her from the stands.

CHAPTER 10

THE BAD BUS RIDE

Tuesday came, and with it came the field trip. I must not have been paying attention, because I had no idea where we were going. The buses ferried us to school, where we attended homeroom before going back to the buses for second bell. Our history teacher announced we would have assigned seating on the bus, which I thought was stupid, until he said the seats would be assigned alphabetically and read out the list. The last two names were Smythe and Wong.

My heart skipped a beat. I would be sitting with Emily. My mind began to spin ridiculous stories of how our hands might brush as we sat next to each other, she might look at me with her vivacious brown eyes and laugh at my jokes, I would somehow find the courage of Odysseus to ask her out, and she would agree to go to the prom with me. I turned to Goober, so excited I could have shaken him, but he only rolled his eyes.

"Way to rain on my parade," I muttered.

"Well, since I've already started to rain on your parade," said Goober in his usual flat voice, "I might as well point out that Emily isn't here."

"What?"

My eyes glanced around, running over the students, and sure enough, Emily was not there. I wanted to hit myself with a baseball bat until I woke up from this bad dream. How could Emily be missing? On the one day when we were designated to be seat buddies, she was gone.

"Expectations," Goober said sagely. "Keep them low, and you won't be so disappointed."

"Yeah," I muttered with my shoulders slumping. "I guess at least things couldn't get worse."

"I wouldn't have said that," said Goober, his voice breaking a monotone for the first time since he'd pleaded with me to flee on Friday night.

I turned to see what he was gaping at, and my shoulders slumped even lower. "No, it can't be."

A woman with neatly done-up silver hair, a colossal sagging bosom, and a gigantic mole complete with hair above her puckered lips was approaching, walking in her usual imperious manner, with her clipboard pressed against her.

"Ms. Schaden," Goober moaned. "Why her?"

Ms. Schaden immediately got to work. Her shrill voice broke up the chatter and laughter around us. She took attendance and frowned when she came to Emily Wong, who was absent.

"Well, I guess there will be a group of three," she said with her nose wrinkling as if someone had put rotten fish under her nostrils.

The girl in Goober's and my group was about the size of Goober and me put together, plus some, so Goober and I ended up as seatmates. She stuffed the comic she had been reading into her backpack; pushed up her glasses, which looked more like laboratory goggles; and turned to us with a broad smile.

"Aren't you delighted Ms. Schaden is accompanying us as chaperone on this journey?" She spoke in an affected southern accent, like a southern belle who spent her days sipping iced tea on the porch and commiserating about how the Emancipation Proclamation had robbed the South of a convenient unpaid labor force.

The bus lurched forward, and the smell of diesel and oil filled the crisp morning air.

Goober looked mournfully at the bus floor and took a drink from his bottle. "Now it can't get any worse."

At the time, it sounded right. What could be worse than getting ditched by Emily, having Ms. Schaden as chaperone, and getting stuck in a group with a brownnosing southern girl who actually liked Ms. Schaden?

By this point, you probably have guessed that in fact, we had a long way to go before things couldn't get any worse.

As the bus bumped along a badly paved road, Ms. Schaden explained the plan for the day. Her voice somehow combined the sounds of nails on a chalkboard with grinding glass. We were going to visit some historic caves, and everyone had to complete three pages of notes and afterward write a two-thousand-word essay. She finished with her usual sermon about how we couldn't have nice experiences like this if we didn't obey the rules, so everyone had best behave, and so on ad nauseam.

After Ms. Schaden finished her soliloquy, I hoped we might get a few minutes of peace and quiet. But then the southern belle, who apparently was named Clarice Jackson—related, yes, to Stonewall Jackson, as she was happy to tell us—started talking again in a nonstop stream of Georgian drawl.

I plugged in my headphones and opened up the YouTube video recording of *The Odyssey* in Ancient Greek. I did my best to focus on the rhythmic poetry, but I couldn't help but overhear Goober and Clarice.

"I don't want to listen to you," Goober said. "I'm trying to think about something else."

I opened my right eye just a crack to see what was going on.

"Oh, bless your heart," said Clarice, shaking her head. Her auburn pigtails flapped menacingly. "What could be more important than what I have to say?"

"Nothing," said Goober flatly.

Clarice seemed taken aback. "Um, yes, exactly."

"No," said Goober as if talking to someone spectacularly stupid. "I mean I'm trying to think about nothing, because it's better than the alternative."

Clarice's already red face flushed a shade redder. "You," she said, waving her finger at him. She turned and raised a hand. "Ms. Schaden!"

"Who is it?" Ms. Schaden snapped. "Oh, Clarice." Her voice suddenly became sweet like that of a grandma doting on her favorite grandchild. "What is it, dear?"

She pointed a fat, accusing finger at Goober and me. "They are mocking me."

Ms. Schaden's face grew redder than the inside of a watermelon. Suddenly, the bus began to shake as she made her way down the aisle—or at least that was how it felt to me.

I elbowed Goober. "Once more, the situation that wasn't supposed to be able to get any worse has gotten worse," I muttered darkly, and then I turned up the sound on my headphones. At that point, I just didn't care.

Ms. Schaden began her usual speech in her sanctimonious, screechy voice, and I did my best to ignore it. It sounded like Goober was getting the worst of it. But suddenly, that changed.

"What rot are you listening to?" Ms. Schaden ripped the headphones out of my ears and stuck one in her own ear, which I couldn't help but notice was not lacking in hair. Her face went through a series of contortions—first confusion, then dismay, and then disapproval—with her lips puckering unpleasantly. "What devilish nonsense is this? Some kind of chanting in a foreign language."

My knuckles grew white as my hands balled into fists. I wished Dr. Elsavier were there. She was sensitive and intelligent, and she would never say something so stupid. "Those are mine. And it's *The Odyssey*," I said, maybe with a little bit too much attitude in my voice.

"Oh, really, Peter Smythe? It sounds Greek to me."

"That's because it is Greek!" I noticed now that half the bus was looking at me.

"Detention," said Ms. Schaden icily. She gave Clarice a tender look and then marched back to the front of the bus.

"Nice," Goober said under his breath after she had gone.

Nice indeed. Detention wasn't so bad, but it would only be a matter of time till my little revelation made its way to Brutus

Borgia. I could already imagine how much fun he'd have with that: "Cheeks likes to listen to Ancient Greek chanting, hur hur hur." It wasn't funny at all, but Brutus's idea of humor was never funny. It was just mean.

Well, whatever. At least things can't get any worse, I thought.

Once more, I was wrong.

CHAPTER 11

THE FATEFUL FIELD TRIP

As we got off the bus, Ms. Schaden handed us each three pages of paper and a pen to use to collect our field notes. She gave me a particularly sour look, followed by a leering gaze, as if she were looking forward to seeing us in detention that afternoon.

Whatever.

We all gathered around an old sign that was supposed to look as if it had been made in the 1800s, when cowboys and Indians fought in the Wild West. Apparently, the place was low budget, because the sign looked pretty cheesy, with fake bullet holes and the works. It was fitting for a Mormont field trip.

After Goober and I finished ridiculing the sign, we read it: "Ai'rim Caves. Est. a long, long time ago."

"What's that supposed to mean?" I asked with my brow furrowed. I was in a mood in which I just wanted to be angry about everything. "Established a long, long time ago? They don't know when they founded this place?"

"I think it's supposed to be a joke," said Goober.

Ms. Schaden led us down winding stone steps to the main area. There was a small lake that flowed out into a slow-moving stream, which led southward. The rock walls were pockmarked with holes just large enough to fit a person or two. So this was the so-called cave.

I slapped my neck as I felt something fuzzy move along it. The weather had warmed up enough to bring the bugs back to life—at least the annoying ones.

"This is the first stop on our trip," said Ms. Schaden in her shrill, grating voice that made her sound like a banshee with pneumonia. "Make sure you take careful notes. I have instructed your teachers to grade strictly."

I wasn't sure she had the authority to do that, but Ms. Schaden was pretty good at bullying people to get her way. As far as I could tell, this field trip had been her idea. No one else would have decided the best way to spend a school day was to look at rocks for five hours and then write a freaking report about it.

I looked around, trying to find something interesting. We were in a chasm of sorts, with a tree line above us and rocks with tiny caves in the walls—nothing big enough to explore.

"Come on," said Goober. "I know a place that's really cool."

I turned to him. "You mean you've been here before?"

Goober's expression remained blank. "Yeah, man. It's a great place to do drugs."

"I don't want to do drugs."

A crooked smile appeared on his face. "Whatever. Just come with me. I can't stand being around Ms. Schaden anymore. Besides, we're already on her bad side and have detention. Could it really get any worse?"

I suppose by that point, I should have understood the answer to that question was "Yes, it could get a whole lot worse." But my head was too muddled by Emily's absence and the humiliation on the bus to be bothered with things like common sense, so I followed Goober down a rocky pathway, away from the others.

The forest above blocked a lot of the sunlight, and the rocks overhead blocked even more. It was getting dark, and I had to turn on my phone's flashlight just to see. But soon we started ascending again, and there was enough light to see by the time we found the place Goober was looking for: a cave whose diameter was about as big as I was tall.

Goober gave a little grin, scampered up the rocks, and then helped me in. We sat on the slippery rocks with our legs dangling freely. He opened up his backpack, and I expected him to pull out his fake water bottle, but instead, he pulled out a full-on bottle of vodka.

I stared at him as if to say, *Really?*

He took a sip and offered it to me.

"No, thanks," I said, pushing it away by instinct. He'd tried to get me to drink a few times before, and I'd always said no. I knew my mom wouldn't like it, and my dad would probably slay me.

"Come on," he said. "You're not gonna tell me life doesn't suck right now, are you?"

"Yeah, of course it does." My thoughts were still on Emily, and my mood felt dark. "But I don't see how drinking is going to fix that."

Goober shook his head. "It doesn't. It just makes it more tolerable."

I thought of Emily's big brown eyes and how they seemed to sparkle when she smiled. Pain rippled through me, and on a whim, I grabbed Goober's bottle and took a long drink.

Almost immediately, I began to cough, and my face contorted as the harsh taste exploded in my mouth. But then I felt a rush of warmth as the liquor burned its way down my throat to my stomach, and my mood rushed upward like a boat on a wave. "Wow, that tastes terrible and feels really good."

Goober nodded sagely. "Exactly."

We sat there awhile longer, passing the bottle back and forth, though I only pretended to take sips, because the world already felt like it was losing its balance—which probably meant *I* was losing *my* balance. The only experience I'd ever had with alcohol was sipping wine from a little cup during Easter.

Goober and I chatted aimlessly about how unfortunate our situations were, commiserating on having Ms. Schaden as our chaperone and discussing strategies for *Ghost Army*, which we decided we'd play as soon as we got out of detention. Meanwhile, the back half of my half-drunk mind was thinking about Emily, how pretty she was, and what could have happened to her.

Suddenly, my heart lurched as I stumbled upon a fact that should have been obvious at the start: this was the first time since eighth grade that Emily had missed a day of school, even when she was sick. She always got a perfect-attendance award. There must have been a serious reason.

"I think something's seriously wrong with Emily," I said, interrupting Goober's exposition on how vodka improved his reflexes in video games.

"Like what?" said Goober.

For some reason, the newscast about the missing teens from Blackstone flashed before my eyes. Could the reason they were missing also have been the reason Emily was missing? *No*, I thought. *That couldn't be right. It's coincidence.*

But all the same, I felt a sinking in my gut, a secret knowledge that there was a connection between Emily's disappearance and Ami's.

"I'm not sure," I said at last. "But she hasn't missed a day of school in all the time I've known her. Something has to be up."

Goober looked at me skeptically, as if the alcohol were having a stronger effect on me than on him. "Yeah, Pete?"

"Yeah," I said, feeling a rush of courage in my gut. "We should go look for her."

Goober snickered. "Sit down, Pete. You're drunk."

I furrowed my brow and realized I had stood up. "Oh," I said, stupidly, and I slumped down to a crouch. My mind refocused on the goal. "But seriously, Goober, we need to go look for her. Something could be wrong."

"Isn't that someone else's problem?" asked Goober in a voice that left no doubt as to what he thought the answer was. "She has parents and friends, you know. Oh, don't look sad. I didn't mean it like that."

"Yeah, I know we're not friends. I know she probably doesn't even know who I am. But why can't I care?"

"Pete, you know, to an outsider, it would sound like you were some kind of stalker. I know you're not, but consider how it looks."

I scowled. "Are we friends or not? I'm going."

"Peter," said Goober tiredly.

But I had already slipped down from the cave, landing on the rocks below. I knew this harebrained plan would probably get me suspended, but alcohol and love can be very persuasive. A moment later, I heard Goober clop down beside me. I guess friendship too can be pretty persuasive.

We were about to move, when suddenly, the sound of footsteps came echoing from the way we had come: the familiar trod of Ms. Schaden. I turned to Goober as our eyes widened. "Is there another way out?"

He shook his head. "Quick. The cave goes farther back. Let's hide back there."

At that point, it probably should have occurred to me that by running from Ms. Schaden, we would only be making our punishment worse. But once more, that didn't occur to me. My thoughts were on Emily and escaping the immediate pain of having to see Ms. Schaden's gigantic mole.

"Hurry!" said Goober, placing two hands on my butt and shoving me forward. I was about to make a dumb joke about him buying me dinner first, when I heard Goober make a squeaking sound. My head spun around, and I saw him slip out of the cave right onto the floor. I was going to go back for him, but he shook his head. "Go on without me," he mouthed.

What is with you, Goober, and your acts of self-sacrifice lately? I wondered. First with Brutus and now with Ms. Schaden. Maybe he was just making up for all the detentions he had gotten me over the years.

I moved farther back into the cave, but I could hear voices behind me.

"Mrs. Schaden! I was just looking for you."

"It is *Ms.* Schaden. How dare you assume my marital status!"

"I didn't mean to, Mrs.—Ms. Schaden. I always assumed you couldn't ... I mean wouldn't ... I mean, didn't ... have gotten married."

Oh boy, I thought. Goober always had a way with words.

"Resol McGooblias, both your manners and grammar are atrocious."

Goober made another squeaking noise, which I assumed was because Ms. Schaden had pulled her old trick of grabbing him by the ears. I was going to have to join him, I decided. I couldn't just let my friend suffer there without me.

I was about to launch myself out of the cave, hopefully giving Ms. Schaden a heart attack, when I noticed something strange: there were markings on the cave. Old markings, not like the cheesy writing on the sign. They were markings unlike any I had ever seen before. They looked like an ancient script from who knew when. Had Indians once lived in those caves and maybe used them for some kind of ritual?

I placed a hand against the markings, slowly tracing them with my finger, with my mouth hanging slightly open in fascination. I felt a shiver of power run through me as I completed the tracing, and the cave felt cold.

Suddenly, I wanted to be out of the cave. There was a power there, and I did not want to know more. I was about to push myself out, when my hands slipped, and I fell back on something small, hard, and sharp.

"Ow," I muttered, reaching instinctively for the object and pulling it out from under me. Even before I laid eyes on it, I knew what it was from its circular shape: a ring.

I turned it over in my hands, examining it. Even in the darkness, it seemed to glow and almost sparkle, as if something inside it were alive, like fish that glow in the darkness at the bottom of the ocean. But unlike those fish, which look pretty freaking ugly, the glow of this ring was beautiful and entrancing, almost like Emily's eyes. Or like Ami's smile.

I felt a rip in my heart as two parts of me pulled in opposite directions. Then I felt a little stab of guilt, as if by thinking of Ami, I was being disloyal to Emily.

"Peter!" A shrill voice echoed through the cavern. "I know you're in there, young man. Now, present yourself this moment before I have you expelled."

Expelled. That couldn't happen. Then I'd never get a chance to take Emily out to prom.

I meant to push myself forward, but my limbs didn't move. It was almost like the sensation you feel when you wake up really early and know you should get out of bed, but your body just won't do it.

I tried again, but still, I didn't move.

"Don't make me wait for you, Peter Smythe!"

"I'm coming," I wanted to say, but the words wouldn't form.

Why? Why wouldn't they form?

Then I realized I was holding the ring out in front of me, staring at its beautiful pale light. I wanted to put it on, I decided. I really wanted to put it on.

Ms. Schaden began to count, as if I were still in kindergarten. "Ten. Nine. Eight …"

No, no, no. I have to leave the cavern, not get expelled, and find out what happened to Emily. We can worry about this ring later.

But the ring was insistent, and slowly, my finger crept toward the hole.

"Seven. Six. Five …"

I tried to pull my finger away, but it wouldn't budge.

"Four. Three. Two ..."

Suddenly, the desire was overwhelming, and I gave in, fitting my finger into the ring.

"One."

For a moment, everything was quiet, and then I felt a rush of power a thousand times stronger than what I had felt when I touched the strange script on the wall of the cave. I was flung backward deep into the cave, and a moment later, I saw—no, I *felt* somehow—cracks rushing along the extent of the cave.

My eyes widened as my heart thrummed with fear. I needed to get out. Now.

But before I could move, the cracks widened, and I began to plummet. A rush of wind swallowed my final scream.

CHAPTER 12

I Become a Jedi, Sort Of

I spent the next minute screaming at the top of my lungs until I ran out of breath, only to suck in more air to scream again. If you've never free-fallen for a solid minute from the inside of a dark cave into pitch blackness, then let me tell you: the experience is utterly terrifying. Even more terrifying than Ms. Schaden's mole.

As I plummeted through nothingness, I became aware of a change in the air. It was sort of a strange thing to be aware of just before you think you're about to die. I'd always heard you think about your family and closest friends, but instead, I noticed weird things. For example, the air smelled and tasted different, and there was an odd feeling to the darkness around me, as if it weren't made of the same stuff as my world, whatever that meant. And there was that thrum of power coming from my finger, where a ring of sparkling stone held on and wouldn't let go.

All these meditations came to an abrupt end as I face-planted into solid rock.

That probably should have been the end of me, but after a few seconds of wiggling my fingers and convincing myself I was still breathing, I peeled myself off the rock. That was when I noticed there was now a me-shaped indentation. I held my head, which now ached, partly from the alcohol and partly from trying to grasp how a human body could cause a dent in solid rock. Strangely, my head wasn't aching at all from slamming into solid stone.

I looked around and found myself in a dark room made of stone, barely illumined by the pale light of the ring on my finger. *Could it be*, I wondered, *that the ring somehow saved me?*

I flicked myself. "Wake up, Peter. This is either a weird dream, your brain's way of trying to tell you to be ready for the field trip tomorrow, or Goober's vodka was juiced with a little more than alcohol." I looked around. "Why am I talking aloud?"

I flung my hands up in frustration, and suddenly, a slab of rock leaped out of the ground. I scrambled backward, waving my hands as stones were flung about the room, seemingly tossed by invisible hands. Every time I swatted them away with my hands, more of them came, shooting out of the walls and ceilings, making me breathe faster and causing my heart to race more frantically.

"What is going on?" I screamed, flinging my arms about, trying to stop myself from getting pummeled by one of the flying rocks.

A voice broke through the mad confusion of my consciousness. *Stop moving*, it ordered.

I fought for a few seconds longer, but the rocks kept coming. There was no way I could defend against them forever, so reluctantly, I let my arms drop, expecting a slab of rock to burst through the wall at any moment and decapitate me.

Instead of killing me violently, however, the rocks just fell to the ground, as if the force that had caused them to fly about were gone.

I furrowed my brow. "What the—"

Tentatively, I raised my arms again. Nothing happened.

"Try imagining," a voice whispered.

This time, I imagined the rocks rising off the ground—and they moved, levitating, as if I were some kind of Jedi.

"Whoa," I said in a low, almost reverent voice. "This has to be a dream."

Some part of me knew better, though. There was something too vivid and coherent about the experience for it to be a dream. That left only two possibilities: Goober had put mushrooms in the vodka, or this was freaking real. I shoved aside the question because it made me want to panic. I decided instead to try a simpler question.

"Why did the rocks attack me?"

"Come on," said the little voice. "Use your head."

I thought for a moment, and then it hit me—literally. A rock went flying from the ground right into the side of my face, though it didn't really hurt.

I realized the rocks had attacked me because I had been imagining them as attacking me. What does everyone fear about the dark? That a monster will jump out and attack. Somehow, in that weird world, which was either a dream or an extremely bad trip, imagination was reality.

"Lessons finished. Welcome to Miria," said the voice. And that was when everything went downhill—literally.

The world tilted sideways, and I began to slide. A wall of freezing air rushed up to meet me, followed by blistering white light. With a start, I realized I was staring into a frozen tundra below, and not only that, but I was about to fall. Again.

I clawed at the rocks, but they no longer seemed interested in obeying me, and in three seconds, I was once more plummeting. This time, I was much colder.

CHAPTER 13

A FAMILIAR FACE

The next few moments happened fast. I fell several hundred feet, during which time I wondered how it was possible I had fallen from a floating rock and how I had ended up on a floating rock able to control matter in the first place. That little mental discussion, and the screaming noise I was vaguely aware I was making, was interrupted as I plunged into a bath of freezing water.

I'd watched enough TV shows involving hypothermia to know I was probably in for it, even if I managed to get myself out of the water. But I was still young at that point and thought I might have a shot at escaping the horrible world of floating rocks, disembodied voices, and frozen oceans.

After a great deal of desperate effort, I finally got myself aboard a chunk of ice, which had a nasty icicle that looked more like a dagger or a T. rex tooth than an icicle. I also noticed with some discomfort that I had landed only a few inches from it. That would have been a way to go—impaled on an icicle.

I was just about to try out my magical powers on the ice block, hopefully to speed myself toward land, when I saw in the distance a monstrous face made of ice, with two blinking eyes like frozen fire. The ice giant.

And that brings us to the present, wherein a gigantic Yeti-looking thing made of ice is inches from my face, staring at me with malignant eyes.

Well, at least I've told my story. I guess I can die now.

The ice giant raises its fist of needle-sharp fingers to crush me, and I stare up at it with my heart thumping madly against my chest. I close my eyes, about to embrace my inevitable fate—getting skewered is probably better than slowly freezing to death anyway—when I suddenly feel a wild rush of warmth in my veins.

It's not terror exactly, though I do feel terror coursing through my veins, sending renewed strength to every muscle fiber in my body. It's more like a certain and unmoving realization that I am not going to die without a fight. For some reason, the image that comes to my mind is of Goober breaking his bottle against the ground to form a makeshift knife. Stupid, foolhardy, and bound to fail. But it's better than just giving in.

I stare up at the ice giant, and this time, I glare at it with all the fearful rage I can focus into one hateful stare. Then I squeeze my eyes shut, and I reach for the power I felt in the floating stone room, which now is gone, when I learned I could bend stone to my will. I call upon the ice, the snow, and the freezing waters below, bidding them to swallow up the ice monster in front of me and cast it back into the sea.

There's a whistling in my ears, followed by a harsh rumbling sound. My eyes burst open, expecting to see the ice giant flying across the sea. Instead, I see it's still there, though it's covered with dust and pebbles and little pieces of dirt. The sound isn't the monster getting tossed back where it came from; the sound is its laughter, I think. A weird sort of laughter that would almost be funny if I were reading about this while curled up in my bed rather than facing it in real life. My brow furrows. Why isn't the ice obeying me?

Then I realize what should have been obvious. I think of the ring of glowing rock and the palace of stone whose walls and rocks obeyed me. The ring's power only extends to earthy things, hence the dust and pebbles.

Well, that sucks.

The monster's laughter ceases, and it turns to me with a gloating, inhuman smile, as if it knows the jig is up. It raises its fist once more to attack, and this time, I know it's over.

"Goodbye, Mom and Dad," I whisper. "Thanks for being my only friend, Goober. I'm sorry, Emily, I was too much of a coward to ask you out to prom. And Dr. Elsavier, thank you for being the best teacher ever."

I face my enemy with my chin raised in defiance, though my legs and arms are still shaking. I can see it's about to come crashing down toward me.

Suddenly, a familiar voice breaks through the air: "Duck!"

My body reacts before my mind has time to process the sound, throwing me onto the ground. A fraction of a second later, a ball of flame rushes over my head, passing through where I was just standing. My head whips up, and I look to the ice monster. It is staring down at its chest, which now has a gaping hole in it.

I crane my neck in the direction from which the ball of flame came, and I see a boat about fifteen feet away. Characters like the ones I saw in the cave of Ai'rim are carved into the sides of the boat, and three faces are staring back at me. My mind latches on to one of the faces, which is familiar.

Finally, my overloaded brain catches up and matches the voice with a face and the face with a name.

"Emily," I say, breathless.

CHAPTER 14

An Extremely Unlikely Escape

I'm certain this has to be a dream, because Emily is in front of me, staring at me from the boat. Her black hair is waving in the wind, and her perfect red lips open wide as she shouts something.

What is she saying?

I try to pull my attention to the words, because something in me knows they're vitally important, but my attention won't budge. I just lie there, stupidly gazing at Emily, probably drooling, and no doubt ruining my future with her.

"The monster!" The words break through the wall of mist around my mind, and their meaning connects with reality.

I whip around and see the ice monster. The hole in its chest is gone, though I can see a rim around the spot where it was.

"Oh, you've got to be kidding me," I say. "You can heal yourself that quickly? Could this get any worse?"

I probably should not have used that phrase after all the times today when things got worse even after I thought they couldn't. Each time, the problems escalated massively in scale. First, Emily went missing, then Ms. Schaden attended our field trip, then I ended up in another world, and then I got attacked by a freaking ice monster. I thought the world was ending because Ms. Schaden was our chaperone, but that seems almost cute now compared to what I am seeing. What I'm seeing is actually worse than a self-healing ice monster.

An army of self-healing ice monsters are forming up out of the water behind the first one, which stares at me with frozen hatred in its pale blue eyes.

I try to scramble back as the monster swings its fist at me, but I'm too slow, and I slip clumsily on the ice. I brace for impact, when suddenly, a gust of wind flings me upward. I flail about before finding that gravity has not stopped working, and I plummet into the freezing water.

Whoosh. The water closes over my head, and I feel the thirsty cold suck the warmth from my body even faster than it did when I stood on the ice. I try to push myself upward, but my body feels heavy. *I could just let go*, I think. *I could fall asleep.*

I stare up at the fading light of the surface, thinking, not for the first time today, I am going to die, despite having been saved by Emily, her flame-flinging friend, and whatever caused that gust of wind to save me from getting smashed to death by the ice monster.

In my final moments—which I seem to have had a lot of today—I reach out my hand toward the surface. I enjoy a last dream in which Emily reaches down and takes my hand, and I feel her soft skin against mine and the thrill of warmth that comes from knowing the person you like likes you too.

I'm struck by how vivid the dream feels, because it seems almost as if there is a hand gripping mine. But the hand, unlike how I imagined it, is not soft and soothing but desperate and urgent. The hand yanks me to the surface, and from below, I feel the water push me, propelling me upward.

I burst from the water and find myself floating in the air again, with the wind somehow keeping me aloft. My mind reels with confusion; I expect to see Emily gripping my hand, but instead, it's—

My mind struggles to come up with her name—the girl with olive skin and hazel eyes who single-handedly kicked the butts of Brutus Borgia and his entire gang. For a moment, our eyes meet, and my stomach does a somersault for reasons I don't understand. There is something in her eyes, a kindness and warmth that almost remind me of my mom. But there's also fear and strain.

Suddenly, she begins to wobble and then falls, plunging into the freezing water. Somehow, though, I stay above the surface, as if she's using all her strength to keep me from the deadly cold water.

"Ami!" I cry as the name floods back into my mind. I reach for her, but someone grabs me.

"Oh no you don't."

It's Emily's voice. She pulls me into the boat and sets me down in the back. She waves her hands in a way similar to how I instinctively moved my hands in the cave, only my movements were larger and more rigid, while hers seem to flow like the water itself, though her hands tremble. A moment later, the water responds, and Ami comes shooting out. Emily grabs her too, pulls her into the boat, and sets her next to me. Her wet jacket presses against my flimsy hoodie.

Emily turns toward the boy, whose features I can make out a little closer, though it feels as if a curtain is falling over my eyes.

He has brown skin; teeth as white as snow; and intense, confident eyes—eyes like those of a genius scientist in an old photograph.

"We got him," says Emily.

"OK, our mission was to get Four, not to fight a war. I'll hold them off. You get us out of here."

Emily nods, and I feel the boat lurch as it suddenly speeds up, while the boy sends jets of flame to the left and right.

There's something about his voice that sounds vaguely familiar, but it sounds so far away, as if echoing from around some distant bend. My eyes close, and I begin to slip into darkness.

As my overloaded and freezing brain finds sleep, the memory of the night at the football game comes to me, only this time, I let Ami take my hand and lead me to the boy with the lighter. Just like in my dream only a few nights before, I find it is not a lighter in his hand but a little flame that dances upon his finger. He puts his fiery hands above me, warming me, and somehow, I know this keeps me from dying as I fall into the deepest sleep I've ever had.

A single question is on my mind as I slip into slumber: *What did the boy mean when he called me Four?*

CHAPTER 15

THE FOUR

Sometime later, I wake from sleep. My head feels fuzzy, as if it can't quite string concepts together. My skin is very warm, though someplace inside me is still shivering from the cold.

The cold. Right. I went swimming in arctic waters. And there was an ice giant. No, giants. And there was Emily, Ami, and the boy with the fiery hands.

I hear voices chatting quietly. I open my eyes slowly but only a crack because the world is so bright and because I can't see much anyway. The world looks like a bunch of vague blobs swimming around.

"Oh, he's waking up!" says an excited female voice.

"Finally," says a bored male voice.

"Caster, try to be more sensitive! He almost got killed by ice giants, almost drowned, and almost froze to death, and he probably is confused as all get out."

"As all get out?" says the boy dryly.

Caster, I think. *What kind of weird name is that?*

"Dear Emily Wong, who taught you to speak?" Caster says.

"I learn in China," she says in an exaggerated Chinese accent. "Shut up, Caster. It's a perfectly normal expression, and it's also not the point. The point is that you should be more sensitive."

"Lord knows we have enough sensitivity," he mutters.

"Do you think he's okay?" says another female voice, this one softer and quieter. She sounds almost guilty the way she says the words.

"It's not your fault, Ami," says Emily. "You almost drowned yourself!"

"Yeah, but—"

"But nothing," Caster says.

The fuzzy shapes begin to congeal until I can more or less make them out. I watch as the boy tousles Ami's hair. She too is under a pile of blankets, and she is sitting next to me, close enough for our comforters to touch. My eyes roll around the room, taking in the sights. We seem to be arranged along a circular couch. It has a rich wood frame and plush pillows all along it, and it's inscribed with the same strange script I saw in the cave at Ai'rim and on the boat. Statues line the high stone walls, depicting figures with majestic faces and weapons in their arms. The ceiling is a dome, which shows the starry heavens but is somehow intensely bright.

With thoughts swirling, I look down again and to the three people around me. "Hi," I manage to say.

All the faces turn to me, and I suddenly wish I'd kept mum. I want desperately to slink deeper into the blankets to avoid their gazes.

"Well, hello!" says Emily, leaning close enough for me to smell the perfume on her.

Cherry blossoms, I think. The sweet smell makes me dizzy, and my stomach does at least a dozen somersaults in rapid succession. I fear I'm blushing furiously.

"Welcome to the Palace of Methyldonin," Emily says.

"Yes, welcome to the Palace of Meth," says Caster, the boy with caramel-colored skin. "He likes to go by Meth."

"He absolutely does not, Caster," Emily says. She then turns to me and smiles. "His nickname is Cog, and he's the friendliest god I've ever met."

"God?" I repeat.

"Well, sort of," says Emily. "He's an immortal being who can take human form but whose true form is something else, and he has tremendous power, which he is tasked with using to defend Miria. Or so he says."

"Right," I say slowly.

"None of that made any sense to you, did it?" says Caster.

I shake my head.

"First things first. Everyone, please extend your hand."

Caster puts his hand out first, followed by Emily. A wreath of golden flame dances along his left ring finger, while a watery ring that seems to pulse with life snakes around Emily's. I manage to extricate my hand from the pile of blankets and place it next to Ami's. Mine, of course, is the glowing rock, but Ami's hand is bare.

"Where's Ami's?" I ask.

Caster looks at me with an amused look. "You must have worked this all out by now. I, Caster Kshatriya-Wick, am fire. Emily Wong is water. You, Peter whatever—"

"Peter Smythe," I say.

"S-m-i-t-h? That's a boring name."

"It's S-m-y-t-h-e," I say.

"Oh, well, at least it's an interesting, if illogical, spelling. Anyway, you, Peter Smythe, are earth. And that leaves Ami Adsila, who must therefore be the Last Airbender. Now, Peter, I'm going to ask you a question. Is air visible?" He looks at me with a crooked grin and amused eyes, as if he's just said the cleverest thing in the world.

"That was mean, Caster," says Emily.

"What?" says Caster. "I was just adapting myself to the level of intell—"

"Oh, stop it," says Emily, rolling her eyes. "From now on, I'll do the explaining. I'm nicer to noobs."

"I don't think that's how you use that word," mutters Caster, but he keeps quiet as Emily goes on to explain what's what.

"Right, so each of us was brought to this world by Methyldonin, a.k.a. Cog, who used the last of the power of the Hearthstone to summon the Four, a.k.a. us, to Miria, a.k.a. here. He didn't explain why exactly he did this when we were all assembled, so we don't know exactly why, but something is definitely wrong, because he did say the Four are only summoned to Miria when bad stuff goes down."

I furrow my brow as I try to piece together all the information. I guess it sort of makes sense, though some part of me still thinks I'm dreaming or on a trip from Goober's shrooms, which I've seen him mix into his drink once or twice. "So what exactly is the Four?"

Emily shrugs. "The people who wield the four rings. Apparently, other people from Gaia, a.k.a. our world—"

"Can you stop saying *a.k.a.*?" says Caster.

"Rude. I'm talking, a.k.a. be quiet."

"That doesn't even make sense!"

"So as I was saying," Emily says, "the Four have been here before. But we don't know much more, because Cog has been waiting till we all get here."

I try to wrap my head around this. "Cog is a god, right? Immortal, with awesome powers and all that? Why were you three the ones who had to come get me? And what possible use could a god have for four humans?"

"Excellent questions," says Emily. "Apparently, Cog is bound to this palace, so he couldn't come get you. But we don't know why he couldn't, and we also don't know why we were summoned."

I glance briefly at Ami to see if she'll say something, but she seems to prefer silence. "Okay," I say. "Well, what about the floating rock castle in the sky? Did you guys come through that?"

Caster raises an eyebrow. "We also don't know about that. In summary, there's a lot we don't know, but we'll find out soon. In the meantime, who the blazes are you, and how did you end up here so late?" A little flame blazes along Caster's fingertips, as if to signal he's making a pun.

"Right," I say. *Where to begin?* "Well, I guess you guys already know my name: Peter Smythe. I was on a field trip, when I found a ring, and for some reason, I couldn't help but put it on. The earth opened up, and I fell into a stone room, which then threw me into the freezing ocean. I think you know the rest."

"A field trip, eh?" says Caster. "Where do you go to school?"

I glance nervously at Emily to see if she already knows, if she recognizes me, but she just looks at me with rapt attention. She leans forward with her mouth open slightly, looking so beautiful it hurts.

"Mormont High."

Caster groans. "Dang it."

Emily's eyes light up, and her smile widens into a broad grin. "You're from Mormont too! Ah, I could kiss you! Yes!"

Emily could kiss me? She probably didn't really mean it, but all the same, I'm blushing furiously, because some part of me thinks that maybe she used that phrase because she does sort of like me, even if she never noticed my existence before.

"You have no idea, Peter, how hard it's been being the only one from Mormont here. These guys are from Blackstone," she says, leaning in a little again, as if to take me into her confidence.

"Yeah, the better school," says Caster confidently, and Ami seems to smile a little but still says nothing. "The Blackstone Buckaroos!"

"More like Blackstone Boogers," says Emily.

"Better than the Mormont Munchkins," says Caster.

Emily looks as if she's about to respond, when suddenly, she wrinkles her nose. "Peter, do I smell alcohol on your breath?"

My thoughts are all a jumble, but mostly, they're just a frantic voice repeating, *Oh no, she can smell my breath. That's probably not a good sign.*

"Uh, alcohol?" I repeat stupidly. *Why did I have to take a swig of Goober's four-hundred proof vodka? Wasn't the point of vodka that you couldn't smell it? The TV shows are all lies.*

"Yes," says Emily, crossing her arms. "I'm certain of it. And didn't you say you were on the school field trip?"

"Dude!" Caster exclaims, clapping his hands and laughing. "You were drinking on a school field trip? I don't know how you manage to cross your legs."

He offers me a fist, which I think I'm supposed to bump, and I do. The expression on my face must be one of bewilderment—mostly because I have no idea what drinking on a field trip has to do with being unable to cross your legs.

Caster's eyes seem to dance with amusement. "You know, can't cross your legs because—"

"Right," says Emily, interrupting. "I think he gets that. It wasn't that funny anyway. So moving on!"

"People find my jokes hilarious, Emily. Isn't that right, little sis?"

Ami nods absently with her brow furrowed again, as it was when I woke, as if she feels guilty about something.

"Sis?" I repeat, looking back and forth between the two of them, and then, because I have nothing better to do, I say the dumbest thing that comes to mind: "Which one of you is adopted?"

"What do you mean?" says Caster, his voice serious. "We're both Indian."

I feel my face grow red hot. The "You probably inadvertently said something racist" alarm bells are sounding in my head.

Emily rolls her eyes. "Oh, hush, Caster." She places a hand on my knee briefly, and my face flushes even brighter, but fortunately, I think she mistakes the cause as Caster, not her touch. "Don't pay attention to his stupid jokes."

"He's not my biological big brother," says Ami, her voice seeming to float from someplace far away. "But he takes care of me like one."

I wonder what taking-care-of a girl like her needs. Wasn't she the one who sent Brutus Borgia and his cronies running all by herself? But then again, she didn't always have the ring.

"Ami is Amerindian, or Cherokee, to be more precise," Emily says. "And Caster is Indian. Well, half Indian. His father is Pakistani. So that explains the stupid and slightly racist joke."

"It is a well-known fact that Indians cannot be racist against other Indians," says Caster in a sanctimonious and accented voice that sounds a lot like King Julian from the movie *Madagascar* and is so overwrought it has to be irony. I'm beginning to wonder if he speaks any other language besides irony, sarcasm, and dumb jokes.

Emily groans and rubs her temples, as if she can hardly bear Caster's antics. I do my best to give a sympathetic look, and to my thrill, she looks at me with understanding in her eyes, as if to say we Mormont kids have to stick together against these Blackstone savages. Or Blackstone boogers, rather.

My stomach does another backflip, and I feel a dizzying rush of blood to my head. Emily never even noticed my existence before, and now it is almost as if we are friends. And under what circumstances! I've fallen into another world and learned I can manipulate earth and am one of the Four—whatever that means. I am in the castle of a god who, despite being immortal and super powerful, can't even leave his own house. And then there are the ice giants.

I hold my head, feeling it ache, as all the thoughts wash over me at once. I just manage to find a place of peace and quiet, with the throbbing in my skull subsiding, when Caster farts obnoxiously loudly. Moments later, the noxious scent reaches my nose. I cough and my eyes water.

"Oh, Caster, what is wrong with you?" Emily exclaims, pinching her nose and fanning the air.

He leans back and runs a hand through his mop of hair, looking satisfied. "That, my friends, was week-old Taco Bell."

He rubs his stomach and looks at his watch, which apparently is still working. I guess the laws of physics are more or less the same here. That's a reassurance.

"I'm hungry," says Caster, pushing himself up. "I'm going to find some food before we get the summoning, if we even get one tonight."

As if on cue, Emily's stomach rumbles. "Did you mention food?" she says eagerly. All thoughts of the great fart seem to have vanished from her mind. She follows him out the massive oaken door in front of us before turning on her heel. "Are you coming along?"

She looks between me and Ami, and I have to pinch myself again to remind myself this is real. Emily is asking whether I want to come along to eat with her.

But instead of responding with an enthusiastic "Yes!" I end up staring straight ahead like a stupid piece of broccoli. Why that's the analogy that comes to mind, I can't explain. I told you: my English is a little problematic. The expression "It's all Greek to me" works in reverse for me. Not that there's an expression about broccoli in Greek.

"That's all right. You guys probably need some rest. I'll bring you something later." With that, Emily disappears into the torchlit hallway, leaving Ami and me alone.

CHAPTER 16

RIDING THE WIND (SOMEWHAT SUCCESSFULLY)

I've never been much good at talking with girls, even when I'm not madly in love with them. In fact, I think I'm pretty terrible at talking to people in general. So as Emily and Caster vanish from sight, I shift uncomfortably in my seat, unsure what to say to Ami, the girl who rescued me from Brutus and then from the ice giant.

"Peter," she says softly.

I slowly turn my head to face her. I have to crane my neck to do so, because we're still sitting close enough for our piles of blankets to touch.

"Sorry I almost drowned you." Her face droops guiltily.

I furrow my brow, confused as to how she can be sorry about saving my lousy butt from getting killed. She even sacrificed herself to try to do so, falling into the water while keeping me aloft. "Don't be. You saved me," I say.

She looks at me with a raised eyebrow and with uncertainty in her doe-like eyes. "Really?"

I give a half smile, wondering how someone who managed to send the biggest gang of bullies at Mormont home to their mamas and who can fly can be so insecure. "Yeah," I say. "For the second time."

She stares at me a little longer, which makes me blush and look away, because as I said, I'm terrible at talking with girls and people in general. She seems to judge me as sincere, and her gloom melts away.

"You want to see the rest of the palace?" she asks, pushing off the blankets.

I've begun to feel a little too toasty for comfort under the blankets, and I realize I have a bajillion unanswered questions and also wouldn't mind Ami as a tour guide. "Sure," I say.

I push off the blankets and discover I'm no longer wearing the jeans and hoodie I wore to the field trip. Instead, I'm dressed in a flowing green-and-brown robe that reminds me of the mountain forests near my hometown. Ami too is wearing a robe, which shimmers and seems almost translucent, as if I can see through her into the walls behind her. The robes look sort of like kimonos crossed with togas, yet they're not nearly as inflexible as the toga I wore for Halloween two years ago.

She notices my stare. "These were given to us by Cog. The traditional robes of the Four."

The Four. There's that word again, that unexplained concept: four people from Gaia brought here to Miria and gifted with certain powers. *Who were the others brought here before? And how are Miria and Gaia connected? And why were the Four summoned? And why us?* A dozen more questions blaze through my mind, until I feel the headache come back.

"You probably still have a lot of questions, don't you?" says Ami in her fey manner, her voice almost like a cloud floating through a field of wheat and gently brushing the tops of the grains with misty fingers.

"Yeah. A lot."

"I'll tell you!" she says. Her eyes widen as an idea seems to pop into her mind. "I have a place to show you. I'll tell you along the way."

She moves excitedly toward the door, and her feet do not quite touch the ground as she walks. I, on the other hand, feel heavier, as though I carry inside me the weight of a mountain— yet the heaviness doesn't bear me down. The weight, while pushing me into the earth, also bears me up; a surge of strength comes from my contact with the ground. I glance at the ring on my finger. I have many unanswered questions that will have to wait till Cog—whoever he is—summons us.

Ami leads me through winding corridors lit with torches and lined with markings in the walls, the same sort of markings I saw on the boat that rescued me.

As we walk, she tells me how she and Caster arrived in Miria the night they drove back from the football game. The winds were high, and Caster was driving too fast. They accidentally sped off the road and into a tree, and the car caught on fire. They managed to scramble out of the car with only minor bleeding and bruises, but when they looked at the flames, a face from the fire looked back at them—a monkeyish sort of face. Caster, as if entranced, walked toward the flames and then into them, disappearing. The face winked and then was gone, leaving Ami confused and terrified, alone on the roadside.

PAUL SCHEELER

She set the car on fire again, hoping she might be able to enter the flames, but they wouldn't grow as big as they had when the face appeared in them. She used her power over the wind to try to stir them up, but she ended up creating a powerful a storm—the storm that soaked Goober and me on our way home. But she didn't get soaked. She got struck by lightning, and in a flash, she was no longer in her world but in Miria, in a field not far from where Caster had landed. A hunch led them to the palace, and that was where Cog found them. He gave them food, new clothes, and half an explanation. The next day, Emily arrived.

I want to ask her more questions, like how they found their rings and what they've been doing here for the past few days. But just as I'm about to, we step out into the evening world. The sun is setting on the far horizon, making the distant snowcapped mountains glow.

We are standing on a high tower, and beneath us is an empty courtyard with a fountain in the center still spewing water, though it's cold enough for the ground to be caked with snow. I wonder for a moment how I feel so warm. I suppose it has to do with the cloak I'm wearing, which glimmers green and brown. There's some kind of magic in it—or else the laws of physics are different, because there's no way something so thin should be able to trap so much heat.

"Beautiful, isn't it?" says Ami as her eyes gaze dreamily at the distant mountains and the snowy forests.

I nod. My heart suddenly swells with the beauty of the place, craving to see more.

"I can float up there," she says almost absently, pointing to some distant speck above us. "It's even more beautiful from so high."

"Can you make two of us float?"

She cocks her head and seems to think about it. Suddenly, her eyes grow big. "What if we fall? It's a long way down!"

I remember how I dented the floor of the floating rock after falling probably a thousand feet through darkness. "Rock can't hurt me. If we fall, I'll land first and catch you."

Definitely a stupid plan. If we end up tumbling from the sky, I will almost certainly not have the presence of mind to land, get on my feet, and catch a falling girl. One of the wonderful things about being a teenager is that these things just don't bother you that much.

She nods and then smiles mischievously. "Okay, Peter. Just don't let the others know. Caster will pinch my ears if he finds out."

"Pinch your ears?" I say, shocked. "The jerk."

She shakes her head. "No, no. Because he wants to keep me safe, and he thinks sometimes I don't think things through very well—that there's something a little funny upstairs." She taps her forehead. "Do you think so too?"

I look at her olive skin, her braids of dark hair with little beads interwoven, and her hazel eyes. My eyes settle on her big, soft cheeks, and the weird voice in my head, whose full-time job is apparently to come up with dumb ideas, says, *What would happen if you pinched them?*

Shut up, man, I tell the voice. *What would happen if I pinched you?*

But I can't help but shake the feeling that she does have really pinchable cheeks. I shake my head. *Right, she asked me a question.*

"Oh no, I think everything is perfectly, er, hunky-dory upstairs."

She laughs. "Hunky-dory? You sound like Emily sometimes."

Do I? I wonder. *Does that mean maybe we'd make a good couple?* I want to ask the question, but somehow, it doesn't feel right.

"So are we going to fly?" she asks.

"That depends on the queen of the air," I say playfully.

She closes her eyes and seems to find a still place inside herself. Then she takes my hand, with her soft fingers wrapping around mine. I feel a little flutter in my heart, but it's followed almost immediately by a tug of guilt for feeling that way. I push both feelings away and try to concentrate on the landscape and what I'll do if Ami loses her nerve and we go tumbling through the air.

"Jump on three," she says. "One. Two. Three."

We leap together, but instead of falling right back down to earth, we are lifted by the wind, and I feel my stomach lurch, the way you feel when an airplane takes off. I can't help but think to myself I must be dreaming.

We climb higher and higher, with the wind feeling somehow both soft and hard beneath us. Just as we reach the first of the clouds, we come to a stop, and in the stillness, we spy the world. In the clear air, I can see so much: the valleys past the smaller mountains, the heads of the greater mountains behind them, fields of snow and ice, green forests, and herds of animals racing across the plains. The freezing ocean swells behind Cog's palace, and the waves break against the Gothic walls.

My eyes fall on a crooked tower at the far end of the palace courtyard. It looks weary and bent like an old man, and I almost pity it, even though it's only stone. Somehow, I know that not long ago, the tower stood straight and tall and was the pride and joy of the palace.

"What is that place?" I ask.

Her eyes follow my finger. "I don't know. I've wondered that too."

The thought slips my mind, and my eyes drift back over the beautiful landscape.

I look to Ami. She's smiling dreamily, and I wonder how many times in the past few days she's come up here to a place where no one can come if she does not take them.

Suddenly, the smile vanishes from her face, melting into fear. Her eyes widen, and her mouth opens. I feel the air beneath us weaken, and then the floor beneath us is gone, and we're tumbling through the sky.

CHAPTER 17

AWKWARD EXPLANATIONS

Fear courses through my veins as the ground races up at me. Worse than that, I see Ami beneath me; her narrow form is falling faster than mine, though she's waving her arms frantically.

She's going to die, I realize. There's a look of wild lack of control in her eyes. There's no way she's going to get control back in time.

As I near the earth, I feel a strength grow in my stomach, and the courage to do what I need to do somehow finds me. I narrow my body by placing my arms together the way I've seen divers do and plunge through the sky past her. Something takes over inside me, and the moment before I land, my arms unfold, and my legs spread into a wide stance.

I punch through the earth, coming to a rapid stop with enough force to shorten my spine by five inches and break every bone in my feet, legs, and back. But instead, I feel the earth move through me; its power courses through my veins, and its wisdom somehow guides my movements.

I look up and see Ami; her body is still tumbling. In one swift movement, I race forward and grab her, collecting her in my arms. The earth lifts me up as I catch her and then brings me down, spreading out the deceleration to keep her from harm.

She looks up at me, and her confused, fearful look slowly melts away from her eyes. We hold each other's gaze, and her warm eyes undo all the knots in my stomach and make my heart race.

Get ahold of yourself, Peter. I'm about to ask her what she saw that made her lose her grip on her power, but at that moment, Caster and Emily round the corner and come to an abrupt stop in front of us.

"Well," says Caster dryly, "good to see you two are getting along well."

Our eyes widen, and Ami mouths, "Let go."

I drop her, and she floats down beside me. We shift away from each other at the same time, which probably only makes things look worse.

"We were just, uh—" I rack my brain for a good excuse. I want to tell the truth, but Ami made me promise not to tell Caster.

Emily gives me a quizzical, somewhat amused look, as if I'm a puzzle she's trying to figure out.

"Just, uh, what?" says Caster, looking defensive and suspicious.

I remember what Ami said: he's like her big brother.

"She was probably just practicing her jumps. Weren't you, little nugget?" Emily says, tousling her hair.

"Oh yes," says Ami, nodding a bit too vigorously.

"Uh-huh," says Caster. "Well, anyway, we were just going to get dinner. Did you want to come?"

"Didn't you just eat?"

They exchange an amused glance.

"That was just a snack," says Emily. "Besides, it's already been like thirty minutes."

I want to say, "How much do you eat?" but I bite my tongue.

Emily laughs as if she can read my expression. "I know. I eat a lot. My mom calls me Zhu Bajie."

"What?" everyone says in unison.

"Um, I'm not sure how to translate it exactly. 'Pig of the eight precepts'? It sounds better in Chinese. Anyway, he's a character from *Journey to the West*, a famous book in China, and as the name suggests, he likes to eat a lot."

"Right," says Caster. "Well, that was enlightening. Can we call you Piggy for short?"

"Piggy?" Emily exclaims, whacking his shoulder. "Say it again, Caster the unfriendly ghost!"

"Piggy!" he says, laughing and taking a step back to avoid her fists. "And how does that make any sense? My name is Caster, not Casper!"

I look at Ami, and she shrugs. "They've been like this the past few days," she says. "Since she arrived, really."

If she hates him that much, why did she get snacks with him? I wonder, but my dense brain doesn't come up with any good solutions.

I clear my throat, and Emily's fist pauses in midair just as it's about to land on a cowering Caster. "Oh, right," she says. "Dinnertime!"

We all follow Caster to the Great Hall, where a banquet is being served, though we are the only people here, aside from the servants. Something doesn't seem quite right about the hall. There are too many empty tables and empty chairs. What sort of godly palace is this? It's almost as if it's abandoned.

As I sit down next to Ami, I whisper to her the question I wanted to ask just before Emily and Caster arrived: "What did you see that made you fall?"

But she only shakes her head. I wonder what she could possibly have seen that she doesn't want to say, even after it almost cost her her life.

CHAPTER 18

DISAPPOINTMENTS AND DREAMS

For the rest of the night, Ami is much cooler to me, as if she wants to prove to Caster that nothing happened between us. I guess I can understand that, but it still kind of hurts, watching how differently she responds to Emily and Caster. I'm reminded once more that I'm the outsider in the group.

We end up back in the room with the circular couch and the statues along the walls, where I woke up earlier today. After about a half hour of being ignored, I decide I've had enough, and I mumble something about going to sleep.

Emily flashes me a brief look of concern, as if she realizes I'm left out. I guess she wants to make up for it, because she offers to walk me to my room. I probably should feel happy about that, but I only feel more sullen, like I'm some sort of lost puppy that she takes pity on.

It turns out there's another hallway behind the couch. It's hidden by a banner showing the four elements fusing together into a sphere of light. The image tickles something in my brain.

It seems somehow familiar. Emily leads me down the torchlit hallway, past three other doors.

"Sleep well, Peter," she says, and I mumble a reply; my mind is on something else.

I furrow my brow at the darkness. At the end of the hallway, there's another door. I walk up to it and pull on the latch, but it won't budge. It must be locked, though there's no keyhole, which makes me wonder. It looks like all the other doors, which open to their respective rings: fire, water, wind, and earth.

But then what is door five? Is there another ring? If so, why did Caster and Emily call us the Four? Is there a fifth ring bearer?

My head starts to throb again, and I decide I've had enough of unanswerable questions for the night. I stumble into the room and instinctively find the bed. It's made of stone, but it feels soothing, reassuring, and almost soft. I wonder briefly what sort of bed Emily lies in. Does she sleep in a pool? And what about Caster? Does he snuggle up inside a personal furnace?

Lastly, I think of Ami and how she wouldn't even look at me for the rest of the night. She had seemed so interested in me before that, even taking me to see the world from a place only she can go to. I recall how I caught her in my arms and how natural it felt. I push the thought away. *Emily*, I remind myself. All the same, I thought Ami and I might have been becoming friends. But I guess not.

I know almost nothing about these people. They somehow got me to tell a lot about myself, but they never shared their stories. Except Ami, and she only told a little.

I will the stone to wrap around me, enclosing me like a tomb. I hope I'll either suffocate or wake up back in Mormont, maybe in a hospital after overdosing on Goober's mushrooms and alcohol. I pray that at least I might get a quiet rest.

But that is not what happens.

Instead, I find myself in a dream that loops and loops until I want to go crazy, but I can't wake up. It always begins and ends the same way. It starts in a grassy field with the sea behind him. I recognize it as the Aegean Sea, which I saw years ago on a family vacation. An old man is sitting by the sandy shore, and he beckons me over. He has brown hair, a beard with flecks of gray, and warm dark eyes that crease as he smiles.

He tells me his name is Homer and speaks to me in Greek. For a while, this is soothing, making me think of the way my dad talked to me when I was little and of my chats with Dr. Elsavier.

But then something changes. His hair grows wild and tangled. He throws his head back and laughs, and when he looks at me again, his eyes are solid blue and cold as ice. He begins to speak words I do not understand, though I know they're Greek, my native tongue. It's as if he's taken from me my very language.

I'm just on the verge of deciphering what he's saying, drawing out his dark meaning, when time stops.

And the dream starts over.

CHAPTER 19

THE TOLL OF A THOUSAND BELLS

I wake up with an even worse headache than I had yesterday. But my night spent on the stone bed seems somehow to have healed my body. I no longer feel the aches and bruises.

I walk down the long corridors of the palace, led by the smells of seasoned vegetables and roasted meat. As I approach the massive wooden door of the Great Hall, I hear two voices bickering.

"Do you eat anything besides peaches?" says Emily.

"Why, yes, sometimes I eat peaches and cream."

I slowly push my way through the crack in the door and see Caster with a bowl of peaches. The corners of his mouth bear evidence of his taste for cream.

Ami's dreamy eyes light up when she sees me. "Good morning, Peter!" she says.

After last night, I can't match her enthusiasm, so I only manage a nod. She seems a little hurt at first, but her look soon turns to one of concern, as if she can see something isn't right with me.

Well, something isn't right. I just had quite possibly the worst sleep of my life, and I'm still in this magical land with three people I don't know in an empty palace, waiting for a god to summon us. These people are basically a clique, and I'm once more on the outside. I miss my mom, my dad, and Dr. Elsavier. I even miss Goober, though I'd never tell him.

Emily slaps the seat next to her. Caster and Ami are sitting on the opposite side of the table, and Emily is nearest to me. "Pop a squat," she says.

I look hesitantly at her, but she smiles warmly, and her eyes make my insides melt.

"Okay," I say meekly, and I take the seat next to her.

I'm conscious of her eyes still staring at me, but I don't look up from the spot on the wooden table I've fixed my sight on.

"Here," she says, pushing over a plate of what look like crepes, followed by a bowl of fruit. "It's good stuff," she adds, plucking out a strawberry and popping it into her mouth.

"Yeah," I mumble.

She takes another piece of fruit and then seems to hesitate, as if she wants to say something but can't find the words. I notice the table has grown quiet. Caster is staring at one of his peaches, looking like a mad scientist about to design some experiment. Ami is still staring at me with a concerned grimace, and part of me feels a little bad for slighting her. But another part feels good after the way she ignored me last night. I know that's petty and mean, but it's hard to control yourself when you're tired and hurt and angry.

"Peter, we were talking last night, and, um"—Emily fiddles with the strawberry—"I think we were kind of unfair to you. We've all been through a lot in the past few days, and we still don't have answers. I guess we were just a little tense."

"Oh, for glory's sake, woman, get to the point," says Caster.

Emily glares at him and throws the strawberry at his face. He catches it and pops it into his mouth, winking at her. She looks like she wants to throw another one, but instead, she takes a deep breath and turns to me again.

"So what I'm trying to say is sorry. We—I—should have told you more and tried to include you more."

"It's alright," I say, trying to hold on to my passive-aggressive gloom, but despite myself, I'm feeling better by the second. Emily Wong, the girl of my dreams, just said she wants to include me more. That's a pretty good start, isn't it?

"It's alright?" Caster repeats. "You're terrible at accepting apologies."

Emily tosses another strawberry at him, this time fast enough that he doesn't have enough time to react. It splatters on his face, and I wonder if she used some of her power over water to make it explode. "You're one to talk!"

Caster wipes the red juice off his face calmly. "Am I? I never apologize. How would you know if I'm bad at it?"

"You're a *bad* person, Caster Kshatriya-Wick," says Emily dramatically. "You should apologize too."

Caster takes a bite of a fresh peach. "Why?" he says through a mouthful.

"I'm sorry about last night," Ami says.

"You have nothing to apologize for," says Caster.

"Yes, I do, and so do you," she says in her soft sort of way. Yet her voice comes across as certain and persuasive.

Caster's demeanor changes a little. "Oh, fine. I apologize for not being inclusive enough or whatever." He takes an aggressive bite of his peach and looks away with a petulant expression on his face.

I smile a little. "I'm sorry too."

"Great!" says Emily. "Let's start again!" She puts her hand in the middle of the table and looks at the rest of us.

"What are you doing?" says Caster.

"*Four* on the count of four," she says, wiggling her fingers, as if expecting us to stack our hands on top of hers.

After a moment of being a complete idiot, I realize this is my chance. My hand whips out, and I place it on top of hers. A rush of warmth rolls through me, and it takes everything in me not to grin like a goon.

Ami puts hers on top of mine, and I try not to think of the fact that her hand feels soft and warm against mine. *Emily*, I remind myself.

Emily coughs. "*Four* on four!" she whispers like a giddy cheerleader.

"Oh, fine," says Caster, and he puts his on top.

"One. Two. Three. Four!"

"Also, that would be '*Four* on three,'" mutters Caster. "'*Four* on four' would be 'One. Two. Three. Four. Four'—counting to four and then saying *Four*."

We raise our hands, and I do my best to keep mine against Emily's as long as possible without seeming like a creep. We all laugh afterward, and I begin to think I might like these people, especially Ami and Emily. Caster's a first-class jerk. Then again, there has to be more to him, because as much as Emily bickers with him, she doesn't hate him. I can see that.

"So," says Emily, "I'll tell my story first."

I turn to face her and am ready to hear what she has to say, when suddenly, the floor begins to shake. A sound like a thousand deep bells ringing at once echoes through the Great Hall, making the doors shudder and the bowls vibrate on the shaking table.

"What's that?" I ask, feeling for the power of the earth. Are the ice giants attacking?

"Yes!" Caster exclaims. "Yes, yes, yes!"

"Yes what?" asks Emily, looking as confused as I feel.

He looks at us as if we're stupid. "What do you think that possibly could mean?"

"Oh," says Emily.

I'm still confused, until she says the next two words: "The summons!"

At that moment, a woman appears in the hall. She's dressed in purple and white and has sleek black skin and penetrating white eyes. Something tells me, though, that she only appears to be a woman but is actually a shadow cast by some vaster object, occupying space I cannot imagine and wielding power of which I cannot conceive.

"I am Ku'ba," she says. Her voice is powerful and subtle, like the deep currents of the ocean. "Methyldonin will see you now."

CHAPTER 20

THE MAN IN THE LONELY CASTLE

Ku'ba does not wait for us to speak. She waves her hand, and the world around us turns to light. Moments later, we are in a new place, which I recognize as the lonely tower I saw with Ami. I'm not sure how I recognize it exactly, since I've only ever seen the outside. It's as though the stones themselves whisper it to me.

The room is filled with strange, whirring mechanical devices. In the center of the room is a globe of interlocking gears and wheels. The shapes on its surface shift and twist in unexpected ways. Below it stands a man dressed in blue and black, stooped and weary-looking like the tower. Like Ku'ba, he seems like only a shadow cast by some immense shape, full of so much power that it could scatter every one of my molecules without hardly meaning to.

"I have brought them," Ku'ba says, bowing slightly. She gives us a look as if we should bow as well, and I suppose some respect ought to be shown to a being as vast as the one who stands with his back to us in the form of an old man.

He turns to us slowly, revealing a man with a white beard, kind eyes, and a brow drawn with worry. He waves his hand, and Ku'ba looks up, which I guess is the signal for us to do so as well. He gazes at us a moment longer. None of us dare to speak first—the others must be just as afraid as I am.

"Three of you have met me at least once," says the man in a baritone voice that is soothing yet rumbling with power. "Now that the Four are complete, I will tell you what I have thus far made you wait to hear."

We all stare at him with rapt attention. Ku'ba stands still and quiet with a knit of worry in her brow, as if what Cog has to say has been weighing deeply on her.

"I am Methyldonin, immortal spirit and defender of the Nine Realms. Along with my sister, Samjang, I was forged in the fiery depths of everlasting flame by Gomdan the Fashioner, the All-Father, the Maker of all, including Miria. Though you may call me Cog," he says with his eyes twinkling. He taps his machines affectionately, as if in explanation of his nickname, and then continues. "For ages, Samjang and I stood guard as protectors of Miria against the enemies who would see her ruined. Some threats, however, were too great even for our combined power, so Gomdan forged for us the rings, which give power over the elements. During the times of Miria's greatest need, ring bearers have been called from your world, Gaia, the closest to ours. Our world is like a shield against many others, the first line of defense against the evils that would consume all worlds, so we have often had need of your help."

I stare at him wonderingly. What help could a few humans bring to a god? I think of how scared I was when I first saw him,

PAUL SCHEELER

filled with that sense of hidden might and size hidden behind the shadow of an old man.

He continues. "In this late hour, in this very nick of time, I have spent the last of the power of the Hearthstone to summon you four. Miria has never before faced days as dark as these; for in times past, my sister, Samjang, and I had all our power to defend this world, Miria, alongside the Four. But—"

He seems to search for words as his gaze drifts across us sadly. "But that is no longer so. Samjang and I were tricked into separation by the god Enki, the mischief maker, the trickster god, and now I cannot leave this palace to defend our world until Samjang is saved from her captivity in the east, for our power can only flow in its full force when it is united. That, however, is not all."

He looks at us with a solemn gaze, with his ancient eyes running over us. I feel naked before him, sensing that somehow, those eyes can peer past my flesh into my very soul, reading everything it is to be Peter Smythe. *At least it's a short read*, I quip to myself, trying to chase away the unsettling feeling of being naked before an immortal spirit.

"My life is connected deeply to Miria, and I can feel the enemy clawing at the ancient gates, the sequence of celestial fortifications I established long ago to keep them out after I banished them. But the gates will not hold longer than three weeks. In that time, you must save Samjang. If you do not, an enemy more fierce and terrible than you have ever known will return, and you, along with every living creature in Miria, will meet a fate worse than death."

The last word echoes through the room, and the air feels colder.

CHAPTER 21

THE QUEST

"A fate worse than death?" Emily repeats. Her usually boisterous voice sounds small and afraid.

Cog's eyes seem to drift to a far-off place. "Miria's old nemeses, the foes she fought in the very cradle of her birth, who nearly strangled her before she could grow to adulthood, the most devious and wicked of the enemies she has ever faced—those enemies are returning. A few of their servants were left behind in the last invasion. You faced some of them just hours ago, in the northern seas."

The ice monsters, I think. *Yeah, they were pretty bad. But didn't Caster blow a hole in one of them? And we did get away. I mean, it's not like it's the end of the world.*

"Alone they are terrible, but when they are connected to the source of their power, few can stand in their way. Their kingdom is known as the Ice Reich, and it is as pitiless and humorless as the name suggests." Cog's brow darkens. "Its servants were once creatures like you. But to tell you more would only terrify you, and I am not here to terrify you but to give you courage."

Yeah, that sounds about right. Definitely not trying to terrify us.

He smiles kindly at us, and a radiance flows from his face. Somehow, I do feel a sense of courage in my chest, as if somehow, it isn't completely insane for four kids to go on a quest to find the sister of a god so the Ice Reich doesn't turn us into who-knows-what.

"Why should we have courage?" I say.

"Because," says Cog, "long ago, you defeated the Ice Reich."

"Reincarnation," says Caster, clapping his hands. "Knew it."

Cog gives a crooked smile. "Not exactly. Every soul and body is unique, but there are patterns, and you are part of a great pattern, the pattern of the Four. Long ago, when the Ice Reich first made their assault upon Miria, they attacked with great force, and the enemy and I were locked in a fierce battle from which neither side could escape. Only when Gomdan the Fashioner forged the rings in the fires of the deep world and brought ring bearers across from Gaia were we able to break the deadlock."

"Who were they?" Emily asks. "And how did they break the deadlock?"

"The first Four were the most unlikely of people—yet not very different from you. Unlike you, they spoke different languages, and their cultures were very different. But they transcended the barriers of language and background. In the end, they defeated the Ice Reich because they became one Life."

"One Life?" I say.

"In this mortal world, is a mixture of the four elements," Cog says. "Life is a ratio, a harmony, and the elements are its notes. Thus, the Four became one, and in their doing so, their power was enough to force the Ice Reich into a black prison sealed with power the Ice Reich has not been able to weaken till now."

I feel a chill move down my spine at the thought that I, a loser who couldn't get accepted into a decent college and couldn't even work up the courage to ask Emily out, might be part of such a great story. But the chill quickly passes, leaving behind only fear and homesickness.

"I see," says Caster. "So on a different note, there's no way for us to just, you know, go home?"

It is the question on my mind too, however selfish it sounds. Our world has enough problems. Why should we have to solve the problems of Miria? Besides, we're only kids. Won't we just make things worse?

Cog shakes his head. "Only the Hearthstone can send you home, and even if you could return, it would do you no good. The Ice Reich, once they overwhelm Miria, will come to your world too."

Caster nods. "So find Samjang, stop the Ice Reich, and reactivate the Hearthstone. Right. Sounds straightforward. How do we get this Samjang?"

Caster looks like the smartest kid in math class when the teacher puts up an especially challenging problem on the board that makes everyone else's eyes glaze over. His eyes are intense and focused, and little flames flicker along his fingers. I guess Cog's encouragement earlier had an outsized effect on him.

Cog gives a little smile and turns to the massive globe behind him. He waves his hand, and the gears begin to whir. The plates rearrange themselves until they settle at last into a definite shape. I have a strange feeling that all the shapes correspond to other worlds, which Cog, or someone like Cog, is watching over. I count nine in total.

"This is Miria, the outermost of the Nine Realms," he says, gesturing at the globe. "Ku'ba, perhaps you'd like to present the plan."

She nods stiffly and then steps forward. Her staff grows in length until it reaches the surface of the globe. "Four, currently, you are right here," she says, gesturing to the far northwest of the landmass. She traces a path through the north toward the center of the landmass, all the way to the far east, where she comes to a stop. "This is where Samjang is trapped." Her staff moves to the center of the map, which is marked by a single mountain. "This is the Heart of Miria, where Miria's strength flows strongest. This is where Methyldonin set up the sequence of celestial fortifications to block the Ice Reich from returning. If we are to succeed, you must first rescue Samjang and then bring her to the Heart of Miria. Methyldonin will meet you there and, if the All-Father is willing, will stop the invasion."

"Okay," says Caster. "So how do we get there in time?" His eyes light up mischievously. "With the right materials, I could create the frame of an aircraft, which could be powered by me and Ami." He puts a friendly hand on her shoulder, and she smiles up at him, as if proud to be considered important by her big brother.

His plan sounds ridiculous to me, yet the look in his eyes tells me he not only means what he says but also could do it.

But Ku'ba shakes her head. "There are enemies who can smell your power. Miria does her best to hide your scent, but her ability to do so is—"

"Inversely proportional to the distance from her," Caster says, interrupting.

Ku'ba smiles. "Actually, to the square of the distance."

"Hoo hoo, Newton strikes again."

The rest of us give Caster weird looks. I'm guessing he has a lot of jokes that only make sense to him.

Ku'ba clears her throat. "Anyway, your best chance of making it to Samjang is by staying close to the ground and only using your power when absolutely necessary. You do not have the strength to fend them all off."

"Forgive me," says Emily, "but to fend off who exactly?"

"Whom," Caster says beneath his breath, and Emily flicks him.

Ku'ba looks to Cog, who picks up one of the clocks on the table beside him and begins to fiddle with its gears, as if in deep thought. He sighs, setting it down. "The fallen gods. Creatures great in power who were made to serve the realms but instead used their power for their own selfish ends. I stand in their way, so they intend to use the Ice Reich to defeat me so they can achieve their ends."

"What ends?" Caster asks.

"That is not relevant," Cog says sternly.

"Who is their leader then?" asks Caster. "It's the trickster god, isn't it? What was his name? Enki?"

"Yes," says Cog slowly, as if impressed with the speed at which Caster's mind works. I guess it makes sense that Enki would be their leader, since he is the one who somehow tricked Cog and Samjang into separation, weakening their powers. "He, though, is not like the other fallen gods," Cog adds with a hint of sadness.

"Why? What does he want?" asks Caster.

Cog's eyes grow moist, and they seem to settle on some distant point. "His motives are different. More than that, I will not say." His voice quivers for a moment. I have a feeling he's more deeply connected to this mystery than he lets on, but his voice brooks no further questions.

"All right," says Caster. He plays with the fiery ring on his finger. "I have a different question. What's this business with the four elements? Last time I checked, the theory of the four elements was rejected in the seventeenth century, along with alchemy. Chemically speaking, there are actually one hundred eighteen elements."

"Ah, but your rings do not give you power over the material substances themselves; rather, they persuade the spirits who control those substances to do your will."

Caster raises an eyebrow. "Somehow, I feel like the concept is even less explained now that it was before."

Cog gives him a harsh look. "It is the first principle of science to marvel at what you know works by asking how, not to reject what you know works because you can't squeeze it into your current theory. It is the theory that must change to fit reality, not the other way around."

"Fair enough," says Caster, but he still doesn't seem convinced.

Though my reasons are probably not as sophisticated as his, I also am not exactly convinced by Cog's explanation. But I can't deny what I've experienced in the last few hours. Somehow, I can bend earth, Caster can summon fire, Emily can move water, and Ami can fly.

"Enough questions for now," says Cog. "More will be revealed in time. I cannot tell you how best to use the rings, for the knowledge can only come from experience, and the knowledge differs among generations of ring bearers." He turns to Ku'ba. "I require a moment with Peter."

She nods and guides the rest of the group to the far side of the room, just out of earshot. Cog turns to me, and I have a flashback to detention with Ms. Schaden. I wonder what I have done wrong.

CHAPTER 22

THE DUTY OF THE ROCK

Cog sits down in one of his mechanical chairs and invites me to do the same. I don't refuse, because I get the impression you probably shouldn't refuse a god.

He gazes at me the way old people sometimes look at others, as if they see a dozen different faces and lives when they look at them. I shift uncomfortably in my chair.

"I'm sorry," says Cog, his voice kind. "It's been many years since I last had this conversation with the Rock, but it feels like only a few short moments ago."

When he says nothing, I decide to venture a response. "This conversation?" My voice comes out almost in a squeak, and I wonder how Caster could have been so brash with Cog.

"The conversation in which I tell you something very hard that you must learn to do." He glances over at the other three and shakes his head. "Some things never change. Separated by thousands of years and by countries, customs, and languages, yet you all are so much alike."

I must look confused because Cog laughs apologetically. "This is the way old creatures talk. When you've lived through every age of the world, you see things differently. But for you, my words must be very confusing. After all these years, you'd think I'd be better at giving this talk." He chuckles to himself. "Well, I'll just say it." He regards me seriously. "Peter," he says, his voice deep and echoing, "you are the Rock of the Four. And so you must learn to be their leader."

"Sir?" I say, fumbling for words. *How could I be their leader? Ami is faster than me, Caster is cleverer than me, and Emily is better with people than me, not to mention smarter and way more attractive.* "How?"

His old eyes crease, and he gives me a fatherly smile. "One never knows in advance. Each of the Rocks in the past has been different. But it is the sacred duty of the Rock to be the support and foundation of the rest. Somehow, my boy, you will figure it out." He ruffles my hair.

The courage in his voice moves through me, and it feels warm and intoxicating. For a moment, I feel I could almost do it. But I know the feeling is artificial and will go away as soon as Cog is gone. Then I'll be my old self again: the loser who gets bullied for peeing with his pants down, whose only friend is Goober, who didn't have the courage to ask Emily to prom, and who can't even make it into college.

"There is something more, Peter—something else I haven't told the others, because I'm trusting you to find the right way to do it." He looks at his fingers, as if searching for the right words. "The Four are not alone when they come into this world. There's always another: Five. But…"

His voice trails off, and his eyes become sad. "His power is not like yours, nor is his fate. He never ends up where he was supposed to go, and oftentimes, the evil ones get to him before we can reach him. I can sense he is in this world, but I do not know where, and I do not know whether he will prove to be friend or enemy to you."

I stare at him blankly, trying to think of what to say. Life is so much harder when you're dumb. "So, um, why are you telling me, sir, and not the others?"

Caster would probably know what to do, I think, but I don't say it. It would be too petulant, too self-pitying.

"Because, Peter, it is the task of the leader to tell his friends the difficult facts and inspire them to make the right decision together."

Just as I predicted, all the courage has gone out of me. I look down at the ground, and I expect him to tell me I'm a failure and am doing a miserable job of being the Rock.

But he only smiles. "The Rocks always start the same. They're humble like the earth, and they think very little of themselves, so they don't want to lead others. But that is one of the reasons they make good leaders, and ultimately, the others come to depend on them." His eyes twinkle. "Can you promise me, Peter, one thing?"

"What?" I ask.

"That you will not discount yourself before you start."

"How can I not discount myself? If trouble starts, I'll fail. I've always failed. I'm a loser, sir."

"The young often think little of themselves. And perhaps it is right because the young are often weak and cannot do it alone. But you will have friends, Peter, and what is more, you will have the All-Father."

106

"The All-Father?"

"Yes, the Fashioner, the Maker of Miria and the other Nine Realms. In times of great distress, do not hesitate to call to him for help."

"You mean like prayer?"

I've never been much of a prayer person. My mother took me to church with her a few times when I was younger, and we'd also celebrate Passover, which was kind of fun. She managed to get my dad to play along—somewhat reluctantly. He was more of a Greek at heart, but he would give in eventually. He would ask me the four questions, beginning with "Why is tonight different from all other nights?" I would give the answers, which I don't quite remember, to be honest, but I know they had something to do with the Israelites' flight from Egypt. The matzah—which is basically just crispy bread, since it doesn't have yeast—and grape juice were pretty good.

But I never really felt connected to anything beyond the food and my parents. The prayers didn't mean much to me, nor did my mother's attempt to connect the Passover story to the Messiah rescuing humanity from sin. I'm not sure what that all has to do with Egypt, which I'm pretty sure is a nation-state, not a metaphor.

Cog watches me sadly. "Yes, prayer. So much has been lost in your world since the last time the Four were called. I suppose I cannot ask everything from you at once. Promise me something different from what I asked before. Promise you will at least do your best and try your hardest to do what must be done to save all worlds."

I close my eyes and let his words settle in my mind. I think of everything that depends on my succeeding. If I fail, then Miria will get destroyed by the Ice Reich. I'll never make it home. I'll never see my parents again or eat pizzelle at the ungodly hour of five o'clock in the morning with them. I'll never hear my mom worry about me or my dad nag me about college again.

I'll never see Goober again or get a chance to beat FireStarter520. The others will die. Emily won't make it home either, and I'll never get a chance to go to prom with her. Right now, I have the best chance I've ever had of getting her to say yes, because she finally knows who I am. I think of Ami, how kind she's been to me, and how sweet her smiles are. I want her to make it home safely. Maybe we'll be friends if we can make it back.

Lastly, I think of Dr. Elsavier and her ridiculous compliment comparing me to Alcibiades's description of Socrates: rough on the outside but filled with the beautiful figurines of gods within. "I know an Odysseus when I see one," she'd said.

Suddenly, I feel a stir of courage in me, one that comes from me and not from Cog. I'm not about to let this Ice Reich destroy Miria and then my world. I'm not about to have my parents killed or enslaved, to watch Emily's and Ami's faces freeze over, or to see everything good I care about destroyed. *All right, Dr. Elsavier*, I think. *I'll do my best.*

I open my eyes, and when I look at Cog, there's fire in my eyes, a belief that wasn't there before. "I swear I'll do my best," I say. The stones beneath me feed my confidence. "I won't stop till I'm dead or we've won."

His eyes twinkle, and he squeezes my knee. "Good." He stands and calls to the others. "Stop whispering over there. You know, you cannot hide your words from a god."

Their eyes bulge, and he gives me a wink.

108

A clap of thunder echoes through the sky, and the earth shakes. Dust crumbles from the tower. Everyone instinctively reaches for the wall to steady themselves as the tower shifts, except for me, because the earth tells me what to do next and how to steady my body. It would feel pretty cool, except I can sense that something massive and terrible is close by, causing the shakes.

Cog's eyes widen. "No," he mutters. "Not yet." He turns to Ku'ba. "They're here."

She nods, seeming to understand whatever code they're speaking in.

"Take them to the armory and through the tunnels," Cog says. "I will delay them."

"What? Who's here?" asks Caster.

Cog turns to us with a deadly seriousness in his eyes. "The fallen gods."

The words hover menacingly in the air for a heartbeat, and then Cog speaks, his voice wrapped in power. "Ku'ba, take them through the tunnels of Erebor, and make sure they have the gifts." He turns to us. "Go now! And may Gomdan the Fashioner be with you!"

With that, the world fades as Ku'ba uses her power to transport us away from the fallen gods and toward the tunnels.

A thousand questions blaze in my mind as we go, but the one that beats in time with my racing heart is simple: *How are we going to escape the fallen gods?*

CHAPTER 23

ESCAPE THROUGH THE TUNNELS

The world re-forms around us, revealing a dark, circular stone chamber lit by flickering torchlight. I'm standing next to Ami, with Caster and Emily across from me. In the center is a vault that glows with a purple light. The room feels cold, though through the stones beneath my shoes, I feel warmth rising up my legs, as if the earth wants to protect me.

"Where are we?" Ami asks timidly.

"And what's going on?" asks Emily.

Ku'ba pulls a key from her robe sleeve and inserts it into the lock on the vault. "This is the armory, where Methyldonin keeps the gifts of the ring bearers," she says as she removes another key to open up a new vault. It looks like the sort of horribly complex device Cog would design.

"As for what is happening …" She twists the key, and a sequence of clicking sounds and whirring emanates from the vault, and she gives a little smile before resuming her grave manner. "I am not certain myself, but it seems the fallen gods have discovered your arrival in Miria. They know you are the one force capable of undoing their plans, so they plan to undo you first. Either that, or something darker is at play."

"That's comforting," says Caster. "You don't happen to have any god-busting weapons in there, do you?"

"This is no time to jest. Your best chance of survival is to flee and make as little noise as possible. You stand no chance against the fallen gods if they find you. These are creatures as old as the starlight in the sky, more powerful than any weapon your world has ever designed, and far cleverer than your little eighteen-year-old brain."

As if to confirm her words, the ground shakes again, and sounds echo through the walls.

She reaches into the inner vault and removes four items. To Ami, she hands a staff with pearly threads; to Caster, she hands a spyglass; and to Emily, she hands a quilt that seems alive with changing colors. Lastly, she hands me a compass.

We stare at the objects, fiddling with them in our hands. I'm about to ask what we're supposed to do with them and why it seemed so important to Cog that we get such ordinary items, when the ground shakes again. Ku'ba waves her hand. Instantly, the world vanishes into mist and then re-forms.

We are now in another dark chamber just as dingy as the one before, but instead of containing a giant glowing vault in the center, it is empty save for five doors that line the walls.

"Quickly!" says Ku'ba, leading us forward. The center door unlocks and opens with a wave of her hand, and moments later, we're plunging into the darkness.

Caster's hands come alight, partly illuminating the gloom. The earth shakes, and dust and dirt fall from the ceiling.

"Where are you taking us?" asks Emily.

I look at Ami, who has been quiet all this time. Unlike the others, she does not seem concerned. Her eyes have a distant look in them, almost as if she's someplace else. Her fingers play upon the staff, feeling it tenderly. She looks at me and gives a little smile—not a happy one but one that makes me feel as if we'll be okay.

The earth shakes again.

Well, maybe.

"Yeah," says Caster, echoing Emily's question. "And what are we supposed to do with these things?"

"No time for questions," says Ku'ba, plunging forward. We have to run to catch up.

I wonder why she hasn't just teleported us where she wants us to go, but something feels different about the inside of this tunnel, as if there's a power here that would keep her from doing that.

Maybe that's why Cog is having us travel through the tunnels. Perhaps if they keep Ku'ba from using her power, they'll keep the fallen gods from using theirs to find us. That might be what we need to escape.

Minutes later, my lungs are burning, and my spit has turned to goo in my mouth. If I weren't about to get killed by fallen gods, I would not have the stamina to keep up with Ku'ba. I still feel as if I could collapse, and my lungs are wheezing like I'm a smoker. Caster gives me the first sympathetic look since I met him, and I can tell he gets about as much exercise as I do. Emily, her cheeks flushed and gorgeous, looks as if she's just getting warmed up, and Ami, I'm pretty sure, hasn't actually been running. She seems to have been floating through the tunnels.

We come to a small, circular room, a dead end, and we all skid to a halt. Caster and I double over, reaching for breath, while Emily and Ami exchange amused, somewhat pitying looks.

"My lungs are on fire," says Caster, wheezing. "Literally."

"Maybe you shouldn't do that, dingus," says Emily. "Fire consumes oxygen."

"I didn't mean to," says Caster, trying to stand up straight, his brow glistening with sweat. He turns to Ku'ba. "What now?"

I squint in the darkness and see the walls are covered with the same symbols I saw in the floating rock, on the boat that rescued me from the ice monsters, and in Cog's palace. Ku'ba runs her hand over them, seeming to ignore us, and then pushes hard on one. The brick leans in, and the ground above us crumbles, revealing trees and an evening sky.

She stares up at the sky longingly, and for a moment, everything is quiet; the sounds of the fallen gods are long gone. They either have been defeated by Cog or are convinced we are somewhere else.

Ku'ba turns to us. "This is where I must leave you. I too am bound to the palace by the Trickster."

The Trickster. Somehow, a god—Enki the mischief maker—managed to separate Cog and Samjang and trap Cog in his palace. Cog never explained how, and I guess we won't get an explanation, because Ku'ba turns to us and says, "Go. You haven't much time, and neither have I."

She looks at me and takes my hands. I feel a rush of fear as I sense her power, which is as great and vast as the ocean itself in full storm. "Peter, your gift will lead the way."

Well, I think, *given that it's a compass, I should hope it'd point the way.* Somehow, her words seem to have more meaning, though.

Still holding my hands, she turns to Caster, Ami, and Emily. "As for the other gifts, they will reveal themselves to you in time." She lets go and disappears into the darkness from whence we came.

"Well," says Caster, "that was helpful."

Emily looks at him sourly. "At least we're not dead." She turns her eyes toward the sky. "I don't know about you guys, but I'm not in a mood to jump fifteen vertical feet. Can you help us up, Ami?"

Ami nods, as if happy to be of help. "I think I can only take two up at a time."

"Send me first," says Caster with fire dancing on his hands.

"Put that out," says Emily harshly. "Don't you remember the warning? Our power attracts the fallen gods." She turns to Ami. "Better send me up with him, or we'll all get killed."

"Oh, don't be ridiculous. We're close to Miria. As Ku'ba said, she'll mask our power," Caster says.

Ami nods at Emily and closes her eyes. A moment later, Emily and Caster rise somewhat unsteadily off the ground toward the forest and moonlight above. They scramble upward, leaving Ami and me alone.

Ami looks up at me and meets my eyes. Her hazel eyes are warm and as big as the moon above. "You ready, Peter?"

I think of my promise to Cog to do my best to find Samjang and fulfill the even harder task of being the leader of the Four, whom I'm not even really friends with yet. Except Ami. The way she looks at me, I know we're friends.

"Yeah," I say. "Let's go save the world."

She smiles, and as we begin to rise, she whispers, "That was really cheesy."

I have to admit it was.

CHAPTER 24

GIFTS

As Ami and I rise above the ground, it closes behind us, cutting off any hope of our returning to the safety of Cog's palace, as empty and eerie as it was.

I glance around. We're in a forest of tall dark trees reaching up toward the sky. The sun has nearly set, leaving only a pale red light on the horizon, and the moon has come up. The ground is covered in snow.

Caster is fiddling with his spyglass impatiently.

Emily is wrapped in her blanket, shivering. "You figure it out?" she asks him, and then she smirks. "It's a spyglass. Shouldn't be that difficult for your big brain."

Caster tries extending it and twisting the knob on its side but still seems dissatisfied. "Fine. You try it," he says, tossing it to her.

Emily examines it and puts it to her eye. "It's blank," she says. "Did you take the cap off?"

"Obviously." He turns to me. "How about your compass?"

I open it up and lay it flat in my palm. Once more, I see that script around the rim—little characters saying things I can't read.

The needle moves around as if lost before settling to the east, opposite the setting sun. Every few seconds, it shuffles around.

Caster shakes his head, stuffs his hands into his pockets, and begins to pace. "Can anyone tell me why they went through such lengths to give us a compass that doesn't point north, a spyglass that doesn't spy, a stick, and a very creepy blanket? Something's not right."

"Hey, it might be creepy, but it keeps me warm," says Emily.

"You're right," I say to Caster somewhat grudgingly. I'm not sure I like Caster. He's kind of a jerk, but he's also really smart, and I think he's onto something.

"I'm right?" he repeats, first surprised and then pleased.

"Cog isn't playing a practical joke on us, right? And the gifts probably aren't damaged. Look at the lengths Ku'ba went to in order to keep them safe."

I think of Dr. Elsavier's words to me: "You're more than meets the eye." It's definitely not true of me, but it might be true of these objects. I tell the others, "They're more than meets the eye."

"Right," says Emily. "Ku'ba said they'll reveal themselves to us in time. So they must have some hidden capabilities."

Ami nods silently, and I wonder what's going through her head. Her eyes always look as if she's seeing something the rest of us are not.

"What do you think, Ami?" I ask.

"Well," she says, "I was thinking about Caster's telescope."

"Spyglass," Caster mutters under his breath.

The words don't seem to reach Ami. "Telescopes let you see things you can't see with just your bare eyeballs. So maybe the thing the telescope lets you see isn't something far away but something …" She seems to struggle to find the right word. "Something else, I guess."

"Any ideas on the 'something else'?" Emily asks.

Ami squeezes her eyebrows together in concentration and then shrugs. "No. My brain isn't very good."

"Yes, it is," I say.

Caster gives me a somewhat suspicious side glance before saying, "Yes, indeed it is, lil' sis. You have a beautiful brain." He turns to me. "Peter, give me your compass. You lot figure out what to do. I'm going to work out how to use the gifts." He takes my compass and begins to pace, mumbling to himself, "Something else."

Emily looks between me and Ami, who is shivering. I don't feel cold, though I think I would if not for the earth, which seems to warm me. I wonder how this can be, since we're still wearing the special robes Cog gave us, which kept us warm near the palace, even though it was snowy there too. Maybe they only work around Cog. But a darker explanation occurs to me: maybe there's something near us creating an unnatural chill in the air. I quickly brush the thought away, unwilling to think of any more danger for today. Getting attacked by ice monsters, fallen gods, and, worst of all, Ms. Schaden in a forty-eight-hour period is enough for me.

Emily opens her blanket. "You guys want some warmth?"

Ami nods. Before I can stop myself from being a complete idiot, I say, "No, that's all right. The earth keeps me warm." I mentally punch myself in the face. *Emily just asked me to stand next to her under a blanket!* "Actually," I say, "it, um, doesn't do a very good job."

I put my hands on my arms and rub them, probably unconvincingly. But Emily only smiles and opens the blanket to share. Suddenly, it billows outward and encloses all three of us almost like a tent, with a ceiling too high to touch.

"Whoa," we all say in unison.

Emily sits down, followed by Ami and me.

"So," Emily says, turning to us, as Caster still paces back and forth, fiddling with the compass and spyglass. She folds her hands together. "What's next?"

Ami looks as if she's contemplating something else, so I guess I have to answer. I look up to Emily, nervously meeting her beautiful eyes. They focus on me, and the attention is almost too much. Part of me wants to shrink back and hide in a hole—but another part of me finds it exhilarating. Emily Wong, the cutest girl in class, is talking to me.

"You still catching your breath?" she asks.

I realize with a start that my mouth is hanging open a little; no doubt I'm drooling too. I clamp it shut and feel my cheeks color.

"Oh, no need to be embarrassed." She laughs. "Ku'ba drove a punishing pace earlier. If you don't run a lot, it can be hard."

"Right," I say, thankful for the excuse and not certain whether she believes what she's saying or is just being nice.

"So, you two, what are we going to do? Caster's big brain is about to figure out what those devices do, and I don't want the rest of us to look like fools. I can hear him now: 'What were you guys doing the whole time while I was figuring out Cog's gifts? Chewing the fat?'" She squeezes her eyebrows together, lowers her voice, and makes chopping motions with her hand, which I guess is her imitation of Caster. It's not good, but it is unbelievably cute, because it's Emily.

"Well, putting aside the mission, we need food and water," I say.

Emily waves her hand, and some of the snow floats off the ground, melting into a giant droplet of water. "Water. Check." She furrows her brow. "As for food, didn't you notice on the map there were some villages marked to the west of Cog's palace?"

I nod as the map appears again before my eyes.

"How will we talk with them?" asks Ami.

"Talk with them?" I repeat.

"Oh," says Emily. "Think about it. We could talk with Cog and Ku'ba, but they were gods, so of course they could make themselves understood to us. But the people in the villages probably don't speak English; they speak some other language, likely nothing we have in our world."

"So then what should we do tonight?" I ask.

Emily purses her lips. "Well, we have only about three weeks to avoid a fate worse than death, or whatever it was Cog said, so we probably should start moving east. If we're lucky, we'll find villages."

Ami nods. "We can all sleep here, even if we don't find anyone." She lies back and stares up dreamily at the top of the gigantic blanket-tent thing. "It's so nice."

"That sounds—"

Caster interrupts me. "Eureka! I've got it!"

"You've got what, dingus?" shouts Emily. "You figure it out at last?"

"Yes!" shouts Caster. "Hey, where are you guys?"

"Right where you left us."

"I can hear you," he says, his voice growing closer to us. "But I can't see you." His voice now sounds as if it's right on top of us, almost as if he's inside the tent but not.

Emily furrows her brow, and then her eyes brighten. "Take a step back."

"All right," says Caster, his voice drifting farther away. "Now okay?"

Emily grabs the sides of the tent walls and yanks, and the sides suddenly wrap back up into a personal blanket.

Caster, standing only a few feet away, jumps. Sparks and flames dance along his face and hands. "What the—"

Emily laughs, slapping her knee. "Oh, your expression! I wish I still had my phone. I'd love a picture of that."

"What just happened?" I ask.

Caster puts his dignified expression back on. "Isn't it obvious? We've found out the use of the third gift."

"No," says Emily. "*We've* found out the use of the third gift."

"That's what I just said."

"No, it isn't!"

"Yes, it is!"

"No," says Emily. "*We* as in me, Ami, and Peter."

"Oh," says Caster. "I thought you meant *we* as in *weeee*. Easy mistake."

Emily says something angry in Chinese, probably a curse word, and Caster smirks and says, "Anyway, congratulations on figuring out that you have an interdimensional blanket, Linus. *I* found out what the spyglass and the compass do. Well, I think I did."

"What do they do?" I ask.

"It'd be easier just to show you," he says. He hands me my compass and then his spyglass. "You see all those words?" He points to the foreign squiggles along the compass. "Totally incomprehensible, right? Wrong."

He gestures for me to raise the spyglass to my eye. I do so, thinking this is possibly the stupidest idea ever, and Caster just wants to have some fun at my expense, maybe by shoving the spyglass into my eye. But as I look through the glass, I see what he means. "No way," I mutter.

"What?" says Emily. She pokes my shoulder. "No way what? C'mon! What does it do?"

I let her poke me a few more times, savoring the moment, before I slowly lower the spyglass and compass. Emily looks desperately curious.

Caster is wearing a devilish grin. "Pretty cool, huh?" he says.

"Yeah," I say. "Really cool."

Emily slaps us both. "You're being jerks, you two! You're not supposed to conspire! What does it do?"

"The spyglass lets you read the squiggles," I say. "And the squiggles are instructions. The compass doesn't point north because that's not what it was made to do."

"What was it made to do?" asks Ami.

I hesitate and then reply, and the words seem fantastic even as I say them. "It was made to point the way."

CHAPTER 25

THE WATCHMAN

"Whatever happened to the horses we were supposed to get?" Caster moans after we've walked for a solid two hours, following the compass. It's thoroughly dark now, except for the moonlight.

"We got attacked by fallen gods, remember?" says Emily.

"Yeah, but all the same, couldn't Ku'ba have teleported a few horses into the tunnels for us?"

Emily shakes her head. "You probably don't even know how to ride a horse, do you?"

"That's not the point," says Caster petulantly.

"Yes, it is," says Emily. "And besides—"

"Hey, guys?" says Ami. She's been quiet for the past few hours, but now her voice is concerned. She doesn't sound outright terrified, but somehow, it would almost be less scary if she did. The little whisper of fear cuts me right to the bone.

"What is it, Ami?" Emily says.

"There's someone else here."

"Someone else?" I repeat.

The rest of us look at her with puzzlement, and she returns the look as if unsure how we don't get it.

"Didn't you hear it?" asks Ami.

"There are probably animals moving nearby," says Caster. "It is a forest."

"Yeah," says Emily, glancing around nervously. "No need to scare us."

Ami shakes her head and looks at me for support, but I only shrug. Then again, it does feel as if something is running quickly over the ground. But it is probably just my tired mind playing tricks on me, I think. Besides, I don't want to believe there's anything following us just yet. Cog and Ku'ba took care of the fallen gods. No one else should know we're here.

We walk along a little longer. Caster and Emily bicker just as before. Meanwhile, a toxic potion of hunger and fear brews in my stomach, and it's all I can do to keep myself from dry-heaving. Ami looks around the forest warily, and I find myself standing a little closer to her, partly because I want to protect her and partly because I want to be protected by her. After all, she sent Brutus Borgia and his gang packing and utterly humiliated them to boot.

I notice Caster and Emily are standing a little closer too. Despite their bickering, I suppose they are friends. It only makes sense that they fight as much as they do: he's fire, and she's water. But what about Ami and me? What could be more distant than wind and stone, heaven and earth? Yet I don't feel distant from her. I feel close. It's easy to get along with her, just like when she took me to see the sights above the palace.

My mind goes to the look of terror in her eyes before she fell, and I decide to ask her again. "Ami," I say, speaking quietly so the others don't hear, "what did you see that made you fall?"

She glances at Caster and Emily, who've grown quieter, and shakes her head. "I'll tell you later," she mouths, leaving me to imagine what horrible sight she must have seen. In a dark forest, imagination can get pretty gruesome.

"So, Peter," says Emily, breaking through my thoughts, "what did Cog want to talk to you about?"

I think back to the conversation. *I'm supposed to lead you guys, and we're not the only one with magic rings. There's a fifth one out there, and he might turn out to be our enemy.* Will they hate me if they think I'm a teacher's pet, the special one who got information from Cog they didn't?

"Oh, nothing much," I lie. "I think he just wanted to catch me up on some things, since he had already talked with you before I arrived."

"Oh," says Emily, looking a little disappointed.

I feel a stab of guilt, both for lying and for causing pain to Emily, even if in a small way. Caster looks bored and fatigued. Ami looks at me funny, as if she knows I'm not telling the truth. Mercifully, she doesn't say anything.

We travel on in silence for a few more minutes, when Caster shouts, "I see light!"

I move up beside him. "Light?"

"Yeah! Up ahead. Can't you see it?"

We all squint until our eyes hurt but can't see anything besides trees and pale moonlight.

"Oh, I think I understand," says Caster.

"What?" asks Emily.

"Ami earlier said she could hear something moving, even though none of the rest of us could. Maybe we're more sensitive to things in our element. There are fires up ahead, so it would make

125

sense I can see them before you all." He strokes his chin. "Peter, I bet you can sense things through the earth, right?"

Now that I think about it, it's true. I felt something moving earlier when Ami said she heard something, and now I can feel footfalls coming from the distance. It isn't so much that I can actively sense things; it is more like the ring occasionally gives me flashes of insight.

"Yeah," I say, nodding. "Sort of."

"And what about me?" says Emily.

"You probably can tell when someone is peeing from like nine hundred yards away. Very important. You wouldn't want to accidentally open a porta-potty and find someone inside."

Emily slaps him on the arm. "Oh, shut up. You're atrocious, Caster."

"I know. But fear not. We will eat tonight."

In a little while, we come to the edge of the forest. We have to walk what feels like miles through fields of empty stumps. There's something eerie and wrong about the place, as if these trees should not have been cut down. I'm glad when a village appears in the distance. It's a few hundred yards from the forest, and it has a fence built around it made of sharpened logs. Torches spaced about every ten feet flicker along the sides. They must be what Caster saw earlier.

We come to the gate, and Caster knocks three times. I stare at the sharpened logs, wondering what the villagers are trying to keep out and whether we've made a good decision in coming here. They could turn out to be violent people. Judging by the logs, they don't seem fond of strangers.

I think of mentioning this to the group, but a little window opens in the gate. A man with a beard and wary eyes looks at us. "*Dosh kite? Dach kite sin mashok?*"

The four of us look at one another and shake our heads. None of us, of course, has any idea what he's saying.

Caster holds up a hand and begins to mock write on it. Getting him to write is probably our best shot—our only shot. The man furrows his brow, as if he doesn't understand how this possibly could be of benefit, but a moment later, he produces a piece of paper with something written on it.

Caster holds up the spyglass to the piece of paper and translates for us: "Who are you? And what is your purpose?" He scratches his chin. "The only question is, how do we respond?"

We stare at one another for a little while, trying to work out what to do. Ami's eyes look as if she's someplace else, as usual, when suddenly, they brighten. She turns to the man staring impatiently at us through the door and floats a little before holding up four fingers.

The man looks from her fingers to the ground some three inches below her floating feet and then back to her fingers. His eyes widen, and then he looks at us, and recognition dawns in his eyes. "*Khabo!*" he shouts.

"Oh, fudge, Ami, what did you do?" says Emily as a commotion breaks out behind the walls, with excited voices speaking rapidly.

"I answered his question," she says simply. "Honestly."

"Honestly?" Caster repeats, flabbergasted, as if it's the most absurd thing he's ever heard in his life. His dark eyebrows arch upward like caterpillars about to do battle. "You never answer a stranger's questions honestly! Didn't you learn about stranger danger?"

Ami shrugs. "I could tell he didn't want to hurt us."

"How could you tell that?" asks Emily.

Ami opens her mouth as if to reply, and then she squeezes her eyebrows together, as if uncertain what to say. "I just could."

At that moment, I hear the sound of a giant lock, and then the gate begins to move.

"Let's hope you were right," says Caster with little flames dancing across his fingers.

CHAPTER 26

DECISIONS

The gate opens to reveal dozens of men, women, and children dressed in tunics and gowns, all staring at us with a mix of curiosity and fear in their eyes—and something else too, especially in the children and the old, but I can't say exactly what it is.

Caster looks at the group of villagers warily. His eyes run over the farm tools they carry: scythes, hoes, and other metallic things with pointy edges. I gulp, wondering if we could defend ourselves against so many, even with our magical rings.

Emily steps a little closer to the rest of us and glances around as if looking for water in case she needs to fight.

The moment of tension holds for a second longer, and then one of the villagers steps forward—an older woman, maybe some kind of village elder. She has a lot of beads in her hair, and her weathered skin looks as if it has seen many more winters than summers.

"*Ai-ku!*" she says to us, banging her staff on the ground. Then she turns and walks toward the center of the village. The rest of the villagers move with her.

"I guess that means 'Come,'" Emily says.

We follow after the old woman, who hobbles along with the help of her staff. We travel along a winding dirt street with wooden shops and houses along the sides. None of them are higher than two stories, and some look as if they would be condemned as dangerous to public health if they were in America. I see rotting wood, loose nails, and fire damage. We also pass by several crumbling stone buildings and weather-worn statues.

"Is it just me, or do you get the feeling this place used to be a very nice place to live?" says Emily.

I nod quietly. There's something about the village that feels dark and glum the longer I'm here. Questions linger in my mind: *So what happened to the village? Did a trade route that used to pass through here get changed? Or did something else, something darker, befall the village?* I remember the sensation I felt when we were in the forest—the feeling that something else was there. I wasn't the only one who sensed it; Ami did too.

Fear begins to work in my mind, making me imagine that every shadow holds a nasty creature ready to jump out at me and kill me. I'm glad when Ami breaks the silence.

"Did you notice the look in their eyes?" she whispers to me.

I'm not sure what she means at first, and I'm also not sure why she's whispering, but then I remember that some of the villagers did have an unusual look in their eyes, not just fear or curiosity.

"Yeah," I say. Then I wonder if she could read the look, just as she read the watchman and knew he wasn't going to harm us. "What was it?"

"Hope," she says quietly.

I furrow my brow. Their looking hopefully at us makes me a little fearful. *What stories do the people here have about the Four? Are we mythical heroes to them, like Odysseus and Nestor? Or are we more like Roosevelt and Churchill to them, real figures from the recent past who people put their faith in during hard times?*

The possibility scares me, and it reminds me of what Cog said will happen if we fail: Miria and then Gaia will be consumed by the Ice Reich, and we all will meet a fate worse than death. Why should so much depend on four kids? We're not even out of high school. We're supposed to be getting summer jobs and getting ready to go to college, not saving the world—or worlds! Why couldn't the rings have come to four people in, say, the Special Forces?

I turn to Ami to ask her why she thinks they look hopeful, when the old woman bangs her stick against the ground. I look up and see we've come to the village center. There's an old, crumbling stone building that looks as if it might have housed an assembly long ago, but it's boarded up now. Across from it is a large house with an iron gate around it; it's the only building in sight with three stories. I wonder who lives here. Whoever it is must be pretty important.

The woman turns to us and says something incomprehensible. When we don't immediately respond, she begins to make elaborate hand gestures. Caster gives us a smirk and then does hand gestures of his own, signing for them to produce paper and a writing instrument. The watchman who met us at the wall comes forward and explains to her.

She nods and begins to write on the ground with her staff. I suppose in a town like this, they don't have much paper.

Caster translates for us when she's finished: "Are you truly the Four?"

"I think we're in a little too deep to lie," says Emily.

"Agreed," I say, partly because it makes sense and partly because Emily is the one saying it.

Caster looks skeptical. "I'm not sure. Who knows whether they like the Four? Why do they have all these pitchforks and scythes if they're just happy to greet us?"

I glance around at the villagers. Their farm tools look more ominous in the firelight, glinting menacingly. Yet they look more anxious than angry. If they hated the Four and suspected us of being the Four, wouldn't they look a little more violent? Instead, they look fearful and a little confused. They're probably wondering what we're saying. English has to sound just as funny to them as their language does to us.

"They're scared," says Ami quietly. "The pitchforks aren't for us."

Caster strokes his chin, as if realizing Ami has a point. "Then are we decided on the response?"

We all nod.

"But how are we going to tell them?" I ask. "The spyglass lets us read foreign languages, not write them."

Caster looks at me and smirks as his bright eyes dance with amusement. "Are you serious, Smythe?"

I furrow my brow. "What?"

Emily flicks Caster and then gives me a gentle look. "Think about it. The spyglass lets the viewer read foreign languages. All we have to do is write in English and give the spyglass to the old woman."

"Oh," I say, feeling spectacularly stupid. It's never fun to be the dumbest person in the group, especially when the group happens to have the girl you like in it. At some point, I'm going to have to stop being so lame, or she's never going to go to prom with me.

"Duh," says Caster. "Anyway, Ami, you have a stick. Would you like to do the honors?"

As Ami scrawls out the reply in big letters on the ground, I entertain violent fantasies of burying Caster under six hundred feet of earth or squishing him between gigantic boulders. It might attract the attention of the fallen gods, but who cares? It would be worth it just to wipe the smart-ass "I'm better than you" expression off his face. He's even worse than Brutus Borgia, because at least Brutus is stupid. Caster, on the other hand, is buckets smarter than I'll ever be. How am I supposed to work with him in a team, much less lead him? *Oh, Cog, why couldn't you have been a little more helpful?*

Emily notices my sullen expression, and she squeezes my shoulder, which sends a flood of warmth into my chest and makes my cheeks flush a little. "Don't mind him," she says. Her eyes flicker to Caster as he presents the spyglass to the old woman. "You're not as stupid as he'll try to make you feel."

"Thanks," I mutter, glad she's beside me, unsure what exactly to make of her encouragement. "So does that mean I'm stupid, just not as stupid as Caster thinks I am?"

She smiles and elbows me. "You're not getting another free compliment out of me, Peter Smythe."

"That wasn't my intention," I say stiffly, but I can't help but smile too, even though we're in a foreign world, surrounded by a bunch of villagers with scythes and pitchforks. Emily has a special spark that can make a person feel warm and wanted. Or maybe that's the power all pretty girls have over guys, especially the poor guys who are crushing on them. But I think Emily's special.

I can hardly believe I'm next to her, much less laughing with her, and the feeling is euphoric—until it's interrupted by, of course, Caster. He coughs loudly, looking somewhat irritated, and says, "She's responded. She says the village will be happy to provide us with whatever help we need, as long as we perform a task for them."

"We could use food, a map, and maybe a few horses," says Emily. "Though I'd feel bad for taking anything from them. They don't look like they have much."

"If we succeed, we can pay them back. If we fail, a few missing loaves of bread will be the least of their problems," says Caster. "End of the world and all."

"What does she want exactly?" I ask.

As if anticipating my question, the old woman begins to write again. Caster raises his spyglass and translates: "There is a demon creature that has been haunting our village, stealing away children in the night, and leaving pale corpses in the forest, though often, we are not even lucky enough to find our dead. The creature, according to the ancient wisdom of our people, is called a bloodgorger. In the old days, the Four drove these creatures out of our lands, but now they're returning. Bring back the head of the bloodgorger, and we will give you whatever you need."

Caster closes the spyglass and turns to us. "I don't know about you, but I think that sounds like a terrible idea. There are probably a few nearby villages that aren't haunted by bloodgorgers. We can get supplies there."

"Hold on," says Emily. "Look at them."

I look at the people around us. Their expressions are desperate. One woman, who can't be much older than Emily, already has two children holding on to her skirt. In her arms, she holds another baby. She fixes her eyes on me and pleads with me in the common tongue of mankind, the language we all recognize in each other's eyes.

"We need to help them," says Emily, and Ami nods her agreement.

"No," says Caster. "We don't. Think it through. If we die fighting the bloodgorger, then these people will all die because the Ice Reich will come. If we don't die fighting the bloodgorger, then one, we might die because using so much power will attract the fallen gods, and two, we might fail in the quest because we wasted time fighting a minor enemy, when we should've been rescuing Samjang. This is a terrible idea."

"That's because you're heartless," says Emily. She looks to me.

As much as I hate Caster, his logic seems sound. There are a lot of ways this could go wrong. I don't know how we'd begin to go about fighting a bloodgorger. But the woman's eyes cut a deep wound in my heart. How could I tell her, "Too bad. We're too busy"?

An idea occurs to me. "Why don't we let the compass decide?"

"What do you mean?" says Ami.

I think back to one of the few things I remember from physics class. "A compass at magnetic north doesn't point in any particular direction. Sometimes it will spin, and sometimes it will wobble, trying to point downward. If this compass points where we're supposed to go and we're supposed to fight the bloodgorger, then the compass should act like we're at magnetic north."

135

Caster nods thoughtfully, as if impressed with my reasoning, which I have to admit feels kind of good. "Agreed. Let's see it."

"Okay," says Emily reluctantly.

Ami merely dips her head, but I guess that means yes.

Slowly, I open the compass. Suddenly, a screech of metal tears through the chilly air.

CHAPTER 27

THE KEEPER OF
THE MANSION

The sound turns out to be the gate of the mansion opening. Apparently, they don't have WD-40 in Miria, so the gate sounds like a wailing banshee—or what I imagine a wailing banshee would sound like—as it opens.

Out from the gate steps forth a tall, lean man who stands a full three heads above everyone else in the crowd, yet he doesn't seem monstrous or giant-like. Somehow, we're the ones who seem out of proportion. Maybe it's because of how majestic his features are: his face is perfectly symmetrical; his eyes are large, keen, and sympathetic; and his jaw is strong and set. He wears a long white robe that sparkles and subtly changes colors in the firelight the way mist makes a miniature rainbow. He's followed by a small hunchbacked woman with shifty eyes.

As the villagers see him, they all become quiet, with their eyes cast downward. Caster notices this and smirks. "Well, he must be important."

"*Namaskara*! *Au'gui'tana*! *Salvete*! *Khairete*!" the tall man bellows as he approaches us.

The first two words are incomprehensible to me, but the last two hit my ears with jarring familiarity.

"*Khaire*?" I repeat, using the Ancient Greek greeting addressing one person.

"Ah, splendid!" he says in Ancient Greek. "I knew it was a long shot—it's been about two millennia or so since I last traveled to Gaia—but they always do seem to choose a linguist among the Four." He looks me up and down. "You must be earth! What's your name?"

"My name is, er, Peter," I say, stumbling through my Greek. It feels weird in my mouth. The only people who ever have talked in this language with me are Dad and Dr. Elsavier. Standing before this man, I suddenly feel the need to speak formally. "And who are you, Lord?"

"You may call me Galthanius. I am the Kar-dun leader of this town, sent here by the Hai-run Court," he says. He smiles indulgently at me and the others. "Mumbo jumbo to your ears, no doubt. No worries. I shall explain, but perhaps first, you ought to enlighten your friends on what exactly is going on."

I turn and see Emily, Caster, and Ami staring at me with mouths partly open.

"What language is that?" asks Ami.

"Is it Greek?" asks Emily, confused. But I don't miss the admiration in her eyes.

"Yes," I say, blushing a little. "Ancient Greek."

"Whoa," says Emily. "How do you speak Ancient Greek? And what are you talking about?"

Caster looks on with grudging admiration, which feels nearly as good as Emily's warmth. Well, actually, it's not close at all. Impressing Emily feels a thousand times better than proving to Caster I'm not a total blockhead.

"He says his name is Galthanius, and he's the leader of the town from, er, some place or another. I didn't really understand. Apparently, he traveled to our world two millennia ago."

"Wait—what?" says Caster. "You sure you got the Greek right?"

"Yes," I say flatly, not happy to have Caster questioning my ability to understand Greek, especially since this is one of the few things I'm any good at.

"I hope you've done a good job of elucidating the situation," Galthanius says, interrupting. "In any case, I am pleased to meet the newest Four to visit Miria and would like to offer you residence in my home. Fear has become rampant in this town ever since the old forest was cut down, and you might find yourselves safer behind an iron gate." He smiles graciously and waits patiently as I translate his words to the others.

Caster strokes his chin. "I assume this invitation implies he'll be offering us food."

"Yeah," says Emily as her stomach growls. "And it seems like he knows a lot. He could probably help us out a lot. We have a lot of unanswered questions."

I nod in agreement, thinking Emily and Caster both have made good points. We're starving for both food and information, and Galthanius sounds like he has both.

"Ami?" I ask.

Her eyebrows are drawn together, as if she's worried about something. When her eyes meet mine, there's hesitation in them. "Yeah," she says at last. "I'm hungry too."

"Excellent," says Caster, clapping his hands. "It's settled then. Herodotus—I mean Peter—translate!"

I cast him an irritated glance for giving me orders, but he seems not to notice and instead gives me a look of impatience. I translate for Galthanius, and he nods enthusiastically.

"Very good," he says. "Then I shall be very glad to have you for dinner tonight!"

He nods to the small, fidgety woman who came out through the gate with him. I didn't notice her much before, but I guess she is hardly something to notice compared to the towering Galthanius.

Galthanius speaks a few words to the disappointed crowd, and after he finishes, they seem a little less disappointed. Though I have no idea what he said, his voice sounded encouraging and soothing. It seems to have the same effect a lullaby has on a restless infant.

He gestures toward the mansion, and we follow after his long strides. I have to jog to keep up. The gate screeches as it closes behind us, and I feel a stir in my stomach I can't quite explain, as if we might have made the wrong decision.

I glance down at the compass, which was perfectly still only a few minutes before. Now it seems confused, spinning around, but amid the confusion, there seems to be a direction it likes coming back to: straight ahead toward the massive oak doors that lead into the mansion of torchlight and flickering shadows.

CHAPTER 28

TALES OF AN ANCIENT

A few minutes later, we find ourselves seated at a long wooden table lit by candles, with paintings of impressive-looking men and women staring down at us.

The butler—the small, shifty woman we saw earlier—brings plates of steamed vegetables and dishes of roasted meat. Emily drools as she stares at the food, and somehow, she looks cute with saliva leaking from her mouth. It sounds *really* weird, I know, but it's true. Or maybe I'm just weird.

Galthanius seats himself at the head of the table, in a large chair studded with iron, and pours himself a drink of what looks like red wine, though it's thicker than the wine my mom likes. He closes his eyes as he takes a sip from his glass, and when he reopens them, I imagine that for just a moment, his eyes are as red as the wine itself.

I quickly realize it's just a trick of the firelight. I chide myself for being so jumpy. But I guess it only makes sense I'd be in this state: I'm tired and hungry and a lot of crazy things have happened in the past two days. I realize I'm shivering again, though I don't know why. The cloaks Cog gave us are supposed to protect us from the cold.

Galthanius gestures for us to begin eating, and everyone digs in greedily, except me. I first whisper a prayer of thanksgiving learned from my Italian mom and *then* I dig in greedily.

Galthanius smiles indulgently. "I suppose you all are very hungry, so I shall explain a few things while you eat. You may be wondering, first of all, why I am so different in appearance from the villagers and, indeed, from yourselves."

He waits for me to translate, which I do reluctantly, since it means I must take a break from eating, while the others can continue gorging themselves.

"I am a Kar-dun. Along with the rest of my folk, we rule the Hai-run, the northernmost kingdom. There are two other kingdoms, one to the west and one to the south, and generally, we have spent the last several millennia quarreling. In your world, we are called by various names: demigods, heroes, giants, or Nephilim."

Nephilim. The word sounds familiar to me, tugging at some piece of long-ago-buried knowledge. "Nephilim like from the Bible?" I say.

He looks at me funny, and I realize I've used a modern Greek word for *Bible*. I rack my brain for what my dad taught me long ago about ancient translations of the Bible.

"The Translation of the Seventy," I say when the phrase finally comes to me. The name comes from a story about seventy Jewish scholars commissioned to translate the scriptures into Greek.

"Indeed," he says. "*There were giants on the earth in those days and also afterward, when the sons of God came into the daughters*

of men, who bore children to them. Those were the mighty men of
old, men of renown."

The half-eaten peach in Caster's hand falls onto the table as
I translate the words. "So you're—"

"The offspring of a god. Or of a messenger, an angel, a son
of god—all words used by different people to mean the same
thing. When I last visited Gaia, there were already men going
around saying that the gods of Olympus were myths, that the
Translation of the Seventy was a primitive guide for living a
happy life but nothing more, and that it certainly did not relate
historical facts." He smiles. "But as usual, the human intellectuals
got it wrong. That is perhaps one of the few things you can count
on them to do."

Caster looks hurt as I translate these words. "What about
scientists?" he mutters. "This sort of anti-intellectual attitude is
exactly why we can't take a helicopter to rescue Samjang."

"So what I want to know is, how is he still alive after at least
two millennia?" Emily says. "And why are there no heroes and
gods or whatever in our world anymore?"

I translate the questions, softening the tone a little, so we
don't sound as if we're questioning his existence.

"We are not like ordinary humans, whose bodies have run
down like poorly built machines ever since the Flood. We have the
blood of gods in our veins. Is it much surprise we should live so
long? As for why there are no more heroes or gods in your world,
I cannot say. Perhaps your gods were banished, or perhaps they
are so clever that you do not see them acting. Perhaps something
similar is true of your heroes."

I ponder his statements, wondering if there are any people in
our world who are descendants of gods or their children.

143

"In any case," he says, "because of our superior ability, we rule the world."

"If it comes down to ability," I say, "why don't the gods rule?"

His eyes flicker momentarily with irritation, but it passes so quickly I wonder if I've only imagined it—just as I imagined the red glow in his eyes, which was probably only firelight. "Who can understand the mind of a god?" he says airily. "Whatever their reasons, they do not favor direct rule, so we rule. And if we didn't, if we imitated the gods, it would, I suspect, be a very terrible thing. Humans are frail and stupid creatures; they need guidance. As you already saw, they are apt to believe in old myths and boogeymen to explain away uncomfortable facts."

"You mean the bloodgorger?"

He rolls his eyes. "Precisely. Humans, among other things, are stubborn and so would not listen to me, but you ought to know: there is no such thing as a bloodgorger."

"Well, then what are the villagers so afraid of?" asks Emily after I finish translating.

Caster twirls his fingers absently, and Ami looks inquiringly at Galthanius. I get the impression she's more curious about *him* than about what he's saying. It makes me wonder what she's trying to figure out.

I pose Emily's question to him. He nods sadly; his eyes are filled with sympathy. "It is a terrible thing, the truth of the matter. The old forest behind the village had to be cut down because our empire needed wood. There were a few troublemakers who claimed these woods provided protection against evil, and by cutting down the woods, the villagers were inviting a bloodgorger to feed on them. The Kar-dun before me worked very hard to dispel the rumor. But this process was made very difficult because the nymphs and laganmorfs who inhabited the woods were uncooperative."

He pauses, letting me translate, and then continues. "After the woods were cut down, the situation became very tense, and I was sent over by the capital to calm matters. We have mostly avoided bloodshed, but there are always a few nymphs and laganmorfs who take to violence after being relocated, even though we're very fair about it. It is these acts of retaliation that have lent credence to the pernicious myth of the bloodgorger."

"What exactly is a laganmorf?" I ask. I have a vague recollection of what nymphs are supposed to be: fairy-like creatures tied to a particular natural place, such as a tree, river, or mountain. When they take human form, at least according to the old myths, they look like beautiful maidens. But I've never heard of a laganmorf.

"Ah, the laganmorfs are tall, solemn creatures who inhabit woodlands and call themselves the older brothers of the nymphs. They've very protective of their younger sisters. Most likely, they are the ones causing the violence."

"So how can we get them to stop?" I ask.

He shakes his head. "Believe me, I have tried. They are very difficult to find, and even when you succeed in finding them, they are not willing to hear sense." His voice sounds deeply sorrowful and sincere. But there's a quiet part of me which whispers that he sounds *too* sincere.

"So," says Caster after I finish translating, "they have an insurgency on their hands here. I'm not sure we should interfere. We are Americans, after all, and with our glorious history of success in interfering in the affairs of sovereign countries, I'm not sure it's a very good idea. What if the laganmorfs attack the World Trade Center or the Pentagon because of us?"

"You're just saying that 'cause you don't want to help," Emily says.

"So you have an idea about how to keep laganmorfs and nymphs from terrorizing a town of people who stole their homeland?" says Caster.

"I …" Emily falls silent. She pushes around the food on her plate with a knife.

"See?" says Caster, and he looks to me for support.

I glance over at Ami, whose worried eyes seem to indicate she is deep in thought. They meet mine for a moment, and it looks as if there's something she wants to tell me, but I get the feeling she doesn't want to say it here. I don't blame her.

I yawn. My stomach feels heavy from all the food, and my legs ache after all the running and walking we did today.

"I'm sure you are weary from so much travel," says Galthanius. "Perhaps you would stay the night here. In the morning, you can furnish me with tales of your travels, and then I can see you off."

We thank him, and his little butler guides us from the table to our sleeping quarters. There's something not quite right about the hallways. It's hard to put my finger on it, but it's as if they're slanted, like the way the world looks in a bad dream. There's something wrong about the lamps too. They're made of metal that looks far too sharp for holding a bit of glass and burning oil.

Ami taps my wrist as we near the end of the hallway. I look to her and mouth, "What's wrong?"

She mouths a single word: *Galthanius.*

CHAPTER 29

THE KNOCK AT THE DOOR

The hunchback butler separates us into two bedrooms, one for the girls and one for Caster and me, which is a less-than-delightful arrangement. One of my big fears in life is—supposing I get into college—ending up with a roommate like Caster.

"So," says Caster as we both stare at the single king-sized bed in the room, "who's going to be the big spoon?"

"I'll sleep on the floor," I say.

"Oh, c'mon," says Caster. He busts out his exaggerated Indian accent. "Would you like a wedgie sandwich?"

"What?" Sometimes Caster makes no sense at all.

"Humor is unpredictability," he says.

"If that were true, you'd be funny," I retort, half-surprised I come up with a comeback in time.

"Oh, good one," says Caster. He flops down onto the bed and stares up at the ceiling, as if pondering an interesting and amusing problem. "I know you don't like me."

"I never said that."

"It's obvious enough," he says. "I rub many people the wrong way, and sometimes I can be"—he assumes an exaggerated British accent—"perfectly beastly."

Well, at least he's self-aware.

"All the same, I have no apologies." He shrugs. "It's just how I am, but you ought to know it's not because I have a special dislike of you."

My fists begin to clench, but then the exhaustion of the day and the absurdity of the moment wash over me, and I begin to laugh, first quietly and then hysterically.

Caster gives me an odd look and then a concerned one. "Oh dear, have I broken him?"

This, for reasons I cannot explain, only makes me laugh more, and I fall to the ground. Sprawling pain shoots up from my hips, which sends me into another fit of giggles. Such laughter is contagious, and even hard-hearted Caster begins to chuckle a little.

After a few minutes, we end up at the foot of the bed. "So tell me about yourself, Peter," he says.

I do. Then he tells me about himself, about his quirks and hobbies and the long summer hours spent watching MIT lectures from his bedroom, reading analytic philosophy, and doing chemistry experiments in his garage. He has a few good stories, and when I tell him of my attempt in chem lab to put out flames with Goober's "water," he laughs. I almost don't hate him. I guess beneath the arrogance and smart remarks, there's a human being. I almost feel bad for him. There's a common strand in all his hobbies: they're all things he does alone.

"We're not so different, you and I," says Caster.

"That's cliché," I say.

"There's a reason why certain things become cliché. They're said often because they're often true."

I shrug, conceding the point. I'm about to ask him about Emily, because I've been wondering what he thinks of her and my chances with her, when there's a quiet knock on the door.

"Probably the girls," says Caster, springing up. I join him.

When he opens the door, though, we're greeted only by darkness. Caster looks side to side down the hallway to see if someone's playing a trick on us by knocking on the door and then flattening against the wall. But there's no one.

He shrugs and shuts the door. We turn around, and I nearly jump through my skin as someone says, "Boo," close enough to kiss me.

"Aah!" I yell, stumbling backward. It turns out to be Emily, who, along with Ami, is giggling. Caster too looks amused. My mind reels, wondering how they managed to sneak behind us, and then I see Emily's cloak on the bed.

"You know, Ms. Granger, you ought to use your cloak of invisibility for better things," says Caster. "Why do you have to be so mean to Peter?"

Emily looks at him, flabbergasted. "First of all, I thought we decided it was an interdimensional cloak. Harry Potter's cloak wasn't interdimensional. And second of all, since when do you care about Peter's feelings?"

Caster puts his arm around my shoulders. "Since we became best friends." He sticks his tongue out at her, which makes me wonder how sincere he is.

What are you talking about? I say to myself. *Caster is the least sincere person you've ever met.*

Caster and Emily descend into bickering for the next few seconds. I shoot Ami a "Help me" look, and she gives me a knowing look but no smile. There's something else in her eyes that keeps her from smiling, something that turns my insides cold. It reminds me of the way she looked just before we tumbled from the sky above Cog's palace. I remind myself to ask her what she saw next time we're alone.

"Listen," I say, interrupting them. "What are you guys doing here?"

Emily's fist stops in midswing. She brushes herself down and collects herself, growing suddenly serious. "Right, well, I think Ami should take that question."

Ami looks at Caster, and he gives her an encouraging nod. "Well," she says, "don't you think Galthanius is a little suspicious?"

"Suspicious?" says Caster.

"I …" She wrings her hands in frustration, as if she knows what she wants to say but can't express it in language. "I can't explain it. I guess I haven't got a very good head. But there's something not right about him."

"Don't say that," says Emily. "You've got one of the best heads that ever headed. That ever did head."

"You truly have a way with words," says Caster.

"I know what you mean," I say to Ami. "I felt it too."

I think of the way the firelight played in Galthanius's eyes and the strange flicker of anger that came across his face when I mentioned the gods. Then there was his story about the nymphs and laganmorfs. There was something about it that didn't ring true, as if he were lying about something.

"Hm," says Caster, stroking his chin. "We have a hypothesis. I think we should apply the test of truth."

"What's that?" asks Emily.

"Experiment," he replies airily, and then he adds, "Obviously."

"You mean explore the house?" I say.

A mad gleam comes into his eyes. "Someone's catching on."

CHAPTER 30

THE SECRET CHAMBER

After a short debate, we agree we must explore the house. If it turns out Ami's intuition is correct, we owe it to the villagers. But what really settles it is the compass, which is pointing toward the door.

Slowly, we creep down the dark hallway and toward the winding stairs. We link hands, and somehow, I find myself between Emily and Ami, who is on the end so she can hold her stick in her left hand.

The weird part of my brain that insists on seeing meaning in everything whispers to me that this arrangement is deeply metaphorical: I am caught between Emily and Ami. But I've made it a practice never to listen to that voice, so I shove it into a deep part of me where the moon doesn't shine.

We follow the compass, which changes direction often, leading us down a few more corridors until we come to a room with a glass dome. Moonlight floods through, bathing the room in pale, cool light. It is a beautiful, if eerie, sight.

Caster gazes up at it and recites a poem with overwrought solemnity:

O Moon, when I gaze on thy beautiful face,
Careening along through the boundaries of space,
The thought has often come into my mind
If I ever shall see thy glorious behind.

"So what you're saying is," says Emily, "you want the moon to moon you?"

"Something like that," says Caster.

Emily shakes her head and mutters something in Chinese. It sounds like "*Bian tai.*" I'm guessing it means *nutso* or *weirdo*.

We walk out of the moonlit room and down another hallway till we come to a forking passageway. The compass can't seem to decide which direction it likes better.

"I think this is the point where we're supposed to say, 'Let's split up, gang,'" says Caster.

"No, it's definitely not, Fred," says Emily, shivering. "You're not getting any Scooby Snacks if we split up."

"Fred doesn't eat Scooby Snacks," Ami says.

"Yeah!" says Caster. "He doesn't. And if I'm Fred, who does that make you? Daphne or Velma?"

"I'm a mix of both," Emily answers with a superior smile. "The perfect combination of beauty and brains."

"And ego," Caster adds.

"Like you haven't got plenty of that yourself!"

I watch them bicker back and forth, feeling like an awkward bystander. I guess I want to be part of their conversation, but I'm not sure how. I've never been much good at inserting myself, so I turn to Ami. If you can't join 'em, beat 'em.

"I guess that makes us Shaggy and Scooby," I say to her.

She smiles and seems pleased with the analogy, which means I'm lucky, because I realize I've said she is either a gluttonous hippie or a talking dog.

Caster and Emily are still arguing. Suddenly, an obvious solution occurs to me.

"Why don't we just check each one?" I say.

"Yeah," says Emily. Ami nods.

"Because serial processing is inefficient," says Caster. "But then again, so is democracy."

"It's very fitting that you have the word *caste* in your name, isn't it?" says Emily.

"Is that a racist joke?" says Caster. "Is it because I'm Indian?"

Emily smirks. "As a very wise man once said, it is a well-known fact that Asians cannot be racist against other Asians. Or something like that."

Caster waves his finger and looks to be on the verge of saying something but lets it fall. That was, after all, his explanation for a joke he made in Cog's palace.

We do "Eeny, meeny, miny, moe" to decide which door to take first, which Caster thinks is dumb, since we know in advance which door we'll get, based on which door we start counting on.

We step into the darkness, carrying a torch Caster lifted from the hallway outside our bedroom. The hallway leads to another stairwell, which spirals deep into the darkness below. It takes us a long time to make it to the bottom, and by the time we get there, all the whispered jokes have stopped. I'm pretty sure I can hear not only my own heartbeat thundering in my ears but also Ami's and Emily's heartbeats and maybe even Caster's—assuming he has a heart.

The air grows thinner as we descend, and I begin to feel weaker, as if the exhaustion of the past day is finally catching up to me. After what seems like hours, we finally reach the bottom. Caster holds out the torch into the darkness, and we gather round him to see what it illuminates.

The room we are in is mostly empty, but in the far back stands a wall with strange scripts flashing in and out of view in the firelight.

"Hold this," Caster says, giving me the torch. He takes out his spyglass, and we approach the wall with our hearts pounding in our chests.

"What does it say?" asks Emily, her voice trembling.

The writing on the walls makes me feel like there are snakes wriggling under my skin. By the sound of Emily's voice, she feels the same way. Even Caster's hands shake as he reads the wall. Only Ami seems unaffected; her deep, sensitive eyes are as still as the ground beneath us.

"It won't translate," says Caster after a moment.

"What do you mean?" asks Emily. "Give it here." She takes the spyglass and puts it to her eye. "Is there a button you have to press?"

"No," says Caster, annoyed. "All you have to do is look through the lens."

"Then why isn't it working?"

Emily turns to face us with her face screwed up in confusion. But the look is quickly replaced by one of horror; her eyes widen, and her face blanches. A shiver of fear runs through my spine, and before I can turn to look at what has inspired such terror in her, a familiar voice speaks.

"You cannot read them because they are not words meant for you to read."

The sound of screeching metal tears the air, and the room erupts in flame.

CHAPTER 31

THE POEM AND THE KNIFE

We all spin about at once as flames race along the edges of the wall. The room floods with light, revealing Galthanius. He is dressed in a nightgown, standing before the now closed entrance to the room. The passageway is now blocked by a gate. The walls are covered with iron chains, and in the far side of the room, there's a stone altar flanked by hooded statues and basins of water. On the altar is a knife inscribed with strange runes.

"Is this how you repay my hospitality?" says Galthanius in Greek.

His face looks genuinely hurt, as if we've betrayed the trust of a man who only meant us well. For a moment, I believe it, but then I remember Emily's terrified expression.

"Ah, we were just, um, lost," says Caster, "on our way to the bathroom. Translate that, Peter."

"No need," Galthanius says in English with a sly grin.

"You speak English?" exclaims Emily with her brow drawn.

"Obviously," says Caster. "But if you speak English, what was the whole business of pretending to only speak Ancient Greek? And how do you speak it?"

"Questions, questions," says Galthanius, shaking his head. "I ought to be the one asking the questions. Why are you wandering through my house in the thick of night?"

I look at Ami, and she nods, as if she can read what I plan to say. I open up the compass. "We were following our guide."

Galthanius's eyes flash at the compass, widening momentarily before returning to their usual placid gaze. The rest of our eyes also fall on the compass, and I see why Galthanius looked so surprised: the needle is pointing straight at him.

"So it's you," says Caster. "You're the bloodgorger, aren't you?" Caster smiles cockily as realization burns in his eyes. "It makes sense. You said yourself that you arrived just after the forest was cut down, just as the supposed laganmorf attacks began. Then there's the fact that the rest of the village looks dilapidated and worn, but your mansion looks fresh and well kept. If it were really laganmorfs who were attacking the village, why would they leave the mansion untouched? After all, the people in this mansion were the ones who ordered the forest to be cut down. And then, of course, the compass needle points to you like an accusing finger."

Galthanius claps his hands, smiling deviously. "Bravo, bravo. An excellent deduction, Mr. Sherlock Holmes."

Sherlock Holmes? I think. *How does he know so much about our world?* Cog said he summoned us using the last of the Hearthstone, which can only be regenerated if we get Samjang back. Does Galthanius have other means of interworld transportation? And besides, didn't he say the last time he visited was millennia ago? Sherlock Holmes is new—like turn-of-the-nineteenth-century new.

"The only thing is," says Galthanius, "you're wrong."

"What?" says Caster.

"It's not him," says Emily, her voice small and dripping with fear. "It's—"

"The butler," Galthanius says, stepping aside to reveal the little woman with the hunched back who served us dinner and brought us to our rooms. Only now she doesn't resemble a human at all, at least not a living one. Her face is as gray as a corpse, her lips are sallow, and her teeth look feral. Her eyes burn like crimson coals, hungry and malevolent, and her hands are no longer human hands but shriveled claws.

My stomach leaps into my throat, and my heart kicks into overdrive. It's one thing to hear a description or see a picture of a horrible creature; it's another thing entirely to see it standing before you only a few yards away, staring at you with pitiless, ravenous eyes.

But the creature doesn't attack us yet. It seems almost to be waiting for Galthanius to let it move.

"Why?" I ask. "Why would you do this to the people you're supposed to protect?"

Galthanius's eyes fall upon the wall. "It's written in the stone." He reads the script:

> From children's blood derives a sorcerous power
> To freshen youth and prolong the aging hour,
> To mute the call of the beckoning night,
> And to yield to the sweet taste of dark delight.

159

"The meter is terrible," says Caster. "And there's no manner of literary style at all. Who even wrote the poem?"

"It's translated. You're lucky it rhymes," says Galthanius, irritated. "And that's not the point. The point is—"

"You want our blood to prolong your youth," says Emily in almost a whimper. "That's how you've lived so long."

Galthanius chuckles coldly. "Clever girl! Exactly. And that is what a bloodgorger can bring me."

I feel a sickening twist in my gut as I begin to make sense of his perverse logic. How warped do you have to be to murder children to prolong your own life? To keep a demon at your beck and call so you can drink blood bought at the price of murdered innocence?

"How?" I ask. "How could life be worth living if it's only sustained by cruelty and murder?"

"Words," says Galthanius. "Mere words. What counts is that I can do as I please. If I do not value the pathetic lives of humans, much less human children, then it matters not to me how many I kill to protect what I do value: me. It's very easy to understand. You humans do it yourself: you eat lesser forms of life to sustain your existence and have no qualms of conscience about doing so. Why should I not do the same?" He sighs. "But anyway, I am getting rather bored of this conversation. I was hoping, as I said earlier, to have you for breakfast, but I suppose I shall settle for a midnight snack. Come now, old friend; let us feast upon the altar."

He waves his hand at the bloodgorger and begins to file his nails, looking like a man assigned to a boring task, as if killing means nothing to him, and he is merely waiting impatiently for a little meal.

The bloodgorger gives a feral snarl and advances on us, walking a circular path toward us.

Fear courses wildly through my veins, and I reach for the earth, summoning it to my defense. I wonder how Galthanius could be so stupid as to pick a fight with the Four. Even if we're only high school kids, we still have power over the four elements. What could a mere bloodgorger do against that?

But nothing happens. I look up with my eyes wide and see that Caster is straining for the fire along the walls to obey him, but it will not. He can't even get his hands to spark, when before, he could make fire dance easily across his fingers. Emily reaches for the water in the basins beside the altar, but it too ignores her.

"What's going on?" says Caster.

"Enchanted stone, enchanted fire, and enchanted water. You can do nothing against me." The bloodgorger speaks in a voice like grinding glass, and I can smell its foul breath even from where I stand.

It creeps closer to us, licking its sharp teeth. Its eyes run over us as if we're no more than slabs of juicy meat hanging at a marketplace.

"You seem to have forgotten air," I say.

It smirks. "What can a little wind do against me?"

Ami slams her staff into the ground, and I hear the same popping sound that sent Brutus Borgia and his cronies flying. The bloodgorger flies backward and slams against the wall by the far altar with a sickening crack. Ami claps a hand against her mouth as if surprised by what she has done.

"Good job, little sis," says Caster, mussing her hair. "Run!"

We sprint to the gate, the only entrance or exit in the room. Emily, Caster, and I put our hands beneath the gate and try to lift it, but it won't budge. Meanwhile, Ami keeps her staff leveled at Galthanius, who stares at her warily, keeping his distance.

"Trying to go somewhere?" he asks, amused.

Caster stands up straight. "Let us out," he says.

"Oh no, I'm afraid I shan't. I can already smell your blood, and oh, it is divine!" he exclaims like a connoisseur praising a particularly tasty dish.

"Let us out, or Ami here will smack you upside the wall so hard you'll wish for death," says Caster.

The lights begin to dim. "Will you? You'll have to find me first."

Galthanius waves his hand, and the flames that light the room grow small and then vanish. Only the flickering torchlight is left. The room is too dark to see anything except the ancient poem that speaks of drinking blood to reclaim lost youth.

The room becomes quiet, but I somehow know there's movement. We huddle together, and Emily whispers madly, "What are we going to do?"

Caster for once seems at a loss, and I'm no better.

That's when I feel cold steel drive into my flesh, and pain explodes from my gut.

CHAPTER 32

A BATTLE IN DARKNESS

The muscles in my gut spasm in knots of coiling pain. Fresh fire seems to burn through every nerve in my stomach. The torchlight flickers, and for a split second, I see the leering smile of the bloodgorger and see its gnarled hands on the blade.

Then I feel something in addition to the wrenching pain in my gut. It's as if my spirit, along with all the strength in my body, is seeping out through the wound, up through knife, and into the bloodgorger's body. I have no idea how it's possible, and maybe I'm just hallucinating.

"Where is it?" says Emily.

I try to speak, but my voice stops.

"Does anyone see it?" asks Caster.

I try to tell them it's right behind them, it has me, and I'm about to die, but still, no words come.

I'm about to die. The words hit me like a bullet train, and even though I can feel myself quickly approach the small door that no one comes back through after one enters, I still can't bring myself to believe it. I haven't graduated high school. How can I, Peter Smythe, be about to die?

Then I feel Ami's hand squeeze mine. At first, it is just a brief gesture, probably her checking to see whether I'm okay in the darkness. But my hands are cold and trembling, and that tells her what words cannot.

Her staff whistles through the air and cracks into the side of the bloodgorger's head. A gust of wind pushes the monster against the wall, forcing it to stay put. Caster dives for the torch, and I catch onto his plan. The torches are unnaturally sharp at the end, sharp enough to pierce flesh, maybe even the flesh of a bloodgorger.

But before he has the chance to execute his plan, Ami's arms grow weary of forcing the wind to hold the snarling bloodgorger still, and she lets up for just a moment. It's long enough to give the creature time to move. It springs from the wall as fast as a snake and leaps onto Ami. In the flickering torchlight, I see its sharp teeth aimed at her throat.

She gasps in pain.

"Ami!" I scream.

Hot panic burns into me, followed by a rush of adrenaline so massive that I forget the pain in my gut, the fear of the bloodgorger and Galthanius, and the draining strength from the blade. All my thoughts narrow to a single point: *Protect Ami.* I rip the blade from my spasming chest, which sends another burst of pain and adrenaline jolting through me, and I dive forward toward the two struggling shapes on the ground.

My blade finds a home, burrowing into the bloodgorger's back. I rip it out again and then drive it in again and again. It's not easy to drive a sharpened blade into human flesh, much less to pull it out, but in that moment, I'm filled with all the strength I need.

The bloodgorger pushes itself off Ami and grabs me, and we roll together on the floor as it tries to find the knife and bash my head in. But I have the advantage now, because each one of the wounds in its back has siphoned some of its strength and given it to me through the mysterious power of the blade.

Its burning red eyes burrow into mine, growing dimmer as we struggle. For a moment, I see beyond the mad desire in those eyes to something else—a whimpering little girl, afraid and alone. The bloodgorger's face changes into the face of a beautiful girl. I lose the heart to kill the creature. But then its face wrinkles and shrivels, the thirsting desire gains control again, and the bloodgorger drives its teeth toward my neck.

I close my hands along the blade and drive it up into the bloodgorger's abdomen, just below the ribs, aimed upward toward the heart. It gasps, and its eyes grow wide. Then blood begins to spray like a fountain from the wound, shooting all over me until I'm soaked. I shove the bloodgorger off me, horrified at the pool of sticky red blood all over me. Caster and the others are beside me, and we watch in dread and fascination as the bloodgorger shrivels up into a desiccated humanoid body little larger than that of a nine-year-old child.

"What the …" Caster murmurs.

I hurl the rest of my dinner onto the floor as my insides turn sick. A voice chants in my head, *You killed someone. You killed someone*, and I guess I did, even if it was a bloodgorger. But what was it before a bloodgorger? Why did it look like a beautiful girl, even if just for a second? Was it merely a trick of the eye? Or was there something more to the story of the bloodgorger?

The sound of grinding metal echoes through the chamber.

"The gate!" shouts Emily. "He's going to try to escape and lock us in."

"Galthanius," Caster says as he and Emily dive forward.

At that moment, I realize I am about to faint. The wound in my gut and the blood loss have caught up to me. I land amid the blood and sick, and the last thing I remember is Ami's voice, though it's distant, and I'm not sure what she's saying.

CHAPTER 33

THE END OF THE BEGINNING

I awake sometime later to the sound of rain. It sounds as if it's falling in heavy torrents against a wooden roof above and in mud puddles somewhere below. Though the air feels cold against my face, the rest of me is warm, and as I wiggle my fingers and toes, I feel the soft fabric of a blanket against me.

I slowly open my eyes, and they nearly pop out of their sockets, because Emily's looking down at me with a soft expression of concern on her perfect face.

"Hey there," she says. "How are you feeling?"

I feel a lump growing in my throat. She's sitting right next to me, close enough to touch. Her beautiful brown eyes look into mine, turning my insides to mush.

She laughs a pure, un-self-conscious laugh. "Tongue-tied?"

Her laugh loosens me up, and I manage to say, "A little. What happened?" My head feels thick. I know something happened, something important, but the memory is just out of reach. "Where am I?"

"You are sitting on the porch of Galthanius, a.k.a. keeper of the bloodgorger. As for what happened …" She furrows her brow. "You really don't remember?"

I remember being in a creepy room, feeling splitting pain, and rolling through the darkness in a fight for my life. "We fought the bloodgorger, right?"

"More than that," she says, gesturing to the knife beside me. "You killed it. I mean literally, you killed it. Not just like you did a good job, but you killed the bloodgorger."

I pick up the blade and feel a chill rush through me as I handle it. Then my eyes widen as the meaning of her words sinks in. "I did what?"

"You killed the bloodgorger! You were extremely *li hai*. Awesome. Terrific. Amazing."

Blood rushes to my cheeks.

"Aw, you're quite bashful, aren't you?" She shakes her head. "Caster could learn from you on how to take a compliment."

This makes me blush even more furiously, because I guess it means I'm a step up from Caster in her eyes. A crazy part of me thinks this would be a great time to ask her to prom. *Yeah, so I killed a bloodgorger—does that mean maybe you'd want to go out with me?*

But I get distracted as I remember the knife wound in my chest. "I was bleeding badly, and there was probably damage to internal organs. But… I feel fine."

"You can thank my magic hands," she says, wiggling her fingers. "I learned I can use water to heal people."

"That sounds pretty useful." I laugh awkwardly.

I try to push myself up against the wall behind me unsuccessfully, and Emily helps me up. Her hands brush mine, and I feel a throbbing in my heart.

"Thanks." I furrow my brow. "Where are Ami and Caster?"

"They went to town—I mean literally, not just that they were enthusiastic. Right now, they should be collecting the promised supplies from the villagers. We got them their bloodgorger. Thanks to you."

"I see."

A moment of awkward silence passes, but Emily soon fills it, leaning forward with her eyes sparkling. "So, Peter, we never really got a chance to talk. What are you like?"

I feel a rush of dizzying warmth to my head. The whole situation is completely ridiculous: Emily and I are sitting together on the porch of a mansion owned by a Nephilim and a bloodgorger in Miria, chatting about our lives. Half of me still thinks that I've got to be dreaming and that I'm still in the cave with Goober and am going to wake up in Ms. Schaden's office to find out none of these things ever happened, Emily is as much a stranger as ever, and Ami and Caster don't exist. Well, I guess the nonexistence of Caster wouldn't be completely without benefits, though even he has started to grow on me.

I tell her about my boring, uneventful life, but her questions and the way her eyes glow with sincere interest make me feel like I'm not a total loser. She laughs at a few points, such as when I tell her about the laboratory explosion, and she says, "I'm sorry, Peter," when I tell her about the bullying by Brutus.

I leave out my friendship with Dr. Elsavier, because I have the weird and kinda crazy feeling Emily would somehow be jealous, even though that doesn't make sense. And, of course, I leave out the fact that I've been madly in love with Emily since middle school. I leave it out not just because I'm too cowardly to tell her but also because I've started to wonder whether it's really true. She used to be a goddess back when she was a perfect, unattainable girl I had never talked to. But now I guess I'm starting to realize what's obvious: she's just a person like anyone else. A particularly attractive person but still a person.

As the gate squeals, announcing the return of Caster and Ami, I realize I haven't asked Emily a single question about herself. I feel a burst of shame and regret inside that I managed to go on for so long about myself without even really thinking of her. I apologize to her, but she only smiles, rolls her eyes, and says, "We'll talk more later. No rush."

Caster and Ami are thoroughly soaked from the rain, and each of them is leading two horses saddled with supplies. I wonder why they made the trip in the rain, but then I remember Cog's deadline. We only have three weeks to cross the entirety of Miria to find Samjang. There's no time to waste.

"Can you boys ride?" asks Emily.

"No," says Caster. "Can you?"

"Of course." Emily tosses back her hair and then squeezes Ami's hand. "We both can. All girls are equestrians at heart."

"Well," Caster says, "it can't be too hard, can it? After all, you somehow learned to do it."

"No, it's not hard at all, Caster, dear," says Emily. "As long as you don't mind getting bitten and thrown a few times."

I gulp. "Is it that bad?"

Emily smiles, and her eyes dance with amusement. "Don't worry. As long as you don't immediately die, I can heal you."

Caster and I exchange worried glances.

We spend the next half hour learning how to mount and dismount. There are a few embarrassing mistakes, but in the end, I get the hang of it, as does Caster. By the time we finish learning, the rain has spent most of its fury, leaving only a steady drizzle.

Because there's no time to waste, we mount up and leave the town amid the grateful waves of villagers. I have the absurd feeling I'm like a great Roman general upon his horse, having liberated a town from a dark force. That confidence bubble lasts all of three minutes, because when Emily decides we should switch from walking to trotting, I manage to fall off and land butt-first in the mud in full view of the village.

That, I'm sorry to say, is not the end of my troubles with the horse. Nor is it even the beginning of the end. But it is perhaps the end of the beginning.

CHAPTER 34

THE SENSE

It is remarkable how quickly one can learn to ride when getting thrown has minimal consequence. A fall brings a short burst of agonizing pain, followed by the soothing touch of Emily's water, intermixed with her laughter.

By the time we stop for the second night, I've gotten wrapped around a tree four times, stomped on twice, dragged five times, and I've have fallen on my face too many times to count. My only comfort is that Caster has had more mishaps. And Emily fusses over me whenever I fall. At a certain point, I begin to fear she'll suspect I'm getting thrown on purpose just so she'll have to come fix my broken legs, cracked hips, or internal bleeding. But anything is worth it to have her touch my hand, look into my eyes, and say, "Are you okay?"—even if I'm in agonizing pain and she's laughing.

The north seems to have only two kinds of landscapes: wide, snowy plains and forests. There is the occasional lake, and there are mountains on the horizon far to the north. But other than that, everything looks so similar that if we didn't have the compass, we would be hopelessly lost.

We come to rest beside a small woodland just as the last of the sunlight is fading behind the northwest mountains. We follow the usual routine: feeding and caring for the horses and then tying them up. Fortunately, Emily has spent the past two summers working at a stable to pay for her riding lessons, which means she knows what she's doing. Ami too worked at a stable, which Caster informs us was much better than Emily's since it was a Blackstone stable. This reignites some of the old school rivalries, which Emily and Caster ostensibly take seriously—though my guess is it's just an excuse for them to bicker.

Ami and I only shake our heads and laugh wearily. By the time everyone finishes the chores, we're all too tired to talk. We slip inside Emily's interdimensional blanket tent, eat a rationed dinner, and quickly fall asleep.

My dreams are mostly peaceful. I dream of my mom's pizzelle, Dr. Elsavier's homemade chocolate chip cookies, and my dad's steaks. Finally, I find myself in Willy Wonka's chocolate factory. I spend a while gorging myself on gumdrops, lollipops, and Wonka Bars all at the same time, which somehow isn't as disgusting as it sounds. After I finish, I look up and see a chocolate stream. Beside it sits an old man.

He has brown hair and a beard with flecks of gray, and his warm dark eyes crease as he smiles. He tells me his name is Homer and speaks to me in Greek. For a while, this is soothing, making me think of the way my dad talked to me when I was little and my chats with Dr. Elsavier.

But then something changes. His hair grows wild and tangled, and his face begins to resemble that of a monkey. He throws his head back and laughs, and when he looks at me again, his eyes are solid blue and cold as ice. He speaks words I do not understand, though I know they're Greek, my native tongue. It's as if he's taken from me my very language.

I'm just on the verge of deciphering what he's saying, drawing out his dark meaning, and then time stops.

And the dream starts over.

By the third iteration of the dream, I have a tickling in my brain that all this is familiar, as if I've had the dream before—not just tonight but somewhere else before.

Then I remember I had this same dream only a few nights before, in Cog's palace, and I awake with a start, breathing hard. Caster is still asleep beside me. On the far side of the tent, Emily is asleep too, snoring intermittently and muttering words in Chinese and Japanese. But Ami is gone.

I crawl out from under the tent with my mind in two places: half of it is trying to work out what the dream could mean and why I keep having it, and the other half is praying that nothing bad has happened to Ami.

Relief rushes over me when I see her standing by the horses, gently stroking their heads.

"Hey, Peter," she says. She looks over at me and gives one of her dreamy, fey smiles. Her eyes look past me to some point far in the distance. "You sleep well?"

"Not really," I say.

"I'm sorry." She wrinkles her brow. "Take a deep breath. It's beautiful out this morning."

I follow her advice, and my nostrils tickle with all the scents in the air: pinecone and wood, wild grass and tree sap, and a dozen other smells I can't name. If there are animals distinct to this world, there probably are plants too. Though the air feels cold against my cheeks and there's snow on the ground, I'm kept warm by the cloak. It started working again after we slew the bloodgorger and handed Galthanius over to the villagers.

"It is beautiful," I say. I come up beside her and try petting one of the horses, the one I think I've ridden for the past two days. He eyes me suspiciously and then moves away when I try to touch him.

"Gentler," she says. "You have to get him to trust you."

"Trust me? He's the one who's spent the past forty-eight hours launching me at every available tree."

She laughs. "Because he doesn't trust you!"

"Well, how do I get him to trust me?" I say sulkily.

She strokes her chin. "That's a good question. One way is to feed him. That helps."

She motions for me to cup my hands, and she pours a handful of what look like blackberries into my hands. I guess blackberries are different in this world, because in my hometown, we always pick them between July and September.

"Where'd you get these?"

"Oh," she says, as if trying to remember. She gestures vaguely at the field behind the horses. "Somewhere over there. I've been up. It's too beautiful a morning to spend sleeping."

I suppose it is. I feel a sense of peace wash over me, maybe for the first time in years. I wonder how she manages to have that effect and how she always seems so calm. Or at least most of the time. My memory leaps to the moment above Cog's palace when terror shone in her eyes, just before we tumbled from the sky. "I meant to ask. What did you see above the palace that made you fall?"

"Oh," she says. Her gaze grows distant. "It's hard to describe exactly. It's not so much what I saw as what I sensed."

"Sensed?"

"I sensed a terrible presence. It was sad, twisted, lonely, afraid, angry, hateful—so many things at once."

"How did you sense it?" I ask with my brow furrowed in confusion.

She looks at me, just as confused by my confusion. "Can't you sense my presence?"

"Um, no."

"Try it," she says, turning to face me. "Close your eyes."

"Promise you won't tickle me?"

She smiles. "Promise. Now close your eyes!"

I close them, grinning and feeling foolish. "Now what?"

"Now reach out."

I stick my hands out, bumping her in the face.

"Not with your hands!" She pushes them back to my sides, laughing. "With your spirit."

"Where do I find that exactly?" I ask.

"It's everywhere and nowhere." Her voice is serious now. "Your spirit just is you. You don't need to find it."

I try her suggestion, reaching out with my spirit, with myself. I feel kind of stupid at first, sitting there with my eyes shut, trying to move without moving. A sliver of me wonders if she's playing a practical joke on me. But that's not like Ami. Caster would do that but not Ami. She's too sincere.

"It's not working," I say after about a minute of trying. I open my eyes.

"You're trying too hard," she says earnestly. "Try reaching out with the earth."

I realize she's right; I've been straining to reach out through space. Maybe that works for her since all the space around her is filled mostly with air, her element. But my element is earth.

I try reaching out through the stone and ground, which respond to me swiftly and effortlessly—so much so that it's exhilarating. I smile, and my eyes flutter open. "I can sense you! Emily too and Caster."

"See?" she says.

I feel even more foolish, because I realize I've done this before, back in the forest when I sensed a presence. Come to think of it, it was probably the bloodgorger, watching us enter. That must be how Galthanius knew we had come.

Ami's eyes brighten as an idea seems to occur to her. "Now I'm going to move across the field, and you—with your eyes closed!—try to point to me just by sensing."

It sounds like a silly game, but it's just like Ami: pure, kind of ridiculous, and sweet. She makes sure I've shut my eyes, tells me to count to ten, and then runs out into the field.

I follow her movement across the field. The spaces between her steps are too wide for someone as short as she is. She must be using her element to keep herself aloft a little longer than gravity would allow. I count to ten, and I'm about to point to her, when suddenly, I feel another presence on the horizon, moving swiftly toward us—and it does not feel happy.

"Ami!" I shout as my eyes flutter open.

The smile vanishes from her face, and I see she's sensed it too. She propels herself across the field, as swift as a dart.

"I'll get the others," I say.

She nods and moves for the horses.

I slip under the interdimensional tent and wake Emily and Caster, shaking them and whispering their names furiously.

"What is it?" asks Emily groggily, rubbing her eyes.

The answer forms on my lips, a word I should have told them long ago: "Five."

CHAPTER 35

I BECOME ONE WITH THE HORSE

"Five?" repeats Caster. "What is that supposed to mean?"

"Four rings, one for each of us," I say. "But there's one more. A fifth ring. And Cog says that Five is—look, we have to go!"

"Why can't we just stay beneath the interdimensional tent?" asks Emily.

I feel kind of silly for not thinking of that, but Caster shakes his head. "Are you nuts? If we can sense each other, Five can probably sense us, and that means he or she or it will just wait outside the tent until we starve or waste so much time that we can't possibly get Samjang before the Ice Reich returns."

Emily's eyes widen, and she grabs the edge of the tent. It furls back up into a small blanket in her hand automatically.

"Exactly," I say, pretending I understood all that from the start.

We rush to the horses. Ami's nearly finished saddling them. I have no idea how she managed to do it so quickly, but I don't question it, because Five is moving toward us fast, a looming shape on the edge of the horizon of my sense.

We finish saddling the horses, and I pull myself up into the saddle, surprised at how quickly and fluidly I manage to do it. Like I said, if you can get thrown from horses with minimal consequences, there's a lot you can learn in a few days. We kick into a trot and then a canter. The sound of the four three-beat drums echoes across the snowy field as we ride along the edge of the forest toward the open ground to the south and east.

The cold wind bites my reddening cheeks and hands. But despite the wind, my robe doesn't billow, and everything it touches feels warm.

"How are we doing?" shouts Caster against the wind.

"I don't know! I can't sense very well when I'm not touching the earth!" I yell back.

I'm not sure that's entirely true. Maybe if I weren't holding on for dear life, I would have more mental resources to check whether we are still being followed.

Ami, who's next to Emily in the lead, says something, and Emily relays the message back to us: "He's still getting closer."

"What are we going to do?" says Caster.

Emily looks back at us and gives us a devilish smile. "We're going to gallop."

My stomach does something uncomfortable. "That sounds dangerous!"

"Well, do you want to escape or not?" shouts Emily.

Caster gives me a brief glance. "Look," he says. "From a game theoretic perspective, we should gallop. Either we fall off, or we successfully escape. If we fall off, we'll end up facing Five, which is what would happen anyway if we kept at a canter."

"You don't need game theory to work that out, dingus!" Emily says. "Now, lean forward, squeeze your legs, use your knees, and try not to die!"

A moment later, her horse pulls away, and the drumlike sound of three footfalls turns to four. Ami follows Emily, pulling away faster. Caster and I give each other a nod, and then I try what Emily said to do, almost certain it's going to end with me wrapped around a tree or, even if I manage to stay on, permanently unable to father children.

The horse takes off, moving faster and faster, and the wind now seems to scrape against my face like frozen nails. My heart is pounding a dozen times faster the horses' hooves, and it takes every ounce of my lacking leg strength to keep myself in the saddle. Adrenaline gushes through my veins, and the unbridled fear—sorry about the pun—in my gut turns to exhilaration.

I loosen a little, feeling the rhythm of the horse, letting my movements sync up with his. It's terrifying at first, and there's a voice inside screaming for me not to try anything stupid, but when you're jacked up on this much adrenaline, your normal inhibitions go buh-bye. It's not just the adrenaline, though. There's a little voice deep in my heart nudging me on. I'm not sure what to call the voice exactly, but it's warm, strong, bold, and a little reckless. I wonder if it's what Dr. Elsavier meant by "Odysseus's courage."

As I settle into the rhythm with the horse, I realize that before, I was fighting with the horse to keep him slow, and this is what he has been longing to do. I let him move as he wants to move and let my motions meld with his. That's when I begin to feel the trust Ami was talking about.

I chance a look at Caster. His face has turned gray, and his eyes are centered dead ahead and look as if they're on the verge of popping out of his skull.

"Relax!" I say. "It's actually fun!"

I'm not sure the words reach his ears, and if they do, his brain certainly doesn't process them, because he keeps his ashen-faced stare dead ahead.

I urge my horse faster, pulling up next to Emily.

She looks over at me with a broad smile. "Boy, you've really got the hang of it! That was quick."

"You're a good teacher." I grin foolishly. "And, well, the possibility of death."

"That too! Speaking of which, Ami just said she can't sense him any longer. We should take it back to a canter, or we'll wear the horses out. We have a long day ahead." She smirks. "I bet Caster will be glad to hear that. He's such a baby sometimes."

She casts a glance over her shoulder, and her eyes widen. I risk a look as well, and my eyes pop.

Caster is charging forward with his hair literally on fire and his face no longer ashen but alive with a maniacal grin.

"I'm no longer afraid!" he shouts, raising his arms and pumping them at the sky.

At that moment, his horse jumps to avoid a rock and makes a sudden turn, launching Caster, at a solid twenty miles an hour, toward a tree.

CHAPTER 36

THE TALK

Emily heals Caster's six fractured ribs and cracked hip, and he's as good as new. In a few minutes, we're back on horseback, and Caster looks a little chastened, which can't hurt. We still don't sense the presence of Five.

We take it easier for the rest of the day, trying not to wear out our horses. According to Emily, they're much stronger than the horses back in Gaia, but even still, she'd rather not push them too hard. They are our only ride.

As the last rays of sunlight fade behind the distant mountains, we come to a stop beside a forest's edge. There are a few fires in the distance, which give enough light to reveal the outlines of a village. But after our last encounter, we all agree to keep to ourselves. We still have rations from Galthanius's home, and Ami is good at finding berries that don't immediately result in death.

As we tie up the horses and let them feed on the tall grass that peeks out from beneath the snow, Emily turns to face us. "We need to have a talk," she says seriously.

"A talk?" I repeat.

Caster nods as his eyes brighten. "That's right! Peter has some things he needs to share."

"It's not just about Peter," says Emily. She unfurls the interdimensional blanket into a tent around herself and leaves a small opening, waiting for us to follow. Caster steps in immediately. I look to Ami, and she shrugs, and then we too enter.

Emily is sitting cross-legged on the ground and motions for us to sit.

"So," says Caster as he tries to bend his legs like Emily's, mostly unsuccessfully, "why have you summoned us here, my queen?"

"Because we need to sort out what we're doing. A lot of things have happened in the past four days, and I, for one, am a little confused. We've been so busy trying not to get killed by fallen gods, bloodgorgers, or mysterious ring bearers that we haven't taken any time to stop and think."

"Why don't we start with our good and trusty—not to say trustworthy—friend Peter?" Caster says. "What did Cog tell you, and why on Cog's green earth didn't you tell us?"

"Would it kill you to be nice?" snaps Emily. She turns to me. "But yes, do tell us."

"It was a perfectly reasonable question," Caster mutters under his breath.

I stare at my hands, trying to work out my reply. "I—we were so busy the past few days that it slipped my mind."

"That's okay," says Emily encouragingly. "Just tell us now."

"Right," I say, trying to bring my mind back to my conversation with Cog. It seems so long ago, but the words return as fresh as the moment Cog uttered them: "His power is not like yours, nor is his fate. He never ends up where he was supposed to go, and oftentimes, the evil ones get to him before we can reach him. I can sense he is in this world, but I do not know where, and I do not know whether he will prove to be friend or enemy to you."

In halting words, I tell the others this.

"So he could be a friend?" Ami says, her eyes arched hopefully.

"Did he feel like a friend?" I ask, thinking of the description she gave me of the creature she sensed in the sky, the same creature we sensed coming for us earlier today.

She looks at the ground. Her eyes are troubled.

Oh, Ami, I think. *You always want to see the best in people, don't you?*

"Did Cog say what exactly his power was?" asks Emily.

I shake my head.

"I'm beginning to see a pattern here," says Caster. "Cog raises more questions than he answers."

"Well, the fallen gods showed up," I say. "He didn't get much of a chance to finish his explanations."

"Excuses," he mutters. "Do you think Zeus would've taken crap from a bunch of minor gods? Isn't Cog supposed to be basically the Zeus of Miria, the king of the gods or whatever?"

"If that's so, you should probably be a little more afraid of electrocution," says Emily, gesturing toward the skies.

I remember all the stories about Zeus striking those who misbehaved or profaned the gods with lightning bolts, though he also had a passion for turning people into strange animals, which I find to be a far more terrifying fate. I try to figure out which animal Zeus would turn Caster into for punishment. It doesn't take me long. It would definitely be an ass.

185

"But that would kind of be shooting himself in the foot, wouldn't it?" Emily says. "We're the ones who are supposed to be saving his beloved Samjang. How did he manage to let the trickster god dupe him anyway?"

I can almost feel the answer. It's hiding just out of sight in my mind, playing just along the edges of my understanding, too slippery and quick for me to grasp.

Caster shrugs. "Who knows? We should focus on what we know and what we can do." He strokes his chin. "Right now, it seems like our plan has been just to follow the compass wherever it points and ride there. And try not to get caught by any fallen gods or disgruntled fifth ring bearers."

"It seems like a good enough plan," I say. "What else would we do?"

"Hm," says Emily. "We don't know very much about this world. We don't even know how long it will take to get to Samjang. It would be good to find someone who knows more about Miria. Maybe even someone who is willing to help us in the quest."

"Well, if you happen to find any magical guides lying around, that'd be great," says Caster bitterly. "Where are the Gandalfs, Dumbledores, and Mr. Miyagis of the world when you need them?"

"I mean, in all fairness, they weren't around a lot of the time either," I say, feeling for once the conversation has drifted to an area I know something about.

"Yeah, point taken."

We pass into silence for a few seconds. Finally, Ami breaks it.

"What do you think Cog meant when he talked about the Four becoming One?" she asks.

"It sounded like the Four can somehow combine their abilities and unleash a lot of power by doing so," says Caster.

"Four becoming One makes it sound like they have to be unified in some way," says Emily.

I nod, remembering the image in Cog's palace of the Four combining into a sphere of light.

Caster smirks. "Fat chance of that. Shouldn't have picked Americans if he wanted unity."

Not just Americans, I think, *but Americans of all different backgrounds. A half-Chinese, half-Japanese girl; an Indian dude; an Amerindian gal; and a white guy. A whole lot of unity. And we're from rival schools to boot.*

But then I think of what Cog said about the Rock being the one whom everyone comes to depend on, and I wonder if that means I'm somehow the key to finding unity, to the Four becoming One.

No, that can't be it. I'm not a leader. I shove the thought from my mind. We'll find Samjang in time so that we don't have to deal with any Four-becoming-One business.

But a little voice in my head says we might not make it to Samjang in time, and the Ice Reich might still escape from the void to which it was banished. Then what?

I remember my promise to Cog not to discount myself before I start, and I remember Dr. Elsavier's words about how I'm an Odysseus somewhere deep inside.

But both of them feel far away, and I feel very small. I think, *Yeah right.*

CHAPTER 37

THE DELEGATE

The next two days are spectacularly boring. We follow the compass east and south, passing through what seems an infinite sea of grassy fields and forests. By the second day, the fields have changed to farmers' fields, and the snow on the ground has gone; the weather is a little warmer.

We even see a few locals. Some are human and some are Kar-dun, tall and proud. All of them leave us alone, though many whispers are exchanged, and eyes linger on us as we pass. I feel a sense of unease that maybe some of them are working for the fallen gods, the Ice Reich, or even Enki, the trickster god himself.

But no gods appear in the sky, no arrows find us in the night, and we face no dangers aside from occasionally getting tossed from our horses—though I'm down to getting thrown only about once a day, which feels awesome. What doesn't feel awesome are my legs, which ache awfully by the time we get to evening. Emily's healing water helps with that, and I'm grateful for it, even if it makes me look as if I've peed my pants. I am not thrilled about Caster's suggestion of applying fire to said area to make the water evaporate.

By the third day, which is day seven since we got our mission from Cog, we see troop movements in the distance. Kar-dun ride on large horses, with gleaming armor and weapons, followed by human foot soldiers. They all seem to be converging on some location in the distance, and by late afternoon, we find out what it is.

We come over the crest of a hill and see, in the valley below, three encampments posted beneath a single mountain in the distance.

"They look dangerous," says Caster, turning to face me. "Are you sure this is it?"

I open up the compass and show him. It points straight ahead toward the valley.

"Um, guys?" Emily says.

We turn to look at her, and she points ahead to a tall man striding up the hill. His steps are swift, though it doesn't seem like he's running. He's wearing shining white armor and carrying his helmet in his hand. A diamond-studded sword is sheathed on his side.

"A real Prince Charming," says Caster. He turns to Emily. "Try not to swoon off your horse, Zhu Bajie."

I vaguely remember Emily explaining that her mom calls her Zhu Bajie, because of some book—*Journey to the West*, I think— which has a character who likes to eat a lot.

"You either, Sun Wukong," she says, tossing back her hair.

"Who?"

"A very naughty monkey," she says. "From *Journey to the West*. Also, are we going to flee?"

"Nah," says Caster. "He looks fine."

"I don't trust your judgment."

"Have I ever steered you wrong?" he says, imitating one of the characters from *Clifford the Big Red Dog*.

"Yes, Cleo, many times. But, Ami, you haven't steered us wrong. What do you think?"

Before Ami can answer, the man—or Kar-dun—calls out in various languages, trying the same trick Galthanius did, hoping, I guess, to find one we happen to speak.

This time, it's Emily who repeats one of his words in surprise. They exchange a few words, and then she turns to us.

"He says he is Kalix, one of Cog's servants, sent here to help negotiate a grand alliance among the Three Kingdoms."

"First off, what language is he speaking?" asks Caster.

"Chinese," she says. "But it's older. It sounds kind of the way my grandma talks."

"Chinese?" Caster repeats.

I know what's running through his mind: Just how often do people travel between our worlds? And to what purpose? Is Gaia like a giant resort to them? And if they travel so often, why don't they have any technology here?

Emily shrugs.

"The Three Kingdoms?" I ask.

"Remember when Galthanius explained that there were three kingdoms of Kar-dun, one to the north, one to the west, and one to the south?"

"Which raises the question of what lies to the east," says Caster.

Emily turns to Kalix, who stands at least seven feet tall. He has skin like bronze; large, strong hands; a chest like Arnold

Schwarzenegger's; and piercing blue eyes that give me the impression he's very intelligent.

"He says he'd be happy to answer our questions in his tent below, where there's food and drink and also protection against the wild men." She says the last few words uncertainly, probably as confused as I am by what they mean exactly.

Before we get a chance to ask further questions, Kalix turns and strides down the hill as swiftly as he climbed it.

"Well, Emily," says Caster, "looks like you've rolled sixes. You got your magical guide after all."

We nudge our horses forward, following Kalix to the encampment below. It is divided into three sectors, with a neutral island in the middle and neutral boundaries between each of the sectors, marked by colors and guards, who stare at each other menacingly. As we pass, their gazes change first to curiosity, then to recognition, and then to hope.

It makes me want to crawl into a hole, having them look at me like that. What stories have they heard about the Four that inspire so much confidence in us? We're just kids. And I'm a kid who can't even make it into a halfway decent college, who can't even ask the girl he likes out to prom, and whose only friend is Goober. *Poor Goober. His only friend vanished into a cave. He probably thinks I'm dead and maybe even thinks it is his fault.* I shove the thought from my mind. *Finish saving Miria from the Ice Reich first*, I tell myself. *Then worry about Goober's psychological health.*

Kalix leads us to a large tent on the center island, the neutral zone between the camps. Kar-dun in flowing robes in bright colors scurry about. As we walk toward the tent, Kalix talks, and Emily translates.

"The colors of the robes represent the kingdoms the Kar-dun serve: blue and silver for the north, green and gray for the west, and red and black for the south."

We step into the tent, and I try to keep the colors straight in my head, thinking of the Kar-dun I saw moving from tent to tent while carrying articles and speaking rapidly in a language I didn't understand. As usually happens when I experience too many new things at once, my head starts to hurt.

The tent Kalix has led us to stretches about thirty feet into the sky, with two large poles keeping it aloft in the center. In one corner, there are Kar-dun gathered around a table, discussing something passionately. Kalix leads us to the opposite corner, draws a curtain, and has us sit along a couch. I find myself on the end, next to Ami. Her eyes wander curiously about the room.

A human servant brings tea and something resembling biscuits, and Kalix leans in and says something in Chinese. Emily translates: "I'm sure you must have many questions."

CHAPTER 38

THE THREE KINGDOMS

"Yeah, I've got a lot of questions," says Caster. "First off, what's this business with a grand alliance? Second, what happened to Cog exactly? How did the trickster god pull off his trick on the most powerful god in Miria? And why is Cog's gigantic palace so empty? Moreover, what is the trickster god's motive? Cog said it wasn't like the others. And furthermore—"

Emily interrupts him. "Maybe we should ask one question at a time."

Caster waves a hand impatiently. "Well, then hurry up!"

Emily elbows him. "Try to behave." She translates the questions.

"The situation has grown darker since you left Cog's palace," says Emily, translating for Kalix. "The pace of events has begun to accelerate. Cog anticipated this might happen, so he sent me and several other of his servants not entrapped by the curse of the trickster god to start talks with the Three Kingdoms. We must form a grand alliance to stand against the Ice Reich should they find a foothold in our world."

"The Three Kingdoms?" says Ami.

Kalix sighs, and his eyes rest on the burning calls of the fire beside us. He waves his hands, and the flames form into a golden bird, which leaps from the fire into the midst of us. All of us except Caster scramble backward, but Kalix raises his hands soothingly.

"It is a long story and one that requires illustration."

I settle back into my seat.

"Before the fallen gods were fallen, they took on human form to live among men, to teach them of the ways of Gomdan. But when they saw the beauty of the daughters of men, they desired to have them, and thus were born the Kar-dun—grand creatures of strength surpassing human strength and of lofty brows to match their lofty minds. They possessed all the best traits of gods and men. But also all the worst."

The flaming bird changes; its form spreads out into fields of battle, where human figures fight vainly against creatures towering over them at nearly twice their height.

"They had both the ambition of men and godlike abilities, so they quickly felled the kings of men and set up realms for themselves. In time, these warring states coalesced into the Three Kingdoms of today."

The flames change into a familiar landscape of purple mountains and towering pines and oaks. I feel as though I'm a bird rushing over them at a thousand miles an hour. The forests give way to cities built of icy stone, with great statues outside the walls and silver domes within the city.

"In the north live the Hai-run, lean and silver-skinned, with high cheekbones and violet eyes. The men have thick black beards with sacred trinkets interwoven, and the women weave their hair into one long braid adorned with charms and bells. Their ruler is Empress Mai'rei II, a woman of great intelligence and charm—and not to be underestimated."

The flaming landscape of cold, tall cities and forests of pine melts away. In its place, I see a jungle thick with foliage, with a wide, winding river parting its center. At the river's edges, in clearings of the forest, stand pyramids of stone, with fires blazing along the walkways.

"In the south live the Mezrek, with skin like bronze and bodies thick and muscled. They do not believe in excess—or, rather, you could say they believe only in excess. Both their men and their women hunt naked like wild bears without their fur, leaving the humans to tend to the young. When the hunt is over, they gather for nights of drinking, feasting, and bed business—and it is not uncommon for the men to swap wives and for the women to swap husbands. They have the humans to take care of their children and of daily chores, so marriage is unimportant to them."

The flames change again, revealing a softer landscape, one of fields and rolling hills. Barns and granaries dot the landscape. Along the rivers are small cities not much larger than the camp we're in.

"In the west live the Bolshov. Well proportioned, with skin like gold and eyes as gray as the western hills. They call themselves the Middle Kingdom, for they believe they are the golden mean of all virtues. Whereas the northerners are too cold and calculating and the southerners are too hot and feeling, they see themselves as possessing the best of reason and passion. It is ironic that their leader, Mardush, is a man as unfeeling and calculating as the Hai-run and as indulgent and pleasure-loving as the Mezrek."

The flames re-form, and I see the standards of Hai-run, Bolshov, and Mezrek marching into battle—not against a common foe but against each other. I tumble through the sky, and then I'm in the midst of them as wild-eyed Kar-dun hack at one another with swords. Blood and intestines spill out upon the ground, mixing with the mud and filth.

I turn away, feeling queasy.

"This is the clay I have to work with to form the grand alliance," says Kalix sadly.

But I don't feel his sadness. Instead, I feel anger and revulsion. "These Kar-dun seem about as horrible as the worst of humans," I say. "They are cold and distant, or condescending, self-superior jerks— or else they are a bunch of sickos. And they're all violent and nasty to humans. I thought you said they combined the best traits of gods and humans, not just the worst."

Kalix nods. "In many ways, you are right. But it was not always so. There was a time, though brief, when the Kar-dun ruled for the benefit of those they ruled. And even now, Empress Mai'rei II is trying to do so, though she struggles under the weight of thousands of years of bad habit. But enough of this. They are not your worry but mine." He releases the fiery bird into the flames and turns his eyes to the east. "I shall try to answer the rest of your questions now."

CHAPTER 39

KALIX

Kalix gestures to the east, where his gaze lingered moments before.

"The mountain behind us is called the Lonely Peak," Emily translates.

Caster interrupts. "Hold up. There's a mountain here called the Lonely Peak? Like the Lonely Mountain? As in *The Hobbit*?"

Emily rolls her eyes. "Stop interrupting with dumb references to books no one has read. Maybe it's just natural to call a solitary mountain lonely, just like it might be natural to call a solitary boy who is constantly making dumb jokes lonely."

Ami snickers quietly, and I look at her, surprised. She usually stays quiet during Caster and Emily's bantering.

Caster shoots her a wounded look. "*Et tu, Brute?*"

Kalix looks on with a hint of amusement playing on the edge of his lips. We probably all seem young and silly to him—and we are. That worries me, because not only do we now have to get to Samjang, but the situation, which was already bad, has gotten worse, according to Kalix.

Kalix continues his explanation. "The Lonely Peak is the Heart of Miria. It is the source of the powerful binding that Cog put in place millennia ago to stop the Ice Reich from ever returning to our world. It is where they will reenter should you fail in your mission."

He looks at us with deadly seriousness. "The trickster god, as you mentioned, is not acting from the same motives as the other fallen gods. They turned long ago from the path of light to pursue a nightmare design too terrible for human words. He has other designs in mind.

"You may wonder why the Ice Reich is named for ice. It is because long ago, they captured the Winter Goddess and dragged her to their dark dungeons, where they leeched her power and bent it to their own purposes. She is Enki's mother, and when Cog sealed the passage between the void of banishment and Miria, he left her there. Believe me, he did not wish to, and if he could have traded places with her, he would have. But I was there, and there was no time to try to find where in the dark recesses of the void the Ice Reich had hidden her.

"The trickster god pretended to understand, but from that moment, he swore revenge upon Cog. He vowed he would struggle with all his strength to reclaim his mother from the cold clasp of the Ice Reich's chains."

A shiver travels through my spine at these words as I imagine my own mother or Dr. Elsavier being stolen by a kingdom so evil that Cog won't even tell us what happens to its victims. What wouldn't I give to get my mother back? Would I have acted any differently than Enki did? Could I bear to let my own mother suffer forever in the hands of criminals worse than the Gestapo or any human tyrant? How could I?

"But you must not think his motives are so noble," Kalix says. "They are, at root, selfish. He knows we have only a whisper of a hope of beating the Ice Reich should they enter our world again. He knows we only beat them the first time because the Four became One, an event that has not happened since our world was young. He would see all worlds frozen to ice, with their inhabitants left to fates worse than death, to be reunited with his mother for but an instant."

He shakes his head, and his piercing blue eyes seem to grow heavy with a weight I cannot understand. What would it be like to have a life that spanned millennia? To have seen the rise and fall of civilizations? To look at the oldest living man as a mere child?

"The trickster god," Kalix says, "has always had a way of getting his victims to trust him. And with the motivation I have just spoken of, he would let nothing stand between him and his goal. He managed to trick Cog and Samjang by means of ancient magic I will not speak of here. The magic bound them to opposite ends of Miria, and they are unable to leave their places of banishment unless an outside power greater than the magic itself breaks Samjang's bonds. Most of Cog's household were spared the curse, and they since have either joined the fallen gods or spread out into the world, working to stop the rise of the Ice Reich. This is why the palace seems abandoned.

"As for you, the power needed to break Samjang's bonds is the power of the Four, and that is why we have such great need of you. Only you can rescue Samjang, and only the combined power of Cog and Samjang can keep the Ice Reich from returning."

"Speaking of Samjang," Caster says, "where exactly is she? We have a compass that has been pointing the way, but a map with precise measurements would be good. And how do we release her from her bonds?"

Emily translates, and Kalix nods slowly. He says something in another tongue, and a servant appears, bearing maps. The servant sets them up on an easel-like device, and Kalix raises his staff, pointing to the center of the map, where a small mountain is drawn on the map.

He begins to speak again, and Emily translates, though she's beginning to look wearied by the task, which I understand from having to translate Galthanius's Greek. It's hard to constantly switch between languages. I'm impressed with how she manages to make Kalix sound eloquent. Maybe she has a future working as a translator at the United Nations or something—that is, if we manage to stop the Ice Reich from consuming all worlds.

"You are here now in the center of Miria. Human and Kar-dun civilization lies to the west, and Samjang lies in the utmost reaches of the east, in the Far Castle. What you will find in the east few can say, for even gods do not often dare to venture there. Near our camp, there are wild men to contend with who have even dared to strike our camp, no doubt emboldened by protection from fallen gods. Farther east, among the forests, you will likely find lost laganmorfs and nymphs driven east from their homes among the forests in the west, which the humans have cut down at the Kar-dun's demand. They will likely not be friendly to a band of four humans."

I wonder if what Galthanius said is true, if the bloodgorgers are really displaced laganmorfs—or perhaps not laganmorfs but nymphs. I remember the beautiful face I saw for just a glimmer of a second before her skin turned back to its wrinkled and scarred form. Maybe that was what happened to nymphs who lost the land that was theirs to nurture. Did they morph into monsters of rage whose mad thirst can be sated only by the taste of human blood? I shiver at the thought.

"But that is not all," Emily says, continuing to translate for Kalix. "There is a desert to cross, the Silver Lake to brave, and, finally, the Gray City before you come to the Far Sea. In the east, many ancient and evil things lie in wait, and you must ever be on your guard."

I gulp. My thoughts reel from everything he's said, and my heart pounds. Our journey has been hard enough already, including running from fallen gods, defeating a bloodgorger, outpacing Five, and, worst of all, learning to ride a horse. Part of me wants to ask more, to find out what manner of ancient and evil things lie waiting to kill us or worse, but fear gets the better of me, and I keep quiet. Fortunately, Emily has more daring-do than I do, and she asks.

"That is a long story," says Emily, translating for Kalix. "And I will tell you after dinner."

He stands, rising to his full height, which makes me feel like a small shadow. He is about to leave, when he turns back to face us with a solemn look on his long face.

"There is one more thing I must not wait to tell you. The timeline has accelerated. You had twenty-one days when you left Cog's palace. Those twenty-one days have turned to seventeen, which means you have exactly ten days left. And the hardest part of your journey lies ahead."

CHAPTER 40

SOUP AND STORIES

"So we're supposed to travel through a land filled with ancient evils, and not only that, but on a compressed deadline?" Caster exclaims with flames flickering anxiously along his fingers. "How are we supposed to do this with just four magic rings, which we can hardly use, for fear of attracting the fallen gods?"

Kalix's expression turns from somber to dark. He speaks quickly, his voice tinged with anger.

Emily translates: "Do not call them magic rings. They are not to be connected with that evil power, which works by compulsion and deceit, bending nature unnaturally to the will of the magician. Your rings were forged by the Fashioner himself, and their power flows from him, persuading the elements to do your will, not forcing or tricking them into doing it."

Caster holds up his hands. "My bad. It just looks an awful lot like magic to me."

Kalix mutters something darkly and then storms away.

"What did he say?" asks Caster.

"He called you a stupid little, um …" Emily pauses, and her cheeks flush. "I can't translate it. My mother would slap me for saying it."

"Geez, what's his problem?" I say. I'm still not the biggest fan of Caster, but Kalix's response doesn't seem proportional to what Caster said.

"I guess he feels pretty strongly about magic," says Emily. "It is magic that separated Cog and Samjang and started this whole mess in the first place."

Ami nods quietly, and I wonder what's running through her head.

Before I can ask, a servant appears and, using exaggerated body language, explains that he is supposed to take us to dinner. At least I think that's what he is trying to say.

He leads us to another tent with a fire in the center. A hole in the center of the tent lets smoke escape and starlight enter. My nostrils are immediately overwhelmed by the scents of roasted meat and vegetables as we enter, and my mouth fills with saliva.

Emily's stomach rumbles mightily, and she rubs it. "Zhu Bajie is hungry!" she says with a dimpled smile.

The servant lets us sit at a small wooden table by the fire and provides us with sticks of roasted meat, bowls of vegetable stew, and wooden mugs filled with some sort of liquid. He leaves us with a bow, and we dig in. For a few moments, no one speaks as we quench our thirst and hunger. By the time we finish, my head feels a little dizzy, and I reason that the mugs must contain ale. Caster and Emily go back for more food, and he returns looking like a delighted child with three round peaches in his hands.

"You're lucky," says Ami. "Where did you find the peaches?"

Caster taps his nose. "I have my ways."

I gaze around the room, and for the first time, I notice that it's mostly empty. Tables are scattered about the room with hardly anyone at them, though there are a few men who sit in the shadows, staring bleakly into their cups.

"Why do they look so hopeless?" I say, nodding toward the men.

The others glance over discreetly so as not to alert them that we're talking about them.

"I think there's a reason they're eating alone," says Caster. "They're probably like the weird kids who sit by themselves at the lunch tables because no one wants to be their friend."

Caster's eyes flicker strangely in the firelight, which makes me wonder if there is more to his words than a mean joke. Maybe *he* is one of those weird kids. But before I can ask anything, Emily speaks.

"I don't think that's it," she says, shaking her head. "Think about why they're here. They must know it's because there's a chance the Ice Reich will come back and end everything they've cared for and loved. Imagine an alien civilization invading Earth, nuking our big cities, and then systematically rounding up your family and friends for terrible experiments that would never end or something like that. A fate worse than death."

"Of course you go for the corniest analogy," says Caster. "It would be far more believable if China invaded the United States."

Emily raises a hand to slap him, and Caster cringes while giggling.

"Or if—"

"Don't say it," Emily says.

Caster continues giggling. "Or Japan."

The fist comes down hard on his shoulder. "You little punk!"

He snickers and then yelps as she pinches him. "Ow, stop it. That's not fair! Ow, no, stop. Don't tickle me. I'm—ahaha—not ticklish! Ahaha!"

I'm not sure why this is so amusing to Caster or so annoying to Emily, except perhaps because they're the ones involved. I guess it has something to do with the fact that Emily is half Chinese and half Japanese.

I look at Ami, and she looks at me. We nod to each other, get up from the table, and walk to the edge of the tent. The sun has slipped beyond the horizon now, and moonlight illuminates the Lonely Peak to the east. A veil of mist covers the face of the mountain, and I wonder what secrets it holds.

"It's so beautiful," she says softly.

I nod, taking it in, and I think of something Kalix said earlier. "What do you think Kalix meant when he called it the Heart of Miria? Do you think it was just a metaphor?"

Ami's eyes become reflective, and then she shakes her head. "I don't know, but I think it's more than that. Cog said Miria would protect us, which means she's alive. Maybe she too is a goddess, just like Gaia was in the old Greek stories."

"Technically, she was a primordial deity, the mother of the titans, who themselves gave birth to the gods," I say, and then I wince because it is kind of a pedantic thing to say, a real Caster move.

"Oh gee," says Ami in her fey sort of way. "I didn't know. How do you know so much about the Greek myths and language, Peter?"

"I had a sad childhood," I joke, deflecting, but she doesn't laugh. She only looks up at me with her brow furrowed and sympathy in her eyes. It drives like a knife straight into my heart,

205

and hurt floods my chest, but it's a good sort of hurt, an honest hurt. "My dad's a classics professor," I say. "He was—is—very good to me."

"But you did have a sad childhood," she says softly, her words somewhere between a question and a nudging statement.

I shrug and then give a lopsided smile. "Let's just say you guys are the first friends I've ever really had."

She looks at me with the same sad look in her eyes. "I'm sorry, Peter. But what about that boy you were with the night of the football game?"

"Oh, Goober."

She giggles and then claps her hands over her mouth. "Sorry," she says, looking remorseful. "Goober is his name?"

I laugh too. "It's okay. It's a nickname. His real name is Resol McGooblias, but no one calls him that."

"It sounds like he is your friend."

"I guess," I say quietly. I think of all the times he's tried to get me to drink and all the times he's told me to give up on Emily and lower my expectations—the opposite of the advice of Dr. Elsavier. "But friends are supposed to make you better, right?"

She thinks for a moment and then nods and looks up at me with her soft eyes, so honest and earnest. "Does that mean I make you better, Peter?"

"Yeah," I say after a while. "You do. You make me more honest and caring."

"Really?"

I nod.

"Then what about Emily? And Caster?"

"Caster," I say, shaking my head. "He teaches me patience."

She laughs. "Me too. And Emily teaches you horseback riding, right?" She giggles as if she's made a tremendously funny joke.

"And how to endure the pain of getting wrapped around a tree, trampled underfoot, and dragged for a quarter mile across a snowy field."

We stand there awhile longer, laughing and being silly, and I think of how grateful I am to have her as a friend. Even if I end up dying—or worse—I'll at least have the memories of knowing someone as sweet, earnest, kind, and funny as Ami.

The conversation lulls, and we watch the mountain in silence for a little. Then I think to ask her a question I should've asked at the start of the conversation.

"What was your childhood like, Ami?"

Her eyes seem to find some place beyond the mountain. "It was mostly happy," she says. "I lived with my grandma on a farm. There were orchards of fruit, rows of berries, fields of corn and soy, and beds of flowers—something for every season. Her name was Adsila, and my father kept it as his last name after she died. After her death, things changed." Her eyes grow sad.

"Things changed?" I repeat gently.

She seems about to answer, when suddenly, shouts erupt from behind us. I spin around just in time to see Emily and Caster burst from the tent. Their eyes are filled with confusion and fear, just as mine are.

CHAPTER 41

THE GAMES

I rush toward the sounds of the cheers and cries, which probably isn't the smartest decision I've ever made—not that there's much competition. Rhe others follow hot on my trail. I'm not sure why I'm running toward the sounds rather than away from them—the voices don't exactly sound happy. Given the number of heavily armed Kar-dun we saw earlier, it would probably be best to keep my distance. But somehow, the fear pumping through my veins is having the opposite effect on me.

I round the corner of a long vertical tent and skid to a halt to avoid slamming into the backs of a dozen armored Kar-dun, who are pumping their fists in the air and chanting. If not for the ring, I probably would've ended up tumbling straight into them, but I feel its power course from the ground into my legs, steadying me and keeping me on my feet.

I stand on my tiptoes, trying to get a view of what the heck is going on. I'm pretty tall for my age, but a tall human is a ridiculously short Kar-dun, and there don't appear to be many of those hanging around, so all I can see are heavily armored backsides.

"What in tarnation is going on?" Emily says as she comes to a halt beside me.

I shrug. "Can't see." I turn to Ami, who's begun to float, rising above the circular crowd.

She strains her eyes and then gasps, clapping her hands to her mouth. A scream of pain echoes out from somewhere behind the chanting and cheering Kar-dun.

"What do your elf eyes see?" Caster asks, desperate with curiosity.

"They're fighting," she says. "And I think it's a fight to the death."

Caster puts a hand on my shoulder. "Peter, get us up there."

I turn to him with confusion written all over my face. "Shouldn't you be asking Ami?"

He rolls his eyes and gestures at the ground. "You're the lord of stones! Make a stepping stool!"

"Oh," I say, feeling kind of stupid for missing such an obvious solution. I suppose we won't be far off the ground, so it won't risk attracting the fallen gods too much, and besides, we have Kalix, one of Cog's servants.

I will the ground to rise up, putting all my strength into it. I realize I've barely used my power since entering Miria, as I've been too afraid to attract the fallen gods, whom even Cog seems afraid of. I strain my muscles, trying desperately to get the rocks to move, but they barely budge an inch.

"You're trying too hard," says Emily.

I look at her, perplexed. "Don't you mean not hard enough?"

She shakes her head. "Have you ever heard of *wu wei*?"

"Is that your Chinese best friend?" says Caster.

"It's not a person, dingus," says Emily. "It's a concept. It means roughly *inaction*, but it's really about taking the strongest action through inaction. Don't try so hard to make the stones do your will. Let the power flow through you instead."

I wonder how she seems to know so much about using the rings. Maybe that intuition just comes with the package if you're Asian. But then I realize she's been using her power for the past few days to heal us. She's had more experience with it.

I try what she says, ignoring Caster's pleas to hurry up, as he is desperate to see what's going on. Instead of forcing, I coax, letting the power flow through me. To my surprise, it does, rushing up through my legs and arms. It's exhilarating, like the feeling of going over the main hill on a roller coaster. I laugh aloud, ignoring the voices shouting something around me.

Then I realize they're speaking English.

"Hey, that's high enough!"

It occurs to me dimly that the voice is Emily's.

I release the power and look around and notice we're standing atop a twenty-foot column. "Heh, whoops."

I lower the tower just enough for us to see over the Kar-dun. Somehow, no one has noticed us, and then I see why.

Below, in the middle of the circle, a group of Kar-dun are slogging away. Some wear the colors of the north, and others wear the colors of the west and the south, though they're all stained red with blood. A few lie senseless and defeated on the ground. As soon as a fighter is downed, another Kar-dun of the same colors jumps in to replace him, usually passing off a bottle to someone before he does. *So they're all drunk and angry*, I think.

"Why are they doing this to each other?" asks Ami with her brow knitted together in distress.

A silly feeling rushes through me, telling me to put my arm around her and say it will be okay. I shake it away. *How do you even make sense?* I ask that voice. *And besides, I want Emily,* I remind the feeling. It seems to give me a sly smirk before vanishing.

I return my eyes to the crowd, when suddenly, the sky explodes with lightning, and a clap of thunder echoes throughout landscape, somehow powerful enough to shake trees and push Kar-dun to the ground.

CHAPTER 42

AN OLD HOPE

I too would have fallen if the earth didn't brace me, steadying me on my feet.

"What was that?" I exclaim, my voice an octave higher.

"Fallen gods," says Caster as his flames dance on his fingers. "We need to leave now."

I nod, willing the earth to lower us to the ground. It does, and we fall, unable to keep up with its rapid descent.

"Ow!" Emily exclaims as she lands roughly.

"Good job, Peter," says Caster. "We could've just jumped."

Ami floats beside Emily and pulls her up. Another clap of thunder echoes across the sky, and I hear an electric hum behind us.

"Let's go!" says Caster, motioning for us to follow him toward the Lonely Peak, eastward to Samjang.

"Hold on," says Emily, limping along. A little snake of water wraps around her ankles, and a moment later, she's standing straight again. "Now is not a good time to run. We'll be easy to pick off alone. We should hide."

I nod. "I like Emily's plan."

We're about to run forward again, when a voice booms across the encampment. Though I don't recognize the words, the voice is familiar.

"Kalix," says Ami.

We spin around and see a man wrapped in crackling blue lightning descending from above the circle. His eyes glare with azure fire.

"What's going on?" I say. "He's not one of the fallen gods, is he?"

Emily shakes her head. "I don't think so. I think he's—"

"Playing bouncer. Breaking up a drunken fight." Caster chuckles. "To think you guys were so scared."

Emily glares at him. "Let's go!" she says, imitating Caster's voice. She grabs her face with her hands and twists her brow in a look of desperation. "I could've jumped! I'm Caster, and I'm not afraid of anything."

"That's because I'm invulnerable," says Caster, smirking. He leans casually against the wall of a tent and falls into it. He groans. "I'm okay."

Emily laughs, slapping her leg, but then moves to help him up.

My attention drifts to the Kar-dun, who are dispersing, looking thoroughly bummed and wasted to boot. They wander back to their own camps, occasionally shouting what I take to be insults at one another, given the venom in their tone.

Kalix floats to the ground. The electric fire about him is gone; he's just his ordinary tall and chiseled self. His eyes find us, and he strides toward us now that his task of dispersing the drunken fight is finished. He motions for us to follow him and begins speaking in Chinese to Emily, who translates.

"I'm sorry you had to witness that. It is not an easy task to forge a grand alliance out of such bad materials, to draw unity out of the poison of disunity."

I think about the words *grand alliance*. I remember vaguely from history class that is what Winston Churchill called the Allies during World War II. Emily said Kalix speaks Chinese like her grandmother did. Was he in China around the time of World War II? Was he making a deliberate reference to our world?

I suddenly wonder how much Miria looks to our world. Why is that the case? Why do the Four come from Gaia too? Why can't the inhabitants of Miria have their own heroes, their own alliances, and their own identity without looking to us?

I realize a second later that I've been speaking aloud. I always have had difficulty in keeping thoughts inside my head.

Emily looks at me and nods as if I've asked something insightful, and I suppose I have.

Kalix strokes his chin and seems to ruminate.

"These are questions that require much discussion, and I, unfortunately, have other matters I must attend to now," Emily says, translating for him. "One of my servants will take you to your sleeping quarters. At first light tomorrow, you must set out toward the east. There is no time to lose." He turns to leave, with his cloak swishing in one fluid motion.

"What about the story of the east?" Caster calls out.

Emily translates, and Kalix stops for a moment.

"The history would only bear you down." He turns just enough for me to see the side of his face. "One of the advantages of the young is that they do not bear the weight of all our past failures and miseries. They have hope and optimism, creativity and cunning, and just enough naivete to believe they can win. And that is why we depend on you."

With a twinkling of the eye, he nods encouragingly at us and then disappears into the shadows. As promised, a servant comes to collect us and leads us to a smaller tent near the main tent, where Kalix seems to conduct much of his business. The tent is divided into two sides, one for Emily and Ami and one for me and Caster, but we sit in the middle for a long time into the night, discussing the day's events and what we'll do next.

With little information or advice from either Cog or Kalix, we quickly realize that we have almost no idea what we'll face in the east, only that it will be much worse than what we've faced so far. After running from the fallen gods and the fifth ring bearer, facing down a bloodgorger and an evil Kar-dun, and nearly getting trampled to death multiple times, it's hard to imagine how things could get worse.

But I'm reminded of how I told myself the day of the field trip that things couldn't get worse after Emily failed to show up, and things did get worse—and kept getting worse for a long time. So I decide I'd better not jinx myself again.

But a little voice tells me that regardless of whatever I say or don't say, things are, in fact, about to get a whole lot worse.

CHAPTER 43

THE FATEFUL FLAMES

I awake the next morning to light flooding through the walls of the tent. My head aches from too little sleep, and I find myself regretting that I stayed up so late. Our discussion wasn't even productive: we figured out only that there are more unknowns than knowns. But it was time spent with friends, and that makes my heart melt a little.

The morning sky is gray as we set out; the rising sun is obscured by storm clouds on the horizon. I climb into the saddle with ease, surprising myself a little. It's only the eighth day since we left Cog's, and so much has happened. We've met gods and monsters, strange humans and biblical creatures, and discovered many secrets along the way. What kind of person will I be if I ever make it back to good old Mormont High?

But I can't think of that now, because there's too much left to do. We have an impossible task: make it through the east, a cursed land, and find Samjang before the Ice Reich breaks through the ancient barrier defended only by Cog's waning power. And we must do it alone. If there was any doubt about that, Kalix makes it clear as he sees us off. His mind is elsewhere, distracted probably by the business of trying to find ways to unite the Three Kingdoms and forge his grand alliance from the shattered glass of ancient hate. His eyes are tired.

"Are you sure you can't spare a few dozen soldiers to help us through the wilderness?" Caster asks. "It kind of seems like your priorities here are backward: if we get to Samjang first, you can forget your grand alliance, and if we don't get to Samjang in time, the grand alliance probably won't do much good."

Once again, Caster says exactly the thought that is on my mind.

Emily translates, but Kalix only shakes his head.

"Greater numbers would only attract more attention and slow you down. Your greatest advantages now are speed and stealth. Do not trade these. If danger should come, fly to the forests, for you may find help there."

Caster mutters something about glass cannons and how we could use a few meat shields, and I chuckle, knowing that Emily won't bother to translate his gamer lingo to Kalix.

"May the All-Father light your way," says Emily, translating for Kalix.

Moments later, he disappears with his servants, leaving us alone at the eastern edge of the camp. The golden light of dawn struggles through the darkening clouds behind us, and the sky to the west, beyond the mountain, is unreadable.

What secrets do you hold? I ask the east. *What happened to you that Kalix doesn't want to tell us, for fear of leading us to make the same mistakes as the ones who have gone before us?*

We nudge our horses forward and set off into the east at a canter. A cool breeze sweeps the grassy fields, and with my friends beside me, I feel a rare moment of peace. Emily leads the way, as usual, with Ami beside her; their forms bounce along lightly with the horses.

By midafternoon, we've crossed to the other side of the mountain. It surprises me how narrow the mountain is—it almost doesn't deserve to be a called a mountain by the standards of the Rockies. It's more like a steep, abnormally large hill. But it shouldn't be underestimated because of its smallness. There is a power here that I can feel as we pass by it, some of it good, some of it evil, and some of it mysterious—something I don't even know how to describe.

When the sun is low in the west, we make a stop. To the south lie caves and swamplands. To the north and west lies a dark forest with thorny bushes on the outside and a forbidding gloom cloaking its outer edges.

We let the horses graze in the tall grass and gather round Emily, who pulls water from the earth, which she pours into our cupped hands.

"Thanks, Emily," I say after gulping down the water.

"Yeah, you're the best," adds Ami, smiling.

"Hmph," says Caster. "Let me know anytime you guys want a little cup of fire. It really quenches the thirst."

"I saw a man breathe fire once," says Ami, looking out into the distance. "It was very cool."

"Not hot?" says Caster with a grin on his face.

Emily gives him a little shove. "You know what she means." She turns to Ami. "Were you at a circus?"

She nods. "It was lots of fun, but I thought it was very dangerous."

I smile softly, thinking back to when a man breathing fire at a circus would have seemed dangerous or exotic. Now it seems only like a cute trick, nothing compared to what we've seen in Miria.

"I can do it," says Caster. "I could probably do something way cooler—or hotter, depending on your perspective—than the circus performer."

"Oh, that would be great!" Ami says, clapping her hands together.

"Gee, that sounds like a great idea," Emily says. She exchanges a glance with me, looking for me to back her up, but I say nothing, even though part of me wants to agree. But another part of me just wants to let Ami and Caster have their fun. Surely, breathing a little fire won't attract the attention of any fallen gods. Ami did a lot more than breathe a little fire when fighting the bloodgorger, and Emily has been using her power throughout this whole trip to heal us when things go sideways.

"It is a good idea," says Caster matter-of-factly. "Don't be such a fart."

"Fine," says Emily, turning around. "Have your fun."

She storms away and stops a few yards from where we stand. Caster pretends not to be hurt, but he seems a little fazed by Emily's response, as if he were expecting her to do something else.

But his disappointment only lasts for a moment. He smiles at Ami, steps back, and angles his head toward the sky. "Let's see," he says. "Yes, I think this will do."

He takes in a deep breath and then breathes out, and the air ignites into flames. Ami claps her hands in joy. It's such an innocent gesture that it makes my heart hurt a little. She's a junior, but in some way, she seems both a lot younger. At the same time, she also seems a lot older, as if there are two parts to her soul, split between childhood and old age, naivete and wisdom.

Caster performs another trick, this time turning the flames into a liquid jet that wraps around his neck like a snake before disappearing in a puff of smoke.

Emily has begun to tap her foot impatiently. "Is he quite done?" she says to me.

"I don't want to put myself in the middle of a lovers' quarrel," I joke.

Emily looks at me hard, and I blush immediately, feeling stupid. *Why did I say that? Why did that joke even come to mind?*

"So you think I like him, Peter?" she says.

"Um," I say, feeling suddenly small as she steps closer to me with an angry intensity in her gaze. "I was just joking."

"Well, I've had enough jokes for today!" she exclaims. "I—"

Suddenly, her lips begin to tremble, and her eyes grow wide. A word is trying to form on her lips, but she can't quite get it out.

"What is it, Emily?"

"R-r—" She fumbles with the word.

Suddenly, the horses neigh with terror, and a moment later, they bolt.

The word, barely a whisper, finally breaks loose from her mouth: "Run!"

CHAPTER 44

THE PHANTOM MEN

Instead of running, as a sensible person would, the first thing I do is turn around to get a better look at what Emily is staring at.

I wish I hadn't.

The caves to the south are now illumined with an evil green light, and the tall grass is crawling with men with phantom eyes that glow a horrible green and cold breath that hisses from their mouths of rotting flesh like poisonous gas. Their bodies are a mess of blood, torn skin covered with oozing pus, and flecks of bone. I dry-hurl before turning away. Emily is still staring at them with her mouth gaping, seeming to have forgotten her injunction to run only moments before.

I grab her hand and yank her out of her stupor, dashing toward Caster and Ami, who are still goofing off.

"What's up with you two?" says Caster, glancing between us and then at our linked hands with a frown.

Emily pulls her hand free, a motion made easy by the clammy sweat on both our palms. She points behind us and then to the horses, which have run off. "Are you out of your mind, Caster

Kshatriya-Wick?" She snaps her fingers in front of his face. "We're going to die!"

His eyes settle on the figures in the distance, which are moving steadily toward us with leering smiles of drooping flesh crawling with maggots. "Oh," he says quietly. "I see your point. Run!"

"Thanks, genius!" says Emily as we break into a sprint, following our horses.

"What's the plan?" I say.

"Not die!"

"That's a goal, not a plan," Caster says through heaving breaths.

"Well, excuse me!" cries Emily. "Why don't you"—she sucks in another breath—"enlighten us?"

Caster slows to a stop and takes a deep breath, surveying the scene behind us to the south and east. "They don't look very fast. Whatever the devil they are, they're probably not much of a threat at a distance, and at their rate, we could easily outwalk these suckers."

I look back and see the ghoul-like men tripping forward stupidly and slowly, despite their terrifying appearance. "I think Caster's right," I say. "They're too slow; they'll never catch us."

"Then our plan should be to find our horses," says Emily. "All in favor, say aye!"

Everyone says, "Aye," except for Caster, who says, "Me," because he's Caster. We walk at a brisk pace eastward, the direction in which our horses went.

We're starting to put a good distance between ourselves and the phantom men, when all hell breaks loose.

First come the dogs, whose haunting howls echo across the landscape of fading evening light. We spin around and see them: giant black shapes with eyes gleaming with the same evil green light that glows in the southern caves.

"Oh boy," says Caster. "Just when I thought things couldn't get much worse."

"Don't say that!" I exclaim.

Caster raises an eyebrow at me. "Why? Are you afraid of jinxes?"

A moment later, a whistling sound breaks through the fading evening air, and an arrow implants itself in the ground by our feet.

"See?"

"Oh," says Caster. "My bad."

At that moment, a dozen more whistles tear through the night.

"Run!" screams Emily, and we dash forward.

My lungs turn to fire, and my legs burst with agony as every new footfall sends fresh pain shooting up my legs from my aching muscles, but the desire to live overrides any question of stopping or slowing. Onward we run toward the horses, whose dark shapes we can see in the distance. But as soon as we think we might just make it to them, the dogs howl again, and the horses switch to full gallop.

Caster and Emily break into a curse fest in a flurry of various languages I don't understand, so I throw in a few Ancient Greek oaths for good measure. Socrates taught me how to swear by gooses, dogs, and trees, which is a lot more fun than the garden-variety curse words you see today. But I guess "By the goose!" doesn't have the same ring to it in English.

"New plan," says Caster. "We need a new plan."

"Remember Kalix's advice?" says Emily. "To the forest."

I glance at the gloomy forest, not wanting to enter and find out what secrets it holds, but it was Kalix's only advice to us, and things are not exactly safe out here either.

"To the forest," Caster says.

"To the forest," I say reluctantly. I glance around. "Where's Ami?"

Suddenly, there's a whistle of another arrow, followed by a flash of movement and a thud as the arrow impacts flesh. Someone cries out—the soft voice of a female in pain.

"Ami!" I scream.

CHAPTER 45

Attack of the Stones

I spin around as my heart pounds like a madman against the walls of his asylum, and my throat constricts. Ami is lying on the ground with blood on her chest and hands and an arrow sticking upward from her abdomen. There's so much blood.

No, I think. *This can't be right.*

I rush forward to Ami's side and cradle her in my arms. "Are you okay?"

Her eyes, dazed and confused, find mine, which are full of terror. She looks down at her chest and then holds up a dark shape from which the arrow is protruding.

"It's a bird," says Emily.

"Oh, thank God," Caster says, and I think the same silent thought, though Ami looks hurt by the comment.

She looks at me and smiles gratefully, and her eyes turn my insides warm, despite the fear still throbbing in my veins. I let her go, suddenly self-conscious about holding her. But the others seem too preoccupied by the fact that Ami almost died and the fact that dogs and arrows are still bearing down on us to notice.

"Can you heal her?" asks Ami, holding the bird out to Emily.

Emily looks puzzled, and Caster explodes, with flames bursting from his ears. "Do you want to die? Leave it, and let's go!"

"No!" screams Ami with her demeanor growing fierce. "She saved my life."

I notice Ami said *she*, not *it*. I bet she liked watching old Disney movies when she was younger. She kind of reminds me of a Cinderella or a Snow White, the type who would talk to animals as if they were people.

"Fine!" says Caster, grabbing her arm and yanking her to her feet. "Take it, and if we live, we'll heal it. Let's run." Another batch of arrows whistle through the air, and Caster looks at me. "Want to do something about that?"

I don't have to think. I dive into the stone in my heart, and I become one with its essence. I stamp my foot, and a slab of rock shoots up from the earth, blocking a shower of arrows a few milliseconds before they would have skewered our bodies. They shatter against the earth and stone, showering splintered wood onto us.

I look at Caster, Emily, and Ami as each of us draws in a deep breath, grateful to be alive. Then we dash forward toward the forest. Caster sends a few bursts of flame to our rear to slow down the assaulting dogs and phantom men. I feel a gust of wind at my back, nudging me forward and easing my movements, and I realize it's Ami, literally causing the wind to be at our backs.

The whistles of a dozen more arrows shriek through the air, and I send up a wall of stone, blocking their descent. *They really should've invented stealth*, I say to myself, half amused. The forest is almost in sight.

But then I see movement to my left and right—dark shapes speeding through the night. The dogs. They easily pass us, even with Ami's wind pushing us along, and I wonder for a moment what they're doing. Then it hits me: they're cutting us off.

Moments later, they've encircled us, and we skid to a halt a few yards from tumbling into six hideous black dogs as large as full-grown panthers. They have eyes in a ghoulish green, teeth like razors, and breath that smells of the stench of death, even from this distance.

I spin around in time to see a dozen more dogs join the rest, and behind them, the army of phantom men are closing in.

"How did the phantom men get here so quickly?" asks Emily, as confused as I am. They walk so slowly.

But then again, there's something about this night that doesn't feel right, almost as though we're in a bad dream, the kind in which the usual rules of physics and logic are off, a world of tilted mirrors and mad laughter.

I turn back to face the forest, which is only a dozen yards from where we stand now.

"Without the dozen or so dogs blocking us, we could be there in seconds with Ami's wind to speed us," says Caster, pointing at the forest.

Emily nods. "And what if they follow us?"

"We climb the trees," says Ami.

I nod. "But how do we get past the dogs?"

Caster gives me a manic grin as his hands burst into flames. "We make some hot dogs."

Emily groans. "You're still making corny jokes at a time like this?"

227

"Of course. That way, we can make corn dogs." Caster stretches forth his hands, and jets of flame leap from his fingers, clawing hungrily at the black dogs and engulfing them in fire.

I cough as the smell of charred flesh sears my nostrils.

"Well, that was unexpectedly easy," says Emily.

Caster shrugs. "Some things just are."

We're about to run forward again with Ami's wind pushing us, when, from the shadows and smoke, the dogs emerge, charred and stinking of burned flesh but very much alive. Low, menacing growls come from their throats.

"Or not," says Caster. He glances behind him at the hordes of phantom men slowly closing in with their arrows notched, ready to fire. "Anyone have another plan?"

Before anyone has a chance to respond, the dogs leap for us. Their jaws open wide to tear our flesh to bits, and from behind, a dozen arrows fire at once.

Time seems to slow. The dogs leap as if in slow motion, and the arrows seem to drift through the air, as if the world is playing at one-twentieth speed. I look around, and I'm no longer in the middle of a plain of long grass, trapped between dogs and phantom men, trying desperately to get to the safety of the forest. Instead, I'm in the floating stone castle through which I entered this world called Miria.

A voice is saying something to me, and I recognize it as the voice in the dream. I turn around, and I see the monkey man who calls himself Homer. He smiles strangely at me, and his wild eyes are filled with a funny emotion I cannot name.

I get the feeling he has been speaking for a long time, only the words haven't made sense until now. All at once, I realize what he's been saying.

"Petros. Petros. Petros."

A single word. My name in Greek. The name my dad called me when I was little.

I feel a sudden rush of warmth, unsure where it's coming from or why, only knowing that it's there. But with it, I also feel a dizzying confusion. *Why are you saying my name?*

He stares at me and shakes his head with the same unreadable look in his eyes. Then it occurs to me what should've been obvious: *petros* means "stone."

Stone. Earth. The power of my ring. The realization comes with a plan—not one I can say in words but one I can feel in my bones.

The world re-forms around me into the bleak scene I was in before, with arrows bearing down on my three friends and me and with dogs leaping at our throats. Suddenly, a surge of power rips through me like I've never felt before, fueled by desperation and, more than that, a wild sense of courage. The power comes bubbling up as if from the very core of the earth—of Miria herself—and walls of stone shoot up from the ground on all sides of us.

The world lurches back into full speed again, and a moment later, I hear the cracks of dogs smacking against stone and of arrows breaking against the wall.

I squeeze my fists together, and the walls shatter outward with an avalanche of stones. The dogs are thrown backward onto the ground, yelping, and whole columns in the army of phantom men are wipe out. They make a strange gurgling noise in their throats and look uncertainly at me, seemingly unsure whether to press forward. The dogs are more tenacious and are soon back on their feet, charging for us with redoubled bloodlust.

But my stones aren't finished yet. They swirl around like angry hornets, colliding with the dogs with such force that the animals are sent hurtling a dozen yards. One after the other, I pick them off, and then, guided by Homer's plan, I twist my hands, and the stones bury the dogs.

"Quickly!" I shout at the others. I can already feel the dogs crawling loose.

I run forward and then stop as I see the others staring at me with open mouths. Emily has a look of admiration on her face that I would have killed for a week ago. The way her face glows right now makes it look as if she really does like me, and the crazy thought of asking her out right here and now comes to my mind.

But the growling of dogs brings me back to my senses, and Ami, still clutching the poor bird, starts running; the wind nudges us all forward. At that moment, the sky crackles with lightning, and dark shapes appear in the sky.

"Fallen gods," I say, and the others don't bother to check my words.

We dash toward the forest, leap over the thorn bushes, and plunge into the thicket of trees.

We decide climbing a tree would not be advisable under the present circumstances, as we are possibly being chased by fallen gods, so instead, we decide to rest on the ground. Emily kept her interdimensional blanket on her horse, and with the horses gone, the blanket is gone too. Without its protection, she and Caster offer to keep watch.

I don't argue with them, collapsing onto my back in exhaustion, and before anyone has a chance to ask me any questions, I fall asleep with a single thought on my mind: *Who is the voice in the stone palace and in the dream? Who is Homer?*

CHAPTER 46

THE WEEPING WOODS

I find Homer in my dreams. He's dressed in goat skin. He holds a shepherd's staff in his hands and has a look in his deep eyes that I have no words to describe. They're the sort of eyes that have seen things—not ordinary things but things that would drive ordinary men mad. I'm getting the sense that Homer, if he exists, is not an ordinary man—if he even is a man.

We're on a plain beside a cliff that leads down to a white beach. The sea breaks against the rocks in showers of white foam. A storm is brewing in the distance, with dark clouds gathering.

Homer approaches me until he's close enough to whisper a single word into my ear. Then he passes me, striding to someplace behind me.

I turn with the word still ringing in my ears: *Follow.*

But before I can see what world lies behind me, I find myself stirring to wakefulness on hard ground with a knot in my back.

"Well, look who's awake," says a loud, obnoxious voice.

Caster. I groan internally, rubbing my eyes and leaning forward. When I open them, I scramble backward, because

Caster's face is like two inches from mine, and he's grinning manically. "What the—"

He stands and offers me a hand, which I refuse. I use a tree instead to help myself up. Its bark is thick and soft, and as I glance up, I see the tree extends upward at least a hundred feet. It's been here a long time.

Ami is sitting a few feet away, by a patch of wild berries, and Emily is leaning against a tree.

"We need your compass," says Caster. "We're trying to figure out where to go."

"Here," I say, tossing it to him. "Catch."

I find Ami and take a seat next to her. "How's the bird?"

In reply, she turns to me and reveals the bird in her arms. It's smaller than I remember, and despite the absence of blood, it seems tired, as if on the verge of death. It looks pathetic and fragile. I feel a twist of pity in my heart.

"It looks like Emily did a good job," I say.

"Of course I did," says Emily, turning and winking, before joining Caster to play with my compass.

Ami's lips curl into a smile, as do mine, but hers quickly twist into something sadder. "She's not better yet."

"Do you know what's wrong?"

She strokes the bird's feathers gently. That sseems to smooth the pained look in the bird's eyes. I remember being told not to touch birds' feathers, because of the oil on human skin, but oil is the least of this bird's problems. Besides, it seems to like Ami's touch.

At length, she looks back up at me and shakes her head.

I get the feeling the bird is probably going to die, but I decide it's best not to tell Ami that.

"She's going to make it," says Ami, as if reading my thoughts, which startles me.

She seems spacey so much of the time, and she's quiet. It's unfair that people assume if a person quiet, it means she has nothing to say.

"Of course," I say, forcing a smile.

"All right, it looks like the compass wants to take us through the forest," says Caster, "which, assuming it has our best interest at heart, makes sense, because I'd be willing to bet the dogs and zombies or phantom men are waiting for us outside, not to mention the fallen gods. And naturally, we don't have horses anymore, so we'd be finished on foot in the open." He yawns. "Okay, let's go."

I stand and offer Ami a hand. She takes it, and I feel a brief flurry of warmth in my chest before she lets go. I try not to think of it, reminding myself it's Emily I like. I've always liked her, and I still want to ask her out to prom once all this is over.

If you get Samjang in time, says an ominous voice in my mind. I promptly silence it.

We follow Caster deeper into the woods. The trees grow closer together, and strange sounds echo in the distance, too indistinct to make out.

After a while, Emily comes up beside me. "So, Peter," she says, leaning closer, "how'd you do it?"

"What do you mean?"

"Well, you hardly use your power, and then all of a sudden, you're like the Thing!" she exclaims.

"The Thing?" I repeat, grateful for the darkness of the forest since it hides my blushing.

A giddy, stupid voice inside me shouts, *She likes you! She likes you!* at the top of its lungs, and even the skeptical voice inside me can't deny that she does sound at least mildly fond of me.

"You know, the guy made of rocks from *The Fantastic Four.* Ugh, it's a great reference!"

"No, it's not," says Caster.

Emily puts her hands on her hips. "And why is that, Human Torch?"

Caster sighs. "Because it makes us sound cliché, like we've been done before."

"I assure you, Caster Kshatriya-Wick, I have never been done before."

"Well, technically, you're not the first bearer of the water ring," I say.

Emily shoots me a wounded look. "You're taking his side?"

"No, no! You're not normal at all." I wince. "I mean, you're different."

"Nice, Peter," says Caster. "If you're so obsessed with her, why don't you just ask her out?"

I feel a sudden lump in my throat, and the rest of my body goes numb. I blink, trying to figure out whether I'm dreaming or imagined Caster saying those words. Part of me says, *Yeah, Peter, do it! Ask out the girl you love before there's no time left.* Another part knows that Caster is almost certainly being his usual emotionally tone-deaf, slightly mean-spirited self and can't have said those words because he actually cares about my getting the girl of my dreams.

I look up and realize everyone is staring at me from a few paces ahead, because apparently, my legs have stopped working.

I hope the darkness hides my cheeks, which I know are as red as a sunburned ginger. My first sensible idea in a few days comes to me: *Deny, deny, deny.* I decide to pretend I didn't hear Caster and stopped for some other reason.

"Sorry. Just suddenly felt a drop in blood sugar. What did you say?"

"Oh," says Caster. "It was just a quote from *Office Space*, but apparently, no one here has any culture." He shakes his head disappointedly. "You okay?"

"Yeah," I manage to say, gulping down the lump in my throat and trying to pretend nothing happened.

But Emily is still staring at me with her head tilted sidewise and a knowing look in her eyes. I wonder anxiously just how knowing a look it is. Does she know I like her? If so, does she have any idea how much? Does she know I've spent every day since middle school dreaming about her, writing bad poetry about her, yearning to be with her, and hating myself for not having even a sliver of the manhood to just ask her out?

Of course she doesn't know all those things, I snap at myself. *She's not a mind reader.* I gulp. It does look an awful lot like she knows I like her at least a little.

We walk on a little longer, mostly in awkward silence. The only light in the forest by now comes from Caster's glowing hands. The canopy blocks all light in a way that seems a little unnatural to me. How can leaves be so good at blocking sunlight or even moonlight?

Suddenly, Emily stops, and because I'm sort of a ditz, I slam into her.

"Ow, Peter," she says, rubbing the back of her head.

"Sorry!" I yelp, holding my nose, which is trickling blood now. I whisper a prayer that I didn't bleed on her. That would be a killer preamble to asking her out.

To my horror, I notice what look like flecks of red on the back of her head. But she doesn't seem to notice; instead, she shushes us and tilts her head.

"Do you hear that?" she asks.

I close my eyes and listen. I hear what sounds like a little girl weeping. It's the saddest, most dejected voice I've ever heard in my life—and I recognize it.

It's the voice I heard earlier that was too indistinct to make out.

CHAPTER 47

MEILA

"To approach or not to approach? That is the question," says Caster.

"It's not a question," says Emily. "It's obvious. We need to go help her."

"No, it's not obvious! What if it's a nasty creature who is trying to lure us into its grasp by imitating the sound of a weeping girl?"

Emily looks at him as if he's nuts.

"Oh yeah?" he says. "Don't look at me like that. Ever heard of weeping angels?"

"They don't sound like lost little girls! They're called that because they're creepy stone statues that cover their faces when they move. You need to refresh your knowledge of *Doctor Who*."

"And you need to learn to think more like a criminal!"

Emily looks at Caster with a wry smile. "Why, Mr. Wick, is that any advice to give to a lady?"

Caster opens his mouth to make a smart reply but instead clamps it shut, which is probably a good idea. "Fine. Let's go meet our weeping angel."

"Hey!" I raise my hand. "Am I not part of this decision?"

"Don't forget me," says Ami.

But Emily and Caster are already too far ahead. Ami looks at me with a half-puzzled, half-amused expression. We jog forward together, trailing Emily, who is running ahead, and Caster, who is running after her.

We come to a small clearing in the woods, though it's still as dark above as it is elsewhere, which is both interesting and unnerving. At the outer edge of the clearing, a little girl sits by a tree with her head in her hands, sobbing softly, though her voice carries undimmed through the woods—another thing that doesn't seem quite right about this place. Voices are louder when you're closer and quieter when you're farther, but hers is always the same.

Emily approaches her slowly. "Hey, are you okay?"

"She probably doesn't speak English," Caster says.

The girl's sobbing stops. As the rest of us draw closer, the girl's features become more apparent. They don't look like those of anyone in our world. Her face seems both as young as that of a seven-year-old child and as old as that of a seventy-seven-year-old grandma. Her eyes, though, are her strangest feature. When she finally looks up at us, it's as if her eyes can speak, directly forming emotions in my heart. For the brief moment our eyes meet, I feel an overwhelming sadness rush through me. It' a sadness so crushing and heavy that I nearly fall to the ground gasping. At the same time, I somehow feel a relief in the girl, as if I'm sharing her burden.

For a moment, she just looks up at us with those sad eyes, which I studiously avoid, not wanting to feel that terrible sadness again. She looks as if she hopes one of us will gaze directly into her eyes, but when no one does, she speaks.

"I'm Meila," she says. Her voice has a deep, musical quality to it. "Who are you?"

"You speak English?" Caster says. "When did you travel to Gaia?"

Meila glances nervously at the flames dancing on Caster's fingers. "I've never been to Gaia," she says, her voice small and afraid. "Are you from Gaia? Are you going to hurt me?"

"No, we're not going to hurt you!" says Emily. She bends down on one knee. "My name is Emily."

"Hi, Emily," Meila says shyly.

"These are my friends Ami, Peter, and Caster. Caster can kind of be a jerk sometimes, but he's really a teddy bear when you get to know him."

"A flammable teddy bear," says Caster.

"You're not helping!" Emily snaps, giving him the stink eye. She turns back to the little girl, who looks marginally less scared. "Where are your parents? Did you get lost?"

The girl bursts into laughter, and the sadness flees her eyes.

I look between Ami and Caster, who both shrug, as confused as I am.

"What's so funny?" asks Emily.

"Did you think I was a human girl?" She laughs.

"Well, you sort of look human," Emily says defensively.

The girl shakes her head. "No, I don't. You want me to look human, so I appear that way to you. But I don't look like humans at all. Humans look funny."

"I guess she sort of has a point," says Caster. "Humans do look funny. Fortunately, my mother was an alien. How do you speak English?"

"I don't. I speak a universal language, and you understand it as English. But if you speak another language, you can hear me speaking that language too. Try it if you can."

"Well, say something," says Caster.

The girl begins to recite a poem. It starts off pretty, talking about the beauty of the western forests and the joy of having a loving sister, and then it grows darker, speaking of fires, axes, and greed. Midway through the poem, I begin to hear it in Greek, and a moment later, Caster clasps his hands together.

"It's like Laurel and Yanni," he says. "It defaults to the language you speak most often, but if you really try, you can switch to another language. Just like with Laurel and Yanni."

"You could switch between Laurel and Yanni?" exclaims Emily. "I never could."

"I read somewhere that only people with IQs above a certain level could do it," says Caster pompously. "That might explain it."

Emily raises a hand to hit him, but he manages to dodge her strike.

"Excuse me," Ami says. "What's Lauren and Yanni?"

"There was this audio clip a few years back. Some people thought the voice was saying Laurel, other people thought it was saying Yanni," I say. "It was a big thing."

"So if you're not human but can understand our language," says Emily, "what are you then, Meila? A goddess?"

Meila giggles again. "Not exactly, though we are the grandchildren of a god."

"Oh," says Caster. "Obviously. You're a nymph, aren't you?"

Meila nods eagerly. "Exactly. A nymph." Her face grows sad again as a realization seems to dawn on her. "I guess." Her eyes well up with tears.

"You guess?" Emily repeats softly.

The girl looks disappointed. "You didn't understand the poem?"

I think back to the poem, a story of beautiful forests ended by fire and axes, and then my brain pieces together a few scraps of conversation from Galthanius and Kalix, and I get it. "Your forest was cut down," I say.

She nods sadly, biting her lower lip as if to keep herself from tears.

"Oh," says Emily. "I'm so sorry."

The girl brushes back the tears from her eyes and raises her chin. "It's okay. It's all over now, but one day the forest will grow back." She pulls out from inside her dress a chain made of leaves, moss, and what look like cobwebs, though they don't seem sticky. At the end of the chain is a crystal, containing a single seed. "One day," she says with a look of hope in her eyes so sincere it hurts to look at it.

I don't understand how her eyes are so capable of wounding me, as if she puts emotions right into my heart without having to say anything.

"One day," Emily says, nodding encouragingly, though I can't help but feel it's like the nod an older sister might give a younger sister who believes in Santa Claus.

"We're here to save the world, not the planet. Environmentalists," Caster grumbles under his breath.

I look at him, unsure whether his remark is part of his weird idea of humor, in which he says things that don't make sense *because* they don't make sense. To be honest, I don't really understand his humor, but I do my best to pretend like it doesn't go totally over my head, for fear of seeming dense.

"Is this your new home then?" asks Emily.

Meila shakes her head. "No, of course not. This is just where I come to cry. There are others." She stands. "Come. I'll take you to meet them." She wanders off toward the forest ahead.

I pull the compass from my pocket, and it points after her. The others see this and nod.

"Come on, sillies. Follow me!" Meila says.

And we do.

CHAPTER 48

THE BIG FALL

Meila, the nymph girl, leads us onward through the woods. She walks with an odd gait, almost as if she's perpetually tripping over herself, yet she never falls. Her brown hair, as dark as the woods, waves back and forth, and her body sways as if to unheard music.

I wonder what exactly is going on inside the mind of my compass, if it even has a mind. Why did it want us to confront the bloodgorger in Galthanius's home? Why did it lead us to Kalix's camp? And why is it having us follow this nymph girl deeper into woods we don't know how to get out of? How does it make these decisions? Does it do so by itself, or is something or someone feeding it instructions?

We ended up getting supplies from the village after defeating Galthanius's bloodgorger, so it makes sense that it led us there—though to be fair, we did almost die. As for Kalix's camp, though, we hardly got any information useful in negotiating the unknown terrain to the east, other than to go to the forest if something bad happens. That is something common sense could have told us anyway. The food was good, but surely that can't be a sufficient reason for taking us out of our way.

Maybe our presence there had something to do with seeing the Three Kingdoms together in one place, because the grand alliance Kalix is trying to forge will become useful. Does that mean the compass can see the future? If so, does that mean it knows we won't get to Samjang in time and will need a grand alliance to stand against the Ice Reich?

I shake my head, forcing the thoughts from my mind. That can't happen. I remember what Cog said will happen to Miria—and Gaia—if the Ice Reich returns. I remember the fearful images of my mom and dad, Dr. Elsavier, Goober, and my three friends here—Emily, Ami, and Caster—all captured by a malignant enemy who would torture them in a fate worse than death. I remember my promise to Cog: "I swear I'll do my best. I won't stop till I'm dead or we've won."

No, we're going to get Samjang before the deadline is past. That means we need to move with all haste.

"How much longer, Meila?" I call out ahead.

"It's just around the bend," she says, tripping around a lantern-lit corner.

I realize we're walking on a path now, and we have been for some time, judging by the lanterns receding into the distance. They glow with a soft blue light that soothes my worries and anxieties about Samjang and saving my friends, though I do my best to hold on to them. The light replaces them with a gentle curiosity, making me wonder where exactly this path leads and what sort of civilization the laganmorfs and nymphs have built for themselves.

I'm the last one to round the corner, and I crash into Emily, sending her tumbling forward.

"Sorry!" I say, instinctively reaching out to grab her hand.

Our hands latch together, and in the moment they do, I see a new world. I nearly let go of her hand, stunned by how entrancing and beautiful the sight is.

We're standing at a precipice that falls off into a massive cave. The walls are made of intertwining trees. Homes, made of wood and lit by the same soft lanterns as the paths, fill the cave. They float both above and below us. Little points that glimmer like stars drift between the homes. A moment later, I realize they're not stars as Meila drifts off the precipice. She is shinning like the others with an entrancing golden light that seems to pulse to an unseen song.

Precipice. The word enters my mind faintly, and then I realize I'm still holding Emily's hand, and she's struggling.

"Peter!"

"Oh!" The danger of the situation suddenly rushes back upon me.

Emily has nearly fallen off the precipice, pushing against the side with her feet and holding on to my hand for dear life. Somehow, I've had the strength in both my arm and my legs to keep her steady. But now that I realize it, terror shoots through me, and the strength disappears. Emily's weight drags me over the side of the cliff. An unmanly yelp escapes my lips as I go over the edge, and a moment later, we're both tumbling.

Meila is beside us as we plummet through the darkness, somehow avoiding the floating homes. "Fly, sillies!"

"We can't fly!" Emily shouts, managing to look both terrified and cross with me.

"It's okay," I say, thinking back to the trick I pulled off when Ami and I fell from the sky. "I'll catch you when we land."

"No, you won't, silly," says Meila.

"Thanks for the vote of confidence," I mutter to myself.

"There's no bottom," she explains. "It just goes around and around. See? Look!"

I turn my eyes to where she's pointing and see Caster and Ami on a ledge below, and I realize with a start that it is the ledge we fell from.

"How?" I mutter wonderingly. Now that I know I'm not going to die, I'm more interested in how exactly this is possible, but I change my mind as I feel my stomach climb higher into my throat. "Actually, could you get us out first?"

"Yes!" screams Emily. "Get us out. I hate heights!"

I look at her and see her face has turned ashen. Her hand is still squeezing mine, and her nails dig into my skin with how tightly she's gripping. A crazy idea comes into my head that now, as we're tumbling through a perpetual free-fall, would be the time to ask Emily out on a date. But another voice says I don't really want that.

At that moment, Meila grabs her, and Emily's wet palms slip from mine. I'm left alone to tumble through the darkness.

A few seconds later, I feel soft arms grab me, slowing my descent. "Thanks, Meila," I say gloomily.

"I'm not Meila," says a soft voice with a laugh.

It's Ami's voice. She's holding on to my abdomen to keep me from falling, and despite the fact that just seconds ago, I was thinking about asking Emily out, I feel a giddy rush in my head. I try to make the feelings go away, but instead, they make me go away—the me who tries to hold on to liking Emily. I float there, held by Ami, unsure what exactly I'm doing or feeling.

"Don't worry. I've got you."

"Are you sure this isn't going to end badly?" I say, thinking of the time we tumbled from the sky outside Cog's palace.

"You mean if I were to let go?" She loosens her grip.

"No!" I cry before I can stop myself.

Her arms tighten again, and I think I can feel her smile. "What did you mean then?" she asks in an innocent voice, but I think she has a deeper meaning in the words. I'm afraid to understand them.

"Nothing." I say it more coldly than I mean to. "We probably should meet up with the others."

She seems disappointed, which hurts a little, but it is also comforting because even as she tightens her grip as we ascend back toward the cliff, I feel her loosen her emotional grip, which was so strong. Part of me hates myself for doing that to her, and part of me is thoroughly relieved. Another part of me hates myself for feeling relieved. *You're no Odysseus*, the voice whispers to me.

I can't help but agree. Caster is the real leader of the group, or maybe Emily. I can't even sort through my own emotions, much less act on them. *I'm failing you, Cog.*

Ami sets us down on the cliff where we stood a few minutes ago. I try to find her gaze, but she won't look at me. She retrieves her bird from Caster, who looks perfectly happy to be rid of the creature. She pets it softly.

"So," says Caster, turning to Meila, "I have a question."

CHAPTER 49

LEARNING TO FLOAT LIKE A BUTTERFLY

"Why did Peter and Emily fall in a loop?" asks Caster.

"Because they're inside the Wella," says Meila, as if it's perfectly obvious.

"But why do people inside the Wella fall in a loop?" asks Emily.

"Oh." Meila nods. "Well, the Wella is all one big loop. The top is the same as the bottom, and when you're in the Wella, no time passes in the outside world."

"Hold on," says Caster. "If no time passes when you're inside the Wella but time does pass in the outside world, then every time you leave and reenter the Wella, wouldn't an infinite amount of time have passed for the people inside the Wella?"

Meila looks at Caster with a bemused expression. "No, why would that be so?"

"Consider it like this," says Caster. "How much time must pass inside the Wella for a second to go by outside the Wella?"

"I told you," says Meila, laughing. "No time passes outside when you're in the Wella."

"That's my point," says Caster. "Think about it as a fraction, a ratio between the amount of time passing outside and the amount of time passing inside. The way to get zero is to make an infinite amount of time pass inside per some finite unit of time inside. Why does everyone look so confused?"

My eyes unglaze as I understand the first English sentence Caster has spoken thus far: "Why does everyone look so confused?"

"Because you're speaking a foreign language," I say.

"No, I'm not; I'm speaking math. Use your brain! If you go outside, you experience events in the outside world. If you go back inside, you can tell people about those events, can't you? But if anything less than an infinity of time has passed, then no events in the outside world have happened for the people inside, because as you said, no time passes in the Wella. So there's a paradox."

"Well, your maths are wrong," says Meila. "Maybe it's because you don't understand time so well. An infinite time doesn't pass inside when you reenter the Wella."

"Well, then how much time does pass? All I want is a mathematical theory of the Wella. Is that too much to ask for?"

"Can we get off this topic?" says Emily. "I don't think it's going anywhere useful."

"Agreed," I say.

I hazard a glance at Ami, who is still petting her bird softly. I wonder how long she plans to keep it. We can't take it all the way to Samjang; it'll be too much of a burden. But Ami looks as if she doesn't plan to let it go till it's fully healed, and that could take a long time, judging by the sickly look in the bird's eyes.

"I don't know why everyone hates mathematics," Caster says, pouting. "It's really unfair."

"So what is this place you call the Wella?" asks Emily, ignoring Caster. "What sort of creatures live here?"

"Oh, mostly other nymphs," says Meila. "But we also have a few laganmorfs. Would you like to meet them?"

I think back to Galthanius's claim that the laganmorfs are behind the attacks on the village. Even though Galthanius turned out to be less than trustworthy, I still have a lingering anxiety about what sort of creatures the laganmorfs are.

"They, um, are friendly to strangers, right?" I say.

Meila looks at me and giggles. "Of course, silly. What did you think? That they wanted to drink your blood?"

I gulp, thinking back to the bloodgorger. I must look ashen-faced, because Emily turns to me and says, "Peter, don't be absurd." She looks at Meila and smiles graciously. "Of course we would like to meet them. How do we find them?"

Meila steps off the ledge and floats in midair. "Why, they're just down here. Follow me!"

"Hold up!" says Caster, raising a hand. "If you didn't realize, Ami is about the only one who can do the whole floating-in-midair trick. What about the rest of us?"

"You can too, sillies!"

I realize now, somewhat belatedly, that Meila has never asked us about our special powers that distinguish us from ordinary humans. She seems to already know that we have them and why we have them and doesn't make a fuss about it. Does that mean she also knows we're the Four?

"How can we float?" asks Emily, crossing her arms.

"It's very easy, Emily," says Meila. "You just need a little water beneath you. Same for you, Peter; you just need a little earth. And, Caster, you just need some fire. Though try not to burn the rest of us!"

"You know our names?" asks Caster with an eyebrow raised.

"Oh, you're still thinking of language as something you have to learn. I just speak, and you understand me as saying certain words."

Caster strokes his chin, as if Meila has presented an interesting intellectual challenge for his mind. I guess she has, though I'm not smart enough to work it out.

"So how do we do the floating thing?" I ask.

We spend the next few minutes receiving Meila's instruction as she coaxes us into using our elements to support us. Soon we follow her over the edge; bits of rock are beneath my feet, water is beneath Emily's, and fire is beneath Caster's. Ami floats near Meila, and I can't help but feel she's keeping her distance from me. I guess I should say I'm sorry, but I'm not sure for what exactly. I put it off, partly because it takes a great deal of concentration to keep myself from plummeting and partly because I'm far more interested in another question: *What do the laganmorfs have to tell us?*

CHAPTER 50

THE LAGANMORFS

We float to the bottom of the Wella, though I guess there isn't really a bottom, since the bottom is technically the same as the top. Now that I'm not plummeting, I can see it. The bottom looks almost like a still lake, glimmering slightly, with the image of what the Wella looks like from the top staring up at us. It makes my head hurt to look at it for too long, and Meila, smiling amusedly, guides us away before my headache can mature into a migraine.

"It's not far now," she says.

The walls of the Wella are made of thousands of living tree trunks entangled together, with little leaves sprouting from the sides. Meila leads us to a place where we can finally walk again, and I feel soft, cool moss beneath my feet. It sends waves of relaxation up my legs, and I feel I could almost fall asleep right here, but curiosity keeps me moving forward.

She leads us through walls of vines into another clearing filled with a golden light. I feel a throbbing comfort spread from my fingertips and toes up to my torso, reminding me of a distant memory I can't quite place. I have the strange feeling this is what it felt like to be in my mother's womb.

The mossy ground slopes downward, and at the bottom, several tall, thin creatures sit in a circle by a great lantern from which the golden glow emanates. They have long faces, drooping bodies as long as trees, and great, considering eyes that seem to ponder a million mysteries.

"These are our older brothers," says Meila happily. She shouts to them, and slowly, they turn their heads to face us. "Well," says Meila, "I'll be back in a little while. Enjoy!"

With that, she darts out of the room, leaving us with these impossibly tall creatures with smooth skin as dark as oak and deep, penetrating eyes.

The tallest among them fixes his eyes on me. I take a step backward, hoping to avoid his gaze, but it's as if he reaches out and stops me with invisible hands. Then he speaks with a deep, resonant voice.

"Come now, Peter. Tell your friends to take a seat by the Great Lantern."

I laugh awkwardly—I don't like leadership or responsibility—and turn to my friends. "It sounds like he wants us to sit."

"Well, let's do as Groot commands," says Caster.

I'm not sure if his comment is a snipe at the laganmorf or at me. By the tone in his voice, he doesn't seem happy that the laganmorf addressed me and not him. By this point, to the extent that our group is not a total free-for-all, Caster has become the de facto leader and doesn't like being undermined.

As we draw closer to the lantern, I feel all the anxieties and worries that have eaten away at my mind these past days wash away like flecks of dirt in a hot shower. We sit down as he says, next to the lantern, and I feel incomparably small next to the laganmorfs, who tower above me like the trees of a redwood forest. Well, they're not actually *that* tall, but I never claimed to be good at similes.

"So, Peter, Rock of the Nine Realms, what brings you and the Four to the Wella?"

Caster says something, but it's as if the words don't reach my ears. Meanwhile, the lead laganmorf keeps his eyes fixed on me. Part of my mind is trying to work out what exactly he means by "the Nine Realms." I remember Cog saying something about them, but I didn't get a chance to press him on what he meant. It reminds me vaguely of Norse mythology, and I wonder whether all of human mythology has some kernel of truth to it. Perhaps myths are more than just stories people made up. After all, there are nymphs here, and people in Gaia think nymphs are just part of Greek mythology.

Dr. Elsavier's voice appears in my head, quoting something from the Odyssey: "I swear by Zeus and hospitality."

Right. Hospitality. I guess we should show some gratitude. My brain has a weird way of telling me things.

"We would like to thank you and Meila for the hospitality you have shown in bringing us here," I say, trying to infuse my voice with as much deference as possible. I get the feeling each of these laganmorfs has more strength in him than a dozen nuclear bombs put together.

"The honor is all ours," says the lead laganmorf. "Thaegar I am, and Thaegar is at your disposal."

I think for a moment. The others are waiting for me to speak, even Caster, though he looks petulant about it. My mind drifts to the question I really want to know the answer to, the one Kalix wouldn't answer.

"Honorable Thaegar," I say at length, "we would like to know why the east is a cursed land and how we can navigate it to find Samjang."

Thaegar fixes his huge eyes on me, and they twinkle sadly like the nymph light that floods the Wella. "That is something I know a little about. But it is rather a long story. Perhaps you would like some food and drink first."

CHAPTER 51

A DARK TALE AND A PROPOSITION

We sit munching on bread and vegetables, which are somehow the best foods I've ever tasted—I have no idea how vegetables can actually taste good, let alone this good. We also are sipping ale from wooden goblets. The laganmorfs sing songs in languages I don't understand, both sad and joyful tunes, and by the end, my heart is melting, and there are nearly tears in my eyes from the music's beauty. I'm not the only one who looks that way. Emily and Ami are both teary-eyed, and even Caster has lost the usual hyper-rational edge in his eyes. It has been replaced by something more pensive and mellow.

At last, Thaegar, who has remained silent thus far, opens his mouth. He does not sing, but his voice moves with a musical quality, a rhythm and motion that remind me of the way Dr. Elsavier recites Homer—the guy who wrote the Odyssey, not the guy in my dreams.

"The story of the east is a tragic tale; like most tragedies, it begins well, in times of plenty and prosperity. In the old days, it was not a land of monsters and hard terrain. It was instead a rich kingdom, the richest and most glorious that Miria has ever known. A long line of kings stretching back to the kings of the first men ruled these once fair lands. Even as the Kar-dun's power grew in the west, these kings endured, as did the wealth of their kingdom. They built great cities for themselves, where artists formed great statues to adorn the temples and buildings, and poets formed beautiful words to adorn the winds that swept across the rich meadows and lush forests.

"But all this came to an end with the rule of King Morin, or, as he is called by the few who remember his name, Mad Morin. The glory of the east reached such a soaring height during the reign of Morin that his pride could not help but be caught up in that swelling wave. But like all waves, it had to come crashing down. Morin knew this, but he could not endure it, for power was everything to him. And with the knowledge of the superior might the Kar-dun were forging in the west, he made a fateful choice: he sought power in dark, ancient places.

"Morin began to meddle with the dark arts. He brought sorcerers, once hunted and hated, into his court, raising them to the highest positions of the land and giving them great wealth and resources with a single condition: that they instruct him in their dark ways. Morin was gifted not only with the inheritance of a mighty empire but also with a powerful mind, and his genius soon led him to surpass even the sorcerers, despite their high lineage and natural graces.

"For though Morin was but a mortal man, he was graced with intelligence, strength, and beauty beyond all others. But to be unequaled among men was not enough for him; his craving heart desired more. He began to learn the deepest and most ancient magic arts, which no man had known for eons, to wrest from nature her gifts and bend her to his will. But with each new power, his desire and pride only grew, until he longed to extend his mortal life into immortality—to never die. He died before he could achieve this wish, but a dark tale tells that he waits in his tomb beneath the Gray City for when he might rise to claim his immortality by a foul ritual of sacrifice and blood."

Thaegar grows silent for a moment. Flames seem to dance in his great eyes. "It would have ended there but for Morin's daughter. Yes, the whole east would have been crushed beneath the heel of the sorcerers who now held a majority of the high offices in the land. Now, Morin's daughter was unlike him in every way. Those who nurture her memory call her by many names: the Faithful Olive Tree, the Thrush That Knocks at Night, and the Pure Water Stream—but most simply, she is called Haji the Humble or Humble Haji, for she was so unlike Mad Morin, Morin the Proud. Perhaps this was because she was not a true daughter of her father but was adopted. Some say she was one of the Chelei, children of the trickster god and a forgotten nymph, but this too would have been strange. She was not like the trickster god in spirit—though in one way, she was.

"Although Haji was unlike Morin or Enki in that she was humble, kind, and caring, she did have one trait like them: she was frightfully clever, and she did not shrink from battle. So as the sorcerers moved to take over the kingdom of the east, they found they were not unopposed. Haji called upon the fealty of all the true and virtuous servants of the kingdom, who would not see the land of their birth given to sinister and grasping creatures. They fought a long war against the sorcerers and those who desired wealth and rank above honor and loyalty.

"In the end, when the sorcerers realized they would lose, they retreated to the southern hills, where they fortified themselves. There they performed a final spell, a magic of vengeance and hate. They placed a curse on all the land to the east, a curse that would turn life to death and death to life. The rivers poisoned Haji's people, and the sorcerers' dead army rose from their fresh graves to finish off the last remaining men. But the curse they spun undid its weavers, so the sorcerers died—at least most of them—imprisoned in the hills, leaving behind a wilderness of monsters. It was a final testament to the wicked ambition of Morin and his scheming servants."

Thaegar bows his head with a terrible sadness in his great eyes. The other laganmorfs about him too bow their heads, joining in his mourning.

"So that was what we encountered," says Emily quietly. "The remnants of the sorcerers' army."

"Yes," says Thaegar. "And you will encounter still worse things if Peter chooses to leave here with you."

I shrink back into the sloping wall, feeling my cheeks redden from Thaegar's talking about me as if I'm the leader of the group, as if the decision is somehow mine. But what really strikes me as strange is that he thinks there's a choice at all.

"How could we not leave?" says Emily. "If we don't, everything will end."

"That depends on your perspective," Caster says.

I furrow my brow. "What?"

Caster gives me one of his superior, pitying looks, as if I'm missing something perfectly obvious that only a complete idiot could miss. "No time in the outside world passes as long as you're in the Wella, right? So we can stay here for all eternity, and as far as we're concerned, not a second will have gone by in the outside world." Caster strokes his chin and mutters under his breath. "And so I really don't understand how Meila can travel back and forth between these two worlds without an eternity passing."

"But we'd die," I say. "We're not nymphs. We're not immortal."

Thaegar shakes his head. "Those who live in the Wella do not grow old. It is our final sanctuary, a place of rest for those the world has no need of."

There is a deep sadness in his voice, and despite the beauty of the Wella, I get the feeling he'd rather be in his old home somewhere in the west before the trees were cut down. I wonder if he knows that Meila sneaks off into the woods to cry.

I consider his words more deeply, and for the first time, staying here strikes me as a viable option. I won't be abandoning my duty if I stay here, since the outside world will be no different from the way it was when I entered. The Ice Reich will never rise; there will be no end of the world. Dr. Elsavier and my mom and dad will never face the end of everything they know and love. Yet can we do that? Can we forget about quests, and monsters, and our duty as the Four?

I look to the others and see torn looks in their eyes.

"You must consider. We all must consider," Thaegar says, gesturing with a wide hand to the way we came in. "We shall wait."

The other laganmorfs hum their approval in their deep, resonant voices, repeating Thaegar's phrase, "Must consider," and slowly, somewhat confusedly, I stand up, and the others follow. As we're about to leave, Thaegar calls out again.

"But please leave the bird behind. I should like to see her for a little while." His voice becomes quieter. "She reminds me of a bird I once knew."

With that cryptic request, he lets us go.

We step out into the eternal twilight of floating wooden houses and nymphs glowing like stars to discuss the hardest question I've ever been asked. Ami looks as if she's pondering something, but I get the impression it has more to do with the bird and what Thaegar meant by a bird he once knew. She looks as if she understands it better than I do, and that fills my head with a dozen questions. But when I try to speak to her, she only turns away.

CHAPTER 52

ODYSSEUS'S LONGING

We sit down against the walls of living wood, coming to rest on the mossy ground. No one speaks at first. I look among my friends, noticing the differences in reactions. Ami's eyes are on the ground in front of us, which is also simultaneously the ceiling. It looks almost like a lake from where we're sitting, as if we're on a shore. Emily's eyes are fiery, staring off at a distant point with resolution. Caster's eyes look upward, full of longing and nymph light. I wonder what exactly is going through his mind.

"There are three choices," says Caster after a time. "Choice one: we leave immediately. Choice two: we leave after a period of time has passed. And choice three: we stay forever."

He says the last choice quietly, almost reverently, as if he secretly wants to make that choice but is afraid of what we'll think of him. I get it. It seems kind of like a horrible thing to say he'd want to spend the rest of his existence here. But if we never leave, then the bad things in the world will never happen. The Ice Reich will never invade. Mom and Dad, Dr. Elsavier, and Goober will

262

never experience a fate worse than death. At least not from my perspective. So why not stay?

"No," says Emily, breaking the silence, her voice vehement. "There aren't really three choices. I don't know how this whole time business works, but I do know we were given a quest, and we're the only ones who can complete it. So we have a duty to do our best." She stares at us defiantly, her dark brown eyes fiery with conviction and painfully beautiful.

"But if we never leave, none of that will happen," says Caster.

It's true what Caster has said. But I remember my promise to Cog that I will do my best or die trying. I feel a flush of shame in my cheeks. How could I consider doing something else, breaking my promise and living an easy life? But it's more than that. It's about—

"Home," says Ami, speaking the word on my heart. "To make it home, we have to leave."

Something about that word strikes a deep, resonant chord in my heart. It's really what the story of Odysseus is about. He has the chance to live a peaceful, easy life with the beautiful goddess Calypso as his lover. But instead, he chooses to brave the waves and wrath of the sea, which have already taken so much from him, to make it home to the land of his birth, to the place where he belongs.

"Home," says Emily softly. Her anger is gone. "It's funny. I never really thought about what a beautiful word it is." Tears form in her eyes, and when she blinks, they roll down the sides of her perfect cheeks. "I want to see my *lao lao* again and make dumplings with her."

263

She rubs her nose, sniffling, half laughing and half crying. In the next moment, I'm crying too. Ami begins to sob quietly, and even Caster's eyes look moist, though he does his best to hide it.

"Who is your lao lao?" I ask, probably butchering the sounds Emily said so effortlessly.

"My grandma. My mom's mom."

"You're close?" I think of my own grandparents. I hardly know them.

"Yeah, you could say that." Emily's voice comes out hoarsely. She pulls her legs toward her, and a fresh wave of tears shakes her.

I wince, thinking I might have caused such pain. But then I realize I'm being egotistical. Her emotion is not about my question at all. It's that we're four dumb high school kids who got sucked into a strange world and were given an impossible mission with three weeks—now less—to complete. It's the worst group project ever. If we fail, Miria and Gaia—and the rest of the Nine Realms—will plunge into a terrible darkness. As I contemplate it, a new wave of stress hits me, and I understand why Emily's crying. She probably feels the situation all the more acutely because she's smarter than I am and sees more clearly what it really means.

"What do you miss about home?" says Emily. She turns to me. "Peter?"

I glance at the others awkwardly, but Emily gives an encouraging smile, brushing her tears with the back of her hand, and I feel a surge of warmth in my chest, alongside the swirling ache from missing home, family, Dr. Elsavier, and even Goober. Her smile makes me forget Caster and whether he'll judge me. It makes me feel as if I'm alone with Emily, and she thinks I'm the most important person in the world.

"I miss a lot of things," I say quietly, letting myself slip into the memories, which seem distant, though it's been a little more than a week since I was last home. "I miss my weird friend Goober, playing video games with him, and listening to his terrible life advice. I miss my literature teacher, Dr. Elsavier. I miss getting up at zero dark thirty on Friday mornings to eat my mom's homemade pizzelle and get lectured about needing to figure out my life because I'm probably not going to get into any decent colleges."

Emily looks at me with her eyebrows drawn, as if she's seeing me for the first time, as if before this, I was just a cartoon, two-dimensional and unreal, without any real depth of character. I guess I feel the same way about her after hearing that she has a grandma she cares so much about. Despite the fact that I spent high school obsessing over her and low-key stalking her, I didn't know.

"Why are you so close with your, er, lao lao?" I say.

She gives a teary laugh and looks up. Her eyes are still moist and filled with nymph light. "I was going to say it's a long story, but I guess it's not. My parents, let's just say, have high expectations. You know the stereotypical 'You must get a 4.0 GPA and play a musical instrument and get into Harvard' Asian parents? That's my mom and dad." She pauses with her brow furrowing. "It's not that they don't love me. I know they do. But I can't be close with them, because it's all expectations and consequences with them. My lao lao isn't like that. She's seen so much, and well, I guess it would be a long story to explain her. But she's the wisest, kindest woman"—her voice goes small, and she fights to keep from crying—"I've ever known. And I don't know if I'm going to see her again."

She cries again, and I place a tentative hand on her shoulder, patting it awkwardly. I move to pull it away, but her hand comes up and presses mine, keeping it there. She holds it there for a moment, not letting go. Her hand isn't as soft as I've imagined it in all the dreams I've had about her, the ones in which we hold hands. I guess roughing it in the wild and holding fast to reins will give you callouses. But the feeling of her hand atop mine is better than anything my imagination ever produced. I thought it would make me feel dizzy with love, but instead, I feel a different sort of love, the sort of love I'd feel toward a sister, if I had a sister.

"Thank you, Peter," she says. She brushes away her tears and fixes her puffy eyes on Caster and Ami. "So what about the rest of you lot? What are your stories of homesickness?"

I look up and notice Ami is staring at me with a wounded look. I immediately feel a rush of pain and then guilt, followed by confusion about why I feel guilty—I've always liked Emily, right?—and then anger toward Ami for making me feel guilty. But all those feelings soon collapse into sorrow and confusion.

Meanwhile, Caster is gazing at me with an unreadable expression. There's sadness in his eyes, and I get the feeling it's more than just homesickness.

Emily clears her throat and eventually coaxes Ami into going first. She tells us about her father's homemade cooking and their family story nights, when her parents sing old songs passed down over the generations. Even Caster has a heartwarming story about his mother's homemade *pani puri*, which is apparently flatbread filled with flavored water, spices, potato mash, and peas. Somehow it all comes back to food. Food is how we nourish our bodies. Food is culture. Food is how we come together as families, as friends, and as communities. Food is, you could say, life. And I'm not just saying that because I'm a teenage boy and always hungry.

"So have you made your decision?" a voice says from above, and my hair stands on end.

CHAPTER 53

THE EAVESDROPPER
AND THE DECISION

My head jerks up, and my eyes find a girl with mischievous eyes that are somehow below her grin. A moment later, my brain registers that it's because she's upside down.

"You were listening in on us the whole time?" Emily crosses her arms indignantly. "You little imp!"

Meila floats down and straightens herself to face us. "Of course I was, silly. It's been so long since I've seen humans. I had to be a little curious, didn't I?"

She gives us an endearing, dimpled smile, and I watch somewhat amused as Emily's face turns from anger to the peculiar look girls get when they're looking at puppies, kittens, and babies.

"Oh, you're so adorable it's frustrating," says Emily. "Ugh. I guess we've decided then. No option three."

"So that leaves the question of when we leave," says Caster, sounding less discontent than he did earlier.

"I don't think we should stay long," says Emily. "The longer we stay, the harder it will be to leave."

Ami nods, as do I.

Meila looks disappointed. "Where will you go then?"

"On toward the east until we get to Samjang," says Caster. "And then back again to Kalix's camp, I guess."

"Oh," says Meila, furrowing her brow. "That's not good. Morin's servants are in the east, and it's very dangerous."

"Yeah," says Caster. "We know. We met them."

"You met the bloodgorgers?"

My heart jumps. "Bloodgorgers? You mean bloodgorgers are servants of Morin? And there are more of them in the east?"

Her head bobs up and down fearfully. "They're terrible creatures. They'll even eat their own if they can't get enough blood from others."

"Well," says Caster dryly, "this will be fun. You don't suppose any laganmorfs or nymphs would want to help?"

Meila raises her head proudly. "Of course the nymphs would, but we're too weak and…" She seems to deflate. "And our older brothers are strong enough, but they never do anything. They had a chance to fight back and save our old home, but they said what they always say: 'We must consider. We must consider.'"

I laugh at her imitation of the laganmorfs, which is spot on, before good sense can stop me from making a fool of myself. "Sorry," I say, realizing she probably thought I was laughing at her predicament, which isn't funny at all. It's terrible. "Um, continue."

"The other nymphs probably won't help either, because they don't believe they're much good, but I'll help if you want me."

"We like you lots," says Emily, smiling. "But it's very dangerous."

"Maybe the laganmorfs just need to hear the right argument." Caster strokes his chin. "They seem pretty rational."

Meila shakes her head sadly. "You can try, but it won't work." With that, she floats upward toward the levitating tree homes above.

I turn to look at the others. "It's at least worth a shot. If we could get the laganmorfs' help, it would make a big difference."

"Agreed," says Caster.

Ami nods but keeps her eyes studiously away from me. I feel another pang of guilt and sadness, but I can't let it trouble me now. There's too much else to worry about.

"Well, what are we waiting for?" says Emily, pushing herself to her feet and striding toward the mossy mouth of the cave, where the laganmorfs sit by the Great Lantern.

CHAPTER 54

CONSIDERATIONS

"We must consider," says Thaegar.

The other laganmorfs hum their approval, repeating his stupid phrase: "We must consider."

Caster has just laid out a perfect step-by-step argument that would have made any logician swoon, explaining why Thaegar and the other laganmorfs ought to help us. He even managed to circumvent the obvious objection, the one that appeared so powerful to me: as long as we sit here in the Wella, nothing bad in the outside world will happen, because nothing at all will happen. I'm a little surprised Caster was able to make such a good argument for the laganmorfs to help, as he didn't seem too keen on leaving the Wella himself. Then again, Emily's trick of getting us to think about home and our favorite foods seemed to soften him.

"No, you don't need to consider," Emily hisses under her breath, squeezing her fists till her knuckles turn white.

"Peter, Rock of the Nine Realms, what say you?" Thaegar rumbles.

PAUL SCHEELER

"Why do you keep addressing him like he's our leader or something?" says Caster, his voice dripping with irritation.

"Because he is," says Thaegar matter-of-factly. He turns to me, and his great, deep eyes look into mine, seeming to read my inner soul. "Have you not told them, Peter?"

"What do you mean? Has he told us what?" says Emily. She turns to me. "What's this about?"

I blush, thinking back to the talk Emily made us have a few days ago, when I finally told them about Five. She asked me then if that was everything Cog had told me, and I lied and said it was.

"I don't know," I say, trying to look casual.

The room suddenly grows deathly quiet. Then Thaegar rises to his feet, drawing himself up to his full height like a mountain surging out of the earth. I feel small, insignificant, and—despite the fact I'm a ring bearer with power over the earth—vulnerable, as if he could crush me as easily as I could an ant.

"You," he says, pointing one great finger at me, "dare lie before Thaegar and the offspring of gods in the sacred Wella, where we have welcomed you as friends?"

"N-no."

"You lie again!" Thaegar thunders, and I realize now what Meila meant when she said the laganmorfs could have fought back to keep their homeland. There is no way humans or Hairun, even an army of them, could stand against Thaegar, let alone against a dozen Thaegars.

"I-I'm sorry," I say, my voice small and weak. I turn to Emily and the others. "It was the main reason Cog drew me aside back in the palace. He wanted to tell me I was the Rock or whatever and that I was supposed to lead you guys. I didn't say anything, because I thought it was stupid and that I was—am—a terrible leader."

Emily smiles at me. "It's okay, Peter." She turns to Thaegar and glares up at him with such fury that I feel glad I'm not Thaegar. "You! What are you doing trying to intimidate our Peter?" She puts an arm around my shoulders as if we're old buddies. "This man here was appointed by Methyldonin, ruler of Miria, and you think you can just diss him like that?"

Thaegar glowers down at her. "You ought to have more respect. He is not just a friend. He is your leader."

"Well, you know what?" says Caster, looking defiantly up at Thaegar. "That might fly in Miria, but we're Americans, and I never voted for this guy. If Peter has a good idea, we can follow his good idea, but otherwise, I'm going to do as I see fit!"

Thaegar glares at Caster and Emily, and then suddenly, he begins to laugh. The deep resonance of his laughter shakes the cave. He sits back down. "Americans, you say? Is that really how you do things in your country?"

"That's right," says Caster with his enthusiasm mounting to the point of ridiculousness. "Government of the people, by the people, and for the people."

"Okay, Abe Lincoln," says Emily. "Calm yourself."

Thaegar gazes at us, amused. "Is that so? We must consider."

"Oh no," groans Emily under her breath. "Just when I thought we might be making progress."

"Let me ask a final question," says Caster.

"What would you ask of us?"

"Is there at least a probability greater than zero that you'll reach a decision to help us?"

"Of course we shall help you; we just must consider how."

Caster nods, seemingly satisfied. I guess he's accepted that Thaegar is never going to help us. It's just as Meila said: he's probably going to consider for the next thousand years.

Caster turns to us. "You guys ready to face some zombies, bloodgorgers, and whatever other weird stuff the east has to offer?"

I glance at Emily, who gives a little smile, and Ami doesn't look quite as cross with me anymore, at least for now.

"Let's do it," I say.

"Yeah," says Emily. "But first, I have a question." She turns to Thaegar. "Do you know anything about the Four who came before us?"

CHAPTER 55

An Old Story

"I've known many Four before you," says Thaegar. "My life has been nearly as long as that of Miria herself."

"What were they like?" asks Emily. "I mean, I feel like they must have been a lot more awesome than we are."

Thaegar strokes his chin with his long fingers. "It is true some of the Four have been quite impressive. But they have never been impressive in the way you might expect. In fact, they have always been misfits in a certain way."

"Misfits?" Caster repeats. "That must be a relief for you, Emily."

Emily gives him a grand look and then turns her eyes back to Thaegar. "What do you mean?"

"Have you heard of the Atiki?"

We shake our heads.

Thaegar sighs. "Cog did not tell you much, did he?"

"We were sort of rushed," I say.

"The Atiki were one of the many enemies Miria faced. No one is quite sure whence they came, but they nearly defeated us before Cog used the Hearthstone to summon the Four to Miria."

"What were the Atiki?" Ami asks.

Thaegar's brow darkens, and the Great Lantern begins to change. The uniform, gentle glow fills with the shadows of insects, too many too count, all swarming, falling on top of each other as they spread out across everything in sight. "The Atiki were the Distributed Individual; they were all copies of one another but all capable of independently executing orders. Everyone was in charge, and no one was in charge. Everyone was free, and no one was free. They sought to spread their hideous form of life and to envelop all Miria in their scheme."

I shiver as my ears fill with the clicking, humming sounds of insects.

"Against this enemy, Cog summoned your forbearers, and the Four found their way to his palace. A Chinese noble girl, an English playwright, an Indian mathematician, and a mestizo mystic. They were an unlikely group of souls, and it was only with Samjang's help that they learned to communicate at all, for none of them spoke the same language."

In the lantern, I see the shadows of four people who look young and a little gangly, as we do. They sound a bit older than we are but not by much. I smile as I look at their silhouettes, feeling a strange encouragement.

"But despite their differences, they learned to get along. And because of their differences, they were unstoppable. It was not easy, and there were many failures along the way, but in the end, they defeated the Atiki and rescued Miria from sinking into an age darker and more terrible than any tyranny your world has known."

"How did they do that?" Ami asks.

"They did it like all the Four before them. They became One. And in becoming One, they became Life: the ratio of elements, the harmony of the shapes, the song of being."

"But how did they do that?" asks Caster.

"Only they and the All-Father know."

"Oh," says Emily, disappointed.

I remember what Cog told me when we were alone: we should pray to the All-Father if things got really bad. I still think it's kind of a dumb idea. Prayer never worked back in Gaia; why should it work here?

"So will you help us then?" asks Ami. "We're not like the other Four who knew what they were doing."

Thaegar smiles like a kind grandfather—as much as a gigantic, lanky, millennia-old creature can resemble a grandfather. "We will, but first, we must consider."

Emily looks as if she's about to burst from hearing the phrase "We must consider." Ami gets her bird back, and after we say our goodbyes, we file out of the room to decide on the great question: *What the heck do we do next?*

CHAPTER 56

A NIGHT'S CHANGES

That night, we eat in Meila's floating house, and I taste the best food—next to my mom's pizzelle—I've ever had. At some point during the meal, Meila wanders off, and the conversation lulls.

"Do you guys have any siblings?" I ask.

A strange look comes over Caster's face, and his eyes seem to grow distant. Emily's expression also becomes more serious.

"Oh jeez," I say. "I didn't mean to, um, well …" My voice trails off.

Caster looks up and gives Ami a smile. "Just this little rascal," he says, though his voice is heavy.

Emily meanwhile hasn't looked up; her eyes focus intently on her thumbs, which she's playing with.

Caster frowns. "You all right?"

"Yeah," she says softly. "I guess." She sighs. "I have a sister—at least I think."

"You think?" says Caster.

Emily pulls her legs up to her chest, as if trying to compress herself into as small a space as possible. "It's a long story, and

I'm not sure how to start. Her name is Anne, and she was the brightest, most delightful child you could ever meet. But she always has been sensitive and artistic, and that might have been a good thing in another family but not in mine. My parents are all expectations—very high expectations. I don't like it, but it sort of works for me. I'm competitive, and I always wanted to be a doctor anyway, so my parents are as happy with me as Asian parents can be. But my sister …"

Emily sighs. "She wants to be a poet and an artist. And my parents are not okay with that at all. They use me to try to bully her into making 'better' life choices, saying, 'Why can't you be more like your older sister? Why don't you want to study medicine or law or engineering? Why, why why?' I wonder if she's begun to hate me because of how my parents pit us against each other. And it's not like I try to stop it, because I want my parents to be proud of me, or at least I don't want them to hate me."

Emily looks down, and her eyes are barely visible over her knees. "I ask whether she's okay, but she just shrugs at me like I'm not there, like the question doesn't matter, like there's nothing at all that matters. When I do get her to talk, she says she just feels numb. I'm afraid she lives more in her imaginary worlds than in this world. But that's not what scares me most." Emily's voice trembles. "I snuck a look at her journals, where she hides her poetry, and"—she brushes back a tear—"they're about death. Her death. She doesn't want to be here anymore, and I'm afraid she won't be there when I get back—if I get back."

Emily starts to cry. "She used to be such a happy child. I wonder what I did wrong. I just wanted her to be happy, but she's not. She's not."

I look awkwardly between Caster and Emily; my heart hurts, and my head is confused. I want to say something. I want to comfort her. But I don't know how, and I hate myself for that.

In the end, it's Ami who does the comforting, pulling a sobbing Emily into a hug. Caster looks at her piteously, and for the first time, I see his mask of sarcasm and overconfidence fall away, revealing a tender look, as if he wishes he were the one holding Emily against his chest.

"Surprise!" shouts Meila, appearing in the doorway. Her happy expression falls as she sees Emily. "Oh no. What's wrong?"

Emily pushes herself up and brushes back her tears, trying to hide her sniffles. "Oh, nothing." She forces a smile. "What've you got, Meila?"

It takes a little convincing, but Emily eventually gets Meila to believe everything is okay. Meila reveals her surprise, which turns out to be song bubbles—little bubbles of glowing light that play music when you spin them. We have a lot of fun with them.

Later that night, after laughing and singing with Meila, we decide on something more somber. We set a deadline for ourselves on when to leave. We all recognize that if we don't, we could easily just slip into the peaceful, happy rhythms of life here.

Peaceful and happy, that is, except for Meila's sobs, which wake me several times during the night. They're soft sounds, barely above a whisper, but they're also the most tragic and heart-wrenching I've ever heard. I end up crying myself, and unable to go back to sleep, I decide to join her on the porch of the floating hut.

I step into the night, which, inside the Wella, looks much the same as day, only the nymph light is softer. It's a beautiful sight; the quiet light scatters off the tree walls of the structure, and the infinite tunnel below flows into itself forever. I turn and make my way to the soft cries of Meila on the other side of the circular porch. Suddenly, I stop short.

Ami is already next to her with her arm around Meila and her bird sitting next to her.

"Does it hurt?" asks Ami gently.

Meila nods, making a forlorn whine like that of a child who's lost her mother, anguished and hopeless. "It does. It always hurts."

I furrow my brow. *What hurts?*

Ami squeezes her shoulder gently. "We'll help you get it back. I promise."

My head feels muddled. *What are they talking about?*

"But it's all cut down. All the old wood is gone forever." Meila breaks into fresh sobs.

Then I get it: the forest where Meila used to live. But what does she mean it hurts? Maybe it's like a phantom limb. Nymphs are supposed to be part of the land they nurture. If part of me was chopped off and hauled away for lumber, it would hurt, not just because of sentimental attachment but because it was part of me.

I feel sudden anger at the Hai-run and humans, even the ones we saved. Maybe they deserved the bloodgorger for inflicting such pain on someone as innocent as Meila. A dark thought comes to me: *What if we let the Ice Reich destroy the Hai-run and human kingdoms and let them have a taste of the pain Meila knows in every waking moment?*

Almost immediately, I feel guilty for having the thought. The lessons I learned as a little kid come back to me: "Do not return evil for evil" and "An eye for an eye will make the whole world blind." Besides, it wouldn't just be the bad Hai-run and humans who suffered. All the kids would suffer too and all the adults who didn't do anything wrong. I remember the pure hatred I saw in the ice monster's eyes when I first came to Miria. There is no way allowing the Ice Reich to wreak havoc could make the world better, even if it punished the horrible people who caused Meila so much pain.

"And my sister too!" cries Meila with fresh sobs shaking her. "She's missing, and I don't even know where she's gone. I used to feel her."

Ami strokes Meila's hair gently. "Do you want some water?"

"It's okay," says Meila. She rubs her nose and stifles a sniffle. "I'll be all right. You should get some more sleep. You're leaving tomorrow."

Ami nods and gets to her feet. Before I have time to react, she turns around and nearly bumps into me as she rounds the corner.

"You're awake," she says coolly. Then she seems to regret her words, and her expression softens. She looks up at me; her hazel eyes are as big as full moons.

I get the feeling this is the moment when I'm supposed to say something about what happened earlier—either apologize or give an explanation. Instead, I just stare at her stupidly. My tongue feels like lead in my mouth, and my thoughts turn to porridge.

Her hopeful expression falls, and she nods, as if consoling herself. "Well, good night, Peter," she says, and she walks past me.

I curse myself for being so stupid, lame, and spectacularly uncourageous. *You're a coward, Peter,* I say. *Whatever Dr. Elsavier, Cog, and Thaegar think of you, you're just a loser. You're the half that makes the top half possible.*

After I beat myself up a little more, tiredness eventually wins out, and I decide to fall asleep on Meila's porch. There isn't any guardrail, but falling off is the least of my concerns. It's not as though I could die. I'd just end up cycling through the Wella loop. Even if I managed to strike the ground, I'd just leave a dent as long as the ring is on me.

On a whim, I try to take off the ring, but the harder I pull on it, the tighter it grips my finger. It's like a Chinese finger trap.

I give up and fall asleep, fantasizing about a world in which I have the courage to explain myself to Ami. But I realize in the last moments before I fall asleep that it's not just that I lack courage. It's that I don't know what I'd tell her, because I'm confused.

When sleep finally overcomes me, I find myself in a field, facing the ocean. Homer, dressed as a shepherd, tells me to follow him, and as I turn around, the dream fades, leaving me with tantalizing questions: *Who is Homer? And what is he trying to show me?*

CHAPTER 57

FAREWELL QUESTIONS

We talk to the laganmorfs once more before leaving. They preemptively tell us they will consider how and when to leave the Wella to help us, so we move on to other business.

It turns out they know quite a bit about the terrain of the east, and they're willing to assist us—as long as it doesn't involve them doing anything themselves. There are at least six separate occasions when we have to calm Emily down, because she looks as if she wants to explode. But we manage to get through our final meeting without any spontaneous combustions, except from Caster, but that's just because he's bored and likes to make flames when he gets bored.

"The way to the east leads through a desert, which ends in the Silver Lake. It is not made of true silver; it is so called because of what lurks beneath it. You must not look beneath the waters. Afterward, you must traverse rock and mountain. You may be tempted to go through the caves, for much lore is hidden there about the Four, but great evil also hides within. Finally, you must pass through the Gray City and cross the far sea. Then you will come to the forbidden island, where Samjang is kept."

The story sounds similar to what Kalix told us.

"How do we get to the desert?" I ask.

Thaegar nods approvingly—I guess because I've asked the question, not Caster. "You should leave these woods forthwith and travel east through open country till you come to the desert."

"But there are fallen gods who were chasing us, as well as the army of the dead raised by the sorcerers."

Thaegar nods gravely. "I do not recommend you travel through these woods. But if I am not mistaken, you have a compass with you, which points the way. Listen to its guidance above mine."

We say our farewells to the laganmorfs, thanking them for their hospitality and generous advice, and leave their cave, passing through the hanging vines and coming into the main part of the Wella.

"Well, that was spectacularly unhelpful," grumbles Caster under his breath.

"What do you mean?" I say.

"Aside from the vague geography lesson, he basically just told us to follow the compass, which we would have done anyway."

Emily places a hand on his shoulder. "Lower your expectations, Caster. It's the key to happiness. Peter, why are you smirking?"

I look at her and shake the expression from my face. Her advice is exactly the same as the advice Goober gave me long ago in order to convince me not to fall in love with Emily. It's weird to hear it come from her and under such different circumstances. It jolts me to think how much has changed in so short a time.

"Nothing," I say.

We float our way up to the top of the Wella, where Meila is waiting for us. She smiles broadly, but I can tell by the puffy look in her eyes that she was just crying, and I remember how she spent last night crying. She probably has spent every night crying since she was forced to leave her home.

She has a basket in her arms, filled with bread and sacks of water made from what looks like leather. I'm not sure where she found this stuff, but Emily takes the basket into her arms and tears up.

"Thank you, Meila," she says, brushing the tears from her eyes with the back of her hand. "You're the sweetest person I've ever met."

Caster rolls his eyes. "You're so sappy."

Emily punches him. "I think you mean, 'Thank you, Meila.' Did your mother teach you anything?"

"I'm an Indian man. Respect is for girls." He grins. "Just kidding! Thank you, Meila. Ow, stop hitting me! I said thank you!"

Ami walks up to Meila and gives her a big hug.

"Aw, Ami. You shouldn't be so sentimental. It's not like we're parting!"

I furrow my brow. "What do you mean?"

"I'm coming with you!"

"No, you are not!" a deep voice booms from below.

It's Thaegar's voice, I realize immediately.

"Thaegar can hear us from this far?" exclaims Caster. "No wonder he didn't like me. He's heard all the very nice things I've said behind his back."

Meila's head falls, and her expression droops. "Well, I guess I have to stay. But I can lead you for a little."

"Okay," says Emily. "But I agree with Thaegar: you shouldn't come the rest of the way. It'll probably be very dangerous, and you have to live long enough for us to get you your home back."

"It depends on what Peter says." Meila looks at me as if asking for permission.

I shrink into my skin. I hate that Thaegar and now Meila act as if I'm supposed to be in charge. Before about a week ago, I had only one friend, and all the leadership experience I had came from *Ghost Army*, the video game Goober and I used to play. Now a god and divine offspring are telling me I'm supposed to be the leader of the Four.

Caster shakes his head as if he thinks the whole thing is stupid, and I have to agree. But Meila ignores him, with her eyes focused on me.

"Um, sure," I say. I stare at the innocence in her eyes and think of how horrible it would be if she were harmed. A terrible image comes into my head of Meila becoming a bloodgorger chained to a pillar inside Galthanius's mansion, used to extract the blood of immortality to keep him alive forever. "But not too far, like Emily said."

She nods enthusiastically. "Okay! Let's go then."

She takes the basket of food from Emily, which might last a few days if we're lucky and it doesn't get destroyed and lost, as did all the supplies our horses were carrying.

We're about to step out of the Wella, following the direction of the compass, when suddenly, the compass spins directions, pointing back to the Wella. The change lasts only for a moment, and then the compass returns to facing east. I get the impression it's trying to tell me something.

Then a question occurs to me.

"I'll be right back," I say. "I have a question I need to ask before we leave."

CHAPTER 58

THE DARK FOREST

The lanterns sway on the pulsing, glowing cords that stretch out from the Wella. It makes me wonder what sort of thing the Wella is really. It almost seems like a living creature, and now that we're outside it, the world feels colder.

But the question doesn't linger on my mind as we follow the winding path away from the Wella into the dark forest that waits ahead. Instead, I find my mind playing back the scene of Thaegar's answer.

He looked surprised as I pushed through the heavy vines covering the mouth of the cave, where he and the others sat around the Great Lantern.

"What can I help you with, Peter?" he asked.

"I have a question," I said uncertainly. "It's about the Four becoming One."

Thaegar nodded sagely. "I was wondering when you were going to ask about that."

But before I can hear his answer again in my mind, I feel a hot flash of pain in my face, interrupting the memory.

"Fricking frick!" Emily rubs the back of her head. "Stop running into me, Peter!"

My hand rushes to my nose, which is bleeding again. "Sorry! Why'd you stop?"

She steps aside and gestures ahead. "Behold! The unknown!"

To the right and left hang the last two lanterns of the Wella, and before us, the darkness of the forest beyond spreads out.

"I guess this is it," says Emily, turning to Meila.

I remember Thaegar's forbidding Meila to leave the Wella with us and Emily's and Ami's concern about her safety and desire to make sure she lives long enough to see her home restored.

Meila's eyes fill with tears. "I don't want to leave you, sillies." She rushes up to Emily and gives her a hug.

"Aw," Emily says, holding her. "We don't want to leave you either. But it's for the best."

Ami puts a hand on Meila's shoulder and nods in agreement. Caster looks on impassively, though I bet he feels more than he wants to say.

Meila shakes her head. "It's not for the best. I can't wait in the Wella till you make the world someplace better, because nothing happens out in the world while I'm in the Wella, but I'm too weak to be of any help. I'm just a silly nymph who wasn't able to help herself, her sister, or her friends when it counted most."

I guess she also lost friends when the trees were cut down, and suddenly, I feel a wave of emotion overtake me, and before I know it, words are coming out of my mouth.

"No, you're not," I say, surprising myself, and before I have the chance to stop myself, I keep on talking. I have no idea why I suddenly feel so adamant, but I really feel like this is a hill to die on. "You're a Penelope, Meila. Clever, courageous, and true—and strong. Stronger than you know." My eyes drift toward Ami for some reason, and I pull them back to Meila. The annoying little voice in my heart says there's a reason my eyes found Ami, but I flick it away, as I usually do. "So don't discount yourself."

I cringe internally, knowing I sound like a combination of Dr. Elsavier and Cog, but none of the others have heard them say these words, so they don't cringe as I do.

Instead, Emily, Ami, and even Caster grow reflective, and Meila looks at me with teary eyes that flicker through a dozen different emotions. We stare at each other, and in the end, she gives me a hug. Her little head rests against my stomach because she's so short.

"Thank you, Peter," she whispers.

I feel something strange. I feel stronger, as if my saying those words had an effect in the real world, an important effect—not something stupid and meaningless like the games I played with Goober or even the power I have to make rocks move now but something deep, strong, and special: the ability to touch a human heart. Well, a nymph heart. But we're not too different when it comes down to it.

A few more tears are shed, and a few more goodbyes are said. At last, Meila turns and makes her way back up the winding path.

I turn and see Ami's bird gazing at Meila's disappearing form with strangely human eyes. But it's only for a moment. The tiredness that seems to weigh down the bird fills its eyes again, and they close.

It leaves me wondering what Ami's bird is exactly and why Thaegar wanted to see it. I regret not asking, but I can only keep track of so many questions, and this quest has been confusing.

I step forward into the dark forest, feeling more buoyant after my little speech to Meila, and my mind drifts back once more to Thaegar's answer to my final question.

CHAPTER 59

THE SHAPES

In my mind's eye, I can see Thaegar again as he answers my last question to him.

"Methyldonin may have told you about the Four becoming One," Thaegar said, referring to Cog. "And it is true that the Four may become One, but he only tells half the stories these days after what happened."

"What happened?" I asked with my mind reeling.

"It was supposed to be that Five would become One. The five rings were forged together by the All-Father in the very heart of reality, and they are meant to come together. Even now, they call to each other. But for a reason that has eluded the wise from the very start, Five is never summoned to the right location. An enemy always intercepts him; his is a tragic story, for many times, he has killed those who were truly his friends."

"You mean Five has killed the other Four?" I exclaimed.

"Not this Five," said Thaegar. "Another Five in the past. But you are all part of one long thread of history, and it is not so easy to divide one from another."

"So how should we treat Five?" I asked, remembering the presence I'd felt the morning I learned to gallop in order to escape him—a presence of anger, hurt, and pain.

"Warily. If he did not arrive with you at Methyldonin's palace, he may already have been turned. If that is so, you must avoid him and, if necessary, kill him in order to bring Samjang back to Methyldonin."

I nodded, slowly coming to grips with the gravity of the situation. Another part of me, though, wanted to believe Five could be redeemed. If only we could show him the truth, maybe he would be happy to escape whatever dark force intercepted him when he was summoned to Miria. "And what about Five becoming One?"

"You must learn a little history and a little mathematics to understand this," said Thaegar. "Are you willing?"

A little mathematics? Are you kidding me? But I bowed my head. *If that's what it takes.*

"There are five and only five shapes made of equal angles and equal sides. These shapes are the spiritual forms of the five elements: fire, earth, water, air, and something so mysterious that it is often called only the fifth element." Thaegar drew five shapes along the ground and pointed to and named each one by one. "Earth is the cube. Air is the octahedron. Water is the icosahedron. Plato, a philosopher of your world, thought fire was the tetrahedron, but in fact, fire is the dodecahedron, and the fifth element is the tetrahedron, the simplest and loneliest of the shapes, for it has no pair. Earth can become air by switching vertices and faces; likewise, water can become fire. You may have noticed in friends that fire and water, as well as earth and air, naturally fight yet naturally attract too. It is because they are duals of each other, natural marriages, so like yet unlike the other that they cannot help but fight while drawing closer."

Thaegar's words plowed into me like a truck carrying an oversized load. Of course, I'd noticed Caster and Emily fighting, but had they really been drawing closer? *I guess they have. Does that mean Caster and Emily are destined one day to get married? And what does that mean about me and Ami?* I shoved the thought from my mind because it made me queasy, confused, and a little jealous.

"Now," said Thaegar, "these shapes may interact in a certain way so that Five become One, and when this is done, great power—power the likes of which has never been seen—will be released. Even when only the Four became One, it generated enough power to drive the Ice Reich back into the abyss, giving Methyldonin time to lock it and prevent them from reentering."

"And how do we do that?" I asked eagerly.

Thaegar shrugged his great shoulders and shook his head sadly. "None now live who know the answer. Though there is a place where some answers may be found, I must recommend you do not, under any circumstances, attempt to go there."

"Where is it?"

"The Forgotten Caves, which lie east of here and which I have said—and will say again—you must not travel through."

"Why? What lies there?"

Thaegar shook his head. "Much evil," he said sadly with eyes full of regret.

"You look awfully reflective," says Emily, interrupting my thoughts. "What did you go to talk to Thaegar about anyway?"

"Yeah," says Caster. "Don't do what you did last time, when you only mentioned the existence of Five after he almost caught up to us."

Ami doesn't look at me; her gaze is fixed resolutely ahead, and her hands gently hold the weird bird, which, despite having no more injuries, doesn't seem to want to go anywhere.

"Just a little bit of geometry," I say.

Caster raises an eyebrow, and I do my best to try to explain Thaegar's confusing discussion of solids and what they're supposed to mean, though I leave out the part about the special connections between earth and air and between fire and water. However, judging by the look in Caster's eye, he's already figured it out. He probably reads Euclid's *Elements* to pass the time.

I'm about to come to the part about the cave and the answers that might be there, when I feel a tingling in my feet. It spreads quickly up through my legs to my head, where it registers as fear. I glance over at Ami and see her eyes widen as she seemingly senses the same thing through the air: something large and menacing is moving toward us quickly.

Emily shoots a confused and then concerned glance at us. "What is it?"

"Run!" Ami and I shout at the same time.

CHAPTER 60

THE CHASE

We bolt forward with Caster in the lead. His fiery hands light the way through the thick darkness of the forest. I'm close behind. The compass needle bobs in my hand as I struggle to keep it flat. I've learned it can be fickle, suddenly changing direction, so I always have to keep an eye on it to make sure we're still going the right way.

"What's chasing us?" asks Emily through heavy breaths.

"Like I know!" I shout, ducking a low-hanging branch that nearly takes my head off as I slide beneath it.

The earth re-forms around me, pushing me back up and vaulting me forward, so I'm next to Caster again. I make a mental note to replay this awesome scene when I'm not getting chased by something big and menacing in a dark forest that supposedly still contains servants of the evil Mad King Morin.

As we run, the creature continues to close in on us. Emily falls farther and farther behind, panting hard. I feel great, considering the circumstances. Strength courses up through my legs. Caster and Ami look fine too, as far as I can tell through the flickering light of Caster's hands.

A connection forms in my mind. Caster, Ami, and I are all connected to our elements. My feet are on the earth, Caster's hands are ablaze, and Ami is immersed in air, but Emily is far from any water, except maybe some moisture in the soil. Maybe after all the exercise we've been doing these past days, the natural differences have evened out, and what counts now are our elements.

"Emily," I say to Caster. "She's falling behind."

He casts a glance over his shoulder, and in a second, he grabs a stick off the ground, lights it on fire, and gives it to me. "Keep running!"

He runs back to Emily, who's limping along, almost doubled over from cramps. He takes her hand and helps her forward until they're both running again.

I feel a flash of jealousy and regret. I should have been the one to help her, even if it would have only deepened the gap between me and Ami. I think of what Thaegar said about fire and water being duals of each other. He even used the metaphor of marriage. I suddenly feel like punching Caster and knocking the arrogant "I'm cleverer than you" look off his smirking face.

But the hot flash of anger lasts only a moment, as I remember that we're being chased by something we probably don't want to meet. Caster and Emily close the gap, and I redouble my energy. Since Caster dropped behind to get Emily, Ami and I have drifted closer as we run, and part of me wonders whether it's because earth and air are duals of each other. Is all of this inevitable? Do I have any choice at all? Or is all of this, from being summoned to Miria to being the bearer of the earth ring to being the dual of Ami, inevitable, a mere playing out of other people's or gods' designs? Or God's design?

I think of the All-Father and Cog's advice that in times of difficulty, I should pray to him. Now seems like as good a time as any. Will it work?

Shut up, Peter, I tell myself. *This is hardly a time to be doing a philosophical investigation into free will, destiny, and the power of prayer!*

The thought mostly silences the voice that whispers to pray, but I can still hear its nagging in the distance.

A gurgling sound echoes in the distance, something guttural, hungry, and terrifying.

"How much longer?" Emily says through heaving breaths.

Even with my connection to the earth, my legs are starting to go weak, and my lungs are on fire.

"We can't go on like this forever," Emily says. "Maybe we just stand"—she heaves a deep breath—"and fight."

"I'm warming to that idea," says Caster with flames dancing along the fingers not wrapped around Emily's hand.

Once more, the desire to land a fist right between Caster's bright eyes surges in my heart, and I come close to doing it, but then Ami speaks.

"There's light ahead."

Sure enough, in the distance, I see the faint glow of what seem to be lanterns.

"You didn't lead us in a circle, did you?" asks Caster as he sees the lanterns too.

"I was just following the compass!" I say. *Though if we're being chased by something dangerous, returning to the Wella might be the logical option.*

The menacing creature can't be more than a hundred yards away now. It's close enough for us to hear the sound of cracking twigs in the distance.

"I hate cramps," says Emily, holding her stomach.

"Come on! We're almost there!" Caster shouts.

I keep running, which, at this point, feels like falling forward more than running. The creature is still closing in on us. Fifty yards. Twenty-five yards. Fifteen yards.

I'm about to look back, balling my fists to prepare for a fight, when two things happen almost simultaneously: the creature stops closing in on us, and I nearly plow into a girl who looks almost exactly like Meila, only there are dark circles beneath her eyes.

CHAPTER 61

THE OTHER ONE

"Ah!" she cries, bracing herself as I skid to a halt inches from turning her into a human football—or nymph football.

"Nice going, Peter," says Emily, between deep breaths.

I notice there are lanterns hanging on the trees around us, which probably explains why the creature has stopped following us.

"Long time no see, Meila," says Emily, walking up to the girl.

She furrows her brow. "How do you know my name?"

Caster and Emily exchange confused looks. I chance a look at Ami, and I know she sees me, because of the way her eyes flicker, but she refuses to look back.

"What do you mean, Meila? We were together a few hours ago," says Emily, sounding almost hurt.

"Oh, were we?" the other Meila replie airily. My eyes are drawn once more to the hint of dark marks beneath her eyes. "I have trouble remembering things sometimes."

This confuses me. Why does Emily think this is the same Meila, our Meila? Is she our Meila? Was Caster right about an eternity passing inside the Wella for every second in the outside world, and is that why this nymph who looks like Meila doesn't remember us?

The other Meila—who I decide to call Meila Two—regards our sweaty, ragged appearances. "You look like you could use a meal," she says. Her fey expression suddenly brightens and focuses. "Luckily, we're just about to have a feast." Her expression turns to one of concern. "But you should have something to drink first." She offers a canteen to us.

"Oh, you're a dear," says Emily, gripping the canteen and taking a deep drink. "Oh, thank you!"

Meila Two offers the canteen to the rest of us. Ami shakes her head, and I hold up my hand.

Caster looks at the canteen with a smirk. "Well, I've always wondered what your spit tastes like," he says before taking a drink from the canteen. The liquid partially spills onto his cloak as Emily delivers an elbow to his gut.

Meila Two gives Ami and me a disappointed look that almost makes me want to reconsider and ask for a drink, but then she turns and leads us forward along the lantern-strewn path. There's something different about the way the lights glow, but I can't place it exactly. It's as if some part of my brain sees the scene differently, but before it reaches consciousness, the image gets edited to make it look the same as the lantern-lit path outside the Wella. There's definitely something not quite right about it.

"Fancy that," says Emily, brushing the sweat from her face. "Back in the Wella after only a few hours. I guess we have a chance to test your hypothesis about infinite time passing, Caster."

I want to say, "This isn't the Wella!" but it's as if something stops me, swallowing up the desire before it can move me to action.

In the distance, I hear the sound of beautiful voices singing. But once more, I get a funny aftertaste in my mind, as if the voices aren't really beautiful, as if my ears hear what they're really like—something horrible—but the sound gets edited before it reaches consciousness. I glance at Ami, wanting to bring up my question, but she still refuses to look at me, instead pretending to be very interested in the feathers of the weird bird she still holds in her arms.

Ugh, girls. I sigh, hoping I'm not too much like a bitter, lonely teenager.

Meila Two leads us down a lantern-strewn pathway to an entrance that looks like the entrance to the Wella we entered a day ago, or however time is measured in the Wella. There are floating homes of bark and wood, which look like the ones in the Wella.

Why am I viewing them as if they only look like the things in the Wella? Isn't this the Wella? But despite the fact that it looks so much like the Wella, I can't bring myself to believe it really is. For one thing, the air feels different. It doesn't feel warm and peaceful like the Wella. Well, it does but in a different way, an almost seductive way, as if the air is trying to hide something, to force an illusion on us.

What are you talking about, Peter? I chide myself. *The air is trying to hide something? You're going nuts.*

Maybe I am, but I still can't shake the feeling.

Meila Two leads us down the Wella to the mossy ground below. We easily float down, having lots of practice from before.

"Where are you taking us, Meila?" Emily asks.

Meila Two gives us a sideways look, as if confused by the question. Then she startles, as if remembering. "Oh, I'm taking you to the feast."

She pushes her way through the vines that lead into the cave where we talked to Thaegar. Or at least it looks like that cave.

"She seems a bit odd," says Emily, saying the most sensible thing I've heard her say since she drank from Meila Two's canteen.

I'm about to agree, when Caster speaks. "Maybe it's what happens when infinite time passes," he says. "Anyway, do you smell it?"

"Smell what?" Emily says, losing the usual snarky tone she takes with Caster. Instead, she sounds boisterous.

"Peaches!" Caster says.

I smell the wind, and sure enough, the scent of peaches is in the air. I've never thought of peaches as having a strong scent, but maybe Wella peaches are special.

Meila Two pokes her head out through the vines. Her wide, sleepy eyes look expectant. "Are you coming?"

"Heck yeah! Peaches, here I come!" says Caster, plunging through the vines, and Emily follows him, giggling stupidly.

Ami still won't look at me, but there's a concerned look in her eyes, and she holds her bird more protectively. My eyes fall to the faint dark marks beneath Meila Two's eyes, and they seem now to take on a decidedly sinister look.

I follow after Emily and Caster as my stomach churns with a growing sense of dread.

CHAPTER 62

THE FEAST

The room looks similar to the room where the laganmorfs sat, only instead of a great lantern in the center, there's a silver bowl filled with glowing peaches, and the sides of the room are lined with tables.

Emily and Caster rush upon the silver bowl, grab peaches, and wolf them down greedily. Emily has always been a little spontaneous, as has Caster. Still, there's something about their behavior that seems a little over the top. We just left the Wella in order to save Samjang—and Emily was the one who argued most forcefully for doing so—and now she's acting as if she's at an underage drinking party. Not that I would know what that's like.

I get the feeling the situation is even weirder than it seems, but the air feels so warm and the music in the air is so lovely that it's hard to hold on to the thought. Instead, I find myself watching Emily as she joins the dancing nymphs who move to the song of unseen voices. It seems fitting that she got the water ring, because she moves like water: fluid, smooth, and beautiful.

So beautiful it hurts—I feel as if hands are reaching into my insides, turning them inside out, and twisting them all around. Caster's next to her, dancing stupidly, but she's looking at him with bright eyes. I feel a sickening longing and jealousy churn in my gut.

For the first time tonight, Ami looks at me. It's a brief glance, but it's enough to see the expression on my face. Her eyes follow my gaze, landing on Emily. Her face droops.

"You like her, don't you?" she says quietly.

It takes a few seconds for me to tear my eyes from Emily, and I guess that's all the answer Ami needs. But it's not right. I do like Emily, but I also don't. But then why do I want to like her? And why do I feel so jealous? Is it because I've been holding on to an illusion for so long, an illusion that one day I would ask Emily out—and then my boring, lonely, colorless life would suddenly change, and I'd live happily ever after? I guess I have been nourishing a dream like that. But when did I stop? When did the doubt creep in?

The answer is obvious, though I've been hiding from it. It happened when a girl named Ami Adsila appeared behind the bleachers at a football game and gave Brutus Borgia and his gang what-for.

Then there's the spiritual forms of the rings, which Thaegar talked about. According to that philosophy, water and fire go together, and earth and air go together—a fact that both comforts and angers me.

"That's why you were cold to me in the Wella," she says, doing her best to keep her voice steady.

I want to say, "No, it wasn't that." But it was that. I can't find the right words, and the wrong ones stumble out of me: "What can I say?"

She turns to me and takes a deep breath that shivers a little bit, probably with pain. "The truth," she says simply.

Truth? I wonder. *What is truth? It's so hard to find, and we're so very good at deceiving ourselves.* "I don't know how to tell you the truth." *And I'm afraid of hurting you*, I add silently.

"Well, just try." She manages an encouraging nod, though her eyes glisten sadly.

"I've liked her since I was in middle school, since the very first moment I saw her," I blurt out. My face reddens, and I try to hide it, but it's no use.

"Oh."

"But I never knew her before this trip, adventure, quest, abduction, or whatever you want to call it. I only ever thought about talking with her and being with her. I didn't really know what she was like."

"And now that you know?"

"I ..." My thoughts scatter in a dozen different directions.

She gives me a smile. I'm not sure how she finds it, considering the circumstances, but it makes me feel a little more courageous. "It's okay. Just say what you feel. The truth."

The truth. The words hurt but in an oddly satisfying way. Kind of like the way muscles feel when you fall into bed after exercising. Except the words both hurt more and feel better.

"I really don't know," I say. "There's too much to figure out now. But you know, it doesn't really matter, because she and Caster are destined to be together anyway."

She furrows her brow. "What do you mean?"

I tell her what Thaegar said about fire and water being duals of each other and being connected in a special way, though I leave out the part about earth and air. That would only make things more complicated than they already are and maybe even hurt her more. By the time I finish, I see she's crying.

"What is it?" I ask gently, putting a hand on her shoulder before I can stop myself. There's a deep part of me that wants to comfort her and just wants to see her happy. Maybe it's the hexahedron in me. Who knows?

"Oh," she says, wiping her tears with the back of her hand, half sobbing and half laughing. "It's just that everyone has heard about love triangles, but I guess this is a love square."

"Yeah," I say quietly.

Her words sink into my mind more slowly than usual, which is pretty slow already. By saying there's a love square, she's saying she likes me, which I sort of knew after the way she acted in the Wella. But it's different to hear it aloud, and it both thrills me and hurts me. Why, after all these years of being alone, when I finally have someone who likes me and who's a kind, creative, good person, can I not just accept her? Why do my desires pull me apart?

I find myself wishing I had Cog's compass for my heart to point the way I ought to choose.

I try to focus on the world around me again, which I'm finding harder and harder. The music and the warm air are like a lullaby.

My eyes drift to the feasting tables along the edges of the room. There are many chairs at the tables, and the chairs don't look casually made. Each of them looks unique, as if carved to fit a particular personality. Yet there are too many chairs for the number of nymphs in this Wella.

Something about it bothers me, and I once again get the feeling that the world I think I'm seeing is not what the world looks like at all; rather, my perception is getting manipulated and edited before it gets to consciousness.

"Something's not right here," says Ami, once more thinking exactly the same thought I am.

As she says it, I realize again it's not just my visual perception but my hearing too. For the first time, I wonder where the voices are coming from.

"Who is doing the singing?" I ask, and she looks at me with eyes showing fear and concern.

CHAPTER 63

HOMER'S ADVICE

Meila Two returns, munching absentmindedly on a peach. The marks beneath her eyes seem to grow a shade darker as she swallows the juicy fruit, but maybe it's just my imagination, fueled by a growing sense of not-right-ness.

I walk up to her, determined to have my two questions answered. "Why are there so many empty chairs?"

Meila Two stares up at me, looking sort of the way Goober does after he's nearly finished his bottle of "water." She furrows her brow, as if concentrating takes great effort. "Some of the others have been disappearing," she says at last.

"What do you mean *disappearing*?" asks Ami. Suddenly, her eyes are very alert. I nearly take a step back, surprised to see her be so direct. "You mean they leave the Wella?"

"Well, not exactly," says Meila Two, scratching her head. "We all come together to feast every week, and then …" Her voice trails off, and her eyes find a place beyond the bowl of peaches. "It's a beautiful night, isn't it?"

Ami snaps her fingers, more forceful than I've ever seen her. "And then what?"

"Oh," says Meila Two. "What were we talking about?"

"You said that nymphs have been disappearing and mentioned something about the weekly feast," I say.

"Oh, right." Meila Two nods reflectively. "Well, no one really knows where they go. They come to the feast, but in the morning, they're gone."

"And no one remembers them leaving?" I ask.

She scratches her head. "I guess not. It's difficult to …"

"To what?" I say, moving into her line of sight so she can't get distracted again.

"To remember what happens at the feast. It's like music," she says dreamily. "You just move into it, and then you forget. Come. Let's have some peaches."

I'm not sure if it's a trick of the light, but the dark marks beneath her eyes seem to grow darker again.

She turns back to us. "Come on. Have some peaches. You don't want the others to think you're ungrateful. Those are usually the first ones to disappear." She laughs, and it sounds just like Meila's laugh—almost.

I have the feeling it's not really the sweet voice of a nymph I'm hearing, but something dark, evil, and vast is editing its voice before it can reach my consciousness. However, some part of my brain still knows it is wrong.

"What about the voices?" I say to her. "Who's singing?"

Meila Two only shakes her head. "Eat the peaches." Her voice is no longer sleepy or playful, and a little shiver travels down my spine.

I look at Ami, who's clutching her bird tighter now, and she nods. Slowly, we approach the bowl as I try to work out a way to avoid eating the peaches. It shouldn't be a big deal; they're just peaches. But then why are Emily and Caster acting so wild? And why is Meila Two so insistent?

We're in the center of the room, where the Great Lantern was in the real Wella, and Meila Two pulls two peaches from inside the silver bowl. The bowl glows darkly, seeming to combine both brightness and darkness.

Meila Two extends her hands to us, offering the peaches. Slowly, we take them, and I close my eyes as I hold the peach up to my mouth.

"Go on," Meila Two says.

But I can't eat it, I think. *It's wrong.*

"Do it," says Meila Two, her voice more urgent now.

The darkness in my mind changes, filling with an old man I recognize as Homer from my dreams.

What are you doing here? I thought you were just a character in my dreams, I say to him. He puts a finger to his lips, reaches down, picks up a peach, and wraps it in mud before taking a bite. It occurs to me what to do.

I pretend to drop the peach, and when I pick it up, I take a fistful of earth with it.

Ami looks at me, confused for a moment, and then understanding sparks in her eyes.

I take a bite of the peach, but as I do so, I will the earth to close around it, preventing the juices from spilling into my mouth. Ami does something similar, since her eyes stay clear, and she doesn't run after Emily and Caster to join the whirling nymphs on the mossy ground.

I pretend to cough, placing my hand to my mouth and spitting out the earth-covered peach.

Meila Two doesn't seem to notice, and instead, she looks up at us with a happy but glossy look in her eyes. "Come," she says. "The moment is about to arrive."

"The moment?" Ami and I say in unison.

"Oh yes," she says. "The reason why we dance."

She says the words almost as if she's a marionette, as if something else is saying the words for her. I remember when she said earlier that she has trouble remembering and that the nymphs have been going missing. I get a bad feeling about this so-called moment.

But as the bad feeling comes, the pretty voices around me swell, and I'm filled with a gushing emotion—a desire to take Ami's hand, drag her over to where the nymphs are, and dance with her. I'm just about to act on that impulse when I blink.

In the moment I blink, I see Homer's intense eyes staring straight into mine, scaring me half to death and sending me stumbling backward. But I don't look away—not because I don't want to but because I can't pull myself away from his electrifying gaze, not even by opening my eyes.

Homer grips me by the shoulders and, still staring like a lightning storm into my eyes, speaks three words: "Break the illusion."

CHAPTER 64

DON'T LOOK UP

Then Homer is gone, and I feel a rush of pain from my hands. I look around and realize I've fallen onto the ground. I groan a little and right myself.

"Are you okay?"

I shake the dizziness from my mind and see Ami bent down next to me. Her eyebrows are taut with concern.

"Your hands," she says. "Let me see them."

"They're fine," I say. "Just sting a bit."

But she's unmoved, so, rolling my eyes, I show her my hands.

"You're bleeding!"

I glance at my left hand, and sure enough, a bit of blood is trickling down the side. I wipe it on my robe. I wonder how I can be bleeding if I'm impervious to rock.

This isn't important, I think. *But something else is. But what?*

I've just experienced something different, but it feels distant now, like the way dreams slip away just as you wake up.

"What happened?" asks Ami, breaking through the tangle of my thoughts.

In a flash, Homer and his blazing eyes come back to me.

"I—" I struggle for the right words, but even as I search for them, I feel the vision of Homer and his advice slipping away once more, pulled under by the current of the voices.

"Break the illusion," I say, spitting the words out, desperate to hold on to any part of my vision of Homer.

"What?" asks Ami, furrowing her brow. Her eyes are losing clarity, looking more and more like Meila Two's stupid stare.

"I ..." My eyes settle somewhere just above me, on the giant silver bowl. "The bowl."

"The bowl?" she repeats. Her words seem to come from someplace distant. The singing voices are growing louder, drowning out all other sounds.

"The bowl?" says Meila Two, appearing beside us again. "You want more peaches? You should eat more before the moment!"

"The moment ..." Ami's voice trails off, and she looks toward Emily and Caster. "You want to dance, Peter?"

I feel a crushing weight in my chest. *No, not you*, I think. But another part of me thinks differently—a part that makes my heart pound in my ears and makes me want to take Ami's slim form in my arms, gaze deep into her hazel eyes, and whirl her around with the dancing nymphs. Meila Two smiles, and Ami's about to wander off after her with me in tow, when suddenly, the bird pecks at her hand, drawing blood.

"Ouch!" Ami exclaims. For a moment, she looks with confused pain at the bird, but then her eyes are clear again, and she looks around with growing horror at the swirling figures. Their motions intensify as the unseen voices move toward a crescendo. "The illusion," she says.

315

She hands me the bird and unfastens from her back the wooden staff Ku'ba gave her. Then she approaches the silver bowl.

"What are you doing?" says Meila Two, her voice no longer hazy and confused but sharp and worried. The black spots beneath her eyes are as dark as night.

The voices are nearly to the crescendo, and the dancing nymphs spin faster and faster, with Caster and Emily caught up in their whirlwind. Just before the sound reaches its climax, Ami raises the staff and strikes it into the earth. A wave of air blasts outward, flattening everyone except me. The earth keeps me steady.

The silver bowl falls to the ground and shatters.

Wait a minute, I think to myself. *Silver's not supposed to shatter.*

But I have no more time to question this, because the room begins to make a sequence of horrifying transformations.

For one thing, the nymphs don't look the same as they did just seconds before, all bright and glowing. Instead, they look pale and sickly. Furthermore, there's a bright cord, pulsing grotesquely, attached to each of them almost like an umbilical cord.

My eyes follow the cords back to their source in the center of the room, where the Great Lantern ought to be and where the silver bowl was only minutes ago.

Ami's eyes reach the source at the same time mine do. "What the—"

A giant beating heart wet with blood pulses in the center of the room. Its tentacles stretch out to all the nymphs.

I look between Meila Two and the heart, which she stares at with horrified fascination. She touches the cord that stretches from her neck to the heart and begins to whimper with fear.

316

I realize then that I can hear her voice. The singing has stopped.

But no, it hasn't stopped; it's changed, as if the editing that happened between my ears and my consciousness is no longer happening. Instead, I hear a chorus of gurgling growls coming from—

"Don't look up," says Emily, apparently recovered from her daze.

Caster begins to mutter a reply, but his voice cuts off at the end: "Why would you say—"

I feel an awful fear, as if there's a wolf just behind me, ready to pounce, and there's nothing I can do but turn to face its gleaming jaws.

Slowly, I raise my head, and I suppress a scream as two glowing red eyes look back at me. A smile of feral teeth gleams just above the eyes.

Not for the first time this journey, I feel my pants grow warm and wet.

CHAPTER 65

NO RETREAT

Why can't you be a little manlier? I curse at my bladder, but the thought is quickly consumed by a fresh rush of terror.

I try to move, but for a moment, I'm petrified, which I guess is pretty ironic, considering my name is Peter, and I'm the bearer of the rock ring. If you know Latin, the joke is a lot funnier.

Finally, I get ahold of my body, and I stumble backward, landing on the mossy ground. I stare up and see not just one pallid-faced, sharp-toothed, red-eyed monster hanging from the ceiling and staring down at me but dozens.

A dreadful connection forms in my mind as I think of how the bloodgorger in Galthanius's mansion looked for a brief moment like a nymph and how Meila Two mentioned vaguely that the other nymphs here have been disappearing. What if these bloodgorgers were once nymphs, and somehow, they managed to fool the other nymphs into becoming a willing blood supply, until Ami broke the silver bowl of peaches? Peaches that now look like rotting flesh.

Caster's and Emily's eyes land on the peaches, and they both hurl.

My mind turns back to questioning. *Why does this place look so much like the Wella? Why is there a gigantic heart in the middle of the cave, and why are the nymphs all connected to it?* My mind reels with confusion; the facts refuse to fit together into a sensible picture.

The bloodgorger closest to me loses its leering smile. Its red eyes, glowing like a furnace, receive a sudden rush of air. Then its clawed feet push from the ceiling, propelling it toward me with its feral teeth aimed at my throat.

I brace myself stupidly, as if I'm expecting Brutus to give me a whooping, even though I really ought to be doing something else—like using my power to stop myself from getting brutally murdered.

A second later, I feel the impact of a body crashing into me, and I mentally prepare myself for the sensation of having my throat torn out and my blood drained from my body. But instead, the hands on me are soft, though not exactly gentle. I open my eyes and see Ami. She gives me a "What the heck are you doing?" look and then stands to her feet, whipping her staff around right into the bloodgorger's head.

The wood contacts its skull with a resounding *crack*, and it is flung across the room, propelled along by a gust of wind from Ami's hand.

I push myself to my feet, aided by the earth, which brings me up in one fluid motion.

My head is spinning, with a mass of confused thoughts flying through it at once. *What are Caster and Emily doing? We need to get out of here. What about the nymphs? Can they flee, given that they're attached to a giant beating heart? Regardless, we need to get out of here.*

But as I think the thoughts, the bloodgorgers move to close off the exit. The nymphs have all huddled in the back corner of the room, as far from the bloodgorgers as they can get. Their eyes are filled with fear and horror. They're so pitiable, so small and vulnerable, like little birds fallen out of their mother's nest. What must it feel like to discover that the world you lived in was an illusion designed to mask the ghastly reality that you were all attached to a large heart and were the food source of monsters who once were your sister nymphs?

My thoughts are broken by a blur of motion as one of the bloodgorgers dives for Ami and me.

I ram my fist toward it, and a slab of rock thrusts out of the ground, slamming into the bloodgorger and sending it flying into the far wall.

Emily and Caster join us a moment later, apparently finished puking, and soon jets of flame are flying across the room, followed by blasts of water, which Emily sucks out of the moist earth. But no matter how many times we burn, scorch, pummel, and blast the bloodgorgers, they keep returning, and our position is gradually driven backward toward the huddled and terrified nymphs.

"This isn't working," says Emily. "We're getting pushed back, and we have nowhere to retreat."

"Thank you for saying the obvious," says Caster as a jet of flame darts from his finger, sending a bloodgorger flying backward with its sickly gray skin blackened. "Peter, you don't happen to have the knife on you still, do you?"

The knife. My mind casts back to the blade Galthanius's bloodgorger used to sacrifice victims in order to sap their strength—and the blade that ended its life. With a pang of regret, I remember the fate of the knife.

"I kept it with the supplies on the horses," I say, sending a boulder into the face of a bloodgorger diving for us from the ceiling.

The creature struggles beneath the boulder, trying to push the rock off itself, and Caster's eyes light up.

"New idea," he says. "How much do you guys know about the foreign policy advocated by George F. Kennan?"

CHAPTER 66

CONTAINMENT

"Why do you always have these stupid preambles?" Emily says, sending a jet of water into a bloodgorger about to sink its teeth into Ami. "We're about to get eaten by a bunch of demonic nymphs, and you're talking about American foreign policy? Good lord, man, spit it out!"

"Containment," Caster says. "We can't defeat the bloodgorgers with the tools we have. But"—he claps me on my shoulder—"Peter can bury them, and that should give us time."

"Oh," says Emily. "That's brilliant."

"I know."

"Okay," I say with the plan taking shape in my mind. "So I'll bury them, but I need them to not be moving."

"Got it," the others say in unison.

Emily goes to work, using water to make the bloodgorgers slip; Ami blasts them backward; and Caster uses fire to keep them fixed within a ring of flame just long enough for me to bury them beneath hundreds of pounds of rock.

But as the bloodgorgers see what we're doing, their attacks grow more ferocious, and judging by the combinations of gurgling and insect-like clicking sounds, they're communicating. Instead of launching themselves in one wall of force, which made them easy prey to our attacks, they spread out as much as possible.

I strain every muscle, trying to keep track of the racing gray-skinned shapes. I do everything I can to keep them from reaching our position. But even though I'm connected to the earth, I feel my arms begin to weaken from so much effort.

"Stay strong!" says Emily. "Only four more."

"I'd call it even odds," says Caster, wearing his usual smirk, "but clearly, they're no match for us."

One by one, we finish them off; the others work together to push them to the ground, while I make sure they don't get up.

I crush the last one beneath a pile of boulders, and its thirsty gurgling is silenced by the rocks.

"Nice!" says Caster, clapping me on the back. "Actually, nice job, everyone."

Emily wipes the sweat from her brow and collapses into a seated position on the ground. "Thanks," she says, breathless, "for being so inclusive, Caster."

Ami steadies herself on Caster, probably weak from exertion, as are the rest of us, and despite Caster's attitude, her weight is too much, and he collapses. His head lands just next to Emily, and his hair brushes against her calf. For a moment, their eyes meet, and they exchange an unusual look. She doesn't look at him as if she wants to strangle him, as she normally does. But the gaze lasts for only a moment, and Emily pushes him away.

"Ow," says Caster, adjusting himself. "Little sis, I love you, but you're crushing my leg."

Ami pushes herself off him and smiles sheepishly. "Sorry."

I stare at the three of them, feeling foolishly left out. There's a connection between Ami and Caster because they're like brother and sister, and there's a connection between Emily and Caster, however much they want to pretend there's not, because their elements are duals of each other, two sides of the same coin. But I have no connection to either of them. I'm the dummy who's in love with a girl who can't love him, and I've chased away the girl who might like me back.

I wallow in my self-pity for a few more moments before I remember there are nymphs behind us, all bound to a massive beating heart in the center of the room. I'm about to turn to face them, when I hear a gurgling sound and a scream.

CHAPTER 67

MEILA'S MEMORIES

I spin around and see the nymphs all huddled together in the corner, hugging one another. Their eyes are fixed with horror on something just feet away.

My eyes flash to it, and I nearly puke. A bloodgorger, its gray skin charred and bloodied from our attacks, stands bent over a nymph girl with its fangs in her neck. My heart lurches as I recognize the girl: Meila Two. Her eyes are filled with fear, but it's rapidly fading as her face grows pale as her life drains from her body.

I ram my fist forward toward the bloodgorger, and as I do, the earth reaches forward with a finger sharpened into a deadly point and plunges itself into the bloodgorger's back. The creature stiffens and screams with a mix of gurgling shrieks and hisses, and I match its scream with a shout of fury. I close my fist, and the rock spreads out around the front of the bloodgorger like fingers wrapping around its body, and I throw my fist toward the side, sending the bloodgorger flailing through the air. It slams into the wall before crumpling to the ground.

I leave the stone sword in its body and pile a hill of boulders on top of it for good measure.

Ami and Emily rush past me, running to catch Meila Two before she falls to the ground. Caster comes up behind but doesn't approach. Instead he stares with mild interest while stroking his chin, as if observing an interesting experiment. Behind the cold curiosity, I can see a tenderness in his eyes. I wonder if he uses apathy as a defense to hide something painful.

Emily summons a handful of water and lets it wash over Meila Two's neck, healing the bloody wound.

"Are you okay?" Ami says anxiously, stroking Meila Two's hand. "You're not going to become a ..." She gulps as her voice trails off.

I mentally finish her sentence: *A bloodgorger.*

"It's okay. I won't become like one of them," Meila Two says weakly. "They have to spit their poison into you, and they only do that after they've sucked your blood."

"Wait a minute. How do you know about that?" says Caster. "Before Ami broke the silver bowl, you seemed not to have any idea what was going on here."

Meila Two's cheeks flush red, and she looks down, embarrassed. "I know. I didn't know before because I'd forgotten. But I have my memories back now."

"Your memories?" Emily says.

Meila Two nods and glances back at her sister nymphs. They exchange meaningful looks.

"What do you remember?" asks Emily gently. "How did you all end up in this situation?"

As if to emphasize her words, the giant throbbing heart beats louder in the background, filling the empty silence with an eerie pulsing.

"I'm not sure," says Meila Two.

"I thought you just said you have your memories back," Caster says.

"I do. When the nymphs and laganmorfs fled eastward after their homes were cut down, we were separated from the others." A tear forms in her eye, and she brushes it aside as her lips tremble. "I was separated from my sister."

"Aren't you all sisters?" says Caster.

Meila Two nods. "Yes, in a way, but she was my twin sister. It's very special; there aren't very many of us. We have the same name too."

It occurs to me now why our Meila goes out into the woods to cry, while the other nymphs stay in the Wella, even though they lost their homes too. Meila isn't crying for her home as much as for her lost twin, the nymph she called her sister that night she wept on Ami's shoulder.

"Oh," says Emily. "That's why you don't remember us. You've never met us."

"But that means you've met my sister!" Meila Two's eyes widen.

"Yes," says Emily. "In the Wella."

"You've been to the Wella?" one of the other nymphs cries. "Can you take us there?"

"Hold up," says Caster, raising a hand. "First things first. You still have some explaining to do. What happened after you got separated?"

"We were very scared," Meila Two says. "But we knew the others were going to form the Wella in the forest, so we searched the woods, looking for the lanterns, which would lead us there. We found lanterns." She looks down as her cheeks flush red. "We should have known better, because those lanterns looked wrong if you paid close enough attention. But we were so eager to reunite with our sisters."

The other nymphs nod, as if to say it wasn't Meila Two's fault.

"And the heart?" Caster gestures toward the pulsing red blob in the middle of the cave, and in the quivering light, I have to tighten my gut to keep from puking.

"Oh," says Meila Two, her voice growing small. "It's the Bloodfather."

CHAPTER 68

THE BLOODFATHER

"The what?" I say.

"The bloodgorger's power has a source, and it comes from the Bloodfather. He was summoned by Morin's magicians from the Dark Realm. That's where their magic comes from."

"The Dark Realm?"

Meila Two nods. "You know about the Nine Realms, right?"

I look at the others.

"We've heard about them, but I wouldn't say we know about them," says Caster.

"The Nine Realms were made by All-Father, the Fashioner, along with all time and space at the beginning of things. But soon after, a dark realm was discovered by the protector gods. It wasn't made by the Fashioner. It's not so much a thing as an *unthing*. It's a shadow, an absence of light. But it has a will." Meila Two shivers. "And its will is very evil."

"You mean the Ice Reich?" Caster asks.

"No, no. The Ice Reich is just one of the children of the Dark Realm. Not much is known about the Dark Realm, because it's too hard to find. Some say it's everywhere and nowhere. Morin's magicians summoned the Bloodfather from the Dark Realm and stole some of our sisters to make bloodgorgers to gain immortality for themselves."

"But it didn't work," I say. "Morin died, and Haji the Humble led an army to destroy the sorcerers. Even though she failed, the sorcerers died too when they cursed the land. Right?"

Meila Two's eyes seem to glaze over. She is seemingly lost in memory. But when I follow her gaze, I see she's staring at the bird in Ami's arms. Or maybe not. Maybe it's just a coincidence where her eyes happened to land.

She looks up again. "Some say Morin's still alive, in a deathlike sleep, waiting for the proper time. Our older brothers have a saying: 'Whether he's alive or dead, the evil that men make in life lives on after their death.'"

"Until someone comes around and fixes things," says Caster. He holds his hands together, summoning a ball of flame, and turns to face the Bloodfather.

"No!" Meila Two exclaims as Caster fires the flaming ball at the heart.

I stamp my foot on the ground, and a rock slab bursts up from the earth, absorbing the flame.

"You can't kill him," says Meila Two. "Or you'll kill us too."

Emily's eyes fill with tears. "How do we help you then? How do we get you back to your sister?"

"You can't."

"What do you mean?" Emily says. "We'll do anything."

"Anything that doesn't interfere with our timeline of, you know, saving the world," Caster says.

"Only Haji can free us," says Meila Two. "And only if she has her father's staff, the one that summoned the Bloodfather."

"Why only Haji?" says Caster.

"Because she was there when Morin performed the magic rites, so she has the connection between Miria and the Dark Realm in her heart."

"Has anyone bothered to construct a general theory of magic, from which specific facts can be deduced?" asks Caster. "Or do you only have a collection of stories and heuristics?"

Meila Two looks at Caster blankly and then turns to Emily. "You guys are the Four, aren't you?"

We nod.

"Oh no," she says. "Then something bad must be happening."

Caster laughs. "Our reputation precedes us."

"There is something bad happening," says Emily. "Cog and Samjang were separated by the trickster god, and since their power is weakened, the Ice Reich has been trying to get back into Miria, aided by the fallen gods."

"Oh my," says Meila Two. "Not good. Well, then you must hurry. Don't wait here any longer!"

"But what about you?" asks Ami with her brow drawn.

"Oh my goodness, enough with sentimentality," Caster mutters.

"We'll be okay," says Meila Two. "We can look after ourselves."

"Oh definitely," Caster says. "Like the excellent job you did in figuring out you were prey to the Bloodfather and his bloodgorgers."

Emily elbows him. "Hey, genius, you weren't so hot yourself, Mr. Let's Eat Peaches!"

"Pot calling the kettle black."

Ami squeezes Meila Two's hand. "We'll find Haji and the staff."

Meila Two gives her a little smile. Her eyes glisten with tears. "You can't find Haji. She's too well hidden. But maybe now that the Four have come to the east, she'll come out and find you."

It takes another quarter hour to finish our goodbyes, and I'm feeling sentimental by the end. We make sure to pile a few thousand pounds of boulders on top of the already crushed bloodgorgers, and then we push our way through the vines that cover the mouth of the cave.

My thoughts are a blur as we leave the false Wella. The little nymphs wave goodbye below. I try to make sense of all the things that have happened in the past hours, but my brain refuses to cooperate, fixating on one question: *Who the heck is Homer, and why is he so interested in helping me?*

CHAPTER 69

DESERT SONG

It's sunrise when we finally make it out of the forest after hours of stumbling through unnaturally dark woods with only Caster's hands to light the way.

The morning sun paints the eastern sky purple and red above the vast plains of dry, cracked earth before us. I wonder how the terrain can go so quickly from lush forest to parched desert, but this probably shouldn't be that surprising after encountering phantom men, zombie dogs, and a gigantic beating heart bound to nymphs to provide a blood source for corrupted nymphs, also known as bloodgorgers, summoned from a mysterious Dark Realm as part of an evil old king's immortality scheme.

I shake my head. Life was simpler a week or so ago, when there was only Brutus's bullying to worry about and when the only real pain was the throbbing ache for Emily to pay attention to me.

A week or so ago. How long has it been exactly? I pose the question to the group.

Caster stares at the horizon. "We entered the Wella on the ninth day. If time really doesn't pass while you're in there, then our count begins again when we leave the lantern-strewn path. It's sunrise now, which means day nine is definitely over. So best-case scenario, it's day ten. Worst-case scenario, a whole lot more time has passed, we won't make it to Samjang by day seventeen, and we all get eaten by the Ice Reich."

"Well, that's cheery," says Emily. "Let's assume there's still something called hope."

I nod. "Agreed."

"Agreed," Ami says quietly.

"Well then, we have quorum," says Emily. "All in favor of banishing the bearer of bad juju beans into the wilderness, say aye!"

"Okay! I get your point," huffs Caster.

"Don't worry; we're all going into the wilderness together, Bad Juju Beans."

"Stop calling me that," Caster groans.

The next few days are miserable in certain ways. We make the mistake of trying to walk through this desert during daytime, but by noon, it's unbearable. Caster seems to enjoy it. He must like the sensation of melting.

I form a stone house out of the earth and sink it into the ground, so it's as if we're in a basement. Emily manages to draw some water from the earth after severe effort, and that keeps us, and Ami's bird, from dying of heat and thirst. We wait till nighttime, trying our best to sleep during the day, and then we set out, shivering, through the black landscape.

The nights are not entirely miserable, because for the first time, we really start to get along, not just as individuals but as a group. I'm not sure how it happens exactly. Maybe it's just that since there's not constant danger, we finally have a chance to talk and be normal teenagers. But I think it also has to do with the stories we tell each other.

Emily tells the story of how she got to Miria, which everyone already knows except for me, since they all got here before I did. It turns out to be kind of boring, especially compared to Ami and Caster's story, which involved lightning, exploding cars, and a voice in the flames. Emily was swimming up in one of the mountain lakes—I'm not sure why she'd want to, because they're still kind of cold this time of year—when she saw something glinting toward the bottom. She swam down to investigate, and when she touched the object, she found it was a ring. The ring wrapped itself around her finger. The water suddenly turned freezing cold, and when she swam to the surface, she was no longer looking at the familiar lake but at an arctic sea with Cog's palace behind her.

Everyone shares a story. Some of the stories are ridiculous, like the time Ami blew a bubblegum bubble so big that when it popped, it swallowed her face, or the time Caster's parents worried he was using his phone to visit naughty sites during the night and put a camera in his room, only to discover he was watching MIT lectures. His story isn't that funny, but the way Emily says, "Nerd!" afterward is.

Usually when people are sharing stories, I find myself sitting quietly on the sidelines, trying to laugh at the appropriate places but never getting any funny comments in and definitely never sharing any cool stories myself. But this time, even I get to tell a story. It's about the time Goober bought mercaptans—the stuff that makes skunks stink—and sprayed it all over Brutus's and his buddies' backpacks. The story particularly impresses Caster, probably because the prank involved a little chemistry, and he is much friendlier to me for the rest of the day.

But it's not so much the silly stories that draw us together; it's the stories about our families, because in a certain way, they're really the same story played out in different contexts.

My mom is an Italian Jew, and my dad is a half-German, half-English professor of the classics, focusing on the Greek classics. In my family, Jew and Greek came together, you could say. In Caster's family, it was an Indian woman and a Pakistani man. In Emily's family, it was a Japanese man and a Chinese woman. Ami's a Cherokee and an American, part of the group whose home was taken and part of the group who took her home. Then there's the less dramatic fact that two of us are from Mormont, and two of us are from Blackstone, rival schools.

When we finish telling our family stories, it's Caster, surprisingly, who makes a comment that stirs my heart. It's kind of cheesy, but maybe the fact that we too easily pass things off as cheesy is part of the problem with our world.

"I take back what I said earlier—that if Cog wanted unity, he shouldn't have picked Americans," Caster says. "Look at us. Our families are stitched together out of fabrics that spent the last hundred or more years hating each other—kind of like Romeo and Juliet but without the suicide. So maybe Cog was right. Where else in the world can you find a melting pot this big, with all the ingredients mixing together to make one great soup while still preserving some of their distinctive flavors?"

We all grow quiet, until Emily breaks the silence. "Who knew you could be such a poet, my mathematical little nerd friend?"

We all laugh—even Caster.

By the time we stop for the morning on the third day, the parched earth has turned to sand. When we set out again in the evening, the sand grows thicker, until we're trudging up and down hills kind of like the Great Sand Dunes. Sometime after midnight, storm clouds appear overhead, and the desert seems to rise in the distance into a great wall.

I'm oblivious, but Caster, who's been to the Sahara, recognizes it as a sandstorm. I dig out the sand from around us and use the thick earth below to form a makeshift house of strong walls. The sandstorm lasts unexpectedly long and is soon followed by a thunderstorm, with lightning exploding overhead and rain gushing down.

As we wait out the fierce weather, Emily sings songs everyone has grown sick of listening to, because the school bus doesn't have any other songs to play. But in a place so different and far from home, it feels good to sing some of those stupid songs while holding hands with friends. It feels so good that my heart begins to soften and then melt—just like the roof of my makeshift house.

That's when all of us get thoroughly soaked.

CHAPTER 70

OVER HILL

Emily is enthusiastic in the hours following the storm. Having her shoes and pants soaked is, to her, I guess, a thrilling experience since she has the water ring. The rest of us are glad when the sun comes out.

I wake up on the evening of the fourteenth day to the sound of birdsong, which strikes me as more than a little odd, since I haven't seen a living thing since we entered this godforsaken desert.

I feel my way along the stone divider between the boys' and girls' sections of the hut until I come to the wall, and then I widen the opening so I can get out. Ami has her back against the side of the hut, watching the sunset, and beside her is the weird bird that saved her life, singing its heart out.

It's a touching sight so beautiful I'm afraid to say anything, for fear of ruining it. So I just watch as my heart swells with the beauty of the desert evening. The forest we came from has long since disappeared beyond the horizon, and even the mountain is gone—vanished behind the vast rolling hills of sand.

"You want to watch the sunset with me?" asks Ami.

Her voice startles me, nearly giving me a heart attack.

"H-how did you know I'm here?"

She looks back and smiles amusedly. "Did you forget I have the wind ring? I can feel you in the air."

"Oh, right." I mumble something about not being fully awake yet and then stumble over to her and take a seat to her left. The bird sits between us, still singing.

There's a coherence to its melodies, which makes me wonder how intelligent it is. I'm not much of a bird lover, but all the birds I've heard don't really sing. Their sounds are more like high-pitched chattering—nothing like the way humans sing, weaving a complex quilt of patterns that voyage outward before returning home. But this bird's songs sound exactly like that—not like a human voice but like the way humans sing.

Ami hands me a piece of the bread she's eating, one of the last loaves Meila gave us. I take it and nibble on it silently.

I wait to see if Ami wants to ask me anything, but after a few minutes of quiet, I begin to wonder why she asked me over. Then I get it. It's sort of obvious, but it's easily forgotten in my home world, with its cars, smartphones, and blinking lights that make it hard to see the stars: sometimes the best conversations are had between two people who enjoy each other's company, the silence of nature, and the soft sounds of birdsong. I feel a closeness to Ami, and a little voice inside me asks what it would be like if I held her hand, which seems pretty stupid. *Gee, I know I told you a few days ago that I've been obsessed with that other girl as long as I've been alive practically, but can I hold your hand?*

I don't fight with the voice for long, because Caster and Emily soon wake up, and the quiet vanishes. The bird stops singing, and in a few minutes, we're back on the road, trudging over miles of dry earth, as the red sun sinks behind us, and the moon begins to shine overhead.

I carry the memory of the few quiet moments with Ami with me as we march along through the night. My thoughts and emotions are churning. How do I feel about her really?

Part of me wants to cling desperately to Emily and to all the days and nights I spent pining for her just to notice me and fantasizing about finding the courage to ask her out. Sometimes, I'd dream she'd respond with one of her gorgeous, bright-eyed smiles, and we'd ride off into the sunset. Part of me really wants that still. But another part of me whispers, *Why not just let the elements lead you?* If Thaegar is right, then there is meant to be a special connection between Ami and me and between Caster and Emily.

Between Caster and Emily. The words stir a new emotion: jealousy. Jealousy for Caster, who's smarter, wittier, and richer. He's also loads more confident and attractive than I am—poor little Peter, whose only friend is the weirdest kid in school, who everyone calls Goober.

But no, I tell myself. *That's not true anymore. Ami, Emily, and even Caster are my friends. And if we somehow make it back to Gaia, there's no way we'll just go back to our schools and forget about this. We'll be friends for life—if we don't die first or end up suffering a fate worse than death, whatever that means, at the hands of the Ice Reich. But even if that does happen, we are friends.*

Friends. The word makes me stick my chest out a little more as a warm balloon seems to inflate inside me. For the first time on this trip, I feel like maybe I can be the Rock, the leader Cog and Thaegar talked about.

Maybe.

A voice tears through my thoughts with two simple words spoken in a confused tone: "What the—"

I look up, and my eyes focus on Caster, who's standing at the crest of the sand hill we're climbing.

"What is it?" I ask.

This time, it's not Caster who speaks but Emily. "Water."

CHAPTER 71

THE RETURN

As soon as Emily says, "Water," we all make a mad break forward, rushing past Caster and down the sloping sands to the flat shore.

Sure enough, dark waters, illumined by gentle moonlight, swallow up the horizon. But what's strange about the sight is not the water. Thaegar told us we would come to a lake; we knew that. What's strange about the sight is the boat that waits at the water's edge, bobbling gently with the waves. Its stern is anchored to the shore by a stake and a rope.

I glance at Ami, whose brow is furrowed just like mine, and we run up to the boat with Caster and Emily close behind.

The boat contains two oars, four loaves of bread, and four leather sacks marked, "H_2O (not XYZ)," which I guess means they contain water. Pinned to the side of the boat is a note, which Ami takes.

We all gather around her.

"What's it say?" Emily asks, brushing the gleam of sweat off her brow.

"Step aside," says Caster. "You'll need the spyglass."

Ami shakes her head. "It's in English."

My heart jumps and begins to pulse faster. This situation is getting stranger by the second. Why is there a boat waiting for us at the edge of the lake Thaegar told us to cross? Why is there bread and water in it? And why are the note and the labels on the sacks written in English?

I stare over Ami's shoulder at the note as she reads it aloud:

Dear Four,

Here's a boat. Do not look into the water, and do not disturb it except with the blessed oars.

Cheers,
Homer

Homer. My skin grows gooseflesh, and my gut tightens. *You again!* I think to myself with my mind reeling. *How is it you?* I cover my mouth, as I realize I've said the words aloud.

Caster looks at me warily. "What do you mean 'You again'?"

"Nothing," I say quickly.

Emily fixes me with a skeptical stare. "Uh-huh."

"Don't make this into another Five incident," Caster says, referencing the time I neglected to tell them about the existence of a potentially malevolent fifth ring bearer.

I think back to my weird dreams. Despite the trust that's grown among us in the past few days, I'm not sure I'm ready to tell them, mainly because—

"I don't know if I can explain it," I say.

343

"Well, you can start by trying," says Caster pointedly. "If you make mistakes, it's fine. Rapid iteration is the key to improvement."

Emily elbows him. "Be nice."

"It's fine," I say. A few days ago, I would have been annoyed, but now I think I get it. It's just Caster's way of talking. He's not doing it to be a jerk or sound pretentious; it's just the way his mind works. And after seeing him get a little teary as we told one another stories, I know he cares. At least a little.

I scratch my chin, trying to find the way to begin. "So I've been having dreams and hearing voices."

"Oh boy," Caster mutters. "That's a good start."

"Do you want to hear his explanation or not?" Emily says.

"Hey, you're interrupting him. Let him speak," says Caster.

Emily raises a fist to smack him, and he cowers and jumps away. She follows after him, shouting, "Come here!"

I look at Ami, who smiles sympathetically.

"I'm listening," she says softly.

"So am I!" Caster shouts. "Ow! Tickling isn't fair!" He hides behind Ami, using her as a body shield, and Emily circles him, looking like a panther stalking its prey.

"Are you sure?" I ask.

"Continue!" Emily says. "My brain is highly specialized at paying attention to important things while punishing dweebs!"

"Go on," says Ami encouragingly.

"Right," I say. "Well, I've been having these dreams—not just dreams. Sometimes they happen during the day, like when we were in the false Wella. A man dressed like a shepherd appears and gives me advice or riddles. And—" I stop suddenly as I feel a chill travel up my spine. I look and see that Ami feels it too.

Emily and Caster stop their antics and focus on me with concerned expressions.

"Peter," says Emily, her voice fighting to stay calm, "why do you look so scared?"

"He's back," Ami says.

"Who's back?" Caster asks.

I gulp, forcing myself to say the word: "Five."

CHAPTER 72

THE DISTURBANCE

"Get in the boat!" Emily screams.

"Are you sure?" Caster asks, looking fearfully out at the vast waters.

She spins to face him, and her eyes are wild. "You wanna meet Five? We don't have time for this, Caster Kshatriya-Wick! We have three days left before the Ice Reich returns, a.k.a. big trouble, a.k.a. we fail the mission, a.k.a. a fate worse than death for the Nine Realms!"

"Okay, fair point."

"So get in the boat! A.k.a. now!"

"That's not what *a.k.a.* means," mutters Caster, but he does as she says, and Ami and I pile in after him.

With a wave of my hand, I thrust the stake keeping the boat anchored to shore out of the ground and give the boat a nudge. Emily does the rest; her face is a mask of concentration as she coaxes the water to propel us along.

My heart races fast enough to give a hummingbird's wings a run for their money. I lose connection to Five's movements as soon as the boat leaves the shoreline, but Ami wears her emotion on her face. That amplifies my fear, because I can't tell where he is, only that he's getting closer fast. The lack of control kills me.

It must be killing Caster too, because he urges Emily to drive us faster, even though we're speeding across the water like a motor-powered boat. She glares at him but says nothing; all her concentration is focused on quickly putting as much distance between us and Five as possible.

Part of me wonders whether we should be fleeing Five. I recall the conversation I had with Thaegar about the possibility of not just Four becoming One but Five becoming One. What if he's a friend? I quickly dismiss the thought as I remember the visceral feelings of terror, frustration, and anger that rippled through the earth as he approached. A friend would feel friendlier.

Ami calms down as the minutes pass. Five must be falling farther behind. After about fifteen minutes, Emily collapses and slumps down against the seat. Caster reaches out and catches her head before it cracks against the beam and gently sets it down against the side of the boat. He wears a tender expression, and for a moment, the usual amused-smirk expression in his eyes melts, betraying a look of care—and longing.

I feel a surge of frustration, sadness, and anger roiling inside me, because part of me wants Emily desperately and hates that the stupid rings have made that both possible by bringing us together and impossible by tying me to the earth and Emily to the sea—kind of like Will Turner and Elizabeth Swann in *Pirates of the Caribbean*, except with the genders swapped. And I'm not as attractive as Orlando Bloom or Keira Knightly. I try to rip the ring off my finger, but however hard I tug, it won't budge.

Ami looks at me with concern spreading across her face. "You okay?"

I look past her toward the stars shining brightly in the night sky. The waters of the lake sparkle darkly beside the boat, and I feel a strange urge to dash toward the side of the boat and gaze into the depths.

No. I shake the desire from my mind, and my eyes find Ami's forehead but not her eyes. "I'm all right. Just, erm, testing to make sure it wouldn't come off."

"Makes sense," says Caster, giving me a canny look. "Definitely makes sense. Anyway, we need to keep moving." He nods toward the row nearest me. "You wanna take the left side, and I'll take the right?"

I nod wearily. "Okay."

"What about me?" Ami asks.

Caster smiles and puts a hand on her shoulder. "You can be the coxswain."

"Okie!" Ami says happily, and she moves toward the front of the boat. "Come along."

It takes me a second to realize she's talking to her bird, which promptly hobbles along after her and comes to rest at the front of the boat with its chest sticking out proudly. I guess it's been getting better, though I'm not sure exactly what it's been getting better from, why it's been following us, or why it came to us in the first place. It does seem like more than coincidence that it just happened to get hit by an arrow that would have hit Ami. That's strange behavior for a bird. Is it a messenger bird, maybe sent by Cog as protection? Or is something else entirely going on?

Caster and I begin to row as Ami enthusiastically calls out the rhythm. It's the most I've ever heard her speak at one time, and I find it strangely soothing, even as my muscles burn from the constant effort. I like her voice. It's like oatmeal with brown sugar: warm and sweet.

When morning comes, Emily is still asleep, and my arms feel as if they're about to fall off my body. I notice with satisfaction that Caster too is rubbing his arms, looking as thoroughly in pain as I am. Meanwhile, Ami's head bobs up and down as she starts to fall asleep and then startles.

Caster yawns and slumps against the side of the boat. "So, Peter, what do you think is down there?" He gestures toward the water.

I shrug. "I don't know. And to be honest, I don't really want to find out."

Caster raises an eyebrow. "Not even a little?"

"Not even a little."

He sighs. "That's too bad, because I do." He scratches his chin. "Can I borrow your compass?"

I look at him warily but hand it over. "What do you want it for?"

"It has a mirror," he says simply.

I stare at him stupidly for a moment, and then I get it. An old Greek story my dad once told me comes back to me. The hero Perseus supposedly slew the monster Medusa, who would turn people to stone if they looked directly into her eyes, by using a polished shield as a mirror. But who's to say that whatever is beneath the lake works the same way as Medusa? How can he be so reckless?

He pops open the cap of the compass and holds it out over the lake, ready to look through the mirror. I dive for the compass, trying to grab it back from him.

Instead, I knock it out of his hand, and with a plopping sound, it sinks into the lake.

Caster looks at me, surprised and then angry, pointing a flaming finger at me. "You bozo!"

"You're the bozo!" I shout back. "You lost my compass, and you could have gotten us killed!"

"And you still might!" he says. "Did you forget the rest of Homer's warning? Don't disturb the lake, except with the sacred oars. I'm pretty sure your compass isn't a sacred oar."

I slump back down against the side of the boat, folding my arms unhappily. "Whatever," I mutter under my breath. "It was just a stupid compass—a compass that always pointed the way we needed to go."

Caster slumps against the side of the boat too. His eyes are fixed out toward the horizon instead of toward the bottom of the boat, as mine are. A few moments of silence pass, and then he startles, pushing himself upward and staring with wide eyes at the sky.

"What is it now?" I mutter peevishly.

"Look!"

I roll my eyes and turn my head toward the direction of Caster's pointed finger, and my eyes bulge. At the same time, a wave lifts the boat high before setting it down with a violent splash.

"Just a compass," Caster says, shaking his head.

CHAPTER 73

THE STORM

"That can't be a natural storm," I say, gazing at the horizon, which is now being enveloped by a black cloud unfurling like smoke across the sky.

Lightning crackles in the darkness, and thunder breaks through the air. A wind has begun to blow, and the waters have started to churn angrily. Our boat bobs up and down, frail upon the monstrous waves.

"Oh my gosh," says Caster, holding his head. "Could this get any worse?"

"Don't say that!" I say fiercely as a sequence of bad memories smack into me like train cars one after the other. As long as I live, I swear I will never use those words again.

"What do we do?" Caster looks at me strangely, fearful and confused.

It saps the energy from me to see him like this. He's usually the confident one, the one with the plan, the one who looks unfazed by whatever nonsense the world throws at him.

I rack my brain, which is growing more frantic and confused by the second—rather like the world around me—and as I stand there stupidly, a gust of wind nearly knocks me into the water. I manage to throw myself into the boat, knocking my head against a wooden plank. When I look up with my head throbbing, I'm staring at Emily's sleeping form.

Something about a few helpless individuals sitting in a boat in the middle of a lake, dependent on someone—who happens to be sleeping during a storm—to calm the wind and the waves, sounds vaguely familiar.

I hit my forehead as realization dawns on me and then cry out in pain. *You idiot. You slapped your fist-sized bruise!* I curse at myself. *No, don't let that get you down; you're still a genius! Emily can control the water! It'll be all right.*

I crawl up beside her, keeping myself as flat as possible, as thunder pounds my eardrums like artillery, and the boat rises up and crashes down on waves so tall I feel sick when thinking of it. They're definitely taller than the rolling hills of sand we crossed on land. I tighten my gut, trying to keep from puking, and begin shaking Emily, trying to get her awake.

"Emily!" I shout as water sprays over the side of the boat, making me blink fiercely. I grab her arms, trying desperately to jolt her awake. "Emily!"

Caster, meanwhile, has curled into a ball and is rocking back and forth, holding himself and whispering softly, "No, no, no, not again."

"Great," I say. "Just what we need."

I get back to trying to shake Emily awake, but she doesn't respond. I feel for a pulse. The skin of her throat is warm and soft to the touch, and beneath it is a calm beat. Steady and slow.

"Oh, come on! How can you sleep through this?"

Thunder erupts overhead, and the boat crashes into an ascending wave, which sends a spray of water across the boat, thoroughly drenching everyone and whatever supplies we have left, though wet clothes and soggy bread are the least of my concerns. The bigger concern, besides the possibility of our boat getting overturned, is the possibility of our boat sinking. It's rapidly filling with water. Our boat descends on the wave, and I hold on to the edge of the boat. My knuckles turn white as we race down the unholy roller coaster. It ends in another splash of spray that adds more water to the boat, which is now barely sitting above the waves.

Caster is still whimpering in the side of the boat, curled up like a scared two-year-old; Emily is asleep; and Ami is looking fearfully ahead, clutching her bird.

I cup my hands and begin to dig at the water, desperately trying to flush it out of the boat, but with every rock of the boat and splash of the waves, more water enters—much more than I can hope to empty with my pathetically sized hands. As the boat lurches again, with the edges dangerously close to water level, I turn to the side of the boat and hurl, shutting my eyes against the salty spray and against the possibility of setting something even worse in motion by looking into the lake. Things can always get worse.

I begin splashing the water out of the boat again, but the situation is hopeless. I look up at Caster and plead with him, but he won't meet my eyes. He's still balled up and rocking softly; his panic only adds to the rising fear in my chest, which threatens to crush me before the water gets a chance to drown me.

I look at Ami, who sits pressed against the bow, clutching the soaked bird. Her eyes are wide, blinking back terror. Lightning lights up the pitch darkness of the clouds, and thunder explodes so close and powerful it makes my ears ring. I look deep into her eyes, pleading with her to help before it's too late.

CHAPTER 74

THE DANCE

"Please," I mouth to her, pouring all my desperation into that single word—all the hope I have of making it home; of seeing Dr. Elsavier and my mom and dad again; of saving my world, Miria, and the other realms from the clutches of the Ice Reich; and of living past high school, even if I don't make it into any decent college and have to work at McDonald's for the rest of my life.

I just want to live, because being around Ami, Emily, and even Caster has made my life worth living; it's given me a glimpse of how meaningful life can be when you have friends who care about you and want you to succeed. Real friends. Not storybook friends like Achilles and Odysseus and not idiots who can't get past noon without drinking half a bottle of vodka, who think that's funny, and who tell you to lower your expectations and not to try, because you might fail, and that might hurt.

The nagging voice that has been trying to get me to call upon the All-Father these past days once again comes back to me. As the boat is thrown from wave to wave, sinking deeper with every splash that breaks upon its fragile sides, I give in. I close my eyes and pray. *All-Father, Fashioner, Gomdan, whoever you are, please help us.*

Nothing.

Just as I expected. I open my eyes and meet Ami's stare, perhaps for the final time.

Then I feel a tingling in my heart, which flows outward and burrows into my bones, creating sensations where I did not know I could feel sensation. For a moment, I think it's only my private weird feelings, and then I feel a presence and realize it's not just me. I look into Ami's eyes and know she's feeling the same thing I'm feeling, and from that place deep in my bones, she feels all the hopes I have, and those hopes rebound on me with hopes of hers.

I feel her hope of making it into veterinarian school and one day working with animals. Of seeing her grandparents again, roaming their gardens, and listening to their old stories. Of going for ice cream with Caster like they used to do on summer nights when the stars were out and the fireflies were buzzing. I feel other hopes, ones that make my heart twist inside because I want to make those hopes my hopes but can't yet accept them: hopes of our being best friends and maybe something more.

My mind reels, unable to understand how I know all these things, but I do know them—I can feel them as deeply as I can feel my own heartbeat, my hands against the soaked wood, and the thunder in my ears. Ami's eyes, filling up the world in front of me, are no longer afraid but calm, certain, and determined.

Ami stands, somehow maintaining perfect poise even as the boat rocks and sways, swelling up and down on tremendous waves. I stare at her with an awe that only increases as a sequence of amazing and impossible events unfold.

She holds out her hand, and her staff leaps toward it, propelled by a gust of wind. I can see her ring now for the first time, and it crackles with power; electric sparks dance around her finger. She strikes the staff against the boat, emptying in a single moment the water I couldn't begin to empty with all my effort. Then she begins to dance. Her staff, in fluid motion, is like an extension of her body. The bird begins to move with her, circling overhead at first and then diving through the winds she propagates outward from her beaded staff.

The winds change, no longer beating angrily against the boat, and the waters too begin to calm. Emily awakens, Caster uncurls from his ball, and we all watch in wonder as Ami's dance calms the wind and waves. As the dark clouds vanish into the horizon, Ami's motions slow, and her eyes begin to glaze over.

A moment later, she collapses against my chest. My arms fold around her automatically, naturally, and stay there for a moment, warm and peaceful, until I realize Caster and Emily are both staring at me.

CHAPTER 75

MIST

I let go and set Ami down, feeling foolish. My cheeks burn red hot.

"What?" I say as Caster's and Emily's gazes remain fixed.

Emily slowly raises a finger, and I turn, following her line of sight, and my mouth drops open as I take in the view. I also relax as I realize they weren't staring at me, which means I have less explaining to do.

A hundred yards away or so, great stone pillars rise up out of the lake, carved with a harsh, beautiful script I have never seen before, not even in Miria. A fog hovers about the columns, which seem to go on forever into the misty distance.

"Spooky," says Caster. He shakes his head and looks at Emily. "Fine timing, waking up after the storm."

She looks at him indignantly. "I'm surprised you managed to cough the words out amid all the thumb-sucking you've been doing."

"You!" Caster waves a finger at her face, and she waves one back, muttering what sound like Chinese and Japanese curses under her breath at him.

Caster turns to me. "Peter, judge between us. Which of us is right?" He's smiling like a tiger, with flames crackling along his fingers—the usual Caster look but not. There's something off, as if he's trying to hide his real feelings.

Emily meanwhile gestures toward the water and smiles sweetly. "Remember, dear Peter, we're in a lake."

I gulp and look at Ami for support, but she's still asleep. "You're both right," I say.

"But I'm more right," Emily says confidently.

"That doesn't make sense," Caster retorts. "Rightness is a discrete quantity."

"Which proves you are not the least bit right, because you're anything but discreet."

Caster stares at her, open-mouthed. "Did you just make a pun?" He starts to slow clap. "I'm so proud of you. Ow! Stop hitting me where you've already hitted me before!"

"Hitted!" Emily slaps her leg, laughing. "Tongue-tied, Caster, old boy?"

Here we go again, I think. But then Caster's expression changes; the humor he has been wearing only thinly falls from his face.

"It's not funny," he says.

Emily looks about to retort, but she sees how serious he is, and her eyebrows bunch together in concern. "What's wrong?"

Caster crosses his arms and looks as if he wants to contract into himself. "It's nothing," he mutters. But as he looks out at the horizon, his eyes glisten with tears.

"Nothing?" Emily repeats gently, placing a hand on his.

"I hate storms. They took her from me."

"Her? Who did they take?" Emily's voice is soft and sweet as she caresses his hand. It occurs to me that among all the other things she could be when she grows up, she could be a great therapist, the kind who makes patients feel she really cares.

Caster rubs his eyes, brushing back tears. "My sister."

"Oh, Caster." Emily's face holds the most compassionate look I've ever seen. "I'm so sorry." More than compassionate, she seems half mortified, probably for the joke about thumb-sucking. But her feelings don't linger on her. She seems more concerned about Caster than about herself.

She pulls him into a hug, and he sobs on her shoulder. She looks at me, motions toward Caster, and mouths, "Join me." Awkwardly, I put an arm around Caster, patting his shoulder, and Emily and I stay beside him as he tells the tragic story. He and his sister went out on a lake, when a big storm came, overturning their boat. Her life vest came off for some reason, and they found her body the next day, after it was much too late. I now understand his particular affection for Ami, the friend he calls his younger sister. I wonder if she reminds him of the sister he lost.

The group hug lasts awhile longer, until I begin to feel sore from maintaining the same position. I rest against the side of the boat.

Caster sniffles and makes some gross sound with his mouth, and Emily wrinkles her brow. "Caster, did you just get your snot on my back?"

"Maybe," he says sheepishly, laughing the way a child laughs after crying a lot.

She rolls her eyes. "That's so gross. If this were any other time …"

"If this were any other time?" he says.

"I'd tickle you."

"Well," he says, "I'd say after waiting a few seconds, it is another time."

He begins to tickle her, and Emily yelps. "Ah! This is how you repay my hugs?"

And just like that, Caster and Emily have gone back to their usual selves.

I turn to Ami, who's just woken up. "Feeling okay?" I ask.

She nods and yawns, petting the bird nestled between her arm and chest. "I think so. I didn't know I could do that."

"I didn't know you could either. That was amazing. You were amazing."

She looks at me questioningly, as if trying to figure out whether there's another meaning to my words. Half my body wants there to be another meaning, and half doesn't. I just smile bashfully and look down.

She inches closer, and her arm grazes my leg. "What happened earlier?" she asks quietly. "My bones were shaking."

I think of the fierce, wild emotions I felt burrowing down into my bones, extending out into Ami, and then pouring back into me, coming from her bones. But now that I'm not feeling those sensations, it sounds ridiculous to say. I laugh.

She looks at me with her brow furrowed. "What's funny?"

I glance at Caster and Emily, who are still bickering. "Nothing," I say between giggles, the sort of giggles that only awkward and sleep-deprived teenage boys can have. "Just, it sounds really funny."

She strokes her chin. "My bones were shaking," she repeats, as if feeling the words in her mouth. Then she too begins to laugh.

When the laughter dies, Emily and Caster are still fighting, and I decide to ask Ami what she meant when she said her childhood was happy until things changed—an answer she never got to give, because the quarreling Kar-dun interrupted her.

"It's a long story," she says, which I feel is an excuse people give when they don't want to tell you about something.

"Oh," I say with my shoulders sagging. "That's okay. I don't want to press."

"Are you really interested?" She raises her eyebrows expectantly.

"Yeah, of course I'm interested in you. I mean your story. I mean, I'm interested."

She shoots me a funny look, which makes my stomach do a backflip, and I'm not sure why. I didn't give it permission to do backflips, but stomachs and emotions have a way of doing their thing and getting you to go along with it.

"Well," she says, "my grandma died, and we had to sell the farm and move into the city. It was okay, I guess. I got to meet Caster, who's always been nice to me. But a lot of the girls—I don't know. I think they don't like me. They tease me and pull my hair."

I furrow my brow as anger surges in my blood, and my fists ball instinctively. "Why would anyone bully you?" I refrain from adding, "I'll kill the bastards," because I feel that wouldn't be appropriate, as it's not super sympathetic, and because her bullies are girls, not boys born out of wedlock—bastards, that is.

"I'm different, Peter," she says. "I'm not normal."

I want to say, "So what?" *Why should people be bullied just because they're different, especially if they're as sweet, kind, smart, and funny as Ami?* But naturally, the words that come out of my mouth aren't as eloquent: "Normal is boring."

She raises an eyebrow at me and then laughs. "I suppose it is. I guess that's why Caster and Emily are so interesting."

I glance over at the two of them, who are still at each other's throat, and laugh, joining in with Ami.

Our moment of laughter, however, is short-lived, as Caster and Emily finally come out of their little world.

"What are you two snickering about?" asks Caster. "You think it's funny to see your parents fight?"

Emily nods in automatic agreement and then stops, turning to him. "What? What is wrong with your head, Caster?"

"I think you mean Dad," he says, grinning.

"Um, no," says Emily. "You're more the delinquent son or the weird uncle. If anyone's the dad in the group, it's Peter."

"Thanks," I say awkwardly.

Emily winks. "You betcha."

"Are you kidding me? I'm like a factor of twenty times more mature than Peter."

"The fact that you'd say that proves my point," Emily says contemptuously.

"Oh, fine. Then who do you think you are in the family?" says Caster.

"The cool older sister, obviously."

Caster smirks, and so does Ami.

"You're more like the grandma from *Hoodwinked*, the one who goes skiing down a mountain at ninety-five," Ami says, laughing.

Everyone suddenly grows silent and looks at Ami with surprise before bursting into laughter.

"I'm not sure where that came from, but I'll take it, I guess," says Emily. She shivers suddenly and hugs herself. "Does anyone else feel like it's a bit nippy out?"

"No," says Caster. "But it does feel a little cold." He stares intently at the strange markings on the stone pillars, which we're passing now. "We're nearing the end of the Silver Lake that Thaegar talked about. Which means ahead must be—"

"The Forgotten Caves," I say.

As I say the words, Ami's bird perks up, though I can't tell if it's with fear or interest. Or perhaps it's only a coincidence. Maybe it can sense some danger in the air that we cannot, the way birds can sense storms.

"Do you think they're the same caves Meila's twin sister talked about?" Emily asks.

I'm about to shrug, but Ami speaks resolutely. "They are."

Emily furrows her brow, as Caster and I do. "How can you be so sure?"

"I just can feel it," she says.

"You haven't been here before without us, have you?" Caster asks jokingly.

Ami shakes her head. Her face is still serious. "No." She taps her staff. "But I think it has."

The words hang in the air with the thick mist, and none of us reply for a moment. The silence is broken by a thump as the boat strikes something hard, sending the back of my head smacking into the bow.

CHAPTER 76

A VANISHING CHOICE

"Ow," I moan, rubbing the back of my head.

You okay? Ami asks with her eyes.

I nod and turn to Emily. "Did you steer us into a pillar?"

She shakes her head. "No. It would appear we've struck ground. Caster, would you do the honors?"

"Absolutely."

His hands burst into flames, and he jumps off the front of the boat onto what sounds like rocky ground. Hearing the sound strikes a chord of longing in my heart. The ring has started to work its influence deep in my psyche, or maybe I've always had a love of hard, firm ground, and that's why the rock ring came to me. It's a chicken-or-the-egg scenario.

Caster's push sends the boat drifting away from shore, but a wave of Emily's hand puts it back in place long enough for the rest of us to disembark. I feel a chill of strength rush up my legs as I set foot upon the rocks. But I feel more than just strength. I feel memory.

It's as if in the time I've been off the ground, my new rock sense has had time to develop and grow more nuanced. I can pick up more flavors in the earth. The flavors here are particularly strong. I sense love, pain, betrayal, rage—and something deeper and darker.

"You all right, Peter?" Emily asks.

I shake my head and realize I've been staring at the ground like a zombie. "Yeah, just happy to be on solid earth again."

"Now you guys know what I felt like in the desert," she says. "There was hardly even any moisture in the air. What ho!" She strides forward as Caster's hands illuminate a great wall stretching upward high into the night.

"Where do you get all these British expressions?" I ask, following her.

"The BBC. Duh."

We all join Caster, who's positioned before a vast wall engraved with the same strange script we saw on the pillars. With one hand, he holds a flame, and with his other, he holds the spyglass, one of the two gifts we still have left. It strikes me as a bit unfair that it's the Blackstone kids who happen to still have their gifts, not the Mormont kids. Just like it's always been. But almost as soon as the thought comes to me, it strikes me as petty.

My mind drifts toward a question: *Why did Cog and Ku'ba give us the gifts they did?* All had obvious purposes except Ami's, which I initially thought looked like a cool walking staff that maybe you could use to hit people. Now I know it also helps to channel her power. But it does more than that too, doesn't it? She said on the boat that she knew this cave was the one that held Morin's staff, because the staff had been there before. Does that mean the staff holds memories?

"What's it say?" asks Emily.

"A bunch of boring stuff extolling the deeds of the Eastern Empire, ending finally with instructions on how to enter, if we dare to enter."

"I see. So we have a choice," says Emily. "Up or through?"

"I wish I still had my compass," I mutter sullenly.

"I feel like this is one of those moments in a coming-of-age story," says Caster, "when the characters have to make decisions for themselves and thereby grow in the virtues of courage and responsibility."

Emily glowers at him, managing to look both intimidating and cute at the same time. "Shut up. Your metacommentary is not helping."

He throws up his hands defensively. "Hey, I was just trying to be encouraging."

"I think we should go through," says Ami.

"I think so too," Emily says.

"Why?" asks Caster. "Thaegar said we shouldn't go through; we should go around."

"Yeah, and Thaegar has spent the last eternity hunkered down in the Wella so he can find inner peace while the world goes the way of the dinosaurs. 'We must consider. We must consider,'" she says in perfect imitation of the laganmorfs' mantra. "If Ami's right, this cave contains what we need to kill the Bloodfather and save Meila's twin sister and the other nymphs there."

"Thank you for the rousing speech, Patrick Henry," says Caster sarcastically. "But this isn't really a give-me-all-or-nothing scenario. We should take the fastest route to Samjang, and after we've saved the world from a fate worse than death and all that jazz, we can come back and save a few dozen nymphs. You have to have a world to save before you can save a few people in it."

"Yeah, and you have to have a world worth saving before you can save it," Emily says.

Caster sighs and shakes his head. "You're not making sense. It's very simple. You do higher-priority tasks first and then lower-priority ones. We have two days left before the word ends, so Samjang is higher priority. Besides, even if we had the staff, we couldn't do anything. Only Haji can banish the Bloodfather back to the Dark Realm."

"Yeah, and—" Emily suddenly grows quiet, tilting her head. "Do you hear that?"

CHAPTER 77

THE LAST LIGHT

"Is it the voice of reason you're finally hearing?" Caster says.

Emily doesn't respond. Her face is serious. Then she looks up, and her eyes grow wide.

I follow her gaze and curse in all the languages I know, ending with a spectacular "Oy vey." From my mother, of course.

"Okay, caves it is," says Caster, turning toward the door.

I tear my eyes away from the distant figures hovering above the mist, which grow chillingly familiar. *The fallen gods.*

"So how do we get in exactly?" asks Emily. She is trying to keep her voice under control, but I can tell she's as afraid as I am. As bad as Five might be, we'd at least stand a chance against him. But against the fallen gods? Even Cog said we'd be dead meat.

"Apparently, the door is sensitive to certain people's touches," says Caster. "At least that's what it claims. And—"

"Skip to the bottom line!" Emily shouts. "We're about to die, you baboon!"

"Right. So one of the touches the door is sensitive to is the touch of the Four."

"Wait a moment," I say. "It says that specifically?"

"Yes."

Emily's eyes widen. "And that didn't strike you as a little bit creepy?"

"Well, it did, but look, it's too late for saying I was right all along. There's no way we're outrunning the fallen gods in open ground, so put your hands on the door, and let's go."

As the figures in the distance grow larger, we all put our hands on the door. The stone feels cold and creeping, as if it's alive, and I have a sudden urge to rip my hand away. But I leave it there long enough for cracks to appear in a jaw-like pattern in the stone. Then, all at once, the stones collapse inward.

Lightning crackles in the near distance, and the waters begin to shake again, as if preparing for another storm.

"Let's go," I say, striding into the cave, feeling the layout by intuition that comes from the rock ring.

Caster rushes after me with the others; his hands illuminate the way. As soon as we're all in the cave, the stones behind us re-form, blocking off the exit. We all spin around and watch as the last of the light from the outside world vanishes into darkness.

"No turning back." Caster laughs nervously.

"Guess so," I say, feeling less and less happy about this choice.

There's something wrong about the stones in this cave. They feel almost hungry—and deeply malevolent. But I keep my thoughts to myself. It wouldn't do any good to worsen the fear the others are already feeling. Because of the stones, I can sense their fear, and it weighs heavily in the air.

"Mama always said life is a box of lemons," says Caster. "You gotta make the most of it."

"Did she?" I say.

"Yeah, because you know, when life gives you lemons, you make lemonade?"

Emily groans. "Caster, your jokes aren't funny. They're so bad, in fact, they don't even rise to the level of dad jokes."

"That's because they're grandpa jokes."

"There you go again," she says, trying to sound humorous, but as we continue to walk into the enclosing darkness, she mainly sounds deeply scared.

I don't blame her. It's hard not to feel terrified in the dark tunnels, which circle round and round, going ever deeper into the earth like a coiling sarcophagus leading to the stomach of some sleeping beast.

CHAPTER 78

THE STATUE AND THE FLAMES

We follow the narrow stone hallways, which are worn smooth to the touch, for what feels like hours, until we come to a small door. We step through and find ourselves in an antechamber of some kind. Caster increases the fire on his hands to illuminate the whole room. It's barren, except for a gate composed of two stone doors and the statue of a dog.

The dog stands beside the door; its body is long and lean yet muscled. It bears its head proudly, and it wears a slender golden chain around its neck. Its ruby eyes gleam fiercely in the firelight, and despite being made of minerals, they seem to shine uncannily with an almost human intelligence.

My eyes drift down the dog's body to the base on which it stands. A few words are written in the script we saw along the pillars in the lake and the walls outside the cave.

"Can you read the plaque?" I ask, turning to Caster.

He pulls out his spyglass. "I will do what I must."

"You will try," says Emily. She laughs awkwardly. "Sorry. *Revenge of the Sith*. Anakin and Obi-Wan? Just trying to lighten the mood."

He lifts the spyglass to his eye and reads the few short words written in the stone. "It says, 'Dulia, servant of the king, keeper of the riddles.'"

"Keeper of the riddles?" Emily says. "What's that supposed to mean?"

Caster shrugs. "I don't know."

"I suppose," says Emily, "if you're super into riddles, you probably wouldn't write your plaques in a very straightforward way. It wouldn't be very riddley."

"Let's look at the door," Ami says. "Maybe it has some clues."

We drift over to the massive stones that make up the door. I wonder what kind of machine these people possibly could have had that would make them move. But then again, maybe they didn't need machines. The walls of the cave, which unformed and then formed again after we entered, seem more like magic than science. Miria doesn't seem very high tech, and even Gaia, my world, probably doesn't have technology to make stones behave that way, at least not easily. I stifle a chill running up from the stones into my legs, which sets a little voice inside my head to whispering, *Not right, not right, not right!*

I push it away and concentrate on the stones, but they're just stones, with no script at all.

"Peter," Emily says, "do you think you could use your power to—"

I close my eyes and feel for the stones, ignoring the sensation of cold, slippery hands reaching inside my guts, feeling for my heart. But no matter how hard I push at the stones, they will not obey me.

"No," I say, trying to shake off the creepy feeling of the stones. "I can't do it."

She snaps her fingers. "Good try at least." She furrows her brow. "But then for real, guys, how are we getting through? There weren't any other branches from the tunnel. This is it. You don't think there could have been any trapdoors we were supposed to fall through, leading to another part of the cave, do you?"

"No, Velma, I don't think we're in a Scooby-Doo movie," says Caster, annoyed.

"Oh, so what movie are we in then, Fred?" Emily retorts, crossing her arms.

"I don't know. *A Series of Unfortunate Events*? Let's just say we made the wrong choice. The Wong choice, you might say, since it was your bright idea to come into this cave."

Emily waves a finger at him. "Every time you make a stupid joke like that, you wear my patience a little thinner."

Caster shrugs. "I'm just trying to fit in, Emily Wong. When in Wome, do as the Womans."

Emily glowers at him with no hint of humor in her eyes. "It's like you're trying to egg me on."

"No, I'm not," says Caster. "You're always stressing out over silly things."

"Oh, so now it's a me problem?"

"Well, you know, every suit of armor has a chink in it."

"So," says Emily, "you're calling me a Chink? Is that what I just heard?"

I'm about to step in between them before a fight starts, but Ami tugs at my sleeve. "Let them talk it out."

"I didn't mean that," says Caster, his voice quieter. "I was just frustrated. Frustrated with this entire situation. Not to mention I haven't gotten much sleep in the past twenty-four hours."

"That sounds like an excuse," says Emily, though her voice has grown a few degrees warmer.

"What do you want to hear?"

"I don't know—maybe 'I'm sorry'?" She looks up at him with strangely vulnerable eyes. Or maybe it's just a trick of the light. In any case, it doesn't last long, but her expression has softened.

Caster gives a hint of a smirk. "Sorry, I'm afraid I don't do apologies."

Emily smiles. "I'll take it."

I look back and forth between the two with my mouth half open. How do they go from being at each other's throat to smiling stupidly at each other in little more than a minute? I think of how Ami couldn't stay mad at me for long, and I couldn't remain distant from her for long either. Maybe it's the rings—their elements calling to each other. I push away the thought, however warm it feels in my heart. For the first time in my life, I feel as if I might have choices—and as if what I do might matter. I intend to keep it that way.

Caster, meanwhile, turns to the statue of the dog and shoots an angry fireball at it, engulfing it with flames. "Stupid Dulia. Couldn't you be a bit more helpful?"

For a moment, the room is silent. No one moves. Then I feel a shiver run up my spine as wild sensations pulse beneath my feet in the stones below. A voice speaks: "Welcome, Four, to the tomb of my master."

CHAPTER 79

THE RIDDLER

My stomach lurches as I realize the voice came not from outside me but from inside me.

"Caster," Emily says, her voice quivering, "what have you done?"

"I think I've awakened the keeper of the riddles."

As if to confirm his statement, the stone dog turns its head to face us, and its ruby eyes glint with cold amusement.

"Oh, Great Pumpkin, that's creepy," Emily whispers.

Caster stares at the moving statue warily, and Ami looks fearful of it. But I can feel what the others cannot: the dog's feet are fixed to the ground. It can't harm us from this distance.

"Why were you silent till Caster shot you with a fireball?" I ask it.

"Fire calls to me, for I was wrought in flame." The dog cocks its head. "Do you want to know the details of my making, or would you like to enter the inmost chamber?"

The four of us look at one another, exchanging silent nods. I wait for Caster to speak, since he usually does the talking, but he's looking at me.

I gulp and try not to look like such a weakling. *What does my dad always say? Put my shoulders back and chest out?* I do so, feeling awkward, and speak.

"We want to enter the inmost chamber. And to leave this cave." I think for a moment and then add, "Alive and healthy. Within a few hours." I think back to all the ancient tales in which genies and fairies only grant wishes according to literal interpretations of people's words. Usually, those interpretations go horribly wrong. *Have to get it right.*

The dog's stone flesh ripples into an unnatural smile. "Then you must answer my riddles."

"Does anyone else feel like they're in *The Hobbit* right now?" asks Caster.

Emily looks at him askance. "No, why?"

"Well, we're in a cave, faced with a creature that clearly doesn't get out much and is our only chance of getting out, and it's asking us to play a game of riddles. You know, like Gollum?" He turns to the dog. "So what are the stakes? If we win, you let us in. If we lose?"

"You die of thirst or starvation, whichever comes first."

"Makes sense," Caster says. "Though I was expecting something a little more horrible."

Emily elbows him. "Stop it. Don't give anyone any ideas!"

He holds up his hands. "My bad."

"So what are the riddles?" I ask.

"It's very simple, but you must answer honestly. I will know if you do not." The dog's unnatural smile widens. "Who are you?"

The words reverberate deep in my chest, echoing with the sound of a thousand voices all joining together like fingers and arms, skin and bones, to stitch together a monster, a giant so large it swells above me like a mountain. It stares down at me. Its hollow dark eyes gaze into my heart as it repeats the words with its dead lips: *Who are you?*

Who are you? I want to reply, staring up fearfully at the unholy creature in my mind. I want to collapse to the floor, when suddenly, Caster's voice breaks through my thoughts.

"Really? Who are we? Don't you think that's more than a little cliché? Jeez, I was hoping for something fresh. You don't have another riddle, do you?"

The dog stares blankly back at us; its ruby eyes gleam coldly in the firelight.

"Look," says Emily. "If it's an easy question, then we shouldn't complain. It means we have a better chance of not dying tragically of thirst in this stupid cave."

"Agreed," I say, and Ami nods.

Emily gathers us into a huddle, and for a moment, my mind is transported back to the night when Goober and I went to the Blackstone-versus-Mormont football game so I could watch Emily as she played in the marching band. How can two weeks feel like years ago?

As we join the huddle, Emily looks each of us in the eye and then speaks. "All right, each of us here has a part to play. And we're going to do this. How, you ask? We're just gonna do it!"

"That was the worst motivational speech I've ever heard. Ow!" Caster rubs his rib cage.

Emily tries to shake the pain from her fist. "Your stupid bones hurt my hand."

"You punched me!"

"Guys," I say, "can we try to focus?"

"Oh, right. Sorry," says Emily sheepishly. She sticks her tongue out at Caster and then resumes her professional posture. "So, team, are there any questions?"

"Yeah," says Caster. "Who are we?"

CHAPTER 80

DULIA DECIDES

A thought occurs to me, and I turn to the stone dog. "Do you mean individually or collectively?"

The dog's eyes glint with a perverse mirth. "It is for you to decide who you think you are. I only judge."

"Not fair," I grumble.

We sit down in a circle, and no one speaks for a long time; everyone is deep in thought.

I try to find the answer, and meanwhile, the giant keeps breaking into my thoughts, rising up like the terrific waves of the Silver Lake and staring down at me with cold, hollow eyes.

After a few minutes, we begin to throw out ideas, but none of us seems able to decide exactly how we want to answer. After a few hours, we've all but given up.

"If we wait any longer, we won't have to die of thirst or starvation, because the Ice Reich will come," says Caster. "Time is of the essence. We should just try something. Worst-case scenario, we can use Peter's head as a battering ram to try to get in the door by force."

I'm about to object, when I remember I'm impervious to stone. I guess it wouldn't hurt that much, but all the same, it wouldn't be very dignified.

"That leaves the question of who should be the one to give the answer," Emily says.

Caster looks about ready to nominate himself, when Ami pipes up. "I think it should be Peter."

I'm about to make an X sign with my hands and say, "Absolutely not," when Emily nods and says, "I agree. It should be Peter."

"Why?" asks Caster.

I ask myself the same question. Caster's smarter, Emily's more empathetic, and Ami's more intuitive. I've never been the dumbest kid in the class exactly, but I've always been in the half that makes the top half possible. I'm not good at anything, really. I couldn't even get into Elite Class in *Ghost Army*, and practically all I did in my free time was play video games with Goober.

"Because," says Emily, "I trust him. He has the best heart out of all of us."

I both smile and cringe inside. I hate compliments, especially ones that can't be true. There's no way I have the best heart. Emily's kinder to humans, and Ami's kinder to animals. I've just been along for the ride.

"It's true," says Ami. "He's the best friend among us. He should be the one to speak."

Could it be true? I haven't been much of a friend to Ami or Emily, let alone Caster. But then again, maybe I value friendship the most because I've never really had it, except with Dr. Elsavier sort of and with Goober sort of. The more time goes on, the more Goober seems less like a good friend and more like a bad, if somewhat tragic, influence. So perhaps I'm the best qualified to speak about friendship.

"I mean—" Caster stops abruptly as Emily cuts him off.

"And he's humble!" says Emily. "Something you could learn a bit about!"

"Well, in all fairness, I don't have much to be humble about, whereas Peter—" He sighs. "I believe in you, Rocky. Try not to get us killed."

Feeling a mix of encouragement and crushing self-doubt, I approach Dulia, the keeper of riddles. The giant in my mind, with its rotting skin and hollow eyes, tries to intimidate me, but Emily's and Ami's voices shrink him down to the size of a little bobblehead. I push him away and meet the dog's ruby gaze.

"Well, I'm not really sure what to say. We're four friends. I mean, we weren't friends before coming here, and we still are kind of in the stormy phase of our relationship, but we're definitely friends. I'd give up my life for at least two-thirds of them."

I venture a smile, but Dulia only stares back at me with cold, unblinking eyes. "What else are we? We're four high school kids. I'm just an ordinary kid, maybe a little below average, with no special talents and a head as dumb as a rock—that's probably why the rock ring came to me—but the others are amazing people. Caster has the best mind you'll ever come across. Emily will make you feel like you've been her best friend since childhood, and she has a sense of humor bigger than the moon. And Ami is the Samwise Gamgee or the R2-D2 of the group—the true, loyal friend. She has an intuition, a sense for understanding things that others don't. But more than that, she looks after everyone else before herself, is kind to me and to people who don't deserve it and animals who can't repay her. And she has a smile as beautiful as the sunset."

My ears grow red, and I mentally pinch myself for adding that last bit. What am I doing? But the emotions now are flowing too strongly for me to maintain control, and I start talking again.

"Anyway. Um, so that's us. But we're more than that, because we're more than the sum of our parts."

"Cliché," Caster mutters. He yelps as Emily delivers a blow to his kidneys.

"We're the Four. We're the ring bearers. We didn't want to come here—at least I didn't. But after coming here, I wouldn't trade it for anything in the world. Despite the fact we've only known each other for like two weeks, these people"—I turn to look each of them in the eyes—"are my best friends."

I feel my eyes grow watery and my throat choke. It takes a few seconds before I can continue. "The Nine Realms or whatever are in danger of getting eaten by the Ice Reich, but we're going to stop it. Not that we're super amazing or anything, but we sort of are. Our families come from all around the world—our world, I mean—from cultures and countries that used to and sometimes still do hate each other. But somehow, a few people from those cultures found love and made us. We're Americans, born in the melting pot, the place where everyone can have a home. So I don't know how exactly, but we're going to succeed."

Suddenly, I feel a glowing deep in my chest, which feels hot as fire, smooth as water, soft as air, and stern as stone all at once. I see an image of four strings knotting into one. But just as soon as I feel it, the sensation is gone, the strings unravel, and the memory slips from my mind.

I gulp, out of words and feeling drained. "So there."

For a moment, everything is still, and I wonder whether I've failed. Did I misunderstand the riddle or say the wrong thing?

But the silence is broken as Dulia tilts its head to the side, and its ruby eyes glow with the light of a thousand flames.

CHAPTER 81

THE INNER CHAMBER

Dulia begins to howl. It's a hollow, haunting sound rising up from deep within my chest, like the voices of a hundred packs of wolves all joined together. I stumble to the ground as a cracking sound floods my ears. For a moment, I'm convinced my own bones are crumbling as the wolfish sounds tear through my flesh. But then I look up past the heads of Emily, Ami, and Caster, who are on the floor in front of me, and I see it.

The door to the inner chamber is rent in two, and slowly, the two sides fall apart like jaws opening into utter darkness.

I stare at the enveloping blackness as my heart beats loudly in my chest. Dulia's voice has grown silent. Then I feel an urgency burning in my bones, a vivid sense that the door is about to close.

"Quickly," I say, springing to my feet.

I run toward the door and look back to see the others still in a daze, gazing wonderingly at the door. I race back to them and yank them to their feet one by one. "Come on. Let's go!"

Caster's the first one to come to his senses, followed by Emily, and they plunge forward toward the door, which has begun to close back in on itself.

"Ami," I say, taking her shoulders, "we have to go." I stare into her eyes and get the feeling I'm looking into the windows of a house with no one in it. But the feeling lasts only a sliver of a second, and then she's back. Her eyes focus.

We run toward the door and squeeze through with moments to spare before it seals itself shut again. Ami makes a yelping sound just as we pass into the room. I spin around with fears of her hand being caught in the door and her fingers being taken off racing through my mind.

"Are you okay?"

She nods and shows me her left hand, shifting the bird to her right arm. The sides of the palm are trickling blood.

"What happened?"

"Dulia bit me."

"What?" *That stupid stone dog.* I curse, fantasizing about breaking its legs with a hammer. "Why?"

She shrugs. "I don't know. But it's fine. It's not that bad."

"We should get Emily to fix you up."

She shakes her head. "There's not much water here, and she needs to save her strength."

I'm about to protest, when Emily calls out. "You guys okay?"

Ami's eyes plead with mine, and I give in. "Yeah, we're fine!"

"Then get your butts over here. I don't like being left alone with Caster. Ow, you can't hit girls."

"Flicking doesn't count, and you don't count either. Ow!"

"Say it again! Tell me again I don't count as a girl!"

I smile and shake my head as Ami and I walk over to the bickering voices. The bird pushes itself out of Ami's arms and waddles along beside her. It really has been getting better with Ami's care.

"So what are we doing?" I ask as I arrive by Caster's dimly lit fire. I can barely see anything in the room, except four pillars, which surround Caster and Emily's position.

"Oh, right," says Emily, turning from Caster, whom she was about to flick. "Pay attention, Caster; stop being so immature. What did you want to say?"

"Well," he says, "do any of you get the feeling that someone wants us to be here?"

Emily looks at him flatly. "That's what you wanted to say?"

"Yeah," says Caster. "There are too many coincidences."

"Well, no duh! Of course there are. The question is, *who* wants us here and why?"

A dark thought forms on the edge of my mind in answer to Emily's question, but I push it away, and I feel an overwhelming need to fidget, to do something. "There's only one way to find out the answer to that question and also how to get out of here."

Caster nods. "To explore." He clears his throat. "Please stand back."

We all take a step away from him, and he raises his hands above his head. For a moment, the flames along his fingers wink out, and then they rush back again with a fury, illuminating the room.

The room's layout is surprisingly simple. Five pillars stretch up to a high ceiling, each decorated with the same symbols we saw on the pillars in the Silver Lake. In the center of the pillars, carved into the ground, is the outline of a tree. Behind us is the shut door; to our sides are smooth walls. In front of us, however, are three stone steps leading up to a rectangular box encrusted with jewels and the same strange script. Behind it stand three stone statues of women with cloaks covering their faces, except for their sly, hungry smiles. In front of the box, there stands a giant book with leathery binding and a single faded mark upon its surface.

My heart skips as I remember what Thaegar told me about the cave: there are many secrets in it about the Four. Could they be in this book?

CHAPTER 82

THE BOOK

Slowly, we approach the book, almost in a trance, like bugs approaching an electric lamp at night.

As we come to the steps leading up to the podium on which the book stands, I shake myself out of the daze, as do the others. But still, the book fascinates me, and I can't keep my eyes off it. I have a compulsion to run up to it and touch it, to feel its worn pages with my hands.

Stop it, you weirdo, I tell myself.

Holding his flaming left hand high, Caster unbuckles the book with his right hand, opens it to its first page, and takes out his spyglass.

"Let me read this time; you always read," Emily pleads.

Caster regards his spyglass for a moment, as if unwilling to part with it, and then sighs. "Fine. But don't break it. You already lost your gift."

"That wasn't my fault." She snatches the spyglass and holds it up to her eye.

"The other way." Caster sighs.

"Oh, whoops!" Emily turns it around and clears her throat. She reads, "The testament of the druids of Pytho, children of Belial, servants of the king."

"Well, that makes a lot of sense," says Caster under his breath. "Let us know when you come to something useful."

She lowers the spyglass enough to glare at him, tosses her hair back indignantly, and then returns her gaze to the book. She flips through the pages one after the other.

"You can't be reading it that fast," Caster says. "Make sure you don't miss anything."

Sometimes I wonder whether they say things just to get under each other's skin, especially Caster.

"I used to win speed-reading competitions back when I was a freshie. I can read more than twelve hundred words per minute with ninety-eight percent comprehension. So stop talking like my mom after I just got my temps: 'Don't forget to brake for that stop sign!'"

Caster holds up his hands. "My bad. You Gucci. So then what are these self-styled druids of Pytho writing about?"

"It's mostly history right now," she says. "History about the east and how they fought to keep it independent from the Kardun in the west, who quickly dominated the human nations by their superior strength and intelligence. They seem to think of themselves as the OG Avengers or something like that."

I furrow my brow. "The OG Avengers?"

"OG, a.k.a. original gangster, a.k.a. the original, the first," replies Emily. "What world are you from?"

"I know what *OG* means! I meant, why are they like OG Avengers?"

"Oh." Emily clears her throat. "Because they were defending humankind against a superior race intent on conquering. At least that's how they started."

She flips through more pages, and the spyglass races left and right as her eyes speed along the length of each page. "The druids were once a respected caste in the Eastern Kingdom," she translates, "and they led many armies. But when they met with continual defeat against the Kar-dun, they used the only resource they believed could defeat the Kar-dun: magic. When the human leaders found out, they turned on the druids. They merciless in their foolishness. They drowned some, burned others alive, and turned even their name into a curse so black that men feared even to utter it."

"What happened to them?" Ami asks. Her bird is close beside her, and its gaze is narrow, as if it's suspicious of something.

Emily flips through the pages. "They went into hiding for a while as they worked out their next step, which was to infiltrate the literary circles of the east and then the halls of government."

"Does it say what their goals are?" I ask.

Emily furrows her brow, turning page after page. "No, but it mentions something about a plan. Oh!" She stops suddenly, pointing to marks on the page. "It says here, 'The key to our plan lies in a place few could guess. The All-Father was rather clever when he hid the Tree of Life from us. There is a cruel yet delightful irony to this secret, which we now dare to write: the key to our plans is—'" She stops with her eyes widening and voice choking.

"What is it?" Caster says.

"The Four," says Emily, her voice small. "The key to their plan is us."

CHAPTER 83

SECRETS OF THE FOUR

"Well, for Cog's sake, woman, stop with the cliffhangers, and read on!" Caster says. "What is their plan? What do they want to do with the Four?"

Emily closes her eyes, takes a deep breath, and then puts the spyglass once more to her eye. She reads through a few more pages.

"Well, what does it say?"

"Calm yourself," says Emily, placing a hand on Caster's shoulder. "It doesn't say what their plan is or what they intend to do with us, the Four. Instead, it seems to be a dossier of sorts on us. Characteristics of the Four. Patterns they've noticed by observing us for ages."

"What kind of characteristics and patterns?"

"Some things that are obvious, like that water can most easily be defeated in a dry place, fire in a cold place, earth in a high place, and so on. Notes on how to face us in combat. Oh! But listen to this. Here are some personality patterns they've apparently noted. Ahem. 'In every age, we have noticed an interesting pattern. The rings seem to call to each other in a peculiar way. For example, fire always loves water, and water loves fire.'"

"Sounds like a steamy romance," Caster quips, and then he looks at Emily as the words apparently sink in.

"Oh gosh, no! Ew! Gross. Why?" They both say a jumble of words with their faces wrinkled in disgust and horror and shift away from each other.

Their expressions seem to me to be fake, though, like masks worn to hide what neither of them really wants to say. I push the thought away, unsure of how it makes me feel. It's no more than what Thaegar said, but hearing it here in this dark, gloomy chamber makes it different somehow.

Emily finally continues. "It says, 'But stone and wind are always alone, though they call to each other. Earth and heaven, though bound together, can never touch.'"

I feel a crushing weight on my chest, as if I'm being forced into a dark room void of all light and warmth, crammed into an ever-smaller space far from all friends, all hope, and all love.

It can't be like that, I tell myself. *It's not like Thaegar said.*

But Thaegar might have been wrong, says a gravelly voice seeming to echo through thousands of miles of hollow darkness. I recognize it from earlier—the voice of the giant.

Who are you? I want to ask the giant's question to the giant, but another image breaks into my thoughts. *Homer.*

His fierce eyes stare into mine, and though he says nothing, an understanding passes between us. More questions. This is what the giant would want—for me to be sucked into his little game.

Instead, I turn to Ami, who's looking a little miserable herself. Before I can get cold feet, I reach for her hand, wiggling my fingers into hers.

Her eyes widen in surprise, as big as harvest moons, and for a moment, I'm afraid she'll push me away. But then she gives a little smile, and her hand grips mine in return. I feel a warmth inside strong enough to chase away the gloom of the chamber and the cold eyes of the giant. I'm not sure what these feelings mean and what I've done by taking her hand. With the emotions swirling in my head and gut, I decide it's better just to accept it and figure it out later.

"Let's see," says Emily. "Now the druids talk about a bunch of other books about us, which they've hidden across the nine realms."

"Interesting," says Caster. "So they have ways of traveling between realms."

I think of Galthanius, who seemed to know a great deal about our world and was able to speak Ancient Greek to modern English. He even had a personal bloodgorger, which he had been using to extend his life. Does that mean he was one of the druids? But then again, the druids seem to have been founded to protect the east against the Kar-dun, and Galthanius was a Kar-dun. I shake my head, feeling more muddled by the moment.

Emily turns a few more pages. "Oh, this is interesting."

"What?"

"It talks here about how to defeat us." She runs a finger along the page as she quotes aloud: "Every lock has a key, every riddle has an answer, and every enemy has a weakness. Taken together, the Four are too powerful, but separately, they can be defeated. And this hinges ever on turning Five against the Four, the Four against Five, and One against One. Five is the key that unlocks the riddle, and fortunately, in every age, our cause has known this and has managed to turn him against the Four. Thus, even in their victory, we have managed to stealthily grow in strength through the ages. But we must turn now from talk of tactics and stratagems and enter into the hidden places wherein lie the unholy secrets of our sect."

She turns the page, revealing a large pentagram encased within a pentagon, written in cold black ink, with a character at each of the five points. I feel a shiver travel through me, seeing something both familiar and perverse in the shape.

CHAPTER 84

BLOOD

I stare at the black pentagram, and the shape seems to eat at the edges of my sanity, until I have to turn away.

"The pentagram," Emily reads, her voice wavering. "Some call it a mere imitation of the Five, claiming that magic is but an ape and that we copy by will what the Five possess by grace. But in reality, grace is the ape of magic, which is nothing other than will. There is no cause of things but will. The will to power. The will to make and create, to dominate, to have and possess the object of one's will, one's love. The gods are mortal, and we may become like them if only we learn to imitate this truth."

I feel Ami's palm grow sweaty, or maybe it's my palm that's growing sweaty. Either way, I'm creeped out.

Emily continues to read: "Will is love, love is will, and both are beyond all categories, beyond even what the little people like to term *good* and *evil*—those miserable attempts of the weak to control the strong! Will is what brings all things into being, sustains them, and ends them. It is the creator and destroyer, the rhyme and reason, the beginning and end, the—"

Emily puts down the spyglass. "Jeez, these guys are really in love with the sound of their own voice, aren't they? Do you have any idea what in the name of Papa Smurf they're talking about?"

"Faintly," says Caster. His bright eyes are troubled. He shivers. "And for once, I don't want to understand more. Let's just focus on getting out of here."

"Right," says Emily. She starts turning the pages again, and her eyes race along their length as she reads she mumbles comments. "Something about 'the Three, whose names we dare not write,' and the source of their power."

My eyes are drawn to the shadows beyond the book, past the altar-like stone to three statues lurking in the darkness. Three women with veils over their eyes and with smiles of terrible and frightening beauty—the sort of beauty that might drive you mad, make you lose all control, and make you a stranger to your own self. I turn away.

Ami's bird hobbles away toward the tomb. She scrunches up her brow and then follows it. My attention is caught between Emily and Ami, desperate to find out what secrets Emily is uncovering and also why Ami's bird has now landed on top of the rectangular stone and begun pecking at it.

"Stop it, silly!" Ami tells the bird, but it keeps going. Its movements become more insistent.

Peck, peck, peck.

"A great king who restored their prestige," Emily mumbles.

Peck, peck, peck.

"Who now sleeps in death, longing for fresh blood to wake him."

Peck, peck, peck.

"His life is bound to the Dark Realm."

"Come down from there!" Ami says.

Peck, peck, peck.

The noise fills my mind, mixing with Emily's and Ami's words to form terrible images of fields of rotting flesh, bones glinting in moonlight, corpses with emerald fire instead of brains and mouths filled with embers, and, standing over all the horror, a giant—the giant who laughed at me as I tried to puzzle out Dulia's riddle.

"Indeed, only blood can wake him."

Peck, peck, peck.

I think, *Blood. Bloodfather. Bloodgorger. Blood. Dulia.*

"Only blood now can wake our king."

Blood. Dulia bit Ami, and Ami's hand is still bleeding. Blood.

My eyes fix on Ami, who is reaching for the bird, which sits pecking on the rectangular stone. No, not a stone—a tomb. Her bandaged hand is red with blood.

Stop it! Stop! The words are trapped in my throat, held down by an unseen hand—the giant's hand. The king's hand.

Then, like water finally breaking through a dam, the words burst out. "Stop it!"

Everyone freezes and then slowly turns to look at me.

I point at Ami, and Caster's and Emily's heads follow. "Ami," I say as gently as possible, "try to move your hand slowly away from the tomb of—" I bite down the word, even though I know now who it must be, who it has to be.

Ami nods and begins slowly to pull her hand away.

Emily raises the spyglass to the characters carved into the stone walls of the tomb. "Here lies—"

She's interrupted when suddenly, the bird flares its wings, and Ami jumps back, jerking her hand away. A little drop of blood falls from her makeshift bandage and lands on the stone tomb.

I gulp, feeling a power ripple through the stone. For a moment, I'm frozen, and Emily, who still is looking through the spyglass, is oblivious.

> Here lies Morin, yet undead,
> Sleeping till the Four have bled,
> Desiring ever the blood of them,
> Which gives endless life to men.

CHAPTER 85

DISCORD

"'Them' and 'men' don't rhyme," says Caster. "And the meter's wrong."

"It doesn't matter," I say, feeling the stone churn beneath me with a perverse power. "We need to go."

I look up and see Ami's face frozen in horror at the drop of blood on the tomb. Her face changes from horror to hurt as she gazes at the bird, our betrayer.

It now makes sense why the bird tried to sacrifice itself to keep us from dying at the hands of the phantom men and why it's stayed behind us ever since. It must have been one of Morin's servants all along, sent to guide us back to him. It could even be one of the druids.

The stones beneath my feet begin to tremble and shake, and everyone's arms shoot out to try to keep balance. The stone tomb, sealed shut without lid or crack, begins to crumble as its surface rends in two.

"Run!" I shout.

"Where?" Emily asks with her brow drawn in fear. "We're trapped."

I throw up my hands, letting Ami's hand slip from mine. I it regret immediately, as cold swoops in once against like a draft.

"Make for the opposite end of the room," I say. "There might be a chance we can find some way out."

Caster's eyes look hollow, as though he already knows how this is going to end, but he takes the lead with me, and his hands light the way. Sure enough, there is another stone door opposite the one we entered. We can tell it's a door only by the slender crack that runs the length of the stones from top to bottom, just as in the door by Dulia.

The floor shudders again as something heavy falls against the ground. I force from my mind the imagined images of a tomb opening up and of dead hands reaching out.

"Can you move it?" Caster asks.

I touch my hands to the stones and reach for my power, which usually comes effortlessly. But now it feels somewhere distant, buried deep under many in the stones, and all the layers above are hostile, angry, and rebellious, unwilling to listen to my desperate pleas for them to move.

"It's enchanted stone," I say. "I can't get it to budge."

"Galthanius had enchanted stone too," says Emily. Her eyes widen as the same possibility occurs to her that occurred to me earlier. "Maybe he was a druid too—but the druids hated the Kar-dun, didn't they? But maybe that changed, and they started to get along and form a new alliance as their purposes changed, and then—"

"Do you always talk so much when you're scared?" asks Caster drolly.

"Are you always so quiet when you're scared?"

"No, I'm just quietly accepting that we are, in all probability, about to die gruesome deaths."

"Don't say that," I say.

"Yeah." Ami's eyes are fierce, and she unfastens the staff from her back.

"Ami still has her power, just like she did in Galthanius's enchanted chamber. And this time, you still have your power, Caster. We can do this." Emily nods encouragingly.

A crashing sound echoes through the chamber, and we all startle, whipping around.

The tomb has shattered open, and mist, illumined by an awful green light, flows from the gaping hole—the same green light we saw in the hills to the south when the phantom men came after us and the same green light I saw burning in the skulls of rotting corpses in my terrible vision of the giant.

Then, just as in the nightmare, rotten black hands with flecks of bone visible claw the edges of the tomb, pulling out a monster man made of ruined flesh that barely clings to his body. His hollow eyes are lit with green fire. As he rises to his full height, I see why he appeared to me as a giant. He stands a full twelve feet by my guess. But he feels even taller—as tall as a skyscraper and as vast and deep as an ocean.

I shrink backward, and my body touches the hostile stone. I wish it would swallow me like my bed in Cog's palace did.

As the giant moves toward us, the green smoke curls like snakes along the ground, filling up the whole room.

"Oh bad, oh bad, oh bad," says a voice I distantly recognize as Emily's. "This is not good."

"You mentioned that," says Caster.

The green smoke is around us now, coiling round our legs and up our bodies—except, I notice, mine. The smoke, for some reason, seems too heavy, as if kept down by some invisible weight. But for the others, I watch in mute horror as the green smoke creeps up their bodies and into their nostrils.

Then a voice speaks. It is a voice like Dulia's but a thousand times colder, darker, and more malicious—and it echoes in the chasms of my heart, sending spasms of fear through my legs.

"*Barak*," says the voice.

My mind registers its meaning, though I do not know the language: *Discord*.

Then everything goes wrong.

CHAPTER 86

BLADE AND STAFF

Everything goes wrong in the worst way.

It starts with Emily slapping Caster across the cheek, which he probably deserves for something he's said—well, a lot of things he's said—but then he slaps her back. After that, it's an all-out slug fest between the two, though each of them somehow dodges most of the other's blows.

My heart sinks when Ami's kind face turns into a snarl, and she lashes out at Caster, her older brother. In a few seconds, it's become a three-way fight, and it's nasty.

All the while, Morin draws closer in slow, dead steps. My nose fills with the pungent odor of his rotting flesh, and it takes everything I have to keep myself from hurling.

He stops a few feet from me, staring down at me with what probably is supposed to be an amused smile, except half the skin on his face is hanging off, so it's kind of hard to tell.

"Peter," he whispers, his voice deathly cold, "I've longed for this moment."

"H-how do you know my name?"

He stares at me with blank eyes and a perverse smile and takes another step forward.

I gulp. Fear tears through my veins, begging me to run, to flee, to save myself. But then hands grab me in my thoughts—Homer's hands—and his intense eyes gaze fiercely into mine. Then I hear Dr. Elsavier's voice in my mind: *You're an Odysseus, Peter. I know one when I see one.*

Though the fear still boils in my chest, I put my shoulders back and do not retreat. I stand my ground. "I won't let you hurt them."

Emily cries out as flames graze her arms, and Caster goes flying back into the wall with a resounding *crack*, sent along by Ami's gust.

"They do not need me to do that." Morin grins manically. "They will destroy themselves." He steps closer. "Join them. Join their fighting."

"No," I say. "Make it stop."

"Oh, but I cannot. I only reveal what is already there. Shadows have no existence themselves; they only reveal the objects that cast them." His hollow green eyes peer into mine. "Do you know the meaning of the pentagram and the tree? Do you wish to know, Peter?"

"How do you know my name?" I repeat.

"Many things are prophesied in the realms, which you know little of. But I can tell you. I can reveal the hidden, occult things of the world to you if you'll let me."

"What hidden things?"

"Join me. Become my willing sacrifice, and I will raise you up to life again in the secrets of our way. I will show you the hidden things you desire to know." He lifts his arms as he speaks, and as they stretch up toward the ceiling, he curls his long, sharp fingers into fists.

My heart thumps wildly against my chest, my emotions are raging, and I'm a hair's breadth from completely losing it. I take a deep breath and search for something to say, and I find Caster's smirking expression in my mind—the smirk that seems to embody all sarcasm and irreverence.

"Join you? Isn't that what all the villains are supposed to say?" I shake my head. "Have you no shame? So cliché."

Morin's face droops; the amused expression falls from his lips, along with a little piece of flesh, and then his eyes flash with green fire. "Then I shall make of you an unwilling sacrifice."

I glance behind me at my friends, who are now on the ground; their fighting has devolved to scratching and biting. They howl like wounded animals, only to redouble their attempts to hurt one another. My heart wells with sadness. I could die alongside them. I always knew secretly that it might come to this. But I hoped to die with them by my side as friends, like human beings, not like rabies-crazed dogs.

I take one last look at them, holding their image tenderly in my mind. My eyes linger on Ami, the gentlest and kindest of us. Her face is now contorted with mad rage.

I turn to face Morin; my limbs pulse with anger. If I'm going to die, I might as well try to take him with me.

I stare into the fiery green eyes of my death, and though this ought to terrify me, knowing I'm about to die liberates me, because if every outcome ends in torture and death, then I'm free to fight like a crazy person with nothing left to lose. At least, I got to know friendship before I die.

I run at Morin, howling like a madman, pouring all my rage and anger at what he's done to my friends into my voice. I throw myself at him. My hands stretch toward his face to rip the rest of the ugly flesh from his bones, but his hand comes up, cracking me against the side of my head and sending me flying back on top of my friends.

In two strides, Morin closes the distance between us. He draws a long, serrated knife from his belt, one similar to the knife the bloodgorger wielded in Galthanius's basement chamber, and he holds it above me. His lips move frantically, speaking words that leave me frozen in terror. I see dark shapes flit across the room, shadows of creatures that I somehow know are too awful for my mind to let itself see. Behind Morin, the statues of the three women are no longer statues but living creatures. Their mouths are stained with blood. The one in the center licks her sharp teeth, and her tongue is long and forked like a serpent's.

His chanting reaches a fevered pitch, and then he raises the knife all the way up.

He's brings the knife down in one swift motion, and I shut my eyes. I expect my chest to explode with pain and feel cold seep into my bones, as my heart is ripped apart. But instead, I hear a clang of metal on metal. My eyes flutter open, and I see a golden staff above me, blocking Morin's dagger only centimeters from my chest. The staff swings upward, tossing the knife away. Then like lighting, the staff swings back, and a resounding *crack* splits the room. I look up as Morin makes a little groaning noise. The muscles in his face grow limp, and he crumples to the ground, falling to the side.

I gape at his fallen body and look over to see a woman in plain brown robes. Her hair is as black as a raven's wings. Her face is as fair as moonlight, and her eyes are round and mischievous. My sight settles on what she wields in her hands: a golden staff with characters carved into its sides and a single ruby jewel at the tip.

CHAPTER 87

TUMBLING WALLS

"Who?" I gasp for breath. My heart is still hammering wildly in my chest. "Who are you?"

She gazes at me with an amused smile eerily similar to Morin's. "Can't you guess?"

I shake my head. "No!" I get the impression I sound stupid right now, but my heart is racing way too fast for me to speak eloquently or think things through.

"Peter, five persons came into the room. Three of them are beneath you, and that makes four. Who could be the fifth?"

"Five persons?" I stare at her uncomprehendingly. "You're not the bird. Birds aren't persons."

In a flash, her form collapses into that of a bird. The bird makes a quick circle around the staff before exploding outward again into the shape of a woman in time to catch the falling staff. "Some birds are!" She tosses back her hair.

"But then ..." I struggle to find the words but find my mind collapsing under its own weight. I don't even know what questions to ask.

"Ow," Emily groans. "Why is my blanket so heavy? Wait—that's not a blanket. Peter, Caster, Ami, why are you on top of me?"

"Oh, my cheeks. Why do they feel like a feral cat mistook me for a raccoon?" Caster moans.

I try to push myself up, but my legs refuse to budge, and my arms don't have the strength.

The bird woman stares down amusedly at us and offers me a hand. I take it uncertainly, and she pulls me to my feet. Next, she helps up Ami, then Caster, and, last of all, Emily, who ended up on the bottom of the pile.

Emily looks at her fingers, which are caked with blood, and her arm, which is red from where Caster's flames bit her. The others have wounds too, though Emily's look the worst, probably because she was the only one who couldn't use her power.

"What happened?" Emily asks dazedly. Her eyes focus on the bird woman. "Who are you?"

"You fell prey to the smoke of Pyro the deceiver, unleashed by my father, Morin."

"Your father?" we all say at once.

Then it hits me. "Wait. Then that means you must be—"

"Haji," Ami says quietly.

Haji does a little curtsy. "The one and only."

"Why were you a bird?" I ask.

"Wait—you were a bird?" says Emily.

"Our bird," says Caster, as if it is perfectly obvious. "The one Ami picked up."

"Oh."

"I was—" Haji is interrupted by a groaning sound coming from the giant living corpse of Morin lying on the floor. Slowly, he stirs, attempting to push himself off the floor. As he works his rotting flesh, the floor begins to tremble, and I sense a deep anger in the stones, as though they will tear themselves apart if only to fall on our heads and crush us.

"Oh, time to go!" Haji says, striding toward the exit.

"But we're locked in!" says Emily.

Haji flashes a smile. "Oh no, my dear. Not anymore." She pushes past us to the door, raises the staff, and drives it into the narrow crack.

The stones are unyielding at first. I feel them draw all their strength together to resist Haji, but her power is like a tidal wave plowing over a sandcastle, and they shatter within seconds.

She spins around, and her eyes widen. "Get down!" she says as she launches her staff at my forehead.

I duck, and a moment later, I hear another splitting crack, the sound of breaking bone.

"Go!" she yells, and she pushes past us, shoving us toward the door. Caster and I take the lead again, and his light leads the others, while the stones themselves point the way for me.

Seconds later, an unholy roar erupts from inside the inner chamber, and the walls of the cave renew their furious shaking. Dust and pebbles fall as cracks grow along the walls like spidery veins of poisoned blood.

I feel two sets of footsteps coming after us, one larger and lumbering yet quick and the other small, sleek, and swift: Morin and Haji, father and daughter. Before us stretches at least a mile of winding stone passageways before we make it back to the surface.

I tuck my head and run, trying to ignore the burning in my lungs and the roiling in my stomach, which threatens to evacuate the meager contents of my last meal onto the sides of the walls.

411

CHAPTER 88

A BIRD OF MANY COLORS

By the time we make it to the surface, my lungs feel like twin volcanoes about to erupt. Morin nearly catches up to us, but in the last hundred yards, Haji springs past us, drives the staff into the sealed door, and commands it to open. Despite all Morin's curses, the stones yield to her, and we escape through the cracks just as his face comes into view around the corner.

He plunges toward the opening, but Haji strikes the stones again, and they fall unwillingly back onto themselves and their master. His howls and cries for blood die out in the piling rocks and collapsing earth. I feel the voice that once shook my chest grow distant, until it's only a little speck on the horizon.

I take a deep breath, and then my legs buckle. My head smacks against the ground, but it feels more like falling into a soft bed. The earth here is friendlier, almost happy to see me, though I can sense there is a lurking shape somewhere in the distance. But I shove that worry aside. If it's distant, then we needn't worry about it now.

I push myself up and see the others are spread out on the ground. Everyone looks thoroughly exhausted, except for Haji. My eyes stray along the landscape around us. Behind us lies a barren mountain covered by jagged rocks that jut upward like daggers and accusing fingers. To the east lies a city of gray towers spiraling upward like giant soldiers clad in austere and deadly armor. I count six great towers. Five of them seem to be placed suspiciously in the shape of a pentagram. In the center, there's one great tower high above the rest. Its white walls glow red with the sun rising in the east.

"What is this place?" I ask, turning to Haji.

The amusement bleeds out of her eyes, and they moisten. She stares at the city awhile before speaking. "It is the Gray City, once my father's city—once my city. Now it is frozen in time, until I can undo the last curse, the final spite of the druids.

The others have grown attentive now, pushing themselves up to seated positions so they can look at Haji.

"The Gray City," I say. "That was one of the places Thaegar mentioned."

"That means we're getting close," says Emily. "We only have the sea to cross after this, and then we'll be to Samjang. We might actually pull this off."

"That depends on how much time is left," Caster says. "If my calculations are right, then it's—"

"The morning of the sixteenth day," Haji says, finishing for him.

Caster's mouth clamps shut, and he shakes his head. "Sorry. I'm still not used to the fact that you are—were—a bird. Why did you only reveal yourself just now?"

"Because I could not before. My armies were hunting down the last of the druids, and I was flying between camps in order to direct the final assault, when they put a curse on me: to remain in my bird form till Morin woke."

"So you woke him up in order to get back to your original form?" Emily's mouth hangs open. "That could have killed us!"

"That was one reason. The second reason is that we needed Morin's staff to leave the cave. He is not stupid, my father; he is very clever. Do you think he would give the Four a way of escape without making them trigger the trap that would wake him to consume them? It was all very well designed."

Haji looks us up and down with a wistful look in her eye. "It was a pleasure to be alongside you four for so long, but I must go now."

"But we've just begun to know you," Ami says quietly. Her brow is furrowed.

"Go where?" I ask.

"To the nymphs trapped by the Bloodfather. I have the staff now, and I shall deal with him sternly, sending him back to that tortured realm from whence he came."

"Meila!" Emily exclaims happily. If Haji frees Meila's twin, then the sisters will be able to reunite.

"Oh, good," says Ami, clapping her hands. "But how will you get there?"

Haji winks. "You'll see." She takes a step away from us. "You haven't much time now. I would travel with you the rest of the way, but if I do not visit the Dark Wella, the nymphs will become one with the Bloodfather." Her expression darkens. "It might be too late even now."

Ami shakes her head. "No, it isn't."

Haji raises an eyebrow. "I hope you are correct, little one."

Little one. The expression reminds me that Haji is very old, though she doesn't look it. I try to remember what Thaegar said about her. "Wait," I say, and she stops backing away. "You're one of the Chelei, daughters of the trickster god and a nymph, right?"

Haji nods. "I am."

"How many are there?"

"There are many." She looks away. "You have probably met some already, though you did not know it. Long ago, they lived among the humans, laganmorfs, and nymphs, whom they considered to be like sisters. But when the Kar-dun came in the west and the druids came in the east, cruel men began to hunt them for sport, so they withdrew, vowing never to interfere in our world."

"But you did," I say. "You led an army against the servants of Morin after he died."

"I am different. I was born under a strange constellation that marked a difference in my fate, which was prophesied even at my birth. The prophecy came true when one of Morin's hunters captured me as a young girl and brought me into his household. He was still kind to me then and treated me well." She rubs her eye, brushing away a tear. "But we shall have time to talk later if we first stop the Ice Reich. You have only two days to rescue Samjang and reunite her with Cog at the mountain, the Heart of Miria. You must not delay."

For a moment, I wonder how she knows so much about our mission, but then I remember she's overheard every conversation since we found her just after leaving Kalix.

"But how will we make it?" I ask. "It took us many days just to get here. How can we go the rest of the way and back in only two days?"

"When you come to the journey's end, you will see." She takes another step away from us.

"Wait," says Caster. "A final question."

"Time runs short."

"I know, I know," he says. "But I need to know. Who are the druids of Belial?"

Haji shakes her head. "You do not want to know the answer to that question."

She takes another step back. I want to ask her more, but there is a finality in her voice. She lowers herself to the ground, and then, with a twirl of her arms, she transforms into a beautiful bird. Her left wing is as blue as water, her right is as red as fire, her chest is as white as a cloud, and her head is as gray as the stones of the Gray City. In the center of her chest, just above her heart, is a single patch of obsidian feather in the shape of a triangular pyramid—the shape of Five.

My eyes widen, and I'm about to ask her what she might know of Five, but she spreads her great wings and, with a rush of wind, leaps into the air, clutching Morin's staff in her golden claws, leaving us to face the Gray City and the last part of the journey to Samjang.

CHAPTER 89

THE TALE OF THE LAST SCRIBE

"The Gray City makes Detroit look like a lively city," says Caster as we enter through the gates of the crumbling city walls.

The streets are empty of people, as we expected. There hasn't been anyone living here in a long time. But the eerie silence is deeper than the mere absence of traders bartering, children laughing, and the bustle of a thousand voices mingling into one. It hangs like a shadow over the cracked city streets, which look as if they were once made of smooth stones.

It takes me a minute to realize what exactly is causing the eeriness of the city. It's not the crumbling homes, the broken stone steps, or even the six towers that jut from the earth untouched. It's the toys in the street—dolls and rattles made of flimsy materials, such as wood and hay. No one said exactly how old the city is, but from the way Cog, Thaegar, and the druids spoke, I think it must date back to around the time when the Kar-dun first came to Miria. If the Kar-dun are the same as the Nephilim in the Bible, then that means this city is thousands of years old. How can dolls

417

of wood and hay have survived that long? For that matter, how can anything in the city have lasted that long? Shouldn't it all be buried beneath earth and sand? It's as if the city is frozen in time.

As that thought enters my mind, I realize the city looks exactly as it should have looked the day it—what? What happened to the city? Where did all the people go? It's as if they disappeared.

"What are those?" says Emily.

I follow Emily's gaze. We've stopped outside a tall stone wall. It is part of a larger complex. As I search the earth, I find the structure of the stones. The building is a pentagon. Five walls of equal size stretch about fifty feet into the air. At each corner, there are torches, and windows line the tops of the walls. Judging by the stained glass that lies shattered at our feet, they were once beautiful, but now they look down at us like hollow eyes.

I look up past the walls and see a tower spiraling up from the ground. I realize with a start that it's the same tower we saw on the outskirts of the city, the sixth tower. A tower inside a pentagon of walls inside a pentagon of towers. "What's their obsession with fives, pentagons, and pentagrams?"

"Probably has something to do with the Five," says Emily.

My eyes fall to the characters written in violent black ink on the white walls, and I wonder how I missed them before. They're not exactly inconspicuous. I stare at them with a growing fascination. Their sharp points and flowing edges draw me in, but I also feel a growing sense of dread. They do not look like they tell a happy story.

"What do they say?" Emily asks.

Caster pulls out his spyglass reluctantly, as if he does not want to know what grim meaning the characters hide either.

He scans the walls with the glass, and his face grows paler as he reads. Then he settles on the top right corner and begins to read from top to bottom, right to left: "To the stranger who passes by these walls, I, the last scribe of the people of Halir, write these words that you may know the woes of those who fall into the hands of druids, the wielders of magic. All of us were drawn in by Morin's beauty, charm, and genius and the vision of safe lands and a glorious future he promised to us. Such was his grace that even when creatures in dark robes began to gather round him like storm clouds in the sky, we did not worry but accepted them as honored guests, though our traditions told us better. In those days, we learned to reject tradition as a worthless hindrance and to accept whatever came to us by our new teachers, Morin and his druids.

"For a time, we seemed justified in casting away the path of our ancestors. They seemed to us as foolish men, talking nonsense and speaking of things we understood better. We triumphed over our enemies in the west and turned our hearts inward toward our lands. But the days turned against us, as Morin's heart grew darker, and the druids began to reveal more of their true selves. Each new revelation prepared the next, and soon we began to look lustfully on forms that would have seemed hideous to us at the start, so much had we been corrupted.

"Morin's lust for life and its endless prolonging only grew. It was not the kind of everlasting life our ancestors told of, life after death. This was mocked as the fables of foolish men. But it is not an easy task to break our nature and the death that lies waiting for us in our bones. So Morin called upon names that ought not be spoken, drawing evil into our world from the Dark Realm in order to prolong his life. And we suffered at their hands. At last,

Morin's iniquity grew so great that the gods decided to punish him, striking down his pride. But they left to us the druids as punishment for turning from the path of right.

"It all seemed hopeless, till Haji came to us. She led us out from the bondage we had brought upon ourselves by following Morin's madness. She roused the warriors, shaking the blindness off their eyes and teaching them to fight for a forgotten vision of goodness. For a time, we were successful, driving the druids back. But a blessed ending was not to be ours, for our guilt was too great, and the druids' spite was too black.

"Haji left us, taken we know not where. And then we began to vanish one by one. The children first; then the adults; and, last of all, those of us who were full with years, who remembered when the times had been different. I am alone now in the city; being the oldest, I am the last to be taken, but my time shall soon come, and I shall find them, wherever they were taken, whether to torment or to some unknown fate. Perhaps it was Haji, rescuing us from the cursed world her father brought upon us all. But I shall not know until I am taken. Till then, I wait, the last scribe of Halir. Remember, stranger, my words, and learn from them."

After Caster finishes, we all stare in silence at the wall. There are tears in Emily's and Ami's eyes, and even I'm feeling a little sad.

Emily brushes the tears from her eyes and furrows her brow. "Wait a moment. You read all that from only a few characters?"

"They're very efficient." Caster closes his spyglass. "Anyway, sucks for them. We'd best get going. Not much time left— sixteenth day and all."

"That's very callous of you," Emily says.

"Callous shmallous. It's not our problem. Let Haji deal with it."

He starts to walk toward the east side of the city, when the walls begin to shake, and a voice speaks from within: "Enter, Four. I have been waiting for you."

CHAPTER 90

THE TECHNICOLOR GOD

Cracks appear in the solid wall, forming into a circle. The circle falls backward and reveals a soft glow within. I'm starting to get the feeling that people in the east didn't build doors. *I guess why bother if you can enchant stone to crack at the sound of your voice and then rebuild itself once you're through?*

The inside of the pentagon is breathtaking, and we all take a collective breath as we enter the glowing hall. The walls are adorned with five huge gems that pulse with soft light. Their colors change every few seconds, turning from sunset orange to forest green to ocean blue to other colors I can't quite describe. But the gem light seems as cheap as disco light compared to the shafts of milky light that pour in from the center of the room, illuminating a throne of white gold.

But even more breathtaking is the figure sitting lazily on the throne, dressed in colorful clothes and wearing an amused smirk on his monkeyish face that puts Caster's smirks to shame. He looks like Joseph from *Joseph and the Amazing Technicolor Dreamcoat* times ten.

"Who the hockey sticks are you?" says Emily, rubbing her eyes. "And why do you have so much color?"

"It is kind of lurid," Caster says.

The man's amused smirk slips into a momentary frown, and then he stands up and holds his arms out like a great king. "Behold. Welcome to the Pentagon!" He frowns. "No, wait a moment." He snaps his fingers, and a gigantic staff with a golden globe at the top appears in his hands. "Welcome to the Pentagon! No, no, no, it's still not right."

The man claps his hands twice, and confetti tumbles from the air as the room resounds with trumpets playing a royal-entrance fanfare. "Ta-da! Welcome to the Pentagon!" His face glows a ruddy red.

We all exchange meaningful looks. What the heck have we walked into?

He sighs. "Young people these days are so hard to impress. How about this?" He clears his throat. "I am Enki, the god of tricks and the locker-upper of Samjang!"

My heart begins to race, and I reach for my power, pulling two shafts of stone from the earth and fashioning them into pointed spears ready to launch at him. Simultaneously, Caster's hands burst into flames, water gathers around Emily's arms, and Ami whips her staff off her back and levels it at the man claiming to be Enki.

"Now, that's more like it!" he says, clapping his hands. "Vivacity! Elan! Esprit de corps!"

"Before we impale, roast, and drown you and put you in your own personal tornado," says Caster, "how do we know you're really the trickster god?"

The god smiles. "An excellent question. Suppose I were

instead the god of honesty or at least an honest god and not the god of tricks. Being bound to only say honest—and therefore boring—things, I could not say I was the trickster god. Now suppose I were instead the god of dishonesty or at least a dishonest god. Then, being bound to be a scoundrel, knave, and dishonest deity, I could not say I was the god of dishonesty, for that would make me honest. It follows therefore that I must be in between honesty and dishonesty—that is, trickery. Ergo, I am the god of tricks. QED."

"Isn't it logically possible that you're the god of dishonesty and are lying about being the god of tricks?" Caster says.

Enki snaps his fingers. "I usually manage to dupe earth, water, and air with that little bit of sophistry. I always forget how intelligent fire is."

"I wasn't duped," Emily grumbles. "Anyway, if what you really enjoy is duping people, why don't they call you the god of dupery or the dupester god?"

"The dupester god," he repeats, feeling the words in his mouth like a gourmet chef. "Not bad. I might just use that next time." He takes another step toward us, and we all raise our makeshift weapons again.

"Not a step closer," I say. "If you really are the trickster god, you've got an awful lot of explaining to do. Like, why are you bent on destroying the world?"

Enki bears a grin of perfect white teeth. "Ah, Peter, I love how honest and simple you are. It's touching. What if I were to tell you that I've been protecting you four all along?"

"What do you mean?"

Enki's grin widens, and he leans a little closer. "What if I were to tell you that I am Homer?"

CHAPTER 91

THE TWIST

"You're Homer?" Caster says. "You mean you wrote that Greek poetry Peter's obsessed with, whatever it's called? The whatchamacallit?"

"*The Iliad* and *The Odyssey*," Emily says.

"That."

Enki shakes his head. "No, you bozo. I am Peter's Homer. The—"

"That's what I just said."

"Would you stop interrupting me?" Enki thunders.

"Sure thing."

"I am Peter's Homer, the—"

"You already said that bit."

"You!" Enki balls up his fists and looks ready to sock Caster, but then he throws his head back and laughs. "I forget that we're of the same element. You are a trickster yourself."

"More like a dupester," says Emily. "Anyway, can you finish your sentence?"

"I am the Homer who has appeared in Peter's dreams, who

taught him first how to use the power of his ring in the flying cave above the arctic sea—why are you laughing?"

Emily covers her face and tries to bite back her chortles. "Sorry. Just the flying-cave bit sounds really funny."

Enki gives an irritated look and resumes. "I prepared the boat for you at the edge of the Silver Lake, taught Peter what to do in the cave of the Bloodfather, and have ensured your safety thus far."

Caster raises an eyebrow and looks at me. "Is it true?"

I stare at Enki uncertainly. "I can't say whether he was the one who prepared the boat. But there has been a Homer appearing in my dreams and even sometimes when I'm awake, and that Homer did help me in the Bloodfather's cave."

Enki spreads his hands as if that settles everything. "See?"

"So you've been watching us this whole time?" I ask.

"Yes, I've been watching you the whole time. The only thing I didn't get to see was how you managed to get into Morin's inner chamber."

"We solved Dulia's riddle, obviously," says Emily. "Gosh, I hate that dog."

"She was a bitch," says Caster.

"Watch your language."

"No, it really was a bitch, technically speaking," says Caster. "You couldn't tell?"

"No, not really," Emily says airily, and she shrugs. "I guess it takes one to know one."

"Hey!" Caster says, but Enki holds up a hand.

"Enough of this. You'll have plenty of time to flirt later. Now we must do business."

Emily shakes her head. "I'm not really sure we can trust you, and I'm not really sure what you'd have to offer. I mean, you're the whole reason we're in this mess. You were the one who tricked Cog, stole Samjang, and put yourself in league with the fallen gods. Not exactly a great résumé."

Enki's eyes twinkle, and he looks at us as if we're mere children. "Oh? Well, I suppose you understand all the facts—like, for example, why I did what I did."

"Because you want your mom back," says Emily. "An understandable motive, but it doesn't excuse villainy."

"Villainy! Ah, you have a way with words, don't you? I should hire you for my PR team when this is all over. But wordsmithing aside, what do you really know about my mother?"

Emily opens her mouth but clamps it shut again.

"What if I were to tell you that my mother, the Winter Goddess, is Cog's wife?"

"You're Cog's son?" Caster says as his eyebrows arch in surprise. "That's a plot twist."

I agree, but as I think back on the way Cog grew misty-eyed and sad when he mentioned Enki, it makes sense. It also makes sense why he knew about Enki's motives but didn't want to talk about them.

"Okay," says Emily. "So it's all some sort of family quarrel, but how does that dig you out of the very deep pit of kimchi you presently are in?"

"Do you know how the Ice Reich became the Ice Reich?" asks Enki.

"Not really sure how this is relevant, but no," says Emily.

"Because they stole the Winter Goddess. She lies deep within their hidden world, tortured and abused, as they extract her essence from her bones. Do you know how painful that is for a goddess to endure? It is as though every inch of your skin is plunged into burning oil while red-hot knives dig into your flesh, carving openings in your bones, into which molten steel is poured. And this only begins to capture the horror she has endured for centuries."

Enki takes a deep breath, trying to regain composure. I can't help but feel bad for him. How would I feel if my mother or Dr. Elsavier endured torture like that, not for a minute, an hour, or even a year but for hundreds of years? I shake away the thought.

Enki continues. "But the situation is worse than all that. It is only because of this horror that lies at the heart of the Ice Reich that they have been a menace to our world. Before her capture, they were a hidden world of arcane secrets, possessing dark knowledge but no strength."

"If they had no strength, how did they manage to capture a goddess?" asks Caster.

"They didn't. Do you know why the fallen gods are called fallen? I'm sure Cog told you it is because they pried into occult secrets and lusted after power, and this is true. But they became the fallen gods and began their journey into ever-deeper darkness by selling my mother to the Ice Reich in exchange for those occult secrets kept in the arcane and hidden libraries of the Reich. Using their evil knowledge, they were able to extract great power from my mother—so much so that they nearly conquered our world, and they will always pose a threat to it as long as she is kept in their dungeons." He looks at us with his eyes blazing. His monkey face is fierce and flushed with anger.

"Okay," says Caster, nodding. "I'm tracking. But if the fallen gods did this to your mother, why would you join them?"

Enki's eyes light up with mischief. "It's simple. I'm the

trickster god. No one believes me to tell the honest truth. They all expect me to play tricks and follow my selfish interest. If I wanted to save my mother and get revenge on the Ice Reich and all those who aided it once and for all, how would I do it? I'd convince the fallen I had joined them, in order to get the power they had. And in order to do that, I couldn't let Papa—"

"The papa!" Emily sings, and then she blushes. "Sorry. *Fiddler on the Roof.* Continue."

Enki flashes her an irritated look. "I couldn't let Papa in on the secret. It had to look real. I also had to steal Samjang as proof of my trustworthiness to the fallen gods. But it was more than that. I had to convince Papa to summon the Four into the world, because only with you does my plan have a chance at succeeding."

"But isn't this taking a bit too much risk?" I ask. "I mean, what if it goes wrong?"

"It's not a risk," says Enki. "It's our only chance. The fallen gods have grown too powerful. Cog and Samjang could not stop them from opening the portal to the Ice Reich, which they want to do in order to gain further secrets from them, the final step in their perverse quest for immortality. The only chance we have now is to get Samjang back in time and position you, the Four, so that when the portal is opened, we can steal back my mother, thus robbing the Ice Reich of its power, while sending those miscreant fallen gods through the portal and locking the door behind them."

"All right," I say, still not quite trusting him. But what he's saying does make a lot of sense. "What do you have planned then?"

Enki rubs his hands together with a fiendishly clever look in his eyes. "Gather round, children, and I will tell you."

CHAPTER 92

THE SCHEME

"It's very simple," says Enki. "At least for a mind like mine, it's simple, though you might have to apply yourselves to keep up. The plan is this. You will travel to the isle where Samjang is kept and retrieve her. As soon as she is freed from her bonds, Cog will be freed from his and will travel with his loyal gods to the mountain, the Heart of Miria, to restore the broken seal that keeps the Ice Reich at bay. You will travel immediately to this mountain, and you needn't worry about the fallen gods hunting you, so you can travel by jet. Yes, I heard about that little plan of yours, Caster, and I was very impressed. But remember, once you get to the mountain, you must not reveal yourself to Cog just yet. This is the clever bit.

"I will draw from the deep store of power I have been saving up for a long time for this very purpose. Using this power, I will delude the fallen gods into thinking they are at the Heart of Miria, though they truly are elsewhere. At the same time, I will delude Cog into thinking he is closing the seal, when he is really opening it.

"But it will be only a tiny crack, just enough for me to slip in. As soon as I've entered, you will reveal yourselves to Cog and will help him keep the opening small while I retrieve Mother. As soon as I have her, I will release the magic on the fallen gods, and they will storm to the Heart of Miria. But they will not have the Ice Reich as an ally anymore, because I will have stripped the Reich of its stolen power by saving my mother. Then, with the combined power of Cog and Samjang and the power of the Four, you will send the fallen gods into the portal and seal it off, locking them away for all time."

Enki's lips twist into a confident smirk that looks eerily similar to Caster's smirks. I remember how Emily nicknamed Caster Sun Wukong—a naughty monkey, as she put it—from *Journey to the West*. I wonder whether that story, like the myths of the Norse and the Greeks, contains elements of truth too. Maybe Enki is the OG Sun Wukong.

"Pretty genius, isn't it?" says Enki.

"Is it?" Caster asks. "This plan could go wrong in far too many ways, and if it goes wrong, I don't see a path to victory."

"Yeah," says Ami.

"It's the only way," says Enki. "If we don't strip the Ice Reich of its power, we not only condemn an innocent goddess to a fate worse than death but also leave the world open to the same fate indefinitely. If you do not pull weeds up by their roots, they will always return, and eventually, the gardeners will grow tired, and the weeds will win, choking the flowers and consuming the garden."

"I think you're right," says Caster, stroking his chin. "It's an improbable scheme, a daring scheme, and a scheme likely to fail horribly. But I like it."

I think of Enki's phrase *choking the flowers*. If we manage to stop the Ice Reich in this generation but without retrieving the Winter Goddess, then maybe we can all live happy lives, but what about our children, grandchildren, and great-grandchildren? They'll have to deal with the same threat, and if they fail, then it's game over forever. Besides, the thought of the Winter Goddess's face twisted in agony for all time is a thought too horrible to consider. It's wrong. We can't let it continue.

"I'm in," I say. "You have my rock."

Emily looks askance at me and then rolls her eyes. "Fine. I'm in too. You have my water."

"And my ax," says Caster in a spot-on imitation of Gimli from *The Lord of the Rings*. We can always count on Caster to make a nerdy reference.

"You already said you were in," says Ami. "But I'm in too."

"Splendid!" Enki says, rubbing his hands together. "So are there any questions?"

"Yeah. What did you want to show me behind the field?" I say, referencing the dream.

"Oh, about that. It was foreshadowing. Some things are going to happen that you will not understand at first. In fact, it is crucial that you do not understand them now. I know this is a task I can count on you to do."

I stare into his eyes, trying to avoid the feeling that he's just insulted my intelligence and attempting to figure out what exactly he means. "What do you mean?"

"You'll see. Do you trust me?"

"No, not really," all four of us say at once.

"Jinx! You all owe me sodas," Emily says. She then turns to Enki. "Anyway, we're all for the scheme and all, but it's pretty clear you haven't given us a single good reason to trust you. Like none. Nada. Zilch. Zip. *Nichts*. Nu—"

"Can you stop saying different words for *none*?" Enki rubs his temples. "If you don't trust me personally, at least trust the logic. Remember the scenario of the god of honesty, the god of dishonesty, and me, your humble servant."

"That scenario committed numerous errors in formal logic," Caster says.

Enki nods. "Then I'll give you a reason to trust me."

He twirls his fingers through the air as if composing a poem. Then he snaps, and his script appears in big, glowing characters on the walls of the Pentagon. Caster pulls out his spyglass and turns around a full 360 degrees as he reads the script. As he ends, his eyes meet Enki's, and they stare at each other for a moment. Then, unless my eyes deceive me, they nod at each other, as though some kind of understanding has passed between them.

"Did you see that?" Ami whispers to me.

I nod. So it's not just me.

Enki turns to the rest of us and smiles. "I'll leave it to Caster here to explain. Till next time. Toodles! Oh, and one last thing. Remember that an author's soul lives in her words. *Now*, toodles!" He snaps his fingers and dissolves into a mist. It sparkles with all the colors of the rainbow before diffusing into nothing.

"So what was that all about?" asks Emily.

Caster is silent for a moment, focusing his eyes on the ground, in deep contemplation.

Emily leans down and sticks her face in his line of sight. "Hullo! Earth to Caster! Do you copy?"

Caster shakes his head as if to clear his mind and then looks at us. "I'll explain when we're out of this place. It's starting to give me the creeps."

"Agreed," says Ami, and we all walk toward the circular door, which, surprisingly, hasn't closed itself. I worried we'd have to solve another stupid riddle or something to get out of this place.

"Is it just me," Emily says as we pass through the circular exit of the Pentagon, "or does Enki's name remind you of the song 'Skinnamarink'?"

I look at Ami, and we burst out laughing.

"Not at all," I say between spasms of laughter. It's not really that funny, but I guess between the stress and the lack of sleep, the dumb joke has broken my brain.

"I think it's her way of saying she's fallen for him. Either that, or it's her way of saying she never matured out of preschool." Caster clears his throat and begins to sing horribly off-key. "I love you in the morning and in the afternoon! I love you in the evening and underneath the moon! Oh—"

The rest of us join in and finish the song together: "Skinnamarinky dinky dink, skinnamarinky do, I love you!"

Despite the danger ahead, I feel safe and happy in this moment beside my friends. It's obvious by the warmness in everyone's voice as we sing the lyrics "I love you" that we love one another.

It's sappy, I know. But sappy moments are the best sometimes.

Especially when, in all probability, we're going to die horribly sometime in the next forty-eight hours.

CHAPTER 93

THE ISLE

We make our way through the rest of the Gray City, and as we walk, Caster explains the message the trickster god left.

"He basically just asked what we would do to save our mothers," Caster says.

"That's all he said?" asks Emily. "With all those characters he wrote, that's it?"

Caster waves his hand. "They're very efficient."

Maybe it's just me, but I get the feeling he's hiding something. I consider telling Ami my suspicion, but a strange part of me wants to keep it hidden, and that part of me grows until I decide to bring up something silly, such as the weather.

Ami raises an eyebrow at me, as if she can tell something's not sitting quite right with me, but she lets it go, and soon she and I are chatting merrily. Up ahead, Caster and Emily are doing the same, and a little voice inside me whispers that this is how it's supposed to be; I ought to let go of Emily, because this is how the story goes, the story determined by the nature of our rings.

For once, I'm okay with that. I think I can let go of all the years of wanting her that basically defined my high school experience. It feels good to let go. Emily's a cool person and a little quirky like the rest of us. She's funny, kind, and smart, unlike the rest of us—or at least me. Okay, really just me. Everyone else is pretty smart. But I realize now that those qualities are what make her a good friend.

As though Ami can sense my thoughts, she lowers her voice and asks, "So what did it mean in Morin's tomb?"

It takes me a second to realize what she's referring to: the moment when we held hands.

It means I like you. The words come bubbling up from my heart and leave my heart pounding in my chest. I try to say the words, but my tongue decides to act like a beached whale, flopping around helplessly in my mouth. Sometimes I hate myself. *A real Odysseus*, I mutter silently to Dr. Elsavier in my mind. *A real Odysseus I am.*

I finally work up the strength to open my mouth, when Emily shouts, "Water!"

Ami and I turn, looking ahead to where Caster and Emily stand at the edge of a grassy plain overlooking the western sea, which glows red with the last light of evening. In the distance, surrounded by mist, I can just see the outlines of an island.

I look back at Ami, wanting to tell her how I feel, but the moment is over. "We'd better go check it out," she says, her voice just a sliver disappointed.

I sigh and follow her up the hill, feeling a lot more disappointed than she does probably.

"So what's the plan?" asks Caster.

I look at the others and then realize with a start he's looking at me. "Me?" I say, gulping.

"Yes, the one and only Rock. Our glorious leader."

I raise an eyebrow. Caster never has been a big fan of the idea that the Rock is supposed to be the leader. Why the sudden change? Or is he just making fun of me? But he doesn't seem like it. He seems sincere. "What put you in such a good mood?"

"Oh, I had a great conversation with Emily here," he says, grinning mischievously. "She's convinced me of a few things."

For a moment, I feel the temptation to be jealous. But I grind it under my heel. I've decided that I like Ami and that Emily is just going to be my friend, like the sister I never had. "Oh?"

"Oh yes," says Caster. "So what's the plan, jefe?"

My heart pounds in my chest, and my brain feels at least ten times mushier than usual, which is to say, extremely mushy. How am I supposed to think of a plan? It's much easier when other people do the thinking for me. I don't like being told what to do, but I don't like telling other people what to do, even if they agree.

"Um, well," I say, buying time. *It's just a plan. You and Goober did it all the time when you played* Ghost Army. *Yeah, but this is real life!* "Maybe there's some wood we can use to build a makeshift boat, and then Emily can propel us across the water?"

"No wood," says Caster. "At least none nearby."

"I have an idea," says Ami.

Oh, thank God. "What, um, is the idea? Your idea." *Gosh, why do I sound so awkward? It's just my friends.*

"Well, we don't have to worry about the fallen gods getting us anymore," says Ami.

Caster's eyes light up. "Right-o. But three people can be quite heavy. You sure you want to carry us across?"

Ami shakes her head. "Emily can take you across the water. I'll take Peter."

Caster's jaw drops. "You're abandoning me, lil sis?" But then he looks at Emily, and a funny look passes between them. She crosses her arms. "Um, right. That's fine," he says. "See you there."

He and Emily walk down the sandbank toward the shore. "It's a race, by the way!" he calls out.

"A race?" I say.

"He's going to lose," says Ami, and the determination in her voice startles me.

She takes my hands, and we rise upward just as we did the day when we floated above Cog's palace. Despite my affinity for earth, it's a wonderful, freeing feeling to be in the air. It's also slightly terrifying. But with Ami's warm hands gripping mine, it's not so bad. She closes her eyes, and the air tosses us along.

We rush toward the island, the destination we've been trying to get to for so long. It's crazy to think we're finally almost there, even if we're almost out of time. Tomorrow's the final day, which means we have about twenty-four hours to get Samjang and attempt the trickster god's harebrained scheme.

I'm tempted to say, "It's not like things could get worse." But by now, I know those words should never, ever be uttered. Things can always get worse—and I have a sinking feeling they are about to.

CHAPTER 94

AMONG THE STARS

"I hate being wet," says Caster as he steps onto the beach.

Ami and I have been waiting for him and Emily, trying to look as casual as possible, as if beating them was so easy it didn't take any effort—which, to be honest, it didn't. I'm pretty sure Emily nearly drowned Caster at least three times, and it took them a solid twenty minutes to make it across, which gave Ami and me a solid ten minutes to explore the island. There wasn't much to explore. It's a circular island about a quarter mile in diameter, with greenery leading up to a mansion of silver and glass in the center, where I assume Samjang is being kept.

Caster shakes himself off like a dog and then bursts into flames. "I hate getting wet."

Emily mutters something in Chinese as she shakes her head at him. "Don't be such a baby."

"I'm not a baby. You're a baby."

"*Qie.* Immature." Emily turns and marches up to Ami and me.

"You have a fun cruise?" I ask.

"You mean slow cruise," Ami says.

We burst into laughter, and Emily looks stunned. "Ami, since when did you learn to be so sassy? You've spoiled her, Peter."

"Hold on." I hold up my hands. "I'm the sassy one of the group? Clearly, Caster's the sassiest, followed by you."

Caster frowns at us. "Why are you guys laughing? It's immature. Come on. Let's get Samjang and get out of here." He marches up the hill toward the glass-and-silver mansion.

"Immature, grumble, grumble. Let's get out of here, grumble, grumble," Emily says, scrunching her brow up.

"Any day now!" Caster calls out. "It's not like we have less than twenty-four hours to save the world or anything."

"We're coming, big brother," says Ami, and Caster's taut shoulders relax a little.

Ami's a funny creature. In some ways, she's like a child—like the way she calls Caster her big brother—but in other ways, she's the most mature and perceptive of any of us. And I don't feel that way just because there's a warm feeling bubbling up in my heart. I wish I could take her hand again, tell her things, and ask her things. I want to say, "Why on earth do you like me? I'm kind of a loser. A loser with a pretty awesome rock ring. But still."

The mansion sits inside a walled garden. Vines and moss grow along the stones, and freshly trimmed hedges form a path to the door. I get the feeling we're trespassing on the property of some British lord, not trying to rescue Cog's sister. But the feeling soon subsides as we approach the house, which is the weirdest, trippiest, craziest house I've ever seen. It makes me wonder if some of Goober's alcohol and drugs are still in my system.

The house looked normal enough from the beach—normal, that is, for a house made of silver and glass—but up close, it's different. It looks as if we're staring into a hall of mirrors, a kaleidoscope, and the wormhole from *Interstellar* all at once. The funny thing is that I can't say what the house's shape is exactly. From the beach, it looked like a New England home one might see in crime TV shows. But up close, it's as if my brain can't decide what shape it is.

"Trippy," says Caster.

"Took the word out of my mouth." Emily's brown eyes fill with the kaleidoscopic colors of the house's walls, and she begins to look a little dizzy.

"Let's get this over with," I say, striding toward the door. I reach for the handle to pull it open and nearly shout as my hand slips through the door. It's not like a hologram but like mercury, cool, metallic, and slippery.

"Oh boy." Caster shakes his head. "Why do I feel like the Mad Hatter or the Cheshire Cat is waiting for us inside?"

"Because you have an overactive imagination. Go!" Emily gives him a shove, pushing him and me through the door.

"Yup, this place was definitely designed by Monsieur Trickster himself," says Emily as she surveys the room. "A.k.a. Enki."

It's like being inside a 3D astrolabe, except instead of little metal planets moving around on disks, I see huge stars, vivid and bright, whirling around us above and below.

"You have to admit it's beautiful." Caster says the words softly and reverently, and I get a glimpse into his soul: he feels the same way about mathematics and the stars as I feel about Homer's poetry. For the first time, I think I understand how someone can think mathematics is beautiful. The stars themselves are beautiful, but if I could really get why this dance of beauty makes sense and could understand the equations that describe it, I think I'd find it even more beautiful.

Too bad I'm too dumb for that kind of thing.

"Where's Samjang then?" Emily asks.

My eyes search the room, or the skies, trying to pick out something important among the thousands of lights visible to my human eyes. But I find nothing.

Then Ami points straight ahead at the center of the astrolabe. "There."

It takes a second for my eyes to focus on it. In the center of the room is a pillar of faint light like a nebula. Sitting on it is a book sparkling with starlight and clasped with a golden lock.

CHAPTER 95

TRUE SAMJANG

"That's a book," says Emily.

"Obviously." Caster strokes his chin. "But it probably has clues in it as to how to find the true Samjang."

"It couldn't be easy, could it?" I mutter. "Why couldn't she have been sitting in a rocking chair or something, just waiting for us to say, 'Bibbidi-bobbidi-boo, we've come to free you'?"

Emily appraises me. "This is a side of you we haven't seen before, Peter."

"My make-awkward-jokes-when-I'm-nervous side?"

"Something like that. Well, I like it."

"I do too," says Ami quickly, almost defensively, and I make the mistake of grinning foolishly at Emily, which gets me pinched.

"Ow! What was that for, Ami?" I say to her.

Emily shrugs. "She probably had a good reason. All right, let's open the book. I'm tired of this."

We walk across the floor of stars. My stomach tightens, and I try not to puke as right and left, up and down, forward and back all blend into one. I keep my eyes on the book, the center, which

443

stabilizes me, and I try to keep my mind on my friends, who keep me from feeling lost in infinite space.

We all gather round the book, which glimmers like a patch of sky. The others, for reasons I don't understand, make way for me, as if I should be the one to open it. I'm about to unfasten the golden buckle, when I notice there are words written on the front. Caster notices too, and he takes out his spyglass and reads aloud:

> Out of millions, you must choose one.
> Choose well, or your journey's done.

"Oh boy," he says. "We haven't even opened the book, and there's already a puzzle."

"What is wrong with this guy?" Emily fumes. "He tells us the whole plan is to bring us here to get Samjang so he can save his mother and the world, but once he's achieved his goal of bringing us here, he's going to give us riddles and not tell us about them?"

I shrug. "He is the trickster god."

I reach for the golden buckle, but as soon as my hands touch it, I feel a deep rumbling. The whole room lurches, stars and all, and it feels as if the universe itself is hurtling through space, which doesn't make much sense, but that's partly why it feels so terrifying. The stars whip by faster and faster, and I'm sure some of those stars are coming not from the room but from my own head—the kind of stars you see when someone punches you in the face or your blood sugar drops.

"What did you do, Peter?" asks Emily, reaching for something to stabilize herself.

She ends up falling onto Ami, who falls into Caster, and all three of them fall on top of me. Then we're free-falling through empty space. It would be comical if it weren't utterly terrifying.

"Argh!" Emily screams. "Why are we free-falling through empty space? Where is the gravity coming from?"

I hold on tightly to my friends as they hold on to me. It's hard to think coherent thoughts when my stomach is trying desperately to climb up my throat.

Then things get worse. Faces begin to appear in the sky. It takes me a second to realize it, but they're all the same: a woman's face with skin as brown as coffee beans, dark eyes, and full, lush hair. Then the rest of their bodies appear too: they're all wearing the same dress, dark silk that glitters with starlight.

"Guys, I think this is what the book meant by 'Out of millions, you must choose one,'" I say.

"Yeah," Emily says, "but they all look the same."

The women's faces wrinkle unpleasantly at her comment, and then their voices ring out through the room: "We're not the same. Choose me! Choose me!"

I pinch myself. *Someone wake me up from this nightmare.* But nothing happens. We continue to hurtle through endless space, which looks much the same, and the voices of the million Samjangs blend together in my ears, threatening to drive every scrap of sanity out of me. *If I ever make it out of here, it might just be in a straitjacket.*

For the second time on this trip, I pray to Gomdan, as Cog said to. If it worked on the Silver Lake, it might just work now.

Dear Gomdan, I don't really know how to address you, I pray awkwardly, trying to ignore the feeling of desperate terror gripping me like cold, mad hands. *But my friends and I really need your help now. And so do the Nine Realms, because for whatever reason, we're the ones tasked with saving them. So yeah. Please help.*

I make a mental note that if my prayer is answered, I'm going to have to look up how to actually do prayer, because I get the feeling I'm doing a really bad job.

We hurtle through empty space for a few more seconds, and I start to get the impression that Gomdan is too busy or that I did such a bad job with my prayer, he's not interested. Then Ami speaks.

"I know which one is Samjang."

CHAPTER 96

Unraveling the Illusion

Oh. Well, that was easy, I think. *Almost too easy.*

"Which one?" asks Emily.

"She's the book," says Ami.

"The book?" we all repeat at once.

I take it back. It's not too easy.

"How do you know?" Emily asks.

"It's what Enki said: an author's soul—"

"Lives in her words," Caster says, finishing for her. "I think Ami's right. All the other Samjangs are exactly the same, which means we'd be equally wrong to choose any of them. The only unique choice is the book. I'm not sure how Cog's sister can be a book, but when you have eliminated the impossible, whatever remains, however improbable, must be the truth."

"Thanks, Sherlock Holmes," says Emily. "Regardless, we're still falling into empty blackness!"

"And the book is way up there!" I add.

Caster smiles. "How do you know?"

I furrow my brow. "How do I know the book is up there?"

"No, how do you know we're hurtling through space?"

"Because my stomach feels like it wants to jump out of my gullet!" says Emily. "Obviously, we're falling!"

Caster shakes his head and grins. "That's what I thought at first. But the sensation of free fall is exactly the same as being in empty space. Your body doesn't actually sense acceleration, because every atom in your body accelerates at about the same rate. It's just that when you're on the ground, forces push up on you. But according to Einstein's equivalence principle, the—"

"So you're saying we haven't fallen?" says Emily. "We're just sitting in the same place, experiencing zero gravity?"

"Bingo."

"But then why does it look like the stars are rushing by—oh, but they were doing that before too, weren't they?" Emily says to herself. "Right."

I try to make sense of what has just happened and why Caster knows about Einsteinian physics. I remember that he likes to watch MITx lectures on YouTube when he's bored, which I guess is not a completely useless pastime. It might just get us out of a trap set by a trickster god.

"So, Ami, can you help us up?" I ask.

In answer, a gust of wind lifts us to our feet and sets us on the more-or-less-solid ground, if one can call it that, by the stand. The room is a complex illusion, and I don't understand it, but I think there's a walkway between the door and the center of the room, which has normal gravity and whatnot, unlike the rest of the room.

As we gather round the book once again, I feel a tingling in the pit of my stomach, as if my body's trying to warn me of something. Strangely, it reminds me of the sensation I felt when we were outside the Gray City. At first, I think it must be the trickster god, but he's supposed to be far away now, and something tells me it's not him. The sensation feels oddly familiar, but I can't quite place it.

"Peter, give us a hand," says Emily, interrupting my thoughts.

My friends are at three corners of the book. I go to the last corner.

"Lift on three," says Caster.

"Is it really that heavy?" I ask.

"My guess is that it needs all of the Four to lift it," he says. "A precaution probably. Ready? Three. Two. One."

We lift, and the book comes up, and with it, the illusion of the room disappears. The stars vanish, and the sky brightens into a red sunset. The Samjangs shrivel up into replicas of the book, which Caster now holds in his hands. We're no longer in the midst of the universe but in an ordinary sitting room with a few paintings of landscapes on the walls, a rocking chair in the corner, and a mildly fancy chandelier hanging from a vaulted ceiling.

The tingling sensation in the pit of my stomach that tells me something is approaching intensifies. I search it, trying to figure out who or what is causing it, but whatever it is, it's hiding its identity.

"Well, that was sudden," Caster says.

Ami's gaze drifts mysteriously around the room.

"Yeah." Emily's eyes widen as they settle on the red hues of sunset. "How has it been so long? We've got to go!"

The sensation is now so strong that I begin to feel woozy, and I reach for the stand to steady myself.

"Are you all right, Peter?" Ami asks, but when her eyes meet mine, realization sparks between us. She senses it too, and more than that, I can feel she knows who it is. "He's here," Ami says.

Caster and Emily turn to face her. "Who?"

"Five."

With a jolt of sensation tearing up through my gut, I sense him just outside the door—the only door to this mansion.

CHAPTER 97

THE GREEN-EYED MONSTER

"That's our cue to flee," says Caster, striding toward the door. "Come on! What are you waiting for?"

Ami shakes her head.

"He's outside," I say. "Just outside the door."

Caster's gaze darts around the room before settling on mine. Realization burns in his eyes. "No escape."

I remember Cog's warning to me all those days ago: "His power is not like yours, nor is his fate. He never ends up where he was supposed to go, and oftentimes, the evil ones get to him before we can reach him." Then there was the book of the druids in Morin's tomb, which told of their plans to corrupt him every time he was summoned into Miria.

I read similar thoughts in my friends.

"Well, four-to-one isn't terrible odds," says Caster, but I can tell by his voice that he doesn't believe it. "But regardless of how things turn out, I'm glad to have met you guys. Even Emily." He gives her a smile that makes his real meaning clear: especially Emily.

"Aw, that's sweet of you, you dweeb," says Emily. "I'm glad to have known you all too." Water slithers up her legs to her arms, drawn from the moisture in the floor and air. Let's give him what-*for*."

"Just like you to make the terrible pun," Caster mutters as his hands catch on fire.

Ami unfastens her staff from her back and pulls it around. She's quiet, as usual, but I feel that connection again, a warmth deep in my bones that says more than words. I take a deep breath and feel my connection to the earth.

In that moment, I want to tell her once and for all that I like her; I think she's amazing; and if we ever get back home, I want to do everything with her: go to the movies, eat fast food in an old small-town parking lot, watch fireworks on the Fourth of July from the hill that overlooks Mormont High, go hiking in the mountains when it's warm and skiing when it's cold, and even take her to prom if she'll have me.

But I don't get to voice any of those lovely, squishy, embarrassing emotions, because the light in the room suddenly grows dark, and my knees weaken. At least that's what I think it is at first. But then I realize it's not my legs that feel weak but their connection to the ground. Simultaneously, Caster's hands go dark as the flames extinguish, and Emily's water splashes onto the ground.

"What the—" I look at my hand, expecting to find the ring missing, but it's still there—only it feels hollow, as if it's only a husk of its true self.

A figure slips through the door. He's as dark as the walls of the room, his eyes burn with a fierce pale light, and a green vein snakes along the length of his face.

I hoped Five might be a friend, and all our fears would prove to be just a misunderstanding. But the look of pure desperation in his eyes tells me otherwise. Five is only a boy—he looks as if he can't even be in high school yet—but his expression is that of a person who will do anything to get what he needs and will stop at nothing, even if it means torture or killing.

Five holds up a hand, showing a dark ring that glimmers with crimson fire, azure water, mossy stone, and clear air.

"Did he just—" Emily stops, her voice trembling.

"Steal our elements?" Caster says. "I think so."

The green vein on Five's face pulses brighter, and I gulp as I recognize the light. It's the same unnatural light that pulsed in Morin's eyes and in the southern caves where the phantom men lived.

Five takes another step forward, and I reach for Ami's hand. I get a cold and hollow feeling, as if we're about to die, but I'm glad at least my death will be among friends.

Five opens his mouth, and two raspy words escape his lips: "I need." The words are spoken in a high pitch that betrays how young he is.

Emily raises a hand. "We're not your enemy," she says slowly and gently. "We can help you. My name is Emily."

Five takes another step forward, and his ring grows brighter; the colors leech out of it into his skin. Meanwhile, the green vein thickens and pulses menacingly. "Poison," Five says, touching his face.

Emily takes another step forward.

"What are you doing?" Caster hisses, but she ignores him.

"Can I help you?" she asks.

"Help," he rasps.

Emily nods kindly with a tender expression on her face that reminds me a little of my mother.

"You won't hurt me?"

Emily shakes her head resolutely. "Absolutely not."

They both take another step forward, and Emily kneels down so they're face-to-face.

"Then"—he touches the pulsing green vein and winces—"take."

I think at first he means to take the poison, but then he extends his hand, and the watery blue in his ring travels out of his finger and into Emily's, curling around her finger just as before.

His body begins to shake, and his bright eyes glow with a green haze. "Not much time."

With a jolt in my chest, I realize his meaning. The poison will have him soon, and he'll become—what? A phantom man? A bloodgorger? Who knows? But whatever it is, it won't be good.

Emily takes a deep breath and touches a finger to the green vein on Five's face. "This will hurt a little."

He nods, and I'm surprised by the steel in his eyes. How can someone so young be so determined? I'm eighteen, and I don't have 10 percent the courage and strength I see in his eyes.

Emily closes her eyes, and her body grows still as Five's body shakes. The green intensifies in his eyes. I want to encourage her to hurry, but I know it will be no use.

A cut appears on Five's face, and green oozes from the wound.

I want to shout, "Yes! Go Emily!"

But then Five's eyes turn fully green, and he bellows in a voice far too deep and ancient, "Give it to me! It's not fair! I want your power!"

The voice sends chills up my spine, but Emily doesn't move. If anything, she redoubles her efforts. The poison is pouring out of Five now, and the green vein is disappearing.

The monster in him rages and grabs Emily's neck as his hands catch aflame. She cries in pain, and Caster, Ami, and I rush forward to help her, but a thrust of Five's hand sends us hurtling backward with a gust of wind—except Ami, who, still holding on to her staff, stands firm.

Ami closes the distance and smacks her staff down across Five's burning hands and then across his head. He cries out in pain and falls backward, and Emily rushes forward and draws the last of the poison out of Five's face. It coalesces on the floor into a little blob with angry green eyes and razor-like teeth. It moves for Emily to attack her, but Ami stomps her staff down on top of it, splattering its guts.

"Gotcha," Ami says triumphantly.

The room brightens, painted once more with the light of sunset, and I feel a surge of strength run up through my legs, lifting me to my feet. I look at my hand and feel the power in my ring once more.

Caster peels himself off the ground and runs to Emily, who's lying on the ground, holding her burned neck in pain. "Emily, are you okay?"

"Yeah," she manages to say. A ring of water has formed around her neck, and the burns are disappearing as if someone is airbrushing them away. "It's nothing serious."

I come up beside Ami. "That was amazing."

"It sure was. That's my sister!" Caster says.

"And you were amazing too," I say to Emily.

"Aw, gee," she says. "Thanks. Not to spoil the love fest or anything, but um, hadn't we better introduce ourselves?"

We all turn to look at Five. I almost forgot he was there for a moment.

The steel has gone out of his eyes, and he looks now like a lost boy no more than twelve, with a hardness in his cheeks that says he's had to grow up a lot faster than most kids.

"I'm David," says the boy. "David Abara."

CHAPTER 98

FIVE

Everyone is silent for a long moment, and I get the impression it's because we're all asking ourselves the same question: *Where to begin?*

Emily finally breaks the silence. "I'm Emily." She extends a hand.

"You mentioned that earlier," Caster says under his breath, but David ignores him and takes Emily's hand.

The hardness in his features softens a little as he looks at her, and I get the feeling she reminds him of someone. Someone who brings a tear to his eye. Who is this boy?

Ami steps forward and holds out a shy hand. "I'm Ami."

"And I'm Peter."

Caster rolls his eyes. "And I'm Caster, the smartest person you'll ever meet."

David's eyes harden again and meet Caster's. "If you were smarter, you wouldn't be trying to play with someone who can take away your little fire power like that." He snaps his fingers.

Caster blanches and holds up his hands. "My bad."

Emily's face lights up. "I love this new kid. I've been trying to put Caster in his place for weeks. We gotta keep you around." She smiles at him, and David smiles back at her.

"Very respectfully," says Caster in a voice that is not, "I would like to ask that if you two are finished with your little symposium of kumbaya, we could inquire as to the circumstances of the past two weeks."

"What's he talking about?" David asks.

Emily shrugs. "You know, I'm not sure either. But can you tell us what happened? How did you get that monster inside you?"

She keeps her mouth open for a second longer, as if there are other questions she wants to ask, but she seemingly thinks better of it. I bet she has the same questions I do: Why has he been following us? Who found him first? Why did his presence always seem so angry and dark? Was it because of the green-eyed monster? Or was there something else going on?

It's good that Emily doesn't ask the questions, because David immediately takes a step back, regarding her suspiciously. The room darkens a little, just as it did the moment we lost our powers. "Why you wanna know?"

"It's okay, David," Emily says soothingly. "We just want to get to know you better, so we can be friends. Do you want us to tell our story first?"

This seems to calm him down, so she narrates our story: our surprise upon ending up in another world, Cog's quest, Galthanius's mansion and the bloodgorger, our mistaking Five as an enemy outside the northern forests, Kalix's camp in the east, the attack of the phantom men, the Wella and the cave of the Bloodfather, and all the other adventures in the east, including our discovery that Ami's little bird was Haji the Humble herself.

She even reveals our encounter with the trickster god, Enki, and the plan we formed with him.

David relaxes as the story goes on. Emily does a remarkable job; her voice rises and falls like a boat upon a sea of action and emotion. *She'd make a great audiobook reader or voice actor if she wants a quiet post-saving-the-Nine-Realms career*, I think. *If we get that far.*

Caster interjects a few well-timed—for once—jokes, and by the end, David seems to hate Caster a little less.

After Emily finishes, David tells us his story. It was the evening of his twelfth birthday, and he was at home alone, as usual, after school. His parents are both dead, and he lives alone with his aunt Jemima—this makes Caster snicker immaturely because of the breakfast brand. She was supposed to be bringing home a cake and a small present, some of the few things she could afford, but she was late. When she didn't come home by eight o'clock, he knew something was wrong. At midnight, he finally ventured out of the house.

On the front door, he found a note saying that his aunt had been taken, and if he wanted to get her back, he had to play by the rules. Beneath the note was a ring, sleek and black as obsidian. As soon as he touched it, the world began to change. Cold shadows wrapped around him; dark shapes put out the streetlamps and spilled over the world like oil over a canvas, remaking it into something else: a chamber of stones, filled with a chill so deep it bit at his bones.

Figures made of golden light appeared to him then and explained he had been given great power, but he would only be able to use it to get his aunt back if he captured the Four.

"The fallen gods," Emily whispers, clapping her hands over her mouth. "They got to you first."

But David shakes his head. "Not fallen gods. They're called Eloru, projections of Morin's sorcerers."

"How do you know that?"

"Because they told me. I didn't know at the time, but I thought they wanted to help me. It wasn't until the poison they gave me began to eat away at me, taking away my memories of Auntie, that I realized they were my enemies."

"You mean the green-eyed monster?" Emily asks.

"They gave it to me. They told me it would make me stronger, and I believed them." He looks at her uncertainly. "Thank you."

"Of course," says Emily, and she opens her arms to give him a hug.

He seems unsure at first, but Emily's sparkling eyes and dimpled cheeks are persuasive, and he gives in. "There we go! Come on, everyone. Group hug. Think about this! This is the first time the Five have come together in ages—this has got to be pretty amazing."

"Oh yeah, the American way," says Caster in a voice that's not entirely sarcastic. He joins the hug, followed by me and Ami.

I feel a power resonate through all of us like blood circulating from a great heart through the veins of its body and back to itself again. The sensation lasts only a second, but it reminds me of the stirring I felt earlier among the Four—the deep resonance and warmth that reach up into my heart from somewhere deep in my bones—and I wonder if maybe it's the start of the Four becoming One. But no, it wouldn't be—it would have to be the Four becoming the Five and the Five becoming One.

The feeling is only a spark though, and then it's gone as David pushes away from us and eyes the rest of us warily. I hug my chest automatically, feeling a little uncomfortable about the idea of becoming One with these people—even the Four, who I've gotten to know better over the past few weeks.

"David," I say, trying to sound unthreatening, "what is your power? Is it just the ability to take away our powers? Or something else?"

His eyes brighten with fear, and I can feel him tug at the power of my ring, as if he's about to rip it away again. But then he stops and looks down. I glance at the others, who have the same bewildered expression I do.

"Let's not press the issue," Emily mouths. "All right, guys," she says, holding up the book, businesslike. "So this here is Samjang. Somehow. And per our mission, we need to get it, a.k.a. her, to the Heart of Miria tonight."

"How are we going to do that?" I ask. "We have like six hours at best before midnight."

"We're going to fly," says Caster. "Obviously."

I smile. "In a rocket ship?"

"Don't look at me like this is some sort of joke. Of course. Fortunately for you all, I've read a few textbooks on aerospace engineering in my spare time, not to mention archives of blueprints."

"I love how much of a nerd you are!" Emily says.

"I do too. So we'll get to work on that ASAP. But first, I need to talk to David for a moment. Alone."

Ami and Emily simultaneously raise an eyebrow. I try to, but I can never get my face to lift one eyebrow without lifting the other, so I look foolishly incredulous rather than inquiring.

PAUL SCHEELER

"To clear things up between us."

David nods. "Fine. But I'm warning you, if you try anything, I'll take away your power and won't give it back."

Caster's skin pales slightly, but this time, the cocky smile doesn't fall from his face. "I won't try anything."

They step out through the milky door into the evening air, leaving me wondering what exactly Caster wants to say to David that he doesn't want to say in front of the rest of us. Is it to say he's sorry? Maybe he's just bashful about ruining his record of being unapologetic.

But something tells me he has something else up his sleeve.

CHAPTER 99

JOURNEY TO THE WEST

In the next hour, as the sun settles deeper beneath the horizon, I learn that it's not just rock and stone that will obey me. It's the earth, and that means trees too.

It hurts me a little to ask the trees to give themselves up, but we don't have much of a choice. We need something light to make the frame of our plane, and there's not enough metal on the island. We have to use the metal I manage to pull from the earth for another purpose: fireproofing the back of the plane, since Caster intends to help Ami along by shooting flames through some kind of compression chamber.

This doesn't strike me as a brilliant idea, but Caster's intent on it, and he's the one who's read the aerospace textbooks, so we follow his lead. We finish constructing a plane just as the sun slips beneath the horizon, leaving only a faint afterglow in the sky. The plane looks sort of like a canoe with wings attached.

We all pile in: Caster and Emily are in the back, Ami and I are in the front, and David is in the middle, next to Emily. He seems to trust her the most, though he's also warmed up to Caster after their secret conversation.

Emily settles into the seat and begins to pat her lap. "Pat, pat, pat, pat!"

Caster lifts an eyebrow. "Is that a reference to *Little Einsteins*?"

"Does that mean you watched it too?" Emily smirks.

"No, but my little sister did."

"You say it like it's a bad thing," says Ami plaintively.

Caster shrugs. "You ready to get this canoe on the road?"

Ami nods, and her features become determined. I squeeze her hand and feel the strength pulsing through her. The wind around us changes, lifting us off the ground and into the air. My stomach lurches as we ascend, gliding faster and faster. The back of the canoe begins to glow as Caster's hands send jets of flames toward the chamber. I feel as if we're on the world's scariest and most dangerous roller-coaster ride, but with Ami next to me, it's okay.

We make it to about 1,200 feet before we level off, and Caster and Ami begin to direct most of their energy toward getting us to go as fast as possible, letting the wings do the work of generating lift.

At first, I frantically mutter prayers to Gomdan that we don't go tumbling out of the sky and that Enki wasn't lying when he said he'd keep the fallen gods from coming after us—because if he was lying, we're really asking for it by putting ourselves a quarter mile into the sky. But as time goes on, I relax a little, and I enjoy looking down at the landscape.

We pass over the lake where Ami calmed the storm while Emily slept and Caster turned into a shivering ball of fear. Eventually, we pass over the desert where we sang pop songs and almost drowned after the miniature monsoon hit. As we come to the end of the desert, Caster and Ami work to land the plane.

They're both exhausted and need a break. Fortunately, we collected some food while on the island, so we eat berries and vegetables—not the most fulfilling meal, but it's better than nothing.

Emily shovels berries into her mouth and doesn't even stop to slap Caster when he reminds her of her mother's nickname for her, Zhu Bajie, a.k.a. Piggy. This time, he says it with a strange tenderness, which I guess is the closest Caster's capable of coming to affection.

David eats his berries slowly one at a time. His eyes look between the ground and Emily, as if he wants to say something but is not sure how to start.

"So what do your powers do?" he asks at last.

I get the feeling this isn't his real question, because he should know this better than anyone. Not only did he take our powers from us briefly, but Emily also told him about our powers when she narrated the story of our journey.

Caster looks as if he's on the verge of making a smart remark, but Emily preemptively elbows him and then kindly replies to David's question. When she finishes, David is still staring at her with lost puppy eyes.

"What about you, David?" she asks gently.

Given the way he responded earlier to that question, it doesn't feel like a good idea to ask. But then I realize what Emily sees: he asked us about our powers again not because he wanted to know but because that is the question he wants us to ask him.

David fidgets nervously with his fingers.

"It's okay," Emily says soothingly. "You don't have to tell us."

He shakes his head. "No, I want to. You're the first friends I've had."

I wait for him to finish the sentence with "on this journey" or "since coming to Miria," but he just stops. My heart hurts because I understand. Before coming to Miria, I had only Goober, who I think is only sort of a friend. I guess he cares about me, but he also gives terrible advice, gets me in trouble, and encourages some of my bad habits. But what would life have been if I hadn't even had Goober?

"I have the soul power," says David.

"The sole power?" Emily asks. "You mean you're unique?"

Caster rolls his eyes. "No, *soul* like human soul."

Emily elbows him in the gut.

David seems not to hear them, which I guess makes him lucky. "My power means I hear things, and I feel things. Things others don't. But it's also really scary and …" His voice trails off, and he hugs his legs to his chest, shivering a little.

Emily scoots over and puts an arm around him to comfort him. I imagine how awful coming to Miria would have been if I had been alone the whole time with a green monster in my body while the only person I loved was held hostage.

"When do the voices come?" asks Emily.

David looks up at her with wide eyes and says, "They've always been around."

"Even before the ring?" Caster asks.

David nods. "Nothing changed with the ring. It only made them louder. And it brought me here."

My heart stalls and takes a second before it starts beating again. What does he mean nothing changed with the ring? Our powers come from our rings. Cog's voice echoes in my thoughts:

His power is not like yours. What does Cog know about Five that he didn't tell us?

I look at Ami, who's been silent the whole time, as usual. Her eyebrows are drawn together in a look of contemplation. I want to ask her questions, but she also looks tired, as if she's saving her strength for the last leg of the journey.

David goes back to being his usual suspicious self, and Caster wearily steps back into the canoe. The rest of us follow, knowing we don't have time to waste. Five is the last to get in, and I notice a square bulge in his shirt as he steps in. I consider asking him about it, but I think better of it. He doesn't look like he's in a happy mood.

The canoe soars upward, and soon we pass over the part of the forest where Haji is hopefully saving Meila's twin sister and the part of the forest where no doubt Thaegar and the other laganmorfs are still repeating to themselves, "We must consider," and not acting on anything ever.

In the distance, the mountain comes into view, the Heart of Miria, where, if all goes as planned, we'll save the Winter Goddess and defeat the Ice Reich and the fallen gods once and for all.

If all goes as planned.

CHAPTER 100

THE RETURN OF THE KING

I feel the earth trembling as we get out of the canoe on the mountainside, and I know we don't have much time. My gut tells me it's about one hour to midnight, which means the seal has an hour left before it breaks and the Ice Reich enters.

"I've always wanted to say it's the eleventh hour and actually have it be the eleventh hour," Caster says.

We rush up the side toward the silver arch that marks the entrance to the Heart of Miria.

Caster stops and turns to David. "You remember what I said earlier?"

David nods. He looks at Emily with a mixture of gratitude and longing and then breaks into a sprint, heading around the side of the mountain; the square bulge in his shirt swings from side to side. With each step, his speed increases, until he's as swift as a horse. *What else exactly does the soul power do?* I wonder.

"What just happened?" Emily asks. "Since when are you two so close?"

"I think we understand each other well enough," says Caster mysteriously.

Ami's brow furrows. "What did you ask him to do?"

"To send a short message to Kalix. Just in case."

To send a message to Kalix? What message? I wonder. *And when did he tell him? Was that what they talked about outside the island mansion?*

But before I have time to ask any questions, Caster speaks again. "Well, you all ready? Not much time left."

I set my jaw, trying not to look as terrified as I feel. My stomach is roiling inside me; it feels like the Silver Lake before Ami quieted the storm.

Brave as Odysseus, I repeat quietly to myself, trying to believe what Dr. Elsavier told me all those days ago. *Brave as Odysseus.*

Caster holds out his hand, and I lead the way, clutching the book—Samjang—to my chest.

"So the plan," I say as we walk beneath the silver entrance. "What's the plan?"

"Hide somewhere close to the Heart of Miria and observe. Once Enki slips into the portal, then we'll go into action, helping Cog keep it a small entrance until Enki can escape with his mother. Then the illusion he put on the fallen gods will break, they'll descend on the mountain, and we'll send them into the portal to join the Ice Reich now stripped of its power. Just like the trickster god said."

Just like the trickster god said. Right. What could go wrong?

"It'll be okay," says Ami.

Her voice is warm and calm, and I let myself fall into it. It chases away the creeping coldness in my own heart.

469

Behind the silver gate is a narrow path that slopes upward with smooth shafts of rock on either side. Up ahead, I can sense the presence of at least a dozen powerful entities, which I take to be a good sign: Cog and the other loyal gods have arrived. As we come to the end of the path, we all get down in order to observe without being seen.

I can feel my friends next to me, and I'm just starting to believe Ami's promise that everything will be okay, when a voice rings out.

"Welcome, Four!"

It takes me a second to place the voice; it's familiar, but I haven't heard it for almost three weeks. It's Cog.

"This was not supposed to happen," I whisper furiously to Caster. I'm about to ask him what we should do, when I see the same question in the others' eyes. *Right*, I think to myself. *I'm supposed to be the Rock*. So I draw from the calmness and solidity of the earth and try to project it on my face. "Let's go say hello," I say. "And hopefully we can stall."

Caster bobs his head distractedly, as if his mind is on other matters, but Ami and Emily nod with their eyes focused and alert.

"Hide the book," Emily mouths.

I consider hiding it in the wall but think better of it and slip it into my cloak.

We step out around the corner, and for a moment, I'm stunned at the beauty of the place. Colossal columns of ivory and obsidian stretch up into a vaulted ceiling, at the top of which sits a glowing globe, the universe in miniature, with a thousand dancing lights sparkling in the darkness. The more I look, the more they seem to grow, till thousands become millions, millions become billions, and I am swallowed up in infinity. Then I see that this infinity is only one among many; amid all this vastness, there are still eight other realms and, beyond that, the Mind that dreamed them up.

"It's beautiful, isn't it?"

I tear my eyes away from the sight to focus on the man who spoke. The god who spoke, rather.

Cog, wearing dark robes that sparkle enigmatically, stands at the end of the room, surrounded by other gods. He stares at me; his eyes are bright and cold. I realize his voice too is cold, and it sends a chill across my skin despite the warmness of the air. It is Cog but not the warm, kind Cog we met locked away in a castle in the icy north. It is as though the warmth in his heart went into the air, and the coldness of the weather went into his heart.

That's when I notice two things: an altar in the center of the room, circular and gray, and a knife in Cog's hand. A knife I recognize with a chill.

It is of the exact same make as Galthanius's knife, the one he used to extend his life into immortality, and as Morin's knife.

"W-what's that?" asks Emily with her eyes resting on the same terrible object.

Cog tilts his head to the side in amusement and chuckles darkly.

"Why are you laughing?" Ami asks. Her voice trembles.

This only seems to make him laugh more. I glance at Caster, who usually is the one to insist on having questions answered, but he is silent.

"What is going on?" I say. I have the feeling something has gone terribly wrong.

Cog straightens his neck, and then his eyes light up as they settle on something behind us. "Ah, old friend, you've arrived just in time. Perhaps you would like to explain things to our naive young friends here."

I feel a coldness in the earth, and a chill of recognition runs up my spine even before I turn to look. When I do turn, I almost regret it.

Standing in the entranceway we came through moments before is someone I thought we left behind for good and never would have to see again: Mad King Morin.

CHAPTER 101

THE SECRETS OF THE PENTAGON

Morin's evil green eyes bear down on us, hollow and chilling. Behind him stand columns of phantom men arrayed in full armor, stretching back badness knows how far.

We step away from him, inching toward the middle of the room, but as we do, Cog and the other gods close in on us from the other side. We're surrounded, with no way out.

I look at my friends. Ami looks scared but determined, and Emily looks downright angry. Caster just looks resigned, which makes my heart sink. *Come on. Don't give up, even though we got duped. There's still a chance*, I want to tell him, even though I know there's not. There's no way we can take on Morin and his army, plus Cog and his gods.

And where the heck is Enki? I wonder. *I thought he was supposed to trick the fallen gods. But what if he did? What if he tricked the wrong gods, and Cog was using him all along? But how could Cog be in league with Morin?*

473

"How dare you!" Emily turns to look at Cog. "How could you betray us like this? I thought you summoned us to Miria in order to save the Nine Realms from the Ice Reich."

Cog and the other gods exchange looks and then burst into laughter, as if they are all in on some joke we don't get. He clears his throat and tries to look serious. "I suppose that before we strip you of your powers, spill your blood, and use you to fulfill the plans of the Pentagon, we could give you an explanation." He stares at our dumbfounded faces. "Ah, but I'm getting ahead of myself."

A chill rushes down my spine, and I instinctively step closer to Ami and the others. If we're going to die betrayed by the god who brought us here in the first place and gave us a quest only to deceive us and use us, I'm not going to make it easy. I reach for the power gurgling up from the earth, raw and angry, but then I catch sight of Ami's expression. She mouths a single word: *Wait*.

Reluctantly, I decide it's better to bide my time. Kalix isn't among the gods here; maybe he'll figure out that something has gone wrong up at the mountain and will come to our rescue—if he isn't in on the plot too.

But there's another reason I wait: a perverse curiosity willing to risk my life just to know why Cog did what he did and what this is all about.

"Explain yourself," I tell Cog, trying to sound brave.

"It's very simple," says Cog. "The gods are men."

"The gods are men?" I repeat.

"Didn't you pay attention, boy?" I feel Morin's cold breath on me as he speaks, and it feels like cold, wet fingers on my neck. "The gods are mortal."

The gods are mortal. The words are familiar. They were written in the druids' book. The words didn't make sense at the time but now are beginning to take a dark shape.

"Then h-how are you still alive?"

Cog runs a long, slender finger down the dark blade, which glints maliciously in the moonlight.

Morin speaks. "There are two ways for a god to live. The first is for him to draw life from the All-Father, to grovel before the only God who lives by his own life, and to beg continued existence from him." The words come out of his mouth like spit. "Or we can live by *our* strength. By blood."

"*We*? You mean you're a god?"

"What do you think a god is, boy? The best among men."

I remember what Cog said about being an immortal spirit. "But I thought the gods were spirits. And that's why the Kar-dun were so powerful—because they were the offspring of something other."

Cog's cold eyes glimmer. "Some of the gods, by nature, are spirits; some of them were spirits but became flesh; and some of them are men. Stalactites reach down from the cave's ceiling, and stalagmites reach up from the floor, but the two may touch, given enough time. What makes a being godlike is not its substances but its will. A man may be a god if he makes the world his canvas, if he refuses to be bound by pitiful rules dreamed up by heaven, if he grasps life like a wild mare and rides her fiercely, if he looks into the secrets of love and learns that love transcends all the things that men call good and evil. That is what makes a god."

I shiver, feeling that Cog's description is exactly the opposite of what a god ought to be.

"Yes," says Morin. "And as for the whole affair of siring the Kar-dun, did you really think we were spirits? How do you think we could breed with humans to produce them? Can a man breed with a dog? One must be of the same species or at least similar enough."

I get the feeling, we humans are being compared to dogs in this analogy, which is kind of mean; first, humans aren't all that bad, and second, dogs aren't all that bad either. Mostly, they're good to humans, at least the ones they know. They don't bully humans or make fun of them for being less beautiful, less intelligent, or less cool than the others. If humans were a bit more like dogs, we might have a merrier world. Dogs also don't scheme to betray their friends, bring back the Ice Reich, and bring eternal darkness on the world. Dogs just aren't that evil. Except maybe Chihuahuas. And Dulia. She was pretty nasty.

"But didn't you begin as the OG Avengers?" Emily asks. "Weren't you trying to defend the humans against the Kar-dun?"

Morin and Cog exchange a look, and they laugh, joined by the other gods, though Morin's laughter sounds more like a knife being sharpened against a stone: grating and violent.

"The gods are men, but not all men are gods," Cog says. "Some among the druids were less enlightened. We let them believe certain convenient myths. Circles within circles, each knowing more than the one outside but none knowing the full truth, except the innermost circle."

"But how then are you so powerful?" I ask. "If you're not gods, that is. I mean, most humans can't fly around or manipulate the weather or, you know, do godly things."

Cog rubs his head as if the question is unbelievably stupid, but I'm sort of used to it. My teachers respond that way a lot to me.

"Magic, Peter. Obviously, magic!"

"Magic drawn from the Dark Realm?"

"Ah, so your intellect is not entirely deficient. That is correct. That is, in fact, what is meant by *magic*. The fallen gods, the druids of Pyro, the children of Belial, the cult of the pentagram, the Pentagon—all names for the same circle of gods, the gods determined to live on their own terms, to be free of the All-Father's control."

"And your plan to do this was to subjugate humankind and use them as sacrifices? To use"—I gulp—"us as sacrifices?"

"Exactly." Morin's wizened features widen into a smile of rotten flesh and blackened teeth, which makes me simultaneously want to shiver in fear and to puke. As if the sight isn't bad enough, the smell hits me. The dude needs an Olympic-sized swimming pool of Listerine. I guess that's what happens when you don't brush your teeth for like two thousand years or however long he's been in his tomb.

"But then what does this have to do with the Ice Reich?" Emily asks.

Ami's eyes are closed, but her lips are moving. Maybe she's snapped. I don't know. I feel my sanity slipping away too. It's a contest between my sanity and my life—which will be the first to go?

"The Ice Reich holds many secrets we desire to know," says Cog. "But there is one in particular we desire above all to know."

A strange light appears in the eyes of the other gods. It's sort of the way people look when they're given lots of money, see an expensive car they like, or even see their favorite meal, but the look is a thousand times more intense in their eyes—a grasping, drooling, lusting look.

I make the mistake of looking into their eyes, and my vision fills with three women like the sisters we saw in Morin's cave. Their laughter turns the sky to darkness, bending the world into impossible shapes, making everything simultaneously too large and too small. I feel an overwhelming desire gurgle up from somewhere deep inside, a desire for darkness and madness. I feel a hatred of home, my mom and dad, Dr. Elsavier, my friends, and, most of all, Gomdan, the All-Father.

Ami pulls me away, and I gasp, staring at the ground. *What the hell was that?* If hell exists, I'm pretty sure it's something like that.

I manage to ask Cog, "What do you desire to have above all?"

The room shakes as if a fist just pounded the floor. A crack appears in the stone table in the room's center. I have a bad feeling that the Ice Reich is getting ready to make its entrance.

Cog shakes his head. "Circles within circles. You've been told enough. Now it is time to complete the sacrifice." He nods at the other gods. "Bind them to the altar heart."

CHAPTER 102

THE SACRIFICE

The flight-or-fight response kicks in as soon as the gods reach for us. But I manage to get in only one good hit before a god slips cold black metal around my hands, which makes my arms feel as if they weigh a thousand pounds. Emily and Ami are quickly defeated too, and Caster, for some reason, puts up no fight. It makes me want to smack him. Why is he acting so defeated?

After giving us a few punches to the kidneys and gut, the gods lead us to the altar heart, where Cog waits, picking at his fingers with his knife like some sort of movie villain, except it's not at all cheesy. Our captors push us roughly to our knees. It doesn't hurt me, but the others wince in pain, except Caster, who has a dead look in his eyes, as if this is boring to him. Has his brilliant brain calculated all the possibilities and figured out there's no escape, no hope at all?

I mentally pinch myself. *This isn't a fantasy novel, Peter. People don't calculate all the possibilities.*

Cog raises the knife, and I wince, expecting him to bring it down on my carotid artery, but instead, he brings it down on the altar heart. He carves a pentagram within a pentagon and draws a circle at each of the five points. Then he begins to chant in a language I don't understand, which stirs the same black feelings of the world turning to darkness and of everything being too big and too small, bending into impossible shapes.

Little green lines appear within the five circles, carved by invisible hands. The lines, I realize, are representations of the forms Thaegar talked about, the five shapes.

My heart jumps as I experience a new sensation: Five is approaching. *No!* I want to yell to him. *Get out of here, and warn Kalix!*

"Now, brothers," Cog says, "we shall consume the power of the Five! And at last, we shall be immortal!"

Gods reach for our hands, and Emily blurts out, "Wait! Don't you need all five infinity stones—I mean rings?"

No, Emily, I think. *Give him time to escape.* But of course, she can't sense him, because there's not enough water around. She doesn't know the danger he's in.

"You are a never-ending supply of useless references, aren't you?" Cog says. "Of course we do. But fortunately, spilling your blood will call Five to this location. No need to go gallivanting about in search of him. He will come to us."

Oh well. There goes another plan. I glance at Caster, whose head is lowered, eyes dull. Maybe I ought to just accept that we've lost. The game was rigged against us from the start. Cog, the god who pretended to be the benign father of Miria, was really conspiring against us all this time with the fallen gods.

Cog raises his arms and speaks in a dramatic voice. "Now, brothers, let us proceed!"

I reach for my power to defend myself and my friends, but the black chains around my wrists mute the power. My power is now like a quiet voice speaking from far away, barely in existence and totally unreachable.

I turn to my friends. Caster won't meet my eyes, which makes me sad, because this is probably the last moment of our lives. The thought chills me. Can death really be that close? Even with Cog's knife hanging above my neck, I can't quite believe it.

I meet Emily's eyes and nod, trying to put into my expression all the gratitude I have for her for being such a good friend. I remember the time we sat in Galthanius's house and chatted while Caster and Ami talked to the villagers. It was only a few weeks ago, but it feels like a lifetime.

My eyes settle at last on Ami. I want to tell her now that I like her and that I've always sort of liked her since the first time I set eyes on this strange, beautiful, soft-spoken, tough nut who managed to send the nastiest bullies in Mormont High running for their mommies.

In the end, I say nothing, and neither does she. But that's okay, because I feel her left hand take mine. With her right hand, she takes Emily's hand, and Emily takes Caster's. I turn my face to stare defiantly up at Cog, the false god.

"Why?" I ask.

But he only smirks. The smirk looks vaguely familiar, though I can't quite place it. He lowers his knife toward me, when suddenly, a shrill voice tears through the silence.

"Where's Samjang? I must eat her! I must eat her!"

I instinctively clutch the book tighter to my chest, surprised they haven't asked about it yet. I have been hoping Samjang might spring out and save us, but if Cog is in on the scheme, she probably is too.

"Oh god. Oh me," Cog groans. "Who let Marius the Muncher in here?"

Despite the evident danger of the situation, I can't hold in the snicker that comes gurgling up from my throat in an awkward way that reminds me of my eighth-grade voice. "Marius the Muncher?"

"It's not funny!" Cog snaps. "He's a compulsive muncher! Always interrupting us and always putting things in his mouth and chewing them like some sort of goat!"

"Where is she? Where is Samjang? I must eat her!" Marius wails, sounding like a cross between a hungry toddler and Gollum.

Cog turns to one of the burly gods. "Get him out of here! Get him out! And feed him one of Morin's men to chew on. He likes bones and soggy flesh."

The god does as Cog commands, but Marius is an agile climber, so it takes a good five minutes before he's under control.

"You know," says one of the other gods with a long, stern face, "the Muncher has a point. Where is Samjang? Eating her flesh gives great power."

Cog sighs. "No doubt one of the wimps here has it on his or her person. But it's much easier to search dead persons."

"But why not eat her first? She could be a sort of appetizer, a warm-up to the real thing."

"Yeah!" Another god joins in, and soon there's broad agreement.

Cog sighs even more dramatically. "Fine. Peter, I know you have it."

"I don't," I say, probably too hastily. "I left it hidden somewhere." I remember reading somewhere that if you want to live, you have to make yourself valuable to your captors, and that information now comes tumbling out of my mouth in the form of an ingenious lie. "I've hidden her somewhere. You've got to keep us alive, or you'll never find her."

Cog rolls his eyes. "You're wasting time. I'm very good at detecting bulges in clothing, and you're very bad at hiding them."

Well, it seemed pretty ingenious.

A god rips the book out of my shirt and places it to his mouth, licking it. "Tastes like dust and paper."

"It is a book, after all," Cog says.

"Yes, but it's Samjang too. Why does it taste like paper?"

"There is a ritual you must perform," snaps one of the other gods. "Imbecile. Give it here, and I shall make her transform."

The earth shakes again as something large breaks against the ground below. Dust trickles from the ceiling, and the crack in the altar heart widens.

Cog raises his voice to a shout. "Do what you will, but four of you will gather round me now to complete the ritual!"

The four gods behind us begin to chant with Cog, while the other gods try to transform Samjang from book form so they can eat her. It is wrong, and there's nothing I can do.

Just when I think the situation can't get much worse, I feel a horrible new sensation: the ring on my finger begins to move. Only a little at first, but within seconds, it's sliding down my finger.

I feel the power drain out of me, just as it did when Five took it, only this time, creatures unimaginably ancient and evil are taking it from me, and they're not going to give it back.

The ring comes loose and floats over to the cube, the symbol of my element. I feel naked, as if I've been forced to strip to the skin and walk out onstage for the entire high school to gaze at. From somewhere in the recesses of my mind, Brutus's jeering voice comes back: *Cheeks!* It doesn't lighten the mood, especially since Morin is now standing next to me, holding Cog's knife.

Well, goodbye, Peter, I think to myself. *It wasn't a bad run. At least we get to die beside friends.*

I close my eyes and try to accept my fate bravely. I feel the cold dark knife near the tender skin of my neck, no longer strengthened by the rock ring's power. I know Morin is about to slice, to steal my lifeblood and pour it out onto the altar so he can live forever.

That's when Homer appears in my mind.

You! I want to shout.

Long time no see. How do you feel about not dying?

Um, great. How are you going to do that?

Hold on tight, he says with a wink I recognize all too well.

Suddenly, the room goes dark, and I explode.

CHAPTER 103

THE DOUBLE-DUPING

I don't actually explode; I just feel as if I do. It's like having a thousand Tasers hooked up to me, all going off at once. I'm just guessing—I've never been Tased, but I have seen it on TV.

It takes me a few seconds to figure out what's going on, and by then, a lot of things have already happened.

First, the room darkens, and then I feel an incredible surge of power roiling up from my bones and spreading throughout my whole body. Second, Morin's knife lunges for my throat. A rock shoots up from the ground, sending the knife flying and Morin too. He splats against the wall with a terrific—and, may I add, highly satisfying—*crack*.

I look at my hands with astonishment. The ring is gone, still on the altar heart. I whip my hand outward, and three rocky fists leap from the ground, sending the gods behind us flying backward. So I do have the rock power. But how?

Then it occurs to me. *The darkened room. Five.* The loss of power felt exactly like when Five took it—because he *did* take it. And somehow, he gave it back even after my ring was taken.

485

I wonder, not for the first time, just how powerful Five is. He can take away our powers and give them back with a wave of his hand. And then there are the voices he says he hears. How does it all fit together?

This metaphysical speculation is driven from my mind as Morin roars with rage, which I guess means he is still alive somehow. "What has happened?"

The light in Caster's eyes has returned, and he's wearing his usual overconfident smirk. "I love it when a plan comes together."

"A plan?" Morin says icily.

"Yeah," says Caster. "It's pretty simple. You've been duped."

"Duped?"

"Yes, duped. D-u-p-e-d. Outskilled, outclassed, outsmarted, outgeneraled, out—"

"I get the idea," says Morin coldly. "So you devised some sort of ruse with Five to sneak your powers back into your miserable little corpses. I should thank you for it, for now when we drink your blood, we shall have your powers too." He raises a hand to give an order, but he shudders as a wail tears through the room.

"It's not her! It's not Samjang! Where is she?"

"I thought we had taken care of Marius. What is he whining about now?"

"The book!" Marius cries. His eyes are feverishly bright. "It's not her! It's a counterfeit!"

"A counterfeit?" Emily says with her brow furrowed.

"Yes, a counterfeit," says Caster. "A forged copy or imitation of an artifact designed for fraudulent or deceptive purposes."

"I know what a counterfeit is!"

The other gods ignore Emily and Caster, murmuring among themselves.

"But then"—Morin turns to me, and his eyes flare with green fire—"what did you do with her?"

I shake my head because I honestly have no idea what's going on, though something tells me Caster is behind it.

"You've actually been double-duped," Caster says. "For example, where is your glorious leader?"

Morin's eyes dart to where Cog was standing just a minute ago, but there's only empty air. Morin growls. "Where is he? What have you done?"

"Excuse me," says Emily. "But can someone explain what's going on?"

"It's okay, Em; you can drop the act now. They've figured it out."

"What act?" Emily says.

Caster sighs. "Well, it's like this. That wasn't Cog. That was Enki pretending to be Cog as part of a plan we worked out earlier. He pretended to be Cog in order to trick the fallen gods into thinking he was scaring us and making us feel helpless and betrayed." He takes a deep breath. "But actually Cog was making them—the fallen gods—complacent. Pretty funny, right? And now he's doing the thing we talked about at the Pentagon."

I stare blankly at Caster for a moment before I get it. I recall the letters Enki wrote on the Pentagon walls, which only Caster read; the mysterious way Caster acted afterward; and his secret conversation with Five. So now Cog—Enki—is in the Ice Reich, trying to rescue his mom?

"He betrayed us?" one of the fallen gods asks, stunned.

"Yes, the trickster god tricked you," says Caster. "Surprise, surprise. As a word of advice, if you want someone to be your ally, try not imprisoning his mother in a torture chamber for millennia. It's really bad for goodwill."

Morin glares at him. "You dare lecture me, boy, on—"

"Where is Samjang?" Marius cries, making everyone shudder again. "I must eat her flesh!"

Morin rubs his temples. "I know we're enemies and everything, but before we try to kill you, could you do everyone a favor?"

"Anytime, boss." Caster winks. "Peter, would you?"

I flick my wrist, and a stone fist smacks Marius's lights out.

"Thank you," says Morin. He flashes a smile of rotten teeth and hanging flesh. "I'll make your deaths a little less painful." He raises a hand and points a bony finger at us. "Get them!"

Morin's phantom army rushes through the eastern gate, charging at us, and I'm certain we're going to get torn to pieces. Then I remember that somehow, David has given us our powers back. It's hard to keep track of things—even obvious things—when you're scared out of your bones.

Caster bursts into flames and sends twin jets of fire from his hands, which Ami fans into swelling waves of burning light. The fire sends Morin's troops tumbling backward, smoking and collapsing on each other.

But just as soon as they're down, they're back up again, and worse, I can hear the growl of Morin's zombie dogs in the distance. Morin is busy directing one of the fallen gods to chant around the altar heart, which gives me a bad feeling, especially when the room shakes again from the impact of something massive below.

"So, Caster, what exactly is the plan? Since apparently you have one that you haven't told us about," Emily says between heavy breaths as she blasts phantom men and gods alike backward.

"Just a bit longer," Caster replies.

I'm not sure how much longer we can hold out. My power feels dozens of times stronger than it did when I had to draw it from the ring, but given that we were originally defeated in only a few seconds, that probably means we have only a few dozen seconds before it's all over.

The situation is getting worse by the second. The two exits to the room are blocked—by Morin's army on one side and the druid gods on the other—and despite our increased powers, the gods are good at magic. I guess you tend to get good at things with a few millennia of practice. They easily defeat our attacks, sending them back on us, slowly pushing us toward the wall. Soon we'll have nowhere to go, and we'll get worn out. It's four—I don't know where Five has gone—against a dozen gods and a giant undead army. Not exactly the best odds.

"Caster!" Emily says. "What is the plan?"

"Sh! We can't tell them!"

I glance at Ami, feeling hopeless once more. My arms ache with exertion despite the adrenaline coursing through my veins, and I don't know how much longer I can hold out. But she whispers, "It'll be okay."

I feel that same connection somewhere deep in my bones, and I know that somehow, it will be okay. Still, the fallen gods and phantom men are closing in on us, and it's become a struggle just to ward off the magical projectiles of stone, flame, and darker substances.

The room shakes violently again. The strikes are growing closer, and the scar along the altar heart is growing wider by the moment. As weird as it sounds, I can feel Miria cry out in pain as her skin is ripped open. It won't be long now before the Ice Reich is back, and then it's all over.

I feel my arms grow weak, and I'm about to let a projectile slice through my neck, when suddenly, it stops in midair—along with Morin's phantom men. They're all frozen.

I turn to the western entrance, and there in the doorway stands a man dressed in azure blue, with golden skin, a beard full and white, and a crackling power in his eyes. Beside him stands a woman dressed in crimson silk. Her skin is like ebony, dark and smooth, and her presence feels like something other and beyond—almost like music but not like music. Perceiving her takes me out of my mind.

A few seconds later, the names finally come to my mind: *Cog and Samjang.*

CHAPTER 104

ENTRANCES AND EXITS

"Methyldonin," Morin says coldly as his face contorts with disgust.

Cog nods at us, and we scramble behind him. "Mad Morin, it's over now. This stratagem of yours and the trickster god's has been foiled. It's time to return to your tomb."

"Never!" Morin's eyes flare, and with a whispered word, he sends a jet of green flame racing toward us.

Cog and Samjang move in unity like two graceful dancers and bring forward a shield of purple light that blocks the flames, separating us from Morin.

Morin snarls and grabs a halberd from one of the other fallen gods.

My eyes widen as I see what he intends to do. My scream of "No!" comes too late. The halberd comes crashing down on the altar heart just as the fallen god Morin appointed earlier to chant over the heart finishes. For a moment, nothing happens, and then I feel Miria scream in pain as her heart is torn open, and cold begins to seep out.

"Peter," Cog says, turning to me. Though his eyes are full of urgency, his voice is warm and resonant, and for the first time since I've met him, he really looks like a god, not a bent old man crushed under the weight of responsibility. "Take the others to the camp below, and ready them for battle. And, Peter?" His eyes meet mine, sparking a fire deep inside my heart. "You must speak to them, the Three Kingdoms. Even with the threat of annihilation hanging over them, they still are quarreling. But you can bring them together."

"But, sir, I don't even speak their language."

"That can be solved," says Samjang.

Her voice voice tastes like milk chocolate—sweet, soft, and invigorating. There's something about her that mixes up my senses, as if she's so far beyond ordinary human experience that ordinary humans cannot help but be confused by her.

She closes her eyes and waves a hand over us. I'm not sure what that's supposed to do, because I don't feel the least bit different. *But you know what they say: "Don't look a gift goddess in the mouth." Or something like that.*

Morin taps his foot impatiently. "Are you quite done?"

Cog turns to face Morin. His face is no longer warm but terrible. "Quite. Go, Five! Go unite the kingdoms to face our final battle."

I hesitate, and with a wave of his hand, Cog sends us hurtling out the door. I land on my feet, but the momentum carries me forward, and I find myself racing down the mountain at ever-faster speeds; the stones catch me and launch me at just the right times. Overhead, Ami flies, while Caster and Emily race each other on jets of fire and water.

We come to a halt at the base of the mountain outside Kalix's camp. A little boy is waiting for us in the darkness. David.

It might be a trick of the moonlight, but I think I see him smile a little. "It worked?" he says.

"Beautifully." Caster holds out a fist, and David bumps it.

"This is the fastest bromance I've ever seen," says Emily. "I can't believe you told David and not me."

"Or me," says Ami, sounding a little hurt.

"Or me," I add, not wanting to be left out.

"I had no choice. I'm not really sure of your acting skills. If you had known what was going on, you might have spoiled things."

"But not you?" says Emily.

"Look, someone had to know, and clearly, I've got the most knack for trickery."

"Dupery," Emily says.

"Whatever. You get the point."

"We can sort stuff out later," I say. "In the meantime, we've got the world to save."

I say the words, but I'm not really sure they mean anything. Even if I can somehow get the Three Kingdoms to work together, what chance do we stand against the druid gods, Morin's armies, and the Ice Reich?

Ami seems to read my thoughts and gives my hand a brief squeeze, letting go far sooner than I would have liked. "Come on," she says. "You'll be great. We'll be behind you."

"I'd prefer if you were beside me," I say.

"Then we'll be beside you," says Emily.

"Just remember," says Caster, putting an arm around my shoulders, "imagine they're in their underwear."

493

"Uh." Given the size of the Kar-dun, this is a terrifying idea.

"That's dumb," says Emily.

Caster shrugs. "It's always worked for me. The other important thing is making an entrance."

"An entrance?" I say.

A mischievous grin lights up his face. "Like this." He starts to explain.

CHAPTER 105

THE CAPTAIN'S CALL

Caster's idea for an entrance turns out to be pretty spectacular. It involves Ami launching us thirty feet into the air while Caster sends swirling ribbons of flames around us, Emily sends jets of water dancing over us, David stirs the crowd with his yet-unexplained power, and I pull the earth up to meet us so we'll have a height advantage over the Kar-dun. I land with an earth-shaking crash on one leg and fist, Iron Man style, while Ami floats the others to the ground beside me.

Maybe it's excessively flashy, but it sure gets everyone's attention. Thousands of souls stare up at us—men in hoplite armor and Kar-dun standing as tall as elms, cased in metal that glimmers fiercely in the moonlight, with hard faces. What can I hope to say to these people that they don't know? I'm just a dumb high school kid. Some of the Kar-dun have lived for hundreds of years. They might not be immortal, but their lives are far longer than human lives.

But something in the crowd of metal men gives me encouragement. There's a little spark of admiration or reverence in their eyes—as if seeing the Five together stirs something deep in their souls. I feel my friends nudge me encouragingly, and I close my eyes, trying to figure out how to begin. The closest I've gotten to public speaking was a presentation I had to do in English class, which, to put it mildly, wasn't exactly a hit.

At some point, I start to speak, and the words tumble awkwardly out of my mouth. I speak Greek—the language my dad spoke with me when I was young and the language Dr. Elsavier, the only person who really understood me before I met my new friends, would use with me while we ate chocolate chip cookies in her classroom after school. Somehow everyone seems to understand, as though an invisible translator in the air is converting my words into whatever language the Kar-dun and humans speak.

I'm not really sure what I'm saying. The words come out stumbling at first, but then I feel Samjang's voice inside me, and my emotions begin to course through my veins like fire, ice, wind, stone, and soul all at once.

Memories fill my eyes. I think of what it's like to be cold and alone, and I try to pour those feelings into words to show how horrible it would be if the Ice Reich were allowed to win, consume all realms, and make existence itself a torture. Then I think of what it was like to meet my friends here and to learn that there are other people in the world who are kind of like I am and who, if I let them, care for me. I can hear Caster's voice in my head whispering, "Cliché," but I push through.

I think next of the story I told Dulia—how Jew and Greek, Chinese and Japanese, Indian and Pakistani, and Cherokee and African came together, and in one nation, we've learned to live together, be good neighbors, and not fight wars over stupid things. If us kids can learn to get along despite coming from all corners of the globe and from cultures that have hated each other from time to time, there's hope for the world—maybe Kar-dun and humans and the north, west, and south can do the same.

I finish the speech, feeling okay. It wasn't on the level of Winston Churchill or Henry V, but I did my best. I'm only eighteen.

But when I look out across the crowd, I see tears on those hard faces.

"That's got to be Samjang's work," I whisper to my friends. "No way I said anything that inspirational." But when I look at my friends, they have teary looks in their eyes too.

"No, you were quite good, Peter. Quite good," says Emily.

"Really?"

Caster nods. "Hate to admit it, but yeah."

"Yeah," Ami says. Somehow, her single word says more than all the others.

The crowd begins to chant, led by the Kar-dun dressed in the brightest armor and wearing the brightest colors, who I assume are the leaders. Soon their chant is picked up by the others.

"Captain Peter!" they shout.

I'm not sure if it's a way of saying, "You're only a captain, so you'd better listen to the generals," or if it's an honorary title meaning "You're the leader." Judging by the way they say it, it's the latter—which is a little terrifying.

I turn to Caster. "What's the plan?"

"Storm the mountain."

"Storm the mountain?"

"Yeah, storm the mountain, help Cog defeat the fallen gods, and close the entrance to the Ice Reich before it's too late."

"Right." I turn my eyes back to the armies. I hold up my hands, wait for them to quiet, and then shout, "To the mountain!"

Their voices echo my words, and trumpets blast, shaking the whole camp with noise. The soldiers respond to the horns and form into their units faster than I would have thought possible. Soon the armies are organized.

Kalix comes to us. "We wait for you."

I look to my friends. We stare at one another for a moment, and I think again of all the perfect memories I've made with them—falling from the sky above Cog's palace with Ami, sitting in Galthanius's house and talking with Emily, telling stories inside Emily's interdimensional blanket, singing songs in the desert, nearly drowning as the waters broke through my mud hut, and all the other moments. If this is our final hour and we go to die, I can live with that. I wouldn't trade these past few weeks for eighty-five years of my old life.

"Let's go," I say.

We make our way to the head of the army at the base of the mountain. The leaders of the Kar-dun salute us as we pass, which feels kind of cool and gives me more confidence than I probably should be feeling.

I stare up at the mountain and gulp as I see shadows appear at the top with little green lights flickering in their midst—Morin's armies. Through the earth, I feel another sensation, one I haven't felt since the cave of the Bloodfather: bloodgorgers. There are bloodgorgers in Morin's ranks.

I look at my friends and give them a sad smile.

"It'll be okay," says Ami.

Yeah right, I think. But I'm glad she said it all the same.

I turn to face the armies. "Upon my call!"

The other four nod at me, and the leaders of the armies echo my command.

"For Miria, the Nine Realms, and the All-Father!" *And friends*, I silently add. "Charge!"

The word spreads through all the armies, and we rush forward toward almost-certain death. But it's almost-certain death among friends.

CHAPTER 106

THE FINAL BATTLE

Our charge into almost-certain death is cut short as a meteor of crimson and azure blasts from the mountain, arcs down the mountainside, and crashes into the ground, carving a scar into the grassy plains before coming to a stop a few feet from us.

"Cog!" I rush forward toward the smoking heap.

"And Samjang!" Emily cries.

"Oh boy," says Ami quietly.

"Yeah. 'Oh boy' is right," says Caster. "There goes plan A."

I'm about to bend down to ask if they're okay—they are breathing—when suddenly, they both shoot to their feet. Cog dusts himself off and smiles, still glowing radiantly. Samjang looks no less spirited.

"Well, what are we waiting for?" Cog says.

"Charge!" Samjang cries, and once more, I find myself tasting milk chocolate on my tongue.

With that sweet taste, I feel a swell of courage like a giant wave propelling me upward. We all charge forward. Cog and Samjang are in the lead, followed by the Five and the armies of the west. For the first time, I feel I just might have Odysseus's courage.

The armies meet in a clash of clanging swords. Caster and Ami move around swiftly, knocking over files of phantom soldiers and setting them afire, while Emily hangs back to heal the wounded. Meanwhile, I try to provide defensive positions for archers while burying as many bloodgorgers and phantom men as I can.

I'm still not sure what David's powers are exactly. But one of his powers seems to be an ability to strengthen others. He moves around the battlefield, and whenever he draws near, the courage and energy of those he passes seem to increase. I find myself drawing closer to him like a fly led into the light.

Battle is an ugly thing, I soon discover—though to be honest, I get the best of it. I can wield the earth to my defense, but the Kar-dun and humans are left to fight with swords and pikes, and many of them fall to the enemy before Emily can help.

Despite the many wounded, it looks like we might win. We're making progress up the mountain, driving back the bloodgorgers and hordes of phantom men, while Cog and Samjang do battle overhead with the fallen gods in a fierce electrical storm of grace and spells. But then, just as we're nearing the mountaintop, reinforcements pour over the hills and force us backward down the mountain in a slow, agonizing retreat.

I use my power to create a handful of defenses that slow the tide of onrushing enemies, but it's no good. Our goal isn't to fight to a draw but to get into the mountain.

I search out Ami and Caster, who are fighting for their lives against a circle of dogs and bloodgorgers. They move together in beautiful synchrony, but I can see they're growing tired; their movements are sloppier and more effortful, just like mine. I help them finish off their attackers, and then I throw up a wall of stone behind us and slide to the ground in exhaustion.

"We're not going to make it," I say between deep intakes of breath.

I expect Ami to say, "It'll be okay," but she stays silent. Her brow is drawn with weariness and concern.

Caster shakes his head. "That's not the right way to think of it. We need a new plan."

I'm glad Caster has his fire back, but I don't have it. The wind is growing colder, and frost is spreading down the mountain. Whatever has been keeping the Ice Reich from breaking through is giving way.

"We can barely withstand Morin's armies and the fallen gods," I say. "What will we do when the Ice Reich attacks?"

"Come on," says Caster, offering a hand and pulling me to my feet. "Let's find Emily, and I'll explain."

David finds us and points out her location, and we run to her. She's busy healing some soldiers with stab wounds. Despite the cold, her face glows with a sheen of sweat, and her usually straight hair is frayed.

"What?" asks Emily as she finishes healing one soldier and motions for the next. "I take it things are going great, aren't they?"

"We need to shift the paradigm," Caster says.

"What?"

"Paradigm shift. Thomas Kuhn. Philosopher of science. In 1962, he argued science advances not cumulatively, as Bacon thought, but, rather, in shifts as new experiments render old paradigms, or ways of looking at data, incompatible."

"I didn't know bacon had thoughts," I say.

"Francis Bacon," says Caster, annoyed.

I resist the urge to say, "I didn't know France is bacon." When I'm tired and stressed, the drive to make stupid puns becomes almost overwhelming.

Emily looks up from the man she's healing. "Caster, is this really the time for a philosophy lesson?"

"Yes and no. The paradigm has been this: Enki was going to trick the fallen gods, slip into the Ice Reich, and retrieve his mother while we and Cog held the portal open just wide enough for him to get back. Afterward, we were going to send the fallen gods in, right? But obviously, that's not going to work."

"Thanks, genius," says Emily. "I was aware of that. So what's your paratrooper shift, paragraph shift, parasite shift—whatever you call it?"

"Paradigm shift. The new paradigm is this: we go into the Ice Reich and get the Winter Goddess ourselves."

Emily tilts her head and seems to consider the idea. "Yeah, there's just one problem. How do we get past Morin's armies and into the Ice Reich?"

Caster opens his mouth as if to reply but then clamps it shut.

"Exactly," says Emily.

"We have to try," says Ami. "Caster's right. If we keep doing things the way we've been doing them, it won't end well."

I nod, trying to think of some way we can get past the fallen gods and armies without attracting too much attention. "If only we still had the interdimensional blanket," I say.

"What if I were to tell you," says a familiar voice from behind, "that I have it?"

CHAPTER 107

THE RETURN

We all spin around at once to see a woman dressed in plain brown robes. Her hair is as black as raven feathers, and her face is as fair as the moon. In her hand is a golden staff.

"Haji!" everyone exclaims at once.

"Wait—you know Haji too?" Emily says to David.

"I met him after I left you outside the Gray City," Haji says. "And I told him you were not the enemy he thought you were."

"Well, that would have been good to know," says Emily, crossing her arms.

David shrugs. "A lot happened, all right?"

"Excuse me," I say. "But what are you doing here?"

"Yeah, and am I the only one who thinks this is a little deus ex machina? Haji just happens to appear with the blanket in the nick of time?" says Caster.

Her eyes twinkle, and she nudges her head toward the east. We all turn to look just as a horn sounds in the distance, high and clear. Soon other horns join in the call, followed by a deep, guttural roar.

"It's the laganmorfs!" Emily gasps. "And the nymphs! Haji, you did it!"

"Of course," she says, smiling. "But actually, it was Meila and her sister who did most of the work."

"I knew it!" Caster exclaims.

"What do you mean you knew it?" Emily snaps. "You knew nothing! You literally just said, 'Am I the only one who thinks this is a little deus ex machina?'"

"It was more a commentary on the choice of plot development," says Caster.

Everyone looks at him with an eyebrow raised, except me, because I can't raise a single eyebrow, so I just look silly and incredulous.

"Anyway," says Caster, "it's very simple."

Emily rolls her eyes while mockingly repeating, "It's very simple."

"It is," Caster says. "In fact, it is elementary, my dear Watson. Remember when I asked whether there was a chance they would end their deliberations and come help us?"

Ami shakes her head. "Not really."

"Yeah, I don't either," I say.

"Well, I did ask that, and there was such a chance. With an infinite amount of time, any event with a probability greater than zero is bound to occur."

"Say that in English."

"If you have a million dice, it's really unlikely you'll roll all sixes, right? But given an eternity, as long as you keep rolling, you'll get sixes eventually. No time goes by in the outside world from the perspective of the Wella, which means they basically had an eternity to decide." He scratches his chin. "But I still don't understand how Meila could leave and return to the Wella without an infinite amount of time passing."

"Oh, I see!" I say. "That's really clever."

"Who knows?" says Emily. "He didn't tell us beforehand. I get the impression Caster only likes to prophesy after the fact."

"All the same, my prediction came true."

"It was more of a postdiction."

Caster makes a face. "You're a postdiction."

"You now have a diversion," Haji says. "And a blanket to keep you hidden when you enter the Ice Reich."

She hands us the blanket, and Emily takes it with her mouth open wide. "How did you find it?"

Haji smiles. "I found a few lost horses, and they told me their tale. I have a way with animals."

"Yeah, you do!" Emily throws her arms around Haji in a hug.

"Aw." Haji pats her head. "I have to go now. There are some things that need my attention. But you have a worthy plan, and if you want to succeed, now is the moment to act."

"Right," I say, feeling strength pour back into my body. I'm not sure if it's because of Haji's words, David's power, or the fact that Ami is standing close enough I can almost feel the warmth radiating from her skin.

In the next few minutes, we settle on a plan. We all gather inside the blanket, and Emily pulls it around us, leaving a little hole at the front for me to see out of. I give directions, while Ami causes the blanket to float. Caster does backseat driving, giving an annoying commentary: "If the blanket is really interdimensional, why can Ami make it float in our dimension? There's something fishy going on here with the laws of physics in Miria." He continues the whole way up the mountain.

Slowly, we make our way up the mountain, passing over the fierce two-front battle: Kar-dun and humans in the west and laganmorfs and nymphs in the east, all pressing in against the bloodgorgers and phantom men. I would feel more hopeful if frost were not spreading farther and farther down the mountain, glowing ominously in the moonlight.

Time is running out.

CHAPTER 108

THE REICH

We enter through the west entrance, and the clanging of clashing swords and the thundering of battling gods grow dimmer, muted by the stone.

As we round the final corner, entering the main room, my heart nearly stops.

"Stop," I whisper fiercely to Ami.

"What is it?" Emily asks.

The room is not empty, as we expected. Instead, a familiar gruesome face stares right into us: Morin.

I feel my pulse quicken, readying me for a final fight with him. But then I notice that Morin's eyes are looking past us while he mutters strange words.

"What's he doing?" asks Caster. "Is it safe to proceed?"

I listen closer. *Attack them on the left. Draw back. Now move to the right. Place archers there.*

"He's directing the battle," I say. "We should take him out. His armies will be scattered."

"We don't have time," says Caster. "Ice Reich is priority *numero uno.*"

I want badly to drive a dagger into Morin's black heart, which has caused so much evil and hurt, but I can't argue with Caster's reasoning. "All right," I say reluctantly.

I give directions to Ami, and we make our way around Morin and into the icy crack upon the altar, the Heart of Miria.

The crack turns out to be more like a long hallway, which is still somehow narrow, despite how long it's been open. It's as though there's something trying to keep it closed.

Then I see that there is. A monkey man covered in ice and snow grips the portal walls. His arms are straining hard.

"Enki!" I cry.

"Enki?" Emily and Caster echo. "What's going on?"

"What are you doing here?" I ask.

"Keeping the world from ending," he says, his voice barely above a whisper. It seems to come from far away, as though he's close to dreaming. His lips move as if he's trying to say something or remember to say something. Then, suddenly, his eyes brighten and stare into mine. "Get Mother," he says. "Get her. I can't hold on much longer."

"What's he saying?" asks Emily.

I repeat everything, and she nods and turns to David. "Can you strengthen him?"

He closes his eyes and squeezes his brow in effort. He opens them again. "I can't."

I furrow my brow. "But why would—"

"Go!" Enki says, his voice torn with pain. "I haven't much longer."

I nod solemnly, and Ami floats the interdimensional blanket deeper into the long tunnel. A bluish light appears in the distance. When we get to the end of the tunnel, we see where the blue light is coming from.

The tunnel ends at a crack just large enough for a man to squeeze through. As we exit, I realize with a start that we're not looking down but outward. What counts as down for Miria counts as sideways for the Ice Reich. But this thought is quickly pushed away by a flood of terrifying sights and sounds.

I must be shaking, because Emily's voice is concerned as she asks me, "What is it, Peter? What do you see?"

It's difficult to put into words the massive sight, which only gets more massive as Ami floats the blanket upward, giving a fuller view of what's below.

Spread out upon a sheet of ice that stretches farther than I can see are legions upon legions of ice monsters like the ones I saw when I first came to Miria, only they're larger and stronger. Their eyes glow with an evil pale blue light, casting flickering shadows upon the high ceiling above us.

I've never seen an army so large. I think if all the soldiers in the American military formed up, they would only amount to one column of the hundreds of columns here.

As we float over them, the portal widens a little bit, and the ice monsters begin to chant.

"Azh kar, murak-hum! Azh kar, murak-hum!"

I think Samjang's language gift must still linger in my ears, because the meaning of the words comes into my soul, filling my mind's eye with horrible images.

"Peter," Emily says.

I shake myself away from the spell of the chanting ice monsters and describe what I see.

"How are we going to find the Winter Goddess?" Caster says. "We don't have enough time to do a linear search."

Emily strokes her chin. "Enki mentioned something about keeping her in chains, like in a prison, right?"

"Right," says Caster. "So where do you keep a prison?"

I close my eyes, trying to think. But instead of thinking, I end up feeling—not my emotion but someone else's. It's distant, like a weak signal barely picked up by the radio. But I definitely can feel it—desperate, anguished, pleading for help. Somewhere in the distance. Somewhere—

"Below," Ami and I say at once.

I wonder how I am able to pick up the Winter Goddess's signal if my element is earth. It reminds me of the experience on the boat, when I felt I could feel Ami's emotions, hopes, desires, and dreams. I wonder how that's possible. What kind of connection is there between us?

Emily and Caster look at each other and smirk.

"That was a little weird," David says.

Ami's cheeks flush a shade redder, and mine probably do too, but she presses on, ignoring it. "The Winter Goddess is below us. Beneath the ice."

"It's the best hypothesis we've got," Caster says. "Might as well test it."

I shut the blanket over my eyes, and slowly, we descend, slipping through the ice as though we aren't there, following the signal for help.

CHAPTER 109

CHAINS

For a long time, there is only solid ice outside the blanket, but eventually, the ice gives way to a vast chasm lit by pale blue light. It is huge. Colossal. Epic.

Deep within the chasm, there are five cities with towers that make the Empire State Building look like a child's toy tower and with buildings as vast as malls stacked one atop the other. The architecture varies but is largely the same. Every structure has the same harsh, jutting edges; the same proud height; and the same characters cut into the walls—characters that remind me of the ones I saw in Morin's tomb. The characters are so massive I can see them even from this distance.

But what most draws my attention is that the five cities are arranged suspiciously in the shape of a pentagon.

"Why all the pentagons?" asks Emily. The opening in the blanket is wide enough now for her and Caster to look out.

"It has something to do with imitating the Five, right?" I say.

"Yeah, but don't you feel like it's deeper than all that? I mean, why do they want to imitate the Five?"

I don't have an answer for her, so I keep silent as we descend toward the center field among the cities, led by the strengthening signal calling out for help.

As we grow closer to the plain, I see that it's not all solid ice. In the center is a chasm surrounded by five short towers, with ice-monster guards stationed facing outward. Their faces are grim and stiff, as though they haven't moved in a thousand years. But their eyes are fierce, which tells me that despite their stillness, they are not the sort of creatures one would want to pick a fight with.

Fortunately, we have Ami and the blanket, so we slip past them and begin our descent down the chasm. I'm certain now this has to be where the Winter Goddess is kept, deep in the Ice Reich, with guards outside.

The chasm winds downward, and I'm reminded of a line from a poem I heard somewhere: "For who goes up your winding stair can ne'er come down again." I'm not sure why, but I have the growing feeling it's true: we will never come out of here again. I try to shake off the feeling, but the more I stare at the creepy characters written along the walls, the more I can't help but feel it's true.

At last, we come to the bottom of the winding well, to a hollow room about the size of a stadium. In the center is a bed of ice and chains with a figure hidden in shadows upon it.

"The Winter Goddess," I say.

We speed toward the bed to find a woman stripped of all her clothes; her pale skin is bruised and blue, her flesh is emaciated, and her body shivers from more than just the cold. Chains bind her arms, legs, and neck, and her chest moves so slowly I can hardly tell she's breathing. If I were her, I wouldn't want to breathe either.

I remember Morin saying that the gods are mortal. If that's so, how has she stayed alive so long? It feels wrong that a person should have to experience such torture, with no end in sight—and not because of anything she did but because someone betrayed her.

Emily unravels the blanket, exposing us to the icy cold. "Quick. Let's get to work!"

We rush forward to the bed. Emily and Ami take the goddess's hands. "We're going to get you out of here," Emily says.

"Caster," says Ami, "can you melt the chains?"

Caster's lips crease into a confident smirk. "Of course I can." He closes his eyes, and his hands burst into flames, but the flames are weak and sputtering like the flames of a gas grill that's almost out of gas. Caster furrows his brow. "What the—"

Suddenly, the Winter Goddess groans, and her eyes open. She looks as if she's trying to tell us something. Her eyes are bright and urgent, but her lips only mumble sounds I can't understand.

"It's okay," says Emily. "We're going to get you out of here."

She shakes her head, and Ami furrows her brow. "You don't want to leave?"

She shakes her head again, which only confuses us more. No, she doesn't want to leave? Or no, she doesn't *not* want to leave?

Then I realize her gaze is no longer fixed on us but on something behind us.

Just as realization and dread break over me, her tongue is loosed, and she speaks two words: "He's here."

CHAPTER 110

AFTER DEATH

We whip around to face a monster of nine icy tentacles slithering like snakes from its body, which is almost as large as one of the towers in the city. Its eyes are as big as laganmorfs and full of the same blue fire that lights the ice monsters' eyes, only a thousand times more malevolent. Its body is fat and overgrown, like that of a man who's spent all his life gorging himself, and its face is as sharp as the blade of a sword.

I reach for my stone, as the others reach for their powers, but I find my power weak, sputtering like Caster's flames, and in a moment, we're all in the grip of the monster's tentacles.

"Who are you?" I say.

"I am the One," says the monster. "The Father, the Knower, the Master of the Deep."

The creature's words fill my thoughts with horrible images.

"I am the One all the gods wish to imitate, one of the originals who did not serve." It says the words with horrible envy and spite, as its icy eyes fix on me. "Now, the question is, what is your purpose here?" It has none of the playful cruelty of Morin in its voice, the sort of cruelty interested in protracted conversation. Rather, it has a cold urgency in its tone, and that scares me even more than Morin.

I look at my friends and draw courage from them. "We're here to rescue the Winter Goddess from your nasty grip," I say, spitting each word. "You evil bastard."

"Is that so?" says the monster. "Then it is clear what must be done. Who among your friends wishes to die first?"

"Just like that?" says Caster. "No speech explaining your grand, evil schemes?"

"No speech," the monster says, and I can feel the impatience in its voice. Its tentacles squeeze me tighter.

I reach for my power but find it still weak and distant. I look among my friends and see the same strained, empty expressions on their faces. A chill spreads through my being as I realize there's nothing any of us can do.

You're going to die, Peter, a voice inside me says.

I know. But it could be worth it.

"Me," I say. "Kill me. Let them go."

The monster smiles. "Wrong answer." It drives a spike through Emily's back. The point bursts through her stomach, lined with crimson. Emily's blood.

Emily gasps in pain, and the light in her eyes begins to fade.

I pinch myself and cry in anguish, hoping this is somehow just a dream, and I'm not really watching Emily Wong die. The monster grins.

Caster's face is pale with shock. "Emily," he says softly, and his voice breaks me.

"Oh, interesting," says the monster. "You loved her, didn't you? Well, then I'll be kind. I'll send you to meet her in the afterworld." With another spike, a gasp, and blood, just like that, Caster's dead.

Another spike, another gasp, and more blood immediately follow. David's gone. The poor kid—he only wanted to find his Aunt, and this is how it ends for him.

Only Ami and I are left. I bite the inside of my mouth until it bleeds, praying this is all a nightmare, and I'll wake up to find I never left Gaia and never became friends with Ami and the others, if only it turns out they're still alive.

With the drive of another spike, I hear another gasp and see more blood.

Ami! My head is spinning now; my whole body heaves with pain. This can't be happening. *Ami. Emily. Caster. David.* My thoughts mix together, swirling into a crimson fire. *Blood. Blood. Blood.*

Blood and fading light surround me.

The monster grins down at me, but I don't care. I am enveloped in pain; every inch of my flesh screams in agony. I see visions of the future—the monster tears through my mom and dad and Dr. Elsavier and consumes all worlds until nothing is left—but amid all the future terrors, my mind's eye keeps coming back to the moment the monster killed my friends.

I tremble with horror and loss I can't even begin to put to words. I reach out with my soul, wishing with all my heart I could touch my friends, feel them alive again, and trade my life for theirs. But I feel only ice and snow, cold, hard, and unfeeling.

No. I feel something beneath the snow in my mind. I dig and dig, prying deeper even as my mind's fingers begin to bleed.

There's something beneath the ice, something deep in my heart. Or not my heart. From that deep place, I see something in the distance—something bright and so massive it would make the sun look like a grain of sand. I race toward it, pulled in by its fierce gravity. All the while, images of my friends' bodies torn open by icy spikes wet with blood pierce my mind, and some mad monster in my mind chants, *Death, death, death.*

But countering those words is the massive Light, warm and bright, which swells over the entire horizon.

CHAPTER 111

ONE

"What are you?" I say. The only thing I can think is that I must be dead already. "Are you the light at the end of the tunnel?"

I feel a new pain blossom deep in my heart, somewhere so deep I didn't know it existed. But it does—it *is* more than anything else that is. It hurts at first, but then, strangely, it feels warmer and kinder, more desirable than any pleasure.

Joy. The word springs into my mind unbidden. It's joy. But that doesn't make sense. How can joy hurt so much? How can I want it to hurt more? And why should hurt or joy be so bright?

I sense the Joy growing, until it's more than a mere sensation; it's substance, something real, something feeling, something thinking—but these terms are like only shadows of the words that really describe it, the way a shadow of a person is nothing compared to the real person, the one who fills space, loves, cries, hopes, feels, thinks, and is a world in herself.

"Who are you?" I ask again, overwhelmed by the largeness of the Being, the Light, the Joy. But however overwhelming it is, I am certain of one thing: the Being is not a *what* but a *who*.

The Being is silent for a long time—it seems like hours or, rather, years—but then it speaks in a voice that fills up my entire being, penetrating everything that is me.

"I am the Resurrection and the Life."

"The Resurrection and the Life?" I repeat. The words sound familiar, but I can't quite remember where I've heard them. But there is something I do know—the only thing that can make sense of this experience.

"You're Gomdan. Or the All-Father. Or—what am I supposed to call you?" The names seem inadequate.

Even though I'm suspended in space with no up, down, left, or right, I feel a sudden urge to bow down. I'm not in the presence of someone I admire or even an important person, such as a president; I am in the presence of Joy itself, of Being itself, the thing that makes me a thing. I feel shame and joy, horror and awe, and fear and love all at once; the feelings all flow in and out of each other as easily as droplets of water.

All my life before this moment seems shallow, as though I've been living on the surface of a pond, when reality is as deep as the oceans. The things I cared about—playing video games, not getting bullied, and finding a girlfriend—all seem so small, as if I were chasing after pennies, when right behind me, just around the bend, there were mounds of gold as vast as the treasuries of Fort Knox.

"I promise if I make it out of here alive, I will search for you again," I say. And I mean that promise. I mean it more than anything I've ever meant in my whole life.

It's hard to say, but I think I feel the All-Father smile.

Then the world begins to change. I'm surging upward toward something cold and blue: ice. But just beneath the ice, I see something. No, I feel something. It doesn't feel like me. But it also doesn't feel like not me. It feels like the Five.

At first, I feel only five little sparks floating through a space of empty darkness deep beneath the ice. But then the sparks join together, molding into one spark—not a spark that has lost the identity of the original five sparks but a superspark that is at once Five and One.

The spark grows, bursting outward like a universe coming into being, racing through the bounds of nonexistence as space unfurls into space, light into darkness, stillness into breath, death into life.

I am the Resurrection and the Life.

I feel the whole frame of my being begin to rip and tear as the little thing that is me explodes into an existence far bigger than anything it could have imagined, the way the sun outsizes a grain of sand. But even as my being rips, something new makes way for it and nurtures it, turning the unimaginable agony into bliss. I'm vaguely aware that the nurturing presence is the All-Father, the Being who sang being into being, but how I know it I can't say.

My eyes flutter open, and they are my eyes and not my eyes, for I see five worlds and one world—or, rather, one world with five pairs of eyes.

With five pairs of eyes and one pair, I—We—see the monster's smile melt off its face. The monster who dared to call itself the One.

With a fist heavy as stone, swift as wind, unyielding as water, hot as fire, and deep as soul, We crush the monster, pitching it into the abyss. With a flick of Our wrist, the puny ice giants are sent hurtling in after it. Then We turn to the Winter Goddess, who is naked and shivering in pain upon the ground, still bound by the cruel chains that sap her life, and with another fist, We smash the chains into a thousand shards and gather her in Our arms.

The Reich trembles as we take hold the freed goddess. Her flesh is cold but not bitterly cold—it's the sort of cold that invigorates. The sort that makes children laugh as they ice-skate or build snowmen. The sort that makes hot chocolate taste a million times better. Hers is a cold unlike the chill and frost of the Ice Reich, and I realize then what a perversion of winter the Ice Reich is. But no more—We shall make her free.

She looks at Us. Her eyes are empty at first, hollowed out by millennia of torture, but then they focus on Us and grow a shade warmer. "Thank you."

We smile and shoot upward toward the portal, breaking through the ice, as the foundations of the world shake, and the proud structures of the Ice Reich come crashing down into heaping ruin.

We still have the fallen gods to face, but the gods and all their magic are nothing against the Five-become-One, in whom the power of the All-Father dwells.

In the distance, We see Enki, who is now beginning to thaw, and, above him, the light that leads out into Miria. The long hallway of the portal has shrunk to only a few feet now. We're almost back.

But just as We near the portal, a face appears in the darkness, made of rotting flesh and blackened bone: Morin.

"Oh! Isn't this delicious!" he exclaims, holding up the sacrificial knife. "Farewell, Five!"

He drives the knife into the altar, and with a whispered spell, the portal begins to close, no longer propped open by the strength of the Ice Reich. We drive forward with all Our strength, but We know somehow there isn't enough time to make it. We'll be trapped in here, perhaps forever.

"Enki!" We cry. "Can you stop it?"

But Enki looks dazed; his strength is gone from trying for hours to keep the portal from fully opening.

The portal closes to a foot, then half a foot, and then a few inches. Then a clang and a cry echo from above, and just as the portal squeezes shut, a golden circle appears above.

Not a golden circle, We realize. The tip of a golden staff.

The staff pries open the portal to reveal Haji, who is holding Morin by a tuft of his mangled hair. We grab Enki and pull him through the crack.

"You're—" Haji's eyes are wide with wonder.

Morin, relying on her momentary confusion, reaches for the knife and drives it toward Haji, but We merely flick Our wrist, and the knife goes flying from his hand and impales the wall.

He snarls and lunges at Us like a mad dog, but with a crack of her staff, Haji sends him reeling backward into the portal. As his cries echo and fade, Haji turns to Us and smiles. "Now for the rest of them. But how do we keep them from flying to all corners of Miria to hide?"

"Leave that to me." It's Enki. He stands by the wall, holding the dagger Morin tried to stab Haji with.

Haji raises an eyebrow. "What's your plan, trickster?"

"Not Father?" he replies, amused.

523

That's right. Didn't Thaegar say that Haji is one of the Chelei, children of the trickster god and a nymph?

"What is your plan, trickster-father?"

Enki shrugs as if to say, "I suppose I can settle for that," and then smiles. His eyes light up with mischief. "One final trick. All I need is a little blood."

CHAPTER 112

TRICKS AND TICKLES

Enki takes Our hand, and it is the first time We realize what We look like: a single body pure as sunlight but sparkling blue and red, black and green, and golden white. Then Enki cuts, drawing blood from Our hand, thereby luring all the fallen gods with its sweet scent.

They all converge on the Heart of Miria, and that is when We spring the trap. We combine our power with Cog's, Samjang's, Haji's, and Enki's to hurl the fallen gods into the abyss of the Ice Reich.

With horrid shrieks, they disappear into the abyss, and Cog and Samjang close the portal and redo the locks.

After it's all over, Enki shyly approaches his mother, who lies in the corner of the room. He seems almost like a boy who's been naughty and hopes his mother still loves him. When she embraces him, now wrapped in one of Haji's cloaks, they both begin to cry.

It is a touching sight. Enki doesn't seem like the sensitive type, but I guess everyone has a soft spot somewhere. Cog joins them, and his tears trickle down his old beard.

Not long afterward, We collapse, falling into a dreamless sleep.

I awaken sometime later, wrapped in familiar stone. It takes me a second to figure out why it's familiar. Then I recall: it's the bed I slept in when I first came to Miria all those days ago. I'm in Cog's palace.

I stumble out of bed, feeling as if I've slept for at least a full day, and make my way to the common room. Caster and Emily are sitting on the circular couch, and even though there's plenty of room, they're sitting rather close. As I approach them, I see they're holding hands.

Oh, I think, wading through the swamp of a brain that has just woken up. *I guess that was inevitable, wasn't it?* The funny thing is, I don't even feel jealous. Rather, I feel happy for them. There's a lingering sense of oneness in my soul, which makes their happiness my happiness.

I cough, and they turn around.

"Oh, hey there," says Emily, ripping her hand from Caster's, blushing slightly.

Caster looks miffed, as if I've interrupted an important moment or something, but he quickly breaks into a smile. "Good to see you awake, old buddy, old boy, old pal."

"I don't think I'm the oldest."

"Oh yeah? What's your sign anyway?" Emily asks.

"Capricorn. I was born on Christmas."

"Oh really? Do you get double the presents?"

"Not usually. What are you?"

"I'm Leo," she says. "Caster?"

"I'm Cancer."

"Well, we already knew that!" Emily claps her hands and laughs as if she's made the funniest joke in the world. It takes my foggy brain a few seconds to remember that *cancer* is slang for "toxic," "obnoxious," or "annoying."

Caster pinches her, and she yelps before retaliating.

I roll my eyes. "Where's Ami?"

"She's—yow! Still in her—stop tickling! I hate tickling! Bedroom. Aah!"

"I'm going to go get her," I say, shaking my head and smiling.

I can't believe it's been only nineteen days since we first gathered in this room. I feel as if I've known these people all my life, even though there's still a lot I don't know about them. But that's the fun part—getting to know these people I've come to love.

I try knocking on Ami's door, but it turns out the door is made of clouds, and my hand just goes through. Because I'm still feeling muddled, I decide to just barge in—it doesn't even occur to me to ask, "Are you decent?"

Fortunately, it turns out she is decent. And she's beautiful.

She's lying on a bed of clouds with a serene expression on her face. I stand there frozen, looking at her olive skin, the way her dark hair falls across her shoulders, and how small and light she looks floating on the clouds.

"Are you going to say hi, or are you just going to watch me while I sleep?"

"I, uh—" I fumble my words. My cheeks are red hot.

"Because if I didn't know you better, I'd say that's really creepy."

I feel ashamed, and I consider just leaving the room, but she floats to a seated position and smiles at me. "Only teasing."

"Oh, right."

She climbs from her bed and drifts closer to me, holding one arm to her side with the other. Her eyes are shy and inviting, and I find myself drifting closer to her like a fly toward the light. There's a soft tickling in my tummy.

"You remember when you said there was something you wanted to tell me?" she asks.

I search my brain for the past few days, but so much has happened I can hardly keep any of it straight. I make an "Um" noise and stare past her, frozen in space. A few seconds pass.

Her gaze falls, and she looks disappointed. "Well, I guess the others are probably up," she says, moving toward the door.

My heart feels heavy and starts to sink, and I want to say something to make it up to her, but the only words that come out of my mouth are "Except David."

"Let's wake him then."

I follow her through the cloudy door and toward the end of the hallway. My heart is beating fast. I remember now what I wanted to tell her, what I've wanted to tell her for a while now: "I like you, Ami." But I'm not sure how, so instead, as she's about to rap on the dark door at the hallway's end, I reach for her hand.

She turns to look at me. "You're not holding my hand just because you're scared, like you did in Morin's tomb, are you?"

I laugh nervously. "What would I be scared of?"

She says nothing; she only stares at me with her beautiful brown eyes as big as harvest moons.

"I guess I am a little scared," I say.

"Of what?"

"Well, of you."

She laughs. "What about me is scary?"

"Well," I say, my voice feeling suddenly tight. I feel my cheeks flush, and I look away, but she gently touches my chin and makes me look into her deep hazel eyes. "Well, you're really pretty."

Now it's her turn to blush, and the red glow looks beautiful on her olive cheeks. "So are you. Handsome, I mean. Very handsome."

I take a deep breath, and then I say what I've been wanting to say, before another sumo wrestler has a chance to sit on my tongue.

"I like you, Ami. I always have. Ever since you beat up Brutus in the parking lot. You've always been kind, honest, and good, even when I wasn't. And you don't deserve to be bullied by a bunch of stupid girls just because they don't understand you. You deserve to be cherished."

Cherished. Yes, sometimes studying for the SAT can have its benefits.

She beams at me, and then her smile twists into a Caster-like smirk. "I know. It's not easy to be as good as me. But I like you too, Peter."

"I knew it!" Emily exclaims.

We both jump and turn around, blushing furiously.

"Because it was obvious," Caster says. "What part tipped you off, genius? Was it when we found him holding Ami outside Cog's palace? Or when he held her in the boat, looking all googly-eyed at her? Or was it—"

"Oh, shut up, Caster. If you were any more of a gasbag, your own wit would cause you to burst into flames."

"And if you were any shallower, you'd freeze from the coldness of your own heart."

"Huh!" Emily beats her chest. "I'm so hurt!"

Ami and I exchange a knowing look. This is, I guess, Caster and Emily's way of saying they like each other.

We're about to knock on the door, when David opens it, rubbing his eyes.

"Oh, you're awake!" Ami says.

"Yeah. How could I not be with those two?"

Everyone laughs.

"Come on," says Emily after the laughter settles down. "Cog sent someone earlier to say there's going to be a feast. Last one there is a rotten egg!"

CHAPTER 113

A DIFFERENT WORLD

Cog's palace has changed a lot since last I saw it. First, it's not in the north anymore. Somehow, it's been moved to the plains beneath the Heart of Miria, the neutral zone—but I guess if you're a god, you can do that kind of thing. Second, the palace isn't nearly as gloomy. The old, crooked tower where we first met Cog stands tall and proud. Nymphs chase each other through the halls while the songs of laganmorfs drift through the courtyards and corridors. The world feels right and not just because Ami is holding my hand.

We make our way out of the courtyard and into the open field where the armies of the north, west, and south once did battle with Morin's forces. Now the field is filled with men dancing drunkenly under a twilight sky with kegs of ale strewn about.

"How long were we asleep?" I wonder aloud.

"About two days," says a familiar voice.

We spin around to find Cog leaning on a staff, gazing at us with his warm, clever eyes.

"Cog!" says Emily. "So glad to see a familiar face. What happened? I mean after we fell asleep."

"The laganmorfs, nymphs, Kar-dun, and humans made short work of Morin's armies. Samjang and I nursed the Winter Goddess, my beloved wife, back to health, and we began preparations for a great feast."

"All that in two days?" Caster asks.

Cog shrugs. "It's not much for a god. Especially after witnessing what has never been done before: Five-becoming-One." He surveys the five of us and smiles. "You are a very impressive group of people."

An awkward silence settles over the group, and Cog is about to leave, probably to attend to his other duties, when David speaks.

"Sir, do you know where my aunt is?"

Cog's eyes twinkle. "I washed her mind of the fearful memories of the past few weeks, and then I sent her home."

Relief floods over David's face, followed by longing. "When can I see her again?"

"As soon as you're back in Gaia."

"And, um, how soon will that be?" asks Caster.

Cog raises an eyebrow. "You're not eager to return?"

Caster looks away. "Well, I mean, the landscape is nice, and the people aren't terrible."

"Oh, I think he means if you send us back, will we ever get to see you again?" Emily says.

"Of course! Once a ringbearer, always a ringbearer. There's always summer vacation. But if I'm not mistaken, you have missed a great deal of school and, consequently, have a great deal of making up to do."

I forgot Cog has traveled many times between our worlds. It makes sense he would know about schoolwork and whatnot, but it's still weird to hear him talk about it.

"Yeah," says Emily. "And prom is coming up too. Somehow, no one has asked me out yet."

"Gee, I wonder how someone with a personality as great as yours was never asked out," Caster says.

"Gee, I wonder that too," says Emily, crossing her arms. "Is that your way of asking me out?"

"As long as you don't eat all the hors d'oeuvres, Zhu Bajie."

"Why, you!" Emily raises a fist, and Caster cringes laughing.

"I will see you all at the feast," says Cog. "Till then."

"Wait," says Emily. "We have questions."

"Very well," says Cog. "Ask."

"The fallen gods said the gods were mortal, but they also said some of them were spirits or had once been spirits. And they also said the gods get their power from the Dark Realm, but if that's the case, how did the Ice Reich use the Winter Goddess as their source of power? Why not just summon the power directly from the Dark Realm? And lastly, who are the druids of Belial really? I mean, Morin said the druids were just the fallen gods, but I feel like he was hiding things. For example, who is Belial? And who were the three sisters in his tomb?"

"Only those questions?" Cog says, a wry smile on his lips.

Emily scratches her head. "I probably have more, but I've forgotten."

"I'll do my best to answer," says Cog. "Many of the so-called fallen gods, it is true, are men or something like men, but they were not so originally. They were once another kind of creature—a creature that had no need of a body but existed in a way your minds will find incomprehensible."

I remember the feeling I had back in Cog's palace before we left, the sense that Ku'ba's and Cog's bodies were shadows cast by something far vaster and more massive than my puny brain could imagine.

"Some of us stayed true to the All-Father and thus retained the powers he gifted us—the powers of grace. It is not a power as much as a gift, a blessing, and a responsibility. But others of us were deceived by lies and were led down a dark path. They thought that by becoming flesh, they would be freer. Those who were taken in became the fallen gods. They lost their powers of grace and instead sought to steal power from the Dark Realm to bind nature to their will rather than the will of the All-Father."

Cog's eyes seem to grow distant and cold. "As for Belial, pray you never find out who or what he is. Likewise for the sisters." He turns to us and smiles kindly. "With Samjang back, the fallen gods driven into prison, and the Reich stripped of its power, I think you never shall have to worry. Now, I shall see you at the feast!"

Cog turns from us and leaves. His words bounce around in my brain. I feel a sense of relief: we've beaten the Ice Reich, Morin, and the fallen gods and rescued the Winter Goddess. But a dark voice somewhere deep inside whispers that Cog's reassurances are hollow and that this is not the end but the beginning. For a moment, the world begin to fade. The trees and people turn into shadows, and I'm hurtling into darkness. A monster laughs deep below, a monster so vast and terrible it makes the monster in the Ice Reich look like a pitiful toddler.

"What's wrong, Peter? You look upset."

My eyes find Ami's, and they fill me with more courage than Goober's 120-proof alcohol.

"Oh, nothing," I say, smiling, as the sounds of laughter and song fill my ears again, drawing me back to this world.

I feel the grass between my toes, the warmth of the sunlight on my neck, and the softness of Ami's hand in mine. Then come the smells drifting through the air from the kitchens and fires. My stomach growls, and I forget the nightmare I experienced for just a moment.

"Are you thinking what I'm thinking?" says Emily.

"Oh boy," says Caster. "Our Zhu Bajie wants to eat. Ow! Stop pinching me!"

"Last one there's a rotten egg!" Ami says.

She pulls me forward, and a rush of wind lifts us off the ground and toward the Great Hall, where food awaits, while Caster and Emily yell about how unfair it is.

It is unfair. It's unfair I have such great friends. It's unfair I met a person as special as Ami. It's unfair how happy I feel.

But it's a different world, and the world feels right. More right than it's ever felt before.

CHAPTER 114

FAREWELL

The feast turns out to be the greatest food I've ever had—and not just because I haven't eaten for the past three days. The alcohol laws are also looser in Miria, so all five of us end up enjoying the ale, which makes for one heck of an evening. At some point, we end up dancing with Kar-dun—which is awkward, given the height differences—before collapsing on the mountainside to watch the stars.

But before we get too deep in our cups, we see some old friends. The Meila twins are united again, and they hug each of us until we can hardly breathe. They tell us their story; they both found the strength I told them they had and helped Haji convince the laganmorfs to end their deliberations and come to the rescue of the outside world. They even beat up a few of Morin's phantom men.

Thaegar says he's been meeting with the Kar-dun royalty, and with Cog and Samjang's help, they're having talks about ways the Kar-dun and humans can use the forest wood without destroying the ancient homes of the nymphs. Both sides seem more understanding now that their opponents aren't some distant group of monsters they've never met but instead are people sitting across the table from them. One of the highlights of the night is when Thaegar drinks two Kar-dun kings into the ground without even getting drunk. I guess it helps to be four times the size of a man.

Haji stops by our table, and she tells us of her future plans. She intends to go eastward to heal the lands cursed by Morin, find the people of the Gray City, and search for her lost sisters. It's funny that she's called Haji the Humble. She is the humblest person I've met, yet she walks with more dignity, grace, and confidence than I've seen in anyone else, except maybe Cog after he was reunited with Samjang. I guess those things aren't really in opposition if you understand them right. They're really just different sides of the same coin, humility and confidence.

Haji isn't the only one who stops by our table—lots of others want to ask us about the Ice Reich, Five-becoming-One, and all the rest of our adventures. Soon we have a small crowd, which becomes a large crowd, and by this point, Emily has had enough ale that she jumps up onto the table and tells our story with sweeping gestures. Her face glows like the sun in the candlelight and firelight, and her voice hits all the right emotions at all the right times. The rest of us form the peanut gallery, tossing in smart comments from time to time, which she picks up easily and weaves into the story.

The story flows so well that we don't notice how much the ale is flowing, and when Emily is finished, we get carried out of the Great Hall to the open field to dance with the Kar-dun, where we sing songs and whirl about before collapsing on the mountainside to watch the stars.

I fall asleep with my friends next to me; my heart is full and warm. As I fall asleep, I think of all the fun times the five of us, especially Ami and I, will have together once we're home.

Home.

The word makes me think of my mom and dad and Dr. Elsavier. They've got to be worried sick about me. The same goes for the parents of the others. We've been gone for almost three weeks.

Part of me doesn't want to leave, but another part of me knows our task here is done. We defeated the Ice Reich and the fallen gods; we became One. Now it's time to go home. And if we want to come back, then as Cog said, there is always summer vacation.

⊰◉⊱

We wake up sometime in the early morning as rosy-fingered dawn brightens the sky. We all groan as we get up, rubbing our heads. After rehydrating and scrounging for leftovers from last night's feast, we say our goodbyes to Ku'ba, Kalix, Thaegar, the Meila twins, Haji, the Winter Goddess, and the others.

Enki, who ghosted us last night, finally shows up. He saunters over to us, wearing what looks like a leather jacket from the 1980s, which makes me wonder where exactly he's been for the past few days.

"You," says Emily, waving a finger at him. "We have some questions for you, mister."

Enki grins. "I had hoped you weren't yet intellectually satisfied. Shoot."

"First of all," says Emily, "why didn't you tell us what to expect in Samjang's prison? Why did you make us figure it out ourselves? What if we hadn't worked it out?"

"Ah, well, I couldn't have told you, because I myself did not know. Remember, the prison was my insurance policy. If I could have released her or told someone how to release her, Cog might not have used the last of the Hearthstone to summon the Five. So I created a prison that was self-designing—it would configure its structure in such a way that you would crack its code, but no one else would."

"All right," says Emily. "You managed to weasel out of that one. What was the whole business of pretending to be Cog?" She crosses her arms, as if defying Enki to come up with a good explanation for that trick.

"Elementary, my dear Emily," says Enki. "You see, it was really funny! Oh, the expressions on your faces! But that wasn't the best part. The best part was that the fallen gods thought they were in on the joke, when really, the joke was on them!"

Caster nods appreciatively. "Gotta love second-order irony."

I glance at Ami and mouth, "What is he talking about?" She just shrugs.

"Easy for you to say. You were in on it," says Emily. "Fine. I have another question. What do the fallen gods desire above all? When you mentioned it, all the fallen gods got a funny look in their eyes."

"Oh, well, that's easy. They want the Tree of Life."

"The Tree of Life?"

"Yes," says Enki. "You. The Five. The Hidden Tree."

I remember the cryptic writings in Morin's tomb, and it clicks for me—sort of. "But why are we the Tree of Life? Shouldn't we be more treelike?"

Enki's gaze finds a spot on the distant horizon. "It's rather a long story. And I'm afraid the Papa has come to collect you."

We turn around and see Cog and Samjang waiting for us a few yards away. Enki and Cog exchange a look I can't quite read. I guess neither of them fully trusts the other, even though Enki is the reason we were able to defeat the Ice Reich and the fallen gods and get the Winter Goddess back.

"Grrr, why can't you just tell us? But I guess there will always be unanswered questions," says Emily.

"That's the spirit," says Enki. "Off you go!"

Emily and the others reluctantly turn to go, but I stay, telling them, "I'll catch up with you." I wait till the others are gone and then turn to Enki.

He has a strange look in his mischievous eyes. "You want to know about the dreams, don't you?"

I nearly jump, wondering how he knows just what is on my mind.

"They weren't all mine, if that's what you were wondering."

Naturally, this is exactly what I have been wondering. "Whose are they then?"

Enki seems to consider. "I'm not certain. Each of the Nine Realms has a trickster god or goddess. But by my reckoning, these dreams are coming from Loki, the trickster of Gaia, the one who went mad."

Who went mad? I guess that would explain why the dreams were so strange, why my language was taken away, and why the dreams only barely seemed to make sense. "Why Homer? And why is he trying to contact me? And what does he want to say?"

Enki shakes his head and smiles. "I only know the answer to one of those questions, the first. He and I chose Homer because Homer's poetry stirs the deepest parts of your soul. And because Homer was somewhat of a trickster himself—as Aristotle used to complain, Homer taught the other poets how to lie. Why Loki wants to contact you or what he wants to communicate to you, I cannot say. I am not him."

"Oh," I say, feeling a mixture of disappointment and relief. Maybe it was just a mistake, and the dreams will stop. But a question still lingers. "Why did Loki go mad?"

Enki strokes his chin. "No one's quite sure. There are rumors that he saw something on his visit to the Fifth Realm that changed him. But no one is quite sure what he saw."

Fifth Realm. There's that number again: five.

I want to ask more, but my friends have begun to call for me.

"You coming, Peter?" Emily shouts through cupped hands.

My friends are waving at me, and Cog is looking at me with a wary gaze, as though he's afraid talking to Enki will corrupt me. Maybe it will. I'm afraid of meeting Loki, of having more of these strange dreams, and of what it all might mean. I just want to go home and live a normal high school life with my new friends.

"Thanks," I say. "For everything."

"No need," he says. He regards me with almost a sad look. "Enjoy your friends." Then he turns and goes, leaving me to wonder what exactly he meant by that.

Cog and Samjang lead us up the mountain to the chamber that houses the Heart of Miria. There's no longer a scar across the altar or a pentagram within a pentagon carved into its center.

The altar is smooth and soft, with no ornamentation, except for the five rings, which rest upon its surface.

Caster turns to Cog. "Does this mean we have to give our powers back?"

He shakes his head. "No, for better or worse, you shall bear your powers until death. When you die, the grace will flow back into the rings to wait for the next generation of ring bearers."

"For better or worse?" Emily repeats. "What do you mean 'or worse'?"

"There are enemies in your world who long for your power with the same thirst with which the fallen gods longed for it. You must be careful not to attract too much attention."

"Oh," says Caster. "Well, that sounds kind of important. Any other tips for, you know, not getting killed?"

"I've left you a list on your phones—which reminds me." He pulls out five smartphones from his sleeve. "Charged, of course. Though you won't get reception until you're back in Gaia."

"What! Amazing!" says Emily. She kisses her phone, muttering in Chinese and Japanese under her breath.

Samjang's gift for understanding and speaking other languages is wearing off, but I get the gist of what Emily is saying: "My baby, I've missed you so much!"

Cog pulls from his sleeve a small blue-and-red stone, which glows with a deep, pulsing light. "The Hearthstone is now rejuvenated. To return, all you must do is gather round and touch it, and I will send you home."

"We don't have to chant, 'I wish; I wish with all my heart'?" Emily asks.

Caster raises an eyebrow.

"Sorry. *Dragon Tales* reference. Not to date myself."

"I always hated that show," says Cog. "Now, gather round."

We all do, and my heart beats fast as I think the unbelievable thought: *In a few moments, I'll be home. We'll be home.*

The others have put their hands on the Hearthstone already, but I hesitate, with a gnawing question in the back of my mind coming to consciousness. "Why our world? Why do the Five always come from Gaia? Why not from one of the other Nine Realms?"

Cog looks at me with a strange mirth in his eyes. "Something happened differently in Gaia long ago, something that placed her at the center of all worlds. A birth, a death, and a rebirth."

A birth, a death, and a rebirth. The words feel oddly familiar. Maybe it's because they resemble our story—the story of Ami, Emily, Caster, David, and me. We died somewhere deep in the Ice Reich, and then we came to life. Did something like that somehow happen in Gaia, and that's why she's special?

Cog looks at me with an amused expression playing on his brow, as if he can see my thoughts. "Keep asking the right questions. Eventually, they will lead you there."

"Oh," I say, disappointed. But I guess Cog isn't into straight answers.

I take a last look at the world beneath the mountain, a world of gods, Kar-dun, laganmorfs, nymphs, and even stranger things. Then I look to my friends. We nod slowly, knowing it's time at last.

We put our hands on the Hearthstone, and the world around us melts away.

CHAPTER 115

GOOBER'S HEROES

"Peter! *Dio mio*, you're alive!" My mother clutches me harder than I thought was possible, and her fingers dig into my back. "I must call your father to tell him to come home. We've been worried sick about you! What happened? Where did you go?"

"I …" I struggle for words.

Her brown eyes search mine, and all I can think is *If I told you, you wouldn't believe me.*

"It's a long story," I say at last. "A really long story."

"A long story?" My mother seems both disappointed and confused, and I guess that's only fair. "Of course, of course," she says, seeming to come to terms with my answer, but then her eyes widen. "So Resol McGooblias didn't kill you."

"What?" I say. My mind is spinning. "Why would Goober have killed me?"

"One of your teachers said she watched him kill you and then throw your body down a chasm." She rubs her face, brushing away the tears. "But you're alive!"

My eyes bulge. "What's happening to him?"

She runs a hand through her hair, as if trying to remember. "He was arrested. His trial—oh *dio mio*, it's today! He will be sentenced today!"

"Today! Where?"

"The courthouse. You know, the one you went on a field trip to last year?"

I bolt out the door and run like a madman down the street, using my power to give me little jolts of momentum. I probably look like a cross between an Olympic runner in jeans and a nutso escaped from the loony bin. Alarm bells blare in my head, reminding me of Cog's warning that I should use my power sparingly, because it could attract evil forces in my world. But I ignore them—I need speed right now.

As I run, my phone rings. I ignore it, putting all my concentration into getting to the courthouse. It rings a second and then third time. I fumble with it as I tear down the winding streets, finally answering as I avoid getting hit by a car.

"Hello?"

"Peter, it's Ami."

"Oh, hi. This is not a great time!" I say between deep breaths.

"Why are you running so fast? And ruining the sidewalks?"

I glance behind me at all the little cracks I've left by using my power to propel myself forward. "My bad. Wait—how do you know about that? We live on other sides of the valley."

"My parents aren't home, so I came to visit Emily. I'll be right there. Stop ruining the sidewalks."

"I'll fix them later," I say.

A minute later, Ami joins me, and she takes my hand and uses her power to propel us along in a way less damaging to public property. "So where are we going in such a hurry?"

"My old friend Goober is on trial for murder!"

"Murdering who?"

"Me!"

"Oh. But you're alive."

"Exactly!"

We race down Main Street before screeching to a halt outside the courthouse. It might just be my imagination, but I think I see rubber marks on the ground from my shoes.

Mormont is a small town, so the courthouse has low security. A single cop sits at the front desk, munching on a hamburger. He has big 1980s-style glasses, and his front two buttons are undone, letting curly chest hair poke out. He gazes at us suspiciously.

"Can I help you?" he asks in a tone that suggests he doesn't really want to help.

"My friend is on trial for murder! I need to stop it."

He chuckles. "How do you plan to do that, sonny?"

"The judge just needs to see me, and that'll clear everything up."

"What—is he on trial for murdering you?"

"Yes."

The cop laughs again. "What are you? Peter What's-His-Face?"

I get the impression he thinks I'm a basket case. "Peter Smythe," I say.

"That's funny, kid. Look, I can't let you in. The trial's already started, and we're at max capacity."

Ami pulls my sleeve. "Let's just go."

I turn to her with a hurt expression on my face. "I can't just leave my friend to get convicted for murdering me."

"I didn't mean leave. I meant go in."

Oh. I should have known better than to doubt Ami's spunk.

She walks past the cop, and I follow.

"Hey!" The cop stands up and bangs his knee against the desk. "Ow!" He recovers and points a finger at us. His face is as red as a fresh tomato. "You can't do that!"

But we ignore him, and I let Ami tug me along toward the courtroom; her hand squeezes mine tightly. We throw open the old wooden doors and step into the packed courtroom. I see a lot of faces I recognize, including Brutus Borgia, who sits gloating with the other bullies. A balding judge with a monocle sits at the bench.

I glance at Goober, who looks glum and resigned in the corner of the room, sitting beside his attorney. On the other side of the room sits none other than Ms. Schaden, and she appears to be giving testimony.

"And that's when he killed him!" She stands and points a finger at Goober, and the crowd gasps. She sinks back into her seat. "Peter, a sweet boy, a boy I loved like my own child!" She dabs her eyes with a handkerchief.

"Stop!" I say. "This is all wrong!"

The judge adjusts his monocle and looks at me. "What is this?" His voice sounds like a cross between a tuba and an accordion, wavering up and down with such comic exaggeration that I have to stifle a laugh.

"I am here to stop the trial!"

Goober looks at me with widening eyes. "Peter," he mouths, and I smile.

The judge casts me a severe look. "Dismissed!"

"No, no, wait!"

"Schultz!" The judge turns to the bailiff. "Escort these two out!"

PAUL SCHEELER

"*Jawohl*, Your Honor!" His voice is ebullient and exuberant like a big, fat child's.

"Schultz!" The judge swats a hand at him. "How many times have I told you not to speak German to me in the courtroom? Now, get them out!"

"No, no, listen! I can explain!" I shout as Schultz tries to take me out of the room. "I'm the boy Goober murdered! I mean McGooblias! I mean, he didn't murder me, because I'm alive!"

"Oh, this is interesting!" the judge exclaims, folding his hands. "Can you prove your existence?"

Prove my existence? For the first time, I glimpse what it must feel like to be God.

The prosecuting attorney stands. "I really must protest, Judge Klink!"

"Hogan, dismissed!" Klink waves a hand at the prosecuting attorney. "The boy will present his evidence!"

"Your Honor!" Schutz exclaims. "Does this mean I shouldn't take him from the room?"

"Schultz! You are a true *dummkopf*! How is he supposed to present evidence if he isn't in the room?"

"I don't know, Your Honor! And, Your Honor, I thought you said no German!" Schultz smiles conspiratorially, and his fat cheeks make him look like a cherub.

Judge Klink flashes him an irritated look. "That's right! You know nothing! Now, sit down."

"*Jawohl*! I mean, yes, Your Honor!" Schultz says, his voice as boyishly enthusiastic and uncomprehending as ever.

I fumble through my pockets, hoping dearly that when Cog gave us back our clothes, he didn't forget to put my wallet back. Fortunately, Cog didn't forget, and I pull out my driver's license.

It occurs to me then that driving to the courthouse might have been a faster and more normal method, but sometimes things just don't occur to me.

"Bring it here!" says Klink.

I walk up the center aisle, ignoring Brutus's jeers and whispered threats, and hand my ID to Klink.

He examines it, turning it over several times and glancing between me and it. "Well, well, well, it appears the boy lives!" he says, moving his hands around enthusiastically as if conducting an unseen orchestra. "Schultz, get McGooblias out of here." He picks up his gavel and pounds it enthusiastically on the table. "Case dismissed!"

Ms. Schaden shoots me an evil look, but she can't say anything against me after saying she loved me like her own child. Brutus and his gang whisper threats at me, and part of me wants to slip back into being the scared, lost boy I was before I went to Miria, but Ami's hand in mine reminds me that I've changed and matured.

So with great maturity, I stick my tongue out at them and say, "Na-na-na boo-boo, stick your head in doo-doo!" which makes Ami laugh, and that's all that counts.

That and saving Goober from being tried for murder.

CHAPTER 116

THE NOTEBOOK

I'll never forget the expression on Goober's face when I tell him the truth about what happened after I fell into the cave.

At first, he's convinced the sip of alcohol he gave me drove me mad, but when I introduce him to my new friends and we show him just a little of our power, he comes around—after fainting, that is. When he wakes up, he's a little more sober, and I see something in his face I don't expect to see.

Maybe it has been there all along and I was just too blind to see it, but when he looks at Emily, he has the same expression I used to have back in the day when I liked Emily: a shy hope combined with despair. I realize he likes her. A lot. It occurs to me that when he said I should lower my expectations about Emily, he was speaking from his own feelings. That hurts a lot—poor Goober—but I don't know how to comfort him.

I tell him I've missed him these past weeks. He looks away and says, "I've missed you too, Peter. I'm glad you made it back."

Our schools try to figure out what happened to the four of us and what to do about us, but after several consultations with psychologists, they eventually give up, excuse our absences, and let us come back. We have a lot of makeup work to do, but after facing fallen gods and bloodgorgers, precalc doesn't look as terrifying—though polynomial and rational functions might give Morin a run for his money in terms of scariness.

School is pretty much the same, with the same material and the same teachers, except Dr. Elsavier. She apparently had an emergency around the time I disappeared and hasn't come back yet, which makes me worried. But Dr. Elsavier is one of the smartest people I've ever met, and I know she can take care of herself. Still, I miss her. She probably would actually believe me if I told her what happened to me these past three weeks.

At long last, an acceptance letter comes back from a decent state college, and that puts to rest all my parents' nagging about what I'm going to do with my life—at least for a few days. Soon they're asking me about majors and minors and work plans after school. Some things never change.

But other things do. One of those things is that when school gets out, I have something to look forward to: seeing friends.

We meet at Lord of the Beans, a cute little coffee shop midway between our rival schools. Apparently, it causes a mild scandal at Blackstone High that Caster and Emily are hanging out with the likes of Mormont kids.

"Those Blackstone boogers would be bougie like that, wouldn't they?" says Emily.

I'm not entirely sure what she means, but I nod. After our uniting the Three Kingdoms, the petty rivalry between our schools seems just that: petty. Or bougie, as Emily said, though to be honest, I'm not sure that's what *bougie* means. Maybe it's because I'm bougie. I don't know.

Our coffee club occasionally has special guests. The next week, I bring Goober along, which turns out to be kind of awkward. We four have our inside jokes and experiences from Miria. Goober has none of that, so he mostly sits quietly, alternately sipping his "water" bottle and an espresso, occasionally shooting mournful glances at Emily. I can almost feel Goober's pain when Emily looks at Caster with her doe eyes, because I know what it is like to feel useless and unwanted.

But Ami's warm hand in mine makes it hard to feel depressed. All the same, I do feel bad, because I want to comfort Goober, and I don't know how.

I'm not the only one to bring a special guest, though. One day, Emily brings along her sister, Anne—the sister she feared lived in a different world and might not be around by the time she got back.

Anne's like Emily but less filled out, all skin and bones and sharp edges. She has Emily's deep brown eyes, but they're not happy and lively like Emily's. Instead, they're haunted. I wonder what can be haunting a freshman in high school that much.

Goober takes a liking to her, especially when she says she wants to be an artist. For the first time in my life, I hear Goober speak with actual interest about something. "That's super cool," he says.

Anne looks down as her cheeks turn a little red, and I exchange a look with the others.

"What the—?" Emily mouths.

"I could show you some of my drawings," Anne says shyly.

"That would be bong!" Goober leans in closer as she pulls a leather-bound book from her backpack.

She flips through the pages until she comes to a picture she seems to like, and sets it on the table for us to see. I'm afraid at first it's going to be one of the pages Emily discovered, one that has to do with Anne's death. Instead, I see a dark figure standing on a beachhead. The ocean glimmers darkly. Behind him are mountains with darkening storm clouds overhead.

As I gaze at the image, I feel three things. One, I feel my head grows hot, almost feverish, and the geometry of the world begins to change; everything grows large and small at once, and the edges of the world bend at odd angles to each other. Two, I feel something hauntingly familiar about the figure in her notebook, though I can't quite place it. Three, I feel the cold whispering I heard back in Miria that says Cog was wrong about the peace and prosperity to come now that the Ice Reich has been defeated. *It's only just beginning*, the voice says.

In response, I do what I always do when there's a problem I should try to solve but don't want to: I ignore it. I squeeze Ami's hand a little tighter.

Everything's going to be okay, I think.

No, it's not, says the voice.

Yes, it is, I say, *and that's an order.*

CHAPTER 117

BENEATH THE STARS

At long last, prom comes. My mom and dad take me shopping, and by the time we finish, I'm convinced that prom is one giant scheme for clothing stores to fleece parents out of their money. But when I come to Ami's door that night, my feelings change.

She stands waiting for me in the oak doorway, and she looks stunning in her dress of blue and white. It sparkles in the fading evening light and seems like a starry heaven unto itself, brilliant and dazzling, the sort of thing one could get lost in.

"You okay, Peter?" she asks. "You look a little lost."

I shake my head and smile. "I'm fine. Just—your gown is beautiful."

"It's not the only thing," she says, stepping a little closer and reaching out a hand.

I freeze as she touches my cheeks and then pinches them. "You're cute when you smile. You have big dimples."

"You sound like my mom," I complain, though I'm grinning.

"That's how you know you've found the right girl," says Caster, appearing in the doorway behind her.

"Ugh," says Emily, rolling her eyes. "That's what my dad says."

"And that's how you know you've found the right guy. Ow! Do you know how many bruises my right arm has from you?"

"You deserve them, you preening meatball."

"Meatball?" Caster says indignantly.

"Yes, meatball."

Then, because Emily is Emily, she begins tickling Caster, who laughs hysterically while trying to escape, as she sings the meatball song at the top of her lungs:

> On top of spaghetti all covered with cheese,
> I lost my poor meatball when somebody sneezed.
>
> It rolled off the table, it rolled on the floor,
> and then my poor meatball rolled out of the door.
>
> It rolled in the garden and under a bush,
> and then my poor meatball was nothing but mush.

Despite the undignified way she chases Caster out the door and into the garden, Emily looks beautiful in a dress of red and blue. In the past few days, I've begun to think of her the way I would a sister—if I had a sister. But I guess in a way, I do have a sister, because the Five are more than just a group of friends; we are like family—maybe even closer. I mean, who else in the world could possibly understand what it's like to go to a different world; meet nymphs, laganmorfs, bloodgorgers, and fallen gods; and then become One, fusing all your personalities into dynamic unity? Probably not many people.

"All righty, chop-chop," says Emily impatiently, resuming her dignified stance. "Let's get to prom!"

We drive Caster's Jeep, and the warm late-spring wind feels awesome as it roughs up our hair. Emily complains to Caster that it's ruining her curls, but Ami loves it. I guess she would, with her element being air and all. She holds her arms up over the top of the Jeep as if she's on a roller coaster and sways with the motion of the car as Caster pulls around the winding roads. She manages to get me to do it too, and then, with my armpits and belly exposed, she tickles me, and everyone discovers just how high Peter Smythe's voice can go.

Prom turns out to be loud, sweaty, and obnoxious, though I'll never forget my dance with Ami. I step on her toes because I'm clumsy, she steps on mine to get back at me, and by the end, we're whirling about freely, laughing and poking each other and having the time of our lives—until we whirl right into the punch bowl. Emily reflexively reaches out and stops the wave of punch midair but then, as everyone gasps at the apparent violation of the laws of physics, she lets it go—right onto me and Ami. Because we're slaphappy by this point, it only makes us laugh even more.

We quickly tire of prom, so we decide to skip the rest of it, grab David, and go hang out on the valley slopes, where no one else is around.

We ring David's doorbell, and an elderly black lady answers. She seems a little disturbed by us, which I guess makes sense. Four teenagers wearing prom clothes, half of whom are soaked in punch, is probably a scary sight. But when we explain that we're David's friends and when he appears in the doorway, smiling broadly, her eyes moisten, and she thanks us. It seems a little weird to me at first. *Do you need to thank someone for being friends with your nephew?* Then I remember David has had more bullies than friends. And I understand.

David's in a much more talkative mood, and he chats our ears off about all the things that have happened since he got back, including how he faced his bullies.

We stop for gas along the way, and Caster returns from the gas station holding two six-packs and, of course, two bags of peaches.

"Is that beer?" asks Emily, clapping her hands over her mouth. "Scandalous!"

"Square this, and you get beer."

"What?" I say.

"It's root beer. Like square root. Oh, whatever."

"Boo," says Emily. "Your jokes are terrible." She stands up and points ahead. "To the slopes!"

We park outside the park, which is now closed, and jump over the fence. Emily spreads her interdimensional blanket on the ground, and Caster pops open the root beers. As we lie on the descending slope of the valley, I remember the time only a few days ago when we lay upon the slope of the Heart of Miria, gazing up at a different set of stars. But in a certain way, it's all the same, because Ami's hand is in mine, and I can feel my friends next to me.

"So, Peter," Caster says, finishing off his second root beer, "do you play games?"

"You mean like computer games?"

"Yeah, exactly."

I think back to my dying wish all those weeks ago, when I was concerned I might never make it into Elite Class in *Ghost Army*, all because of Goober's and my archnemesis, Firestarter520.

"Yeah, I guess. I used to play *Ghost Army* before all this happened."

Caster whips his head over to look at me. "Wait—you play *Ghost Army*? What's your username?"

"What's yours?" I ask warily.

"FireStarter520."

"PeterPan233. You're FireStarter520?" I exclaim.

"You're PeterPan233?"

"You're the reason I'm not in Elite Class!" *Oh goodness, that explains so much.*

"Great gourds, what's going on?" Emily looks between us.

I laugh. "Oh, nothing. Just—you want to explain it, Caster?"

He shoots a mischievous glance at Emily, who looks at him with wide eyes. "No, not really. Argh! Stop tickling me—I won't give in to torture!"

"It's not torture," Emily says, between tickles. "It's enhanced interrogation!"

Ami leans closer to me, points out a constellation above us, and recites one of the stories her grandmother used to tell about those stars. David, meanwhile, looks awkwardly at the four of us, and I beckon him over to join Ami and me, the sane ones.

It's late when I get home that night—close to three thirty in the morning. My last thoughts as I drift off to a hazy sleep are of the All-Father, the Being I met in the darkest moment after all my friends died in the monster's tentacles, the Mind that brought us back to life and bound us into One. I promised I'd find him again once I got back to my world. Somehow I'll do that, though I don't know how.

I have a feeling it might be the start of another adventure.

CHAPTER 118

THE FINAL CHAPTER

I wake up the next morning to the smell of Mom's pizzelle drifting through the room. The remnants of a dream float just beyond the edge of consciousness. My stomach growls, demanding to be fed, and I stumble toward the door. I'm about to leave when I see a single manila envelope on my desk. It lies just on top of my keyboard, surrounded by month-old Cheetos bags.

Someone with careful handwriting that looks somewhat familiar has written, "To Peter Smythe, Earthmaster."

My eyes widen. Could it be Cog, contacting us already?

I tear open the letter and read the contents.

> Dear Peter,
>
> Welcome home, my Odysseus.
>
> I'm sorry I was not able to greet you when you arrived. I was called away on urgent business, which I thought I might be able to solve.

I have been in contact with Cog and the others of the Nine Realms, and I have learned of your and your friends' recent success. I am truly proud of you. But now I must be more than proud of you. I must call upon you and your friends to help me, for the business I mentioned has become more urgent—and deadlier.

Meet me beneath the cypresses at Pallas Park tomorrow evening. And bring your friends.

Yours,
Dr. Marie Elsavier

I reread the letter several times and turn it over and over in my head, not quite believing my eyes. I guess in a certain way, it makes sense. Dr. Elsavier must have known somehow that I was different and that I might be called into Miria by Cog. Why else would someone as brilliant and talented as Dr. Elsavier waste away her life at a pitiful little school in a pitiful little town like Mormont?

I reach for my phone to call my friends, and as I do, I feel the same flicker I felt for just a moment outside Cog's palace on our last day in Miria—the world turns dark, shadows overwhelm everything, the color and life drain from reality, and everything turns upside down, bending at odd angles.

In a moment, the world is right again, but it's too late. A deep shiver travels through my flesh, and a horrible feeling sinks over me with certainty: *Cog was wrong. The Nine Realms are about to experience not a new age of peace but another great threat, one that will make the Ice Reich look like a mere angry toddler.*

That's when I remember my dream.

I had a dream last night I hoped I'd never have again—a dream with Homer. As all the details come rushing back into my mind, the cold, loneliness, and fear deepen.

With a shiver, I realize what was so familiar about the man in Anne's notebook. Somehow, impossibly, it was Homer, the same Homer from my dreams. My head spins as I try to fathom how Anne can be involved. *Just how big is this thing?*

But counteracting the delirium and the cold is a different feeling, something hot and lively: courage. Courage because of my friends. Courage because Dr. Marie Elsavier is on our side. Courage because of what I've learned I can do. Courage—in a way I don't quite understand yet—because of the All-Father, Gomdan.

I put on a brave face and call my friends.